A Better Part of Valor

Gary Corbin

Double Diamond

P U B L I S H I N G

In memory of my dear friend

Richard Gray,

1958-2020

Contents

Part One

Val Finds a Body

Chapter One

The sun sank low over the Torrington River, peeking below the angry storm clouds threatening to ruin the last mile of Valorie Dawes's evening run. Dressed in running shorts and a gray cotton sweatshirt with "Property of Clayton PD" stenciled across the chest, she'd keep warm enough if the rain held off. But mid-March storms in western Connecticut often turned brutal. She picked up the pace and considered the bright side. Maybe she'd even beat her best six-mile time.

She passed a couple of twenty-something men dressed in name-brand running outfits and ignored their catcalls. Why couldn't guys her age keep rude comments about her ass to themselves? She dialed up the music volume, preferring the Jonas Brothers' energetic riffs over their lewd shouts.

Approaching the pedestrian bridge over the river, she slowed to allow a mother pushing a stroller to exit first. The two men behind her gained enough ground to return within earshot, and one of them shouted something to the effect of thanks for reconsidering his offer. She sprinted onto the bridge without looking back. Reconsider this, asshole.

Halfway across, lightning flashed, reflecting off the green window glass of the food processing plant on the river's far embankment. Seconds later, thunder exploded around her, and the skies opened up in a torrential downpour. The metal grates beneath her feet grew slick, and she debated slowing her pace. But the risk of lightning striking the steel structure outweighed the danger of a twisted ankle. The high-pitched shrieks from the men behind her made her laugh. Such tough guys. Afraid of a little rain.

Lightning flashed again as she approached the end of the half-mile crossing, accompanied a half-second later by a loud thunderclap. She stumbled and caught herself on the side rail, breathing hard. The last thing she needed was to fall into the frigid, choppy current of Berkshire snowmelt thirty feet down—or worse, the jumble of rocks that lined the embankment. Slowing down seemed like a much better idea.

Val took a few deep breaths and pushed herself away from the rail to resume her run, then stopped, and paused the music. Something caught her eye on the river's rocky beach below. A pile of clothing—no, not a pile. A blue parka, backside-up, arms outstretched, with gloves protruding from them. Long blonde hair floated around the edges of the hood. Women's slacks extended from the bottom of the parka. And bare feet.

A body—from what Val could tell, a woman's body— appeared to have gotten snagged in the rocks, pushed there by the river's relentless current.

The two runners slowed to a stop behind her. The shorter of the two, a once-athletic white guy in matching Adidas shorts, shirt, and shoes, shared a sweaty grin and wiped his brow. "Hey, gorgeous," he said, just loud enough for her to hear. "I knew you'd stop and wait for me eventually. How about we head to my place and—"

"Call 9-1-1!" Val yanked out her earbuds and ran ahead, veering off the running path toward the riverbank.

"Something I said?" the guy asked. His buddy, a taller, thinner Black guy in Nikes, laughed and slapped him on the back.

Val picked a route among the rocks, a steep, slippery, fifty-foot descent toward the water's edge. Before she could reach it, the body shook free and rocked in the river's wake.

If she hesitated, the current would wash the body away from her, and it would be lost downstream.

She wiped rain from her face and waded into the shallow water. The icy cold shocked her skin, and her teeth chattered. She slipped on the slimy rocks on the riverbed, and the strong current threatened to knock her down. She paused a moment to regain her footing and rubbed her arms for warmth. The body drifted farther away, picking up momentum. She reached for it, missed the woman's arm by inches. Another step closer…her foot skidded out from under her and she fell on her butt, the water splashing up to her armpits and onto her face. So. Fucking. *Cold*!

Above, Mr. Adidas shouted down to her, holding a cell phone to his ear. Val couldn't make out what he said and didn't care. "Send an ambulance!" she shouted back.

She rolled forward onto her knees, reaching again for the body. Almost. She crawled toward the woman, scraping her knees on the rocky bottom, frigid waves soaking her hair and neck. When she got close enough, she grabbed the woman's arm, stopping her journey into the center of the river. The current tugged back, knocking Val over, and her entire body went underwater for a moment. Her mouth filled with water, choking her. She broke the surface and spit it out, gagging on the water's bitter, mineral taste. But she held onto the woman, somehow. She regained her footing and dragged her back to the shore.

The other runner, Nike-man, met Val on the rocks and helped her pull the body to the grass along the path. Val thanked him and checked for signs of life.

"Is she…do you think she's dead?" Nike-man asked, wide-eyed.

"I don't feel a pulse, and sh-she's not breathing," Val said. "Do you have a phone? Mine just got soaked."

The man nodded, unlocked an iPhone, and handed it to her. "I never touched a dead body before," he said, then ran a few feet away and fell to his knees, retching.

Val sympathized. She'd never forget the first dead body she'd ever touched. Then again, it happened only five months before. It was also the first person she'd ever killed, a gang member who'd shot at her first, whom she'd stopped from raping a teen-age girl. But she couldn't dwell on that at the moment.

She dialed her boss's number from memory. "Clayton Police, Blake here," her sergeant answered. "How can I help you?"

"Travis, it's Val Dawes," she said. "I just pulled a body from the Torrington, east of the ped crossing. A young woman, possibly a teenager. White, about five-five, one-forty to one-fifty, blonde hair, dark brown eyes. Dressed for winter, other than being barefoot."

"No shoes, huh?" Travis said. "I'm guessing no flippers, either." He chuckled, suddenly grew serious again. "Any signs of foul play?"

"Some bruises on her face. Is anyone missing that meets her description?" Val's entire body shivered. As the excitement of the moment abated, bitter cold crept deeper into her bones.

"I'll check missing person reports," he said. "Dawes, are you okay?"

"I'm soaking wet," she said. "The sooner you get someone out here, the sooner I can change into dry clothes."

"On it," Travis said. "Actually, it appears someone else called it in, too." Sirens sounded, as if on cue. "Shouldn't be more than a minute. I'll send fresh clothes out to you ASAP."

Val waved thanks to the white guy, still leaning over the rail on the bridge overhead and talking on his cell phone. She strolled over to his buddy, still puking on the riverbank. "You gonna be okay?" she asked him.

He rolled over to a sitting position on the wet grass, rain splashing his face. Lightning lit up the sky again, and thunder rumbled in the distance. "I guess I need to get used to this," he said with a sheepish grin. "I'm going to UConn Med School in the fall."

"It gets easier, I'm told," she said. "What's your name?"

"Diego Collier." He took a deep breath. "Up there, that's my friend Kent Mercer. Sorry about what he said to you earlier. He can be kind of a jerk sometimes."

Val waved it off. "Thanks for your help tonight, Diego. Can you stick around for a few minutes? Detectives will want to ask you a few questions."

"Sure," Diego said. He pointed to the logo on her sweatshirt. "But aren't *you* a cop?"

Val sighed. "Believe it or not, this is my day off."

***

Val hustled into the Liberty Heights Precinct break room the next evening, a few minutes before the start of her 5 p.m. shift. The aroma of burnt coffee almost, but not quite, overwhelmed the sour smell emanating from the garbage can in the corner of the cramped room, dimly lit by overhead fluorescent lights. Someone on day shift had sloughed off on cleanup duty again.

She set her cap on one of the four empty laminate-topped tables and double-checked the duty roster posted on the wall. No surprises there: patrol duty, swing shift, Thursday through Monday, no overtime. She sighed. The life of a rookie.

Rico Lopez, Val's patrol partner since January, ambled in and poured coffee into two chipped mugs, each sporting Dunkin' Donut logos. "I heard you had a fun day yesterday," he said. He handed her one of the mugs and leaned his compact, muscular frame against the counter, facing her. He rubbed the white scar that stretched across his forehead, a souvenir of a domestic violence case six months before that put his then-partner, Brian Samuels, on long-term disability with a gunshot wound.

Val toasted him with her mug and took a sip. "Any word from the medical examiner on the victim's identity or how she died?" she asked. "She had no ID on her when she washed up on the riverbank. No phone, nothing."

"The vic's name was Olivia Lambert," intoned a deep, rumbling baritone from the break room door. Sergeant Travis Blake, a 6'5", barrel-chested white man in his early forties, took up the entire doorway, and his voice occupied any space his hulking frame didn't. "We matched the body to a missing persons report this morning, and the family identified her a few hours ago. Cause of death: drowning, according to the ME."

"Suicide, homicide, or accidental?" Rico asked.

"Three guesses," Travis said with a sardonic smile. He shuffled in, holding a manila envelope under one arm.

"Give me a hint," Rico said. "Any evidence of foul play?"

Travis elbowed Rico aside so he could access the coffee pot. "Plenty. Choking, sexual abuse, even some mutilation."

The room fell silent, each officer paying their own private tribute to the young woman's suffering. "What else do we know about her?" Val asked to break the silence.

"Seventeen years old, a junior at Liberty High School—your alma mater," Travis said to Val. "Varsity volleyball, honor roll, student body treasurer. Volunteered on weekends with the mayor's literacy program. Oldest of three girls, parents still together."

"That rules out suicide, doesn't it?" Rico mused aloud. "She had the world by the ass on a downhill pull."

"Don't be so sure," Val said. "You never know what a teenager's going through. Sometimes the people you think are the absolute happiest suffer from depression."

"But something has to trigger it, right?" Rico said. "Break-up with a boyfriend, maybe? Or trouble at school?"

"Nope and uh-uh." Travis stirred four scoops of sugar into his coffee. "Her parents said she wasn't dating, and her sister confirmed it. Apparently, she was too busy with her extracurricular activities. And the girl had a 3.8 grade point average. You found yourself a smart one," he added with a smirk. "And high profile."

Val and Rico exchanged glances. "Why 'high profile'?" Val said. "I've never heard of her, so—"

"Because Mayor Iverson made it so," he said. "Which is why I'm here, Dawes. There's an emergency meeting at City Hall to brief her on it. Lieutenant Gibson wants you there." He handed Val the sealed envelope with "Olivia Lambert" scrawled across it. "That's the ME's report. Memorize it. You have twenty minutes."

"The mayor?" Val frowned. "Why is Megan Iverson all worked up about this case?"

"Lost future voter?" Travis said, his eyes twinkling.

Rico grimaced. "That's not as far-fetched as you think. Iverson's considering a run in next year's governor's race on a law-and-order platform. She's looking for a headline to ride into the primaries."

"Whatever the reason, we'd better get on the road," Travis said. "Rico can drive us over while we read."

"Beats desk duty," Rico said. "I'll get the car."

Travis rode shotgun, leaving Val no option but the back seat—where perps ride. She and Travis scanned the ME's report while Rico fought Clayton's rush hour traffic jams. That gave them plenty of time, as it turned out. Despite the region's declining population and economy, the city's narrow, decaying streets clogged daily with the vehicles of the nearly 100,000 bankers, mill workers, and restaurant staff inching their way to or from work. Rico blipped the sirens a few times to scoot past the ugliest backups, but they remained stuck in traffic at 5:30 when the meeting was supposed to begin.

Val didn't mind. She appreciated the opportunity to dive deeper into the report. The M.E. had ruled out accidental death, but not suicide or homicide. He laid out his reasoning deep in the background pages—an explanation that left Val numb and silent for several moments.

"Check this out," she said when she could speak again. "Bruising on the thighs in various stages of healing—some fresh. Scar tissue and traces of semen and lube in the vaginal canal."

Travis stared at her. "And our all-American girl allegedly has no boyfriend."

Val nodded, a lump rising in her throat. "No boyfriend," she said, exhaling a long, uneasy sigh, "but what this tells me is, she does have a history of violent sexual abuse." She gazed out the window, unable to focus further on the details of the case. It all hit too close to home, conjuring memories she fought daily to forget. The invasion of her bedroom by the large, sweaty man, a family friend entrusted to provide safety while her parents rushed her brother to the hospital. His hot, whiskey-laden breath on her, making it nearly impossible to breathe. His massive frame, pinning her to the bed—

For most of her teenage years, notions of suicide flared up inside her, temptations she resisted with therapy and the unflagging support of her older brother, Chad. Did Olivia Lambert have that type of support?

Travis's deep voice brought her back to the present. "Sexual abuse? Where'd you see that?" He flipped through the report's pages.

"Page seven." Her voice sounded dull—as preoccupied as she felt.

Travis let out a long, low whistle and dove back into the report. For the rest of the ride, only Rico's muttered curses at Clayton's idiot drivers broke the somber silence.

****

Val and Travis joined their precinct commander, Lieutenant Laurence Gibson, in the hallway outside the mayor's office at City Hall. Gibson's bearlike figure seemed small only compared to Travis. His dark brown skin, broad nose, bulbous eyes, and untamed salt-and-pepper hair gave the impression of an impatient man, always ready to explode. But his gentle, intelligent demeanor and sonorous baritone put even the most skittish observer at ease—a key attribute in a high-profile political meeting.

"You ready?" he asked them.

"Like a village idiot with cash," Travis said. "Dawes?"

"Not speaking unless spoken to," she said with a mock salute.

A receptionist showed them into the meeting room, already occupied by enough people in suits to staff a small bank. A long mahogany table, with eight chairs on each side, filled most of the rectangular space. Windows took up most of one wall, filling the room with the soft glow of evening light reflecting off the tall, glass buildings lining the river to the east. The opposite wall featured a crisp, clean whiteboard, bordered by cork panels and a handful of upcoming event announcements, news releases, and policy statements affixed with push-pins.

At the head of the table stood a woman in her forties with bright green eyes and perfect skin—tanned, unblemished, and wrinkle-free. Val had never met the mayor, but she recognized her from television. Tall—at least 5'10", Val guessed—and runway-model-slender, Megan Iverson wore a conservative blue suit and, on closer inspection, a little too much makeup, as if she expected to go on camera any second. She sported a politician's smile and a diamond ring that—if real—would make Elizabeth Taylor proud. Only the woman's shoulder-length, chestnut-colored hair seemed authentic.

"Welcome, officers," she said, extending her hand. Gibson shook it and introduced Travis, Val, and himself.

"It's a pleasure meeting you all. Especially you, Ms. Dawes." Iverson held onto Val's hand for several seconds, shaking it with a firm grip. "I'm so grateful for all the work you've done to rid the streets of violent thugs like Richard Harkins."

Val shuddered at the mention of the name. She'd shot and wounded Harkins three months before, but only after he'd raped multiple women and girls in the area. "The whole team contributed," Val said, stammering. "But thank you, Madam Mayor."

A tall man wearing a tailored black suit offered his hand next. "Curtis Iverson, Vice President of Constitution Finance," he said, smiling. "I help Meg out from time to time."

"My most trusted unpaid advisor for over twenty years," the mayor said, beaming. "And we all see through that false modesty, Curt."

"That's the first time she's ever called me modest," Curtis said, grinning. "Except in reference to my looks."

Val chuckled along with the others. No one would criticize Curtis Iverson's appearance. His athletic build, bronze tan, and black hair, graying at the temples, reminded Val of a TV sports personality. But she found his presence in the meeting bothersome. Local pundits called him "the power behind the throne" for his fundraising acumen. Many criticized the mayor for providing her husband unfettered access to city government, despite holding no official title.

"Let's get down to business," the mayor said. She waited until the officers took their seats at the far end of the table. "The media are going crazy over this Olivia Lambert murder," she went on. "A high school girl, evidence of rape—"

"Excuse me, Madam Mayor," Gibson said. "We haven't yet reached a conclusion whether this is a murder, a suicide, or accidental death. All we know is the cause of death: drowning. As for the rape, I'm a little concerned. The details about that weren't shared with the media, so how did—"

"Well, somebody told them," the mayor said with an edge in her voice. "Regardless, the press is making this out to be the latest occurrence of a crime wave targeted at young women, and to be honest, I'm inclined to agree. Mike?"

Val shot a questioning glance at Travis. "Michael Kim, the Mayor's liaison to the department," he whispered, pointing to a twenty-something Asian American man with shaggy black hair, dressed in a blue blazer and khakis.

Kim pulled some papers out of a manila folder and cleared his throat. "Preliminary statistics for last year show a twenty percent rise in violent crimes against women in the city, and twelve percent in the prior year. Calls to the Women's Crisis Center have spiked in recent months, according to my, uh, colleague that works there."

"His girlfriend," Travis whispered again to Val.

"Women don't feel safe in this community," the mayor said. "We need immediate action. As of right now, that's my number one priority. What does your department plan to do in the coming days to help make that happen?"

Gibson stared open-mouthed at her for a moment. "We're doing everything we can to resolve the Olivia Lambert case as quickly as possible," he said. "As for women's safety, naturally that's always a priority—"

"Bullshit," Mayor Iverson said. Her husband smirked, and her staffers ducked their heads, but the mayor seemed not to notice. "Mike just gave you the official numbers, and as we all know, most crimes go unreported. Women are under attack in Clayton, and that's unacceptable."

Val glanced at the lieutenant, wondering if he'd challenge the mayor's information again. Criminologists debated the extent to which different types of crimes went unreported, particularly rape, attempted rape, and domestic violence against women. Overall, she agreed with the mayor, but it seemed unfair to pin the blame for unreported crimes on Gibson.

The lieutenant cleared his throat and nodded. "We agree that it's unacceptable," he said. "But I'm a little confused, to be honest, Madam Mayor. I thought we were here to brief you on the Lambert case, which we're happy to do. As for the department's overall strategy on women's safety, I'd have to refer you to Chief MacMahon. He'd have a better sense of—"

"With all due respect, Lieutenant, if the mayor wanted bureaucratic stonewalling, she *would* have invited the chief to the meeting," Curtis Iverson said. "We'd like to hear what you officers on the front lines are seeing and hearing. Because if it doesn't happen at your level, well, that means it isn't happening." He finished with a reassuring smile at Gibson and Travis, and not so much as a glance at Val.

The veins on Gibson's temples pulsed and his breathing grew tense. Val held her breath. Gibson didn't suffer fools gladly, and Curtis Iverson had "fool" written all over him.

"Mr. Iverson," Gibson said, his voice even, "my officers put themselves in harm's way day, night, and overtime to keep our citizens safe. Two of Sergeant Blake's officers are recovering from gunshot wounds as we speak, resulting from domestic violence calls. Officer Dawes was nearly killed by the same rapist a few months ago. To insinuate that nothing is happening is, frankly, ridiculous." He set his mouth on a line and glared at the well-dressed man sitting across from him. For a moment, the room fell silent.

Michael Kim drew a deep breath. "I think what Mr. Iverson means—"

"I'll speak for myself, thank you," Curtis said, holding up his hand. "Lieutenant, of course that's not what I meant. What I'm saying is, strategies and speeches don't matter if they don't turn into action on the street."

"Which is why we invited Sergeant Blake and Officer Dawes," Kim said. "We want to find out whether they're getting the support they need to solve cases like Olivia Lambert's. Sergeant Blake?"

Travis darkened. Val could almost feel his discomfort. "Lieutenant Gibson bends over backwards to give me the resources I need," he said, "within budgetary limits. It's been my understanding that departmental requests for additional funding in this area have been ignored by City Council." He wiped away a momentary smirk before continuing. "As far as solving the Lambert case, right now that's up to the detective squad. If we suspect it's a murder, we'll assign it to their Homicide Unit."

"More bureaucratic buck-passing," Curtis muttered.

"My impolitic husband has a point," the mayor said. "You're not answering the question. Are you supported by your superiors, or not?"

"I am," Travis said, reddening, but his eyes fell to his hands.

Several seconds passed. The mayor's staff exchanged wary glances, but said nothing. Curtis Iverson turned toward his wife and shook his head.

"Very well," the mayor said. "Officer Dawes, I'll turn the question to you. When walking your beat in Liberty Heights, is the city doing everything it can to help you keep our citizens—particularly the women in our community—safe from predators like Richard Harkins?"

All eyes shifted to Val. Her face grew warm, her breathing shallow. Gibson's expression turned sour, as if he disapproved of the question, or having it directed at her. Travis's face took on an air of amusement, as if he enjoyed seeing Val being put on the spot. The mayor, her staff, and her husband all wore skeptical expressions.

Val swallowed and licked her lips. She wasn't prepared for questions like this, nor for being thrust in the middle of a political tug-of-war between the mayor and her bosses. Worse, while she hated to make Gibson and Chief MacMahon look bad, she tended to agree with Iverson—much more could and should be done to protect the most vulnerable, particularly young women.

"Officer Dawes?" Kim frowned at her. "The mayor asked you a question."

"Lieutenant Gibson has made community policing a priority in our precinct," Val said. "I believe that makes Clayton safer by establishing closer relationships between officers and our residents." She paused, swallowing hard. "But we could do more."

"Namely?" Curtis said in a sharp tone.

Val cleared her throat, wishing someone, anyone, would take the spotlight off her. "Boost staffing levels, beginning with the nearly fifty open uniformed positions in the department. Retrain officers in each precinct to follow Lieutenant Gibson's community policing approach," she said. "For starters."

Gibson smiled and nodded at her. He and the chief had made a similar pitch during budget hearings a few months before, and she'd overheard him complain about how their pleas fell on deaf ears in City Council.

"Fifty?" The mayor turned to face her staff. "Is that true?"

Kim drew in a deep breath. "All police departments claim to be underfunded and understaffed."

"Answer the question," the mayor said with a growl.

Kim ducked his head, face reddening. "Yes, it's true."

The mayor nodded at Val. "Continue."

"Once we reach full staffing levels," Val said, gaining confidence, "we implement best practices in policing, such as allocating more officers to the Domestic Violence Unit, the Rape Unit, and the like. Studies show—"

"I don't need studies. Those are good ideas," the mayor said. "Anyone disagree?" Her eyes darted around the room, and her staff shrank into their seats. "Good. Curt, work with Chief MacMahon and my staff to draft a proposal. Lieutenant, can you make Officer Dawes available to review what they come up with?"

Gibson gestured to Travis. "Sergeant?"

Travis locked eyes with Val for a moment. Her heart raced. Please say yes! she wanted to shout. Instead she allowed a quick nod. Travis gave Gibson a thumbs-up.

"Looks like we have a plan," Gibson said.

"Great!" Megan Iverson stood and wrote "Women's Safety Initiative" on the whiteboard. "Now," she said, "tell me everything you know about Olivia Lambert."

Chapter Two

After returning to Liberty Heights precinct, Val found herself behind a desk in "The Bullpen," a windowless cubicle farm filled with ringing phones on dented metal desks separated by low, shabby dividers. Constant foot traffic brought loud snippets of conversation within inches of her every few minutes. The dim, flickering overhead fluorescent lights added a final layer of mindless distraction.

"The mayor wants this data by morning," Gibson said. "I'll brief her on whatever you come up with, so don't worry about coming in for that. Travis will patrol with Rico until you get back on the street." He donned his cap and strode out the door, his shift done for the evening.

Val sighed. She'd rather walk the streets in freezing rain than get stuck in an office, though she enjoyed and excelled at research. Because of that, she'd graduated a semester early from UConn a year before, fast-tracking her admission into the police academy. She resolved to complete the task before Rico broke for dinner, usually around 8:00 p.m.

She began by pulling together basic facts about Clayton itself. Connecticut's fifth-largest city and the largest in Litchfield County, the city's population had suffered a steady decline in recent years—from nearly 180,000 in the 1970s to about 125,000 at the 2010 census. Probably even fewer now. Like many East Coast cities, Clayton became a "minority-majority" entity around the turn of the twenty-first century, largely due to "white flight." That much she already knew.

What surprised and depressed her was that the city's crumbling industrial economic base had pushed over a third of its residents into poverty. That drove property tax collections down, drying up funds needed to keep the police department—and other city services—fully funded.

Unfortunately, defying national trends, violent crime rates in Clayton—including violence against women—had continued to climb. Val attributed that to another pair of interesting facts: first, a high percentage of the population were males aged eighteen to thirty-five, a high-crime group. Second, the region suffered from crazy levels of unemployment. Worse, the lack of jobs hit that same 18-to-35 demographic hard. On one hand, banking, insurance, and internet service companies went begging for qualified staff. But manufacturers of guns, bicycles, and household appliances—once the backbone of the local economy—had shuttered one after the other. That left a hollow core of empty industrial buildings lining the east side of the Torrington River—the area where she'd discovered Olivia Lambert's body.

That thought prompted her to review the case file for clues. The medical examiner had ruled her death a homicide after all. The autopsy revealed bruises around her neck and cloth fibers under her fingernails, consistent with those used in men's dress shirts. None of the girl's clothes were torn or damaged, other than her missing shoes. She'd been found fully clothed, an unusual occurrence in rape-murders. The ME also detected traces of seminal DNA and condom lubricant and had sent it to a lab for further analysis. That, along with the vaginal bruising, strongly indicated sexual assault prior to her death.

Val shuddered and closed her eyes for a long moment. Too close to home.

She searched Olivia's social media accounts next. She constructed a profile of the girl as a somewhat introverted over-achiever. Smart, hard-working, and active in her Presbyterian church. An obsessive fan of actor Bradley

Cooper. And a member of the "nerdy" clubs at school—student government, the Association of Future Entrepreneurs, yearbook, and the Academic Quiz Bowl team. Her only "cool" activity: varsity volleyball. How she held it all together, Val couldn't fathom. The girl must have never slept.

"Whatcha got?" Travis's towering form filled the opening in her cubicle and cast a shadow over her workspace, startling her.

"I thought you were on patrol with Rico," Val said. "Change of plan?"

He ran a massive paw through his short, graying hair and grinned. "We came back to fetch Rico's hat. It's raining out and he didn't want to melt. So, have you crunched the magic numbers that will let us fill our open positions—and, more importantly, get you back on street patrol tonight?"

"Trade you assignments."

"No, thanks." He took a seat, his knees nearly touching hers. "Come on, help a guy out. Details, and don't be afraid to talk slow."

Val glanced at her computer screen. "Not sure if this will convince Her Honor, but our ratio of citizens to police is almost 700-to-1. That's far below the national average of one officer per 600 residents," she said. "We're also well below average on women and minorities. Fixing that would raise public trust and can help sensitize officers to community concerns."

"What would it take to reach a 600-to-1 ratio?" Travis asked. "How many bodies?"

She cleared her throat. "After filling the open spots? About forty."

He whistled. "That's almost six million bucks." He shook his head. "The budget office says we need to cut spending, not increase it. That's a tough sell. Gibby's gonna freak."

The use of Gibson's unfamiliar nickname threw Val for a moment. "That's why he gets the big bucks," she said. "So, is this enough to make the case for more officers?"

"Nope," Travis said. "You need to tie it to the corpses. Olivia Lambert and any other floaters you can find in the database."

Val winced. "You're a sick man, you know that?"

"Thanks," he said, grinning. He stood and stretched. "I guess I'd better find Rico and wander down the yellow brick road." He sauntered off.

Val turned back to her computer, even more despondent about her task. Travis had made a good point, but it meant even more research—and being stuck in the office. Worse, it meant looking for more cases of violence against women—and probably finding way too many.

***

The sun sank low over the Torrington River, peeking below the angry storm clouds threatening to ruin the last mile of Valorie Dawes's evening run. Dressed in running shorts and a gray cotton sweatshirt with "Property of Clayton PD" stenciled across the chest, she'd keep warm enough if the rain held off. But mid-March storms in western Connecticut often turned brutal. She picked up the pace and considered the bright side. Maybe she'd even beat her best six-mile time.

Ahead of her on the trail, two men jogged side by side, both in their forties or fifties, judging by their gray hair, apple-shaped bodies, and achingly slow pace. One of them glanced back at her every fifteen or twenty seconds, revealing a tired, wrinkled face, red and sweaty. He looked familiar, but she couldn't bring his face into clear focus. Still, he made her nervous.

Val passed the men where the trail split, one side veering off to continue upriver, the other crossing the pedestrian bridge over the swift, swirling current below. She took the bridge route, hoping the pair would choose the riverside path. Running alone beat running with creepy old men, any day.

A quick glance back at them revealed she'd earned half her wish: one of the men had gone on upriver, but the other followed her onto the bridge. Weird. Perhaps they weren't together after all.

Having one man following her seemed even creepier than two, so she picked up the pace. She reached the end of the bridge and peeked back again. She didn't see him. Maybe she'd been mistaken—

Val collided with someone in front of her, a guy who hadn't been there moments before. She tumbled to the ground, landing on the rocky riverbank atop a large, overweight man with gray hair and a red, sweaty face. So close she could smell his sweat, a dank aroma, not pleasant.

"Sorry, I didn't see you," she said, scrambling to climb off him. But she couldn't seem to stand up, or roll to the side, or move at all. His arms gripped her back, holding her down—when had he grabbed her? He rolled on top of her, pinning her under his knees, undid his belt—weird, who wears a belt and trousers while running? He gazed down at her, and his face came into focus: Uncle Milt, the man who had raped her a few weeks before her thirteenth birthday. He shushed her screams, ordering her not to tell anyone, or else. "You know what they say about girls who do this," he said.

Milt groped at her, breathing hard, almost grunting in sick pleasure. Val bucked under him, trying to push him off. He slapped her, then punched her, and blood trickled down her face. She tried to free her arms, but he was too heavy, and wriggling made it hurt more. He laughed at her. "I bet you have a pretty little pussy, don't you?" he said.

And then his face changed. No longer Uncle Milt, it was Richard Harkins, and he had a gun pointed at her, and his finger tightened on the trigger—

***

Val sat up in her bed, cold sweat drenching her body, her heart pounding. She sucked in deep, calming breaths, hugging her elbows to stop shaking. The gloom of the dark, spare room amplified her fear, so she stumbled out to the living room. She flicked on the light, then the television, hoping the noisy screen would take her mind off the nightmare. But the program, a thriller about a creepy rapist-murderer, only magnified her grim mood, and she turned it off.

It was just a dream, she repeated to herself. Milt left town ten years before and never contacted the family again. Harkins was in jail, and castrated by a well-aimed shot from Val's gun. Neither man could hurt her. She was safe.

Unlike Olivia Lambert. Someone an awful lot like Milt and Harkins had gotten to her. Violated her, and either killed her or led her to take her own life. The ME's report hadn't proven it, but Val was convinced that Olivia Lambert's death directly resulted from what she'd suffered at the hands of a rapist. One who remained free to hurt other women.

That had to change.

***

That afternoon, bright sunshine took the edge off the cold, early spring air. The streets Val and Rico walked teemed with shopkeepers, teenagers shooting hoops on school playgrounds, young parents pushing strollers, and shoppers lugging totes laden with recent purchases. The clear weather and bustling street activity put Val in chipper spirits.

"I love days like this," she said when they stopped for a coffee break. "Everyone's in such a good mood out there, I sometimes forget how many of these guys rob stores and deal drugs when I'm not looking."

"Huh." Rico frowned into his coffee and glanced away from her.

"What?" She waited for him but got no further explanation. "Something on your mind?"

Rico shrugged, still not meeting her eyes. "I just thought, now that you're a big shot adviser to the mayor, you'd be trading in your uniform for one of those tailored suits she likes so much. A desk job with a fancy office in City Hall—"

"Don't be ridiculous. I hate that life." Val pushed her coffee away. It tasted bitter all of a sudden. "What makes you think that? Because I got yanked in for one meeting? I didn't even want to be in that one."

"Doesn't it piss you off that they've taken the case from you?" he asked.

She grimaced. "That's just how it goes. As you know." Gibson had transferred the case to the Homicide Division minutes after receiving her research data. But she had to admit, Rico was right: she'd thought of little else besides Olivia Lambert since discovering her body in the river.

"You gonna ask for a special assignment?" Rico asked. "Sometimes they allow it."

Val shook her head. "I'm a rookie. No way they'd go along. Technically, I'm still in training." Her mood soured. Her first partner, Sergeant Gil Kryzinski, took a bullet for her in a shootout two months into her probationary period. Alex "Pops" Papadopoulos, her second partner, got reassigned to Rico after harassing her, emotionally and sexually. Pops took medical retirement weeks later after an encounter with the same perp that shot Gil.

"Doesn't hurt to ask, right?" Rico sipped his coffee. "I mean, it's no secret you're unhappy being partnered with me."

Shock silenced Val's reply. It had taken weeks to find another experienced cop willing to work with her. As the only unpartnered cops on street patrol, Travis had paired them up more by default than by choice. No doubt Rico felt stuck with her. But after Pops retired, he'd also had no luck finding another partner—probably because of his sour disposition.

"Look, I get it," Rico said. "I'm no Valentin Dawes. Nobody measures up to him. Not even Gil."

"I don't compare you to my uncle, or Gil, or anyone else," she said. "I'm fine partnering with you. You're a good cop and a good guy."

"You're 'fine' with it," he said, nodding. "As in, 'he'll do. At least he's not Pops.' Right?"

Air rushed from Val's lips, and she sank into her seat. She needed no reminders of her short but insufferable assignment as junior partner to Pops. If the dictionary used illustrations, Pops's face would appear by the term "old-school chauvinist pig."

"Rico," she said, "what I meant to say was, I'm proud to serve alongside you. Where's all of this coming from, anyway? Did I do something to upset you?"

"Forget it," he said. "I'm 'fine' with being your partner, too. Speaking of which, let's get back out there. It's too nice a day to waste inside." He slid out of the booth without waiting and strode to the exit.

Great. Another partner relationship going south. Would she ever find a cop she'd mesh with like she had with Gil? Maybe the fresh air would improve his mood.

They walked the beat in tense silence for a few blocks and stopped at a busy intersection, waiting for the light. Suddenly, a white woman in her twenties ran out of a multi-story apartment building across the street about a half-block ahead of them.

"Police! Help!" the woman screamed. She wore a torn blouse, holding it closed with one hand and waving at Val and Rico with the other. A male figure in a sleeveless T-shirt and jeans appeared behind the woman, covered her mouth, and pulled her into a nearby alley, out of view.

"Up there!" Val said to Rico, pointing, and dashed into the street. Car horns blared and tires screeched, one vehicle stopping less than a foot from Val's hip.

Rico's footsteps pounded behind her on the pavement. "Christ, Dawes, where are you going? We need to call for backup."

"She could be dead by the time backup arrives," Val said. At the mouth of the alley, she peered into the shadows. Dumpsters lined the far end. Doorways with "Emergency Exit" signs interrupted the monotonous pattern of barred windows and brick walls of the apartment buildings on either side.

"They must have gone back inside," she said when Rico caught up to her, "You take one door, I'll take the other."

"Protocol says—"

"Screw protocol! Now you *are* acting like Pops!" Val regretted saying that as soon as the words popped out, and Rico's darkening expression made clear she'd pay for it later. He turned away and spoke into his mic. "Possible 10-16 at MLK and Maplewood. Unit A-27 requesting backup."

"Roger that, A-27," the male dispatcher replied. "All units in the area of MLK and Maplewood..."

Val knocked on the heavy metal door, tried the handle. Locked, of course.

"Nobody home!" a male voice shouted.

"Help me!" a woman screamed, sounding desperate. "He'll—"

The sound of fists beating flesh interrupted her. The woman screamed again.

"Open up! Police!" Val shouted back.

"Go away!" the man yelled. "It's a private matter. None of your business!"

Something—a body?—slammed into the door from the inside, followed by a yelp of pain. "Stop that!" the man demanded.

Val glanced at Rico, who stood frozen in place, his hand gripping his baton. "Rico?" She tapped his arm. "You okay?"

He started, cleared his throat, and shook her hand away. "Your circus, your clowns," he said. "How do you want to play this?"

Another slap of flesh on flesh sounded inside, another scream. Val looked again to her senior partner to take the lead. He licked his lips, took a half-step backward.

That settled it. "Open up or we'll rip this door off its hinges!" She pulled her weapon and aimed it at the handle.

That shook Rico out of his daze. He grabbed her arm, pushing it downward. "Are you nuts? That's reinforced steel. You're more likely to shoot your own leg off, or worse!"

"Then what the hell—"

"Wait for backup, that's what," he hissed. "Five minutes, tops."

"That guy will beat her to a pulp by then!" But Rico had a point. Val re-holstered her weapon. "Tell you what. You guard this door. I'll go in the front."

Val took off running before he could respond, ignoring his shouts. She dashed around the corner to the building's front entrance and tugged on the door. Locked. On the wall to one side she found an array of call buttons, one for each unit. She pressed them all in rapid succession.

"Who's there?" an elderly woman said over the scratchy speaker on the building's wall.

"Clayton PD, in pursuit of a suspect who entered on the east entrance of your building," Val said. "Buzz me in, please?"

"I'm not on the east side," the woman said.

"It doesn't matter," Val said, her voice rising. "Just let me in!"

"You're crazy," the woman said in a scolding tone, "if you think I'm allowing a stranger into my building. How do I know you're really a cop?"

"Oh, for heaven's sake," Val said, fuming. "I'm Officer Valorie Dawes. Badge number—"

"Just a minute. Let me get a pen," the woman said.

"Don't leave, just—oh, screw it!" Val pressed the buttons for the other apartments again, waited ten seconds. Twenty. No replies. She reached out to press them again.

The door burst open toward her, and a man stood in the opening. He held a woman's white blouse in one hand…and a gun in the other. Pointed at her.

Val ducked and pushed the door shut in his face. A moment before the door hit the jamb, a loud "*pop*" reached her ears—the sound of low-caliber pistol fire. The bullet ricocheted off a trash can, and the booming echo of the slamming door resounded in the alley. Footsteps inside faded away at a fast pace.

"Rico," she radioed her partner, "suspect attempted to flee from the front entrance, and has now re-entered the

building. May be heading your way. I'll check for more exits!"
She ran toward the west side of the building.

"Backup expected in two minutes," Rico said. "What's your 20?"

"I just told you where I was," Val said under her breath. She turned the corner and followed the building's perimeter along the side street, scanning for doorways. Another secure entrance appeared halfway up the block, also with call buttons. She pushed them all as she had before, and the same woman answered.

"Stop harassing me or I'll call the police!" the woman yelled at her.

"I *am* the police," Val said. "Please open the damned door?"

"Not if you're going to be rude," the woman said. "Now go away!"

Val groaned in disgust and banged on the door. "Police! Can someone please open up?" She banged again. A few moments later, the speaker buzzed and the lock clicked. She yanked open the door and ran down the hallway, making her way to the exit on the opposite side. The hallway ended at the landing of a set of concrete steps that continued to descend into the building's dark basement.

But she found no gun-wielding man, and no shirtless, beaten woman.

She paused, gathered her wits, and took a few breaths. The rancid aroma of mold, tobacco, and urine gagged her. She took another deep breath and held it.

Then she heard a low whimper below her. Val crept down the stairs, shining her flashlight ahead of her, until it lit upon the shape of a woman, curled up into a fetal position, crying and shivering. The same woman, though she looked younger up close, perhaps not even twenty. Shirtless, her back and side revealed deep blue and purple bruises in various stages of healing. More bruises surrounded a red welt above her left eyebrow, and her lid had swollen shut.

The woman lifted her head and gazed up at Val through her one good eye, her face wet with tears. "Thank you for coming," she said, "but I think you're too late."

Chapter Three

Val rode with the young woman in the ambulance to Mercy Hospital, leaving Rico to interview potential witnesses at the scene. She waited while doctors stitched the woman's lacerations and checked her for internal injuries, which thankfully hadn't yet escalated to rape. Then she interviewed her, hoping to get some useful information before the painkillers made her too groggy.

Val sat next to the woman's hospital bed. "Do you know the man who did this to you?"

The young woman, who gave her name as Destiny Mathers, nodded. "Hunter," she said. "My mom's boyfriend."

Val retched a little. "How old is he?"

"I dunno, old," Destiny said, her words slurring. "Forty-five?"

Val jotted down his name and age. "Is Hunter his first name or last?"

Destiny stared at her and, after several seconds, shrugged.

"What's your mom's name and number?" Val asked.

Another shrug. "Brandy. She's at...Bedford Hills."

Val's heart skipped a beat. "Prison?"

The woman sneered. "Thanks to you fucks."

Val took a calming breath. "Would she know how to find Hunter, or...?" Her voice trailed off when Destiny's head shook a firm No.

"He don't really live anywhere," she said. "I think he's out of Bos..." Her head lolled to the side, and drool spilled onto her chin.

Val ran to the hallway. "Nurse? Help, anyone!"

A thirty-ish man in scrubs rushed in and checked Destiny's pulse and breathing. "She's reacting to her meds," he said. "Sorry, Officer. Interview over." He called for a doctor and ushered Val out of the room.

Waiting for her ride back to her precinct, Val fumed, frustrated by the dead end. Another crime she and her partner had failed to prevent. Another predatory male might get away with a violent attack on a young woman, and there was nothing she could do about it.

Maybe the mayor's task force wouldn't be such a giant waste of money and effort after all.

***

Around 9:00 the next morning, Val helped Gil Kryzinski, her former partner, lift his sturdy six-foot-two frame off his crutches and into the passenger seat of his Ford Explorer. She braced herself when his body tipped back toward her. For a moment she feared he would fall on top of her—two hundred pounds of dead weight, crushing her onto his paved driveway. But with a grunt and another shove, his momentum shifted up and into the car.

Val chided herself for the "dead weight" thought. Thanks to her, Gil had come close to becoming exactly that a few months before. Fortunately, the bullet he'd taken to the hip missed his vital organs. But it had taken him out of action from the job he loved—and, if Val could allow herself a brief, selfish thought, from the role of mentor that she'd so cherished.

Val shook off the memory, stowed his crutches in the back seat, and jumped in on the driver's side. "Stop and Shop, Big Y, or PriceRight?"

"Fred's Produce Market," Gil said. "No chain stores for me, especially on a Saturday." A thick lock of wavy black hair fell in front of his eyes. He'd let it grow out since going on medical leave. "So, the guy in the tenement escaped? Take a left at the light."

"I know the way. I grew up here, remember?" She exited the cul-de-sac and pulled into traffic. "Yeah, but he'll be back, and then we'll nail his ass."

"Maybe. He got away with, what? A purse, a few hundred in cash, some jewelry? I can't see the department prioritizing it. Was she hurt?"

Val nodded. "A little beaten up, and scared half to death. Still, it's attempted rape and aggravated assault, right? That ought to make someone's radar. Jesus, where do these people learn to drive?" She stopped the car short, jerking them hard into their seat belts.

"Good thing I just had the brakes done," Gil said after catching his breath. He braced himself with a stiff arm against the dashboard. "What concerns me more is you and Rico. It doesn't sound like you're on the same page."

"He's *so* conservative." Val changed lanes to prepare for her next turn. "He's almost as bad as Papadopoulos. In my head, I've begun calling him Pops Junior."

"Come on, nobody's that bad," Gil said. "Remember, Rico faced off against Harkins, too. Got conked on the head, saw his partner get shot. I'm betting that's made him a little gun-shy."

Val drew in a deep breath. "I saw Harkins shoot my partner, too," she said, her voice heavy. "Remember that day?"

"Oh, was that your partner?" Gil said in mock surprise. He winced in pain. "Like I could ever forget."

Val drove in silence for a while, her mind locked on the same memory: Gil, lying on the pavement, blood pouring from his hip where Harkins's bullet had ripped into his body moments before. "I'm glad to see how well you're getting around," she said to break the mood. "Your therapy must be going well."

"Seems slow as hell to me," Gil said. "I thought I'd be walking unassisted by now." He sighed. "At least I don't need that stupid walker anymore, or God forbid, that crappy wheelchair. Even now, I can't stand for more than fifteen minutes at a time." He leaned back, stretched his legs out, and winced. "Freaking hurts."

"What's your timetable?" She pulled to a stop in front of the produce market. "Still expect to come back by Memorial Day?"

He shook his head. "Three to six more months, minimum, the doc says. Hey, what the hell are you doing?"

Val cast him a puzzled look. "Letting you out at the front door. I'll park and catch up to you."

"The hell you will. Come on, go park. I need the exercise." He pointed toward an open spot.

"I can't park in the disabled zone. You don't have the sticker. Which you should get, by the way. You're entitled."

He waved her off. "Park in a regular spot. I'm fine. Really."

She gazed at him with a combination of amusement and frustration, then smiled. "You are one stubborn old coot, aren't you?"

Gil laughed. "If that ain't the pot calling the kettle black, I don't know what is. And who are you calling old? I'm only thirty-four."

"Two hundred, in dog years." Val pulled into the closest spot she could find and stopped the engine. "Race you to the door," she said with a grin.

"If we were both on crutches, I'd win," he said, grinning back. Then he grew serious and reached out to her. "Thanks for doing this. It's above and beyond."

"It's no such thing." She squeezed his hand. "What are friends for, right? Just don't ask me to cook, unless you like burnt toast."

He held on a little longer, and their eyes met. "Val," he said after a pause, "there's a chance I might not go back to patrol when I return."

"So, you go on desk duty for a while," she said, putting on a brave face, "while I suffer along with Pops Junior. Seems like appropriate punishment, since all of this is my fault."

"Don't go there again," Gil said. "Besides, Rico's a good cop. He'll train you well. As it is, I had to fight Gibson to get out on patrol last year. 'Sergeants are managers in Clayton PD,'" he said, imitating Gibson's deep, rumbling voice. "But he wanted you trained right. But now, with this situation..." His voice trailed off, and he looked away. "Val, it may be...*quite* a while."

A lump formed in Val's throat. "For how long? Nine months? A year?"

"Or longer." He blew out a noisy breath and shuddered. "I might never walk a beat again."

"Gil, I'm sorry," she said. Her heart grew heavy. "Does this mean..."

"You're going to have to walk a desk beat, too," he said with a wry smile. "Because I'm not giving up on us being partners."

"Never!" She pulled her hand out of his grasp. "That's too high a price to pay!"

His face fell. She laughed and punched his arm. "You goof. I'm only kidding. Sort of."

His expression turned wistful. "That's what I'm afraid of," he said. "The 'sort of' part."

"I don't have a brilliant solution for that," she said. "We need to think of one. Because not partnering with you, long-term, would just suck."

Gil smiled and held her hand again. "Maybe we just spend more time together outside of work."

Val stared at her hand, suddenly clammy inside his. Warmth spread over her face. She looked away, gave him another quick squeeze, and clicked the door locks open. "We should get on with shopping," she said. "I have to get to work soon."

He didn't respond for several seconds. She met his gaze and found sadness in his eyes. He blinked and nodded. "Lucky you. And lucky Rico."

She slid out of her seat and pressed the door shut, pausing a moment to calm her racing heart before circling around to assist him.

***

Megan Iverson poured herself a second glass of cabernet sauvignon and gazed out of her living room's eight-foot-wide picture window. She adored the view from their hilltop contemporary-style home, a mix of city lights and lush, hilly greenery bisected by the white-capped Torrington River. She and Curt bought the house brand-new two decades before, where they'd intended to raise a family.

But cruel fate had intervened, a double whammy of ovarian and breast cancer slamming her within a span of five years during her thirties. Between the disease and the chemo, her body gave up the struggle to maintain fertility.

Unfortunately, as their dream for a traditional family died, so, too, did the physical attraction that brought them together. Maybe Curt's libido had died from lack of interest, or due to age. Either way, over time his sexual interest in her waned, and he initiated love-making less and less often. On the rare occasion that he did, though, the fire still burned hot—a welcome surprise that Megan never turned down.

She'd wondered if he'd strayed—that maybe his bursts of passion came about during dry spells between flings. But she never found proof, or even a solid reason to suspect him. No specific women ever crossed her radar. Over time, she concluded, their passion for each other had simply faded, replaced by mutual respect, comfort, and dull familiarity.

Instead, politics became her passion, and the entire city had become their family. Especially the female half of the city. After winning the battles against the cancers that so often victimized her gender, Megan made it her life's mission to fight all dangers to women. Women's health concerns led to the fight for a woman's right to control her own body, and more recently, to combat threats from predatory males who victimized young girls like Olivia Lambert.

Megan shuddered. She never should have set eyes on the girl's photos or read the stories of Olivia's happy childhood. The girl's prom-queen smile in her school picture clashed with the bloated, bruised face and body in the forensic photos. Whether the girl had taken her own life or had it stolen from her, the sexual abuse the police had uncovered no doubt had led to her demise. Megan's resolve to find the killer redoubled.

"Is there more wine where that came from?" Her husband's voice preceded him into the room. She turned from the city view toward Curt, ambling across their expansive living room and weaving his way around the plush black leather furniture. He sidled next to her and kissed her neck. "Mmm, you smell good."

"I smell like sweat and exhaustion," Megan said, but her smile belied her grousing. His surprisingly warm embrace pulled the tension out of her better than any wine could. She leaned into him and offered a sip.

"Delicious." He rested his hands on her hips. "Is this the Paso Robles 2012?"

"You know your wine." She set the glass onto the bar and refilled it. "I needed the good stuff after today."

"Typical Monday?" he murmured into her ear. Curt's deep, smooth voice calmed her.

"Worse," she said. "I had to explain the police budget again to those idiots on City Council. You'd think they'd never heard of community policing before. Or simple math." She sighed and took a long sip of cabernet.

"They're grand-standers," Curt said. His lips caressed her neck, tiny tastes of her skin that sent a shiver down her spine. "Budgets are boring. They need something shiny and new to focus on."

"Yeah, well, passing a budget is Council's actual *job*." She shivered as his fingertips traced tiny circles across her abdomen. "Until we fund the basics, we can't afford the bright and shiny."

"Basics like keeping women feeling…safe?" Curt's fingers dipped inside the front waistband of her slacks, making it increasingly difficult for her to concentrate on their conversation.

"Yes," she said. "Like…that." Megan set down the wine again, afraid she'd spill it.

"Well," he said, "I had an idea that could help you. About what we discussed with Lieutenant Gibson and his officers the other day." His fingers abruptly ended their exploratory mission.

She sighed, grabbed his wrist, and pressed downward. But he continued talking. Just. *Talking.*

"Maybe you could repackage your requested increases in police funding around a big, flashy policy initiative of some sort," he said. "Create a whole new unit, dedicated entirely to women's safety. Put a woman in charge, with a female celebrity spokesperson—a UFC fighter, say, like Holly Holm or Ronda Rousey. Then do a big PR push—TV, billboards, social media. Attach a woman's face to something they think of as 'man's work.' Think it'll fly?"

Megan turned toward him, excitement building. She leaned her body into his. "I like it, Curt. But would it actually work with these bozos?"

He smiled. "It works for you either way. Either they buy into it and pass the budget you want, or..." His smile broadened. "You have yourself the centerpiece of a gubernatorial campaign."

She returned his smile and pecked him on the lips. "You're a genius." She let her breast brush against his arm. That always got a rise out of him. Her voice dropped a register. "Where would I be without you?"

Curt's breathing grew shallow. He wrapped his arms around her and squeezed her rump with both hands. "I hate to think about that," he said.

"What do you like to think about?" She pressed against him. His body responded—finally!—in the way she wanted, and she ground into him, harder.

"Thinking's for fools," he said, and his lips found hers, their shared tastes of wine mingling on their tongues. Moments later, they landed together, legs and arms entwined, on the soft, plush carpet.

Chapter Four

After a quick morning shower, Val stepped out of the tub onto the cold tile floor and shivered. She dried off hastily and wrapped the towel around her head, turban-style. Goosebumps formed on her skin, an artifact of the low setting at which she and Beth kept the thermostat to save money. Her straight, fine hair, cut to a jaw-length bob, wouldn't take long to dry, but already her head—hell, her entire body—felt like an icicle. She pawed through her stack of clothes on the bathroom counter and sighed—she'd forgotten to bring underwear in with her. No matter—her roommate, Beth, stayed at her fiancé's most nights, so she had the place to herself.

She rushed into the hall and had her hand on the knob of her bedroom door when she caught movement out of the corner of her eye. She glanced around—

"Company!" Beth chanted, sing-song. She covered the eyes of her slack-jawed fiancé and spun his lanky frame away from Val's naked form. "Josh, don't you dare turn around."

Val shrieked and bolted into the bedroom, shutting the door behind her. She leaned against the door, panting, and chiding herself: Get a grip, girl. So he saw you naked for one second. Big deal.

But it was a big deal. No man had seen her naked in over ten years. Not since the worst day of her life…

The man straddled her, his weight pinning her to the bed, and tore at her pajamas, his whiskey-laden breath hot on her face and neck—

Val shook off the terrible memory, recalling the centering exercises her counselor had taught her years before, the ones that brought her back to the present. Val shut her eyes, listening, bringing to mind the details of her surroundings: the queen bed, unmade, centered on the wall opposite her; the nightstand with the ancient digital alarm clock-radio she'd owned since junior high; the closet's sliding door, open—no, wait, closed—and her laptop on the tiny desk in the corner, its screen dark. Her heart rate slowed, and she shivered from the cold. But she could breathe again.

She reopened her eyes, pulled on the underwear she'd dropped on the floor earlier, and covered up with a pair of shorts and a sweatshirt. She glanced at her seldom-used make-up mirror. Her deep blush had subsided, if not the humiliation.

She scolded herself for her reaction. Josh wouldn't want to see her, anyway. If he liked Beth's body type—tall, voluptuous, lots of makeup, highlights in her long dark hair—he'd take no interest in Val's no-makeup look and lean, athletic build.

Yeah, right.

Val returned to the bathroom—only to find it occupied and locked. She sighed and stumbled toward the cramped galley kitchen, where Beth awaited her, offering a full cup of fresh coffee.

"Sorry about that," Beth said. "We just got home—I needed a change of clothes, and...I should have warned you."

"Forget it," Val said, but her weak voice belied how much the incident had shaken her.

Beth extended her arms wide, and Val couldn't resist Beth's warm embrace. Beth was, hands-down, the best hugger on the planet.

"I don't think he saw much," Beth said in a soft voice.

"There's not a lot of me to see," Val said, choking out a laugh. "You big liar." She squeezed Beth harder. "Thank you for that, though."

"Now, if Gil caught a glimpse of your naked butt, how would—"

"How long is Josh going to be in there?" Val pushed her way out of the embrace. "I need to dry my hair."

Beth's face scrunched into an apologetic frown. "He might be awhile. He brought his phone in with him. And it might be kind of tough to breathe in there after."

Val grimaced, sipped her coffee, and surrendered a wan smile. "Ah, well. The perils of roommate life, I guess."

Beth inhaled a deep breath and paused, apprehension clouding her big brown eyes. "Yeah, about that," she said. "I wanted to tell you sooner, but...Josh and I are...I'm moving in with him next month. Officially, I mean."

Val's heart sank. "I thought you were waiting for the end of the lease, in June!" She slid into the dining area, sat at the table, and took a deep swig of her coffee. Sadness crept over her. Beth had roomed with her since freshman year of college, and despite their differences, they'd spent almost every waking moment together since junior high. But lately, Beth-time had become far more scarce. After she and Josh announced their engagement in the fall, Beth had practically moved in with him. Now, it would happen for real.

She met Beth's gaze again, and guilt replaced her melancholy. "Oh, jeez, what am I saying? That's wonderful. Congratulations!" She jumped up and hugged her friend. Besides showing the proper affection, it hid her tears from Beth's view.

Beth returned the hug in another rib-crushing squeeze, lifting Val off her feet. "Thanks for being so understanding," she said.

"Of course." Val patted her friend's broad back, hoping Beth would get the message that the hug had gone on long enough. She didn't. "All right, put me down," Val said with a laugh.

Beth set her down but kept her arms around Val's shoulders, dragging her to the living room sofa. "I'll cover my share of the rent through June," she said. "I'll need the extra time to pack and move, anyway. But I can help you find a roommate, if you want."

"Thanks. You'll be tough to replace. Impossible, really." Val choked up, unable to go on. No one could *replace* Beth. Not as a friend and confidante. Anyone else would just be a roommate.

Before Beth could respond, the bathroom door flew open, and Josh emerged, still pulling up and zipping his pants. "Hey," he said, grinning at Val. "Nice outfit."

Val sighed. Then again, living alone had its advantages.

***

Thanks to steady rain and a slow bus, Val arrived at the precinct station fifteen minutes late for her 5:00 p.m. shift on Thursday. She signaled "back in a minute" to an impatient Rico Lopez, sipping coffee in the break room with a murderous expression on his face. She still needed to change into her uniform, which meant she would clock in close to a half hour behind schedule. To make matters worse, Travis Blake stopped her twenty feet from the women's lockers.

"Before heading out on your beat," he said, "you've got some paperwork to do." He shoved a sheet of paper at her. "Her Honor the Mayor would like some answers."

Val scanned the page, a list of a dozen or so questions about best practices employed in other cities to fight rape and domestic violence. "Don't they have interns available to do this research?" she said. "This could take hours."

Travis grunted and checked his watch. "You have twenty minutes."

"But I—"

"Have a job to do. Yeah, I know. Welcome to city government." He waved her toward a cubicle and wandered off.

A few minutes later, Rico plunked into a chair beside her. "What's the mayor's favorite cop working on today?" he said. "A new anti-crime initiative, balancing the Parks budget, or redesigning the Torrington River Crossing?"

"I don't know what her *favorite* cop is working on," Val said without looking up. "But she has *me* researching what Hartford and New Haven are doing to keep women safe. And I have all of fifteen more minutes to get it done. Believe me, I'd rather be doing anything else."

"Could've fooled me," Rico said.

She paused, saved her file, and swiveled her chair to face him. "Give me a break," she said. "I didn't ask for this."

"No?" He shook his head. "That's not what I heard."

Val inhaled a deep breath, held it, and let it out, tapping her pen on one knee. There was no avoiding the conversation; it might as well happen now. "Rico, what's bugging you?"

"Nothing." He stretched and yawned. "I'll just wait—"

A loud *bang* echoed through their space, followed by several more—the sound of rapid gunfire. Rico jumped out of his chair and squatted low, right hand reaching for his sidearm. "What the fuck was that?"

"Sorry," someone said from the next cube over. A young male cop with shaggy, sandy-colored hair stood and waved. "Just watching a training film. I guess my headphones got unplugged."

Rico, his breathing calmer, got back on his feet and brushed himself off. "Call me when you're done." He shuffled off, muttering about idiot rookies.

Val turned back to her computer, deflated. Rico's crappy mood didn't exactly motivate her to rush the research and rejoin him on patrol. His reluctance to talk only made matters worse. Still, Travis had made it clear: the mayor's orders came first. She dove into her work, hoping the subject matter would keep her focused on getting the job done.

The research took almost an hour, meaning she blew the mayor's deadline big time. Whatever. Nobody died waiting for these statistics. Val set a copy of her report on Travis's desk and went searching for Rico shortly after sunset. As she walked, the evening's persistent drizzle slowed and halted.

"I'll take that as a good sign," she said when she joined him on the beat, pointing at the sky's thinning clouds.

Rico grimaced and shook his head, saying nothing. They walked down Martin Luther King Boulevard side by side in silence. With the clearing weather, the sidewalks grew crowded with kids bouncing basketballs toward the park, young couples pushing strollers, and old men smoking and talking in low voices.

Val found her mind wandering to Olivia Lambert. While desk work held no appeal, a small part of her resented losing the case to Homicide. No doubt Rico sensed that.

"Hey, I'm sorry I got pulled—"

"Let's drop it," Rico said, his gaze straight ahead.

She sighed. Okay. Give him time to cool down.

They reached the corner, the site of a defunct theater and a large parking lot where a juvenile street gang, The Disciples, hung out. A few broken-down cars filled spaces on the edge of the lot. Only two of the lot's half-dozen overhead lights cast any illumination on the grim scene. A group of twenty or thirty Black youths stood in a circle, some cheering and yelling. Closer inspection revealed two youths rolling on the ground, fighting.

"You want me to take the lead on this?" she asked Rico.

He stared at her. "You really want to jump in on that? What for?" He shook his head. "This is how they entertain themselves. Let them have their fun."

She returned his disbelieving stare. "You can't be serious?"

"Look," he said. "Either they're unarmed, and they'll wear each other out in a few minutes, or they're armed, which means they're a threat to whoever tries to break it up. Either way, we're better off staying out of it." He walked on, ignoring the fight.

"That's ridiculous!" She stared after him. He couldn't possibly believe that ignoring a brawling gang fit their job description. But he kept walking, never once looking back.

Val sighed and pushed her way into the group. A few Disciples pushed back until they saw the badge and uniform. Once the crowd let her through, she pulled the two brawling youths apart with ease. She stood between them, arms wide. "All right, party's over," she said. "Everybody settle down."

"Damn, Copette," said a short, stocky Disciple with a twisted pile of long, black curls. "We just having some fun."

She recognized him as Gunner, a mid-level lieutenant in the gang. Two gold loops dangled from each ear, signifying his mid-level rank in the group. "Have fun some other way that doesn't get people hurt," she said. "You two okay?"

The two youths she'd pulled apart glared at her, then each other, and nodded. The onlookers grumbled about who owed whom money. Bets, she surmised, now had to be covered, somehow. Whatever.

"Try not to kill each other tonight, guys," she said, channeling her inner Travis Blake. "At least not until the end of my shift."

Val caught up with Rico a block up the street. "I could have used your help back there," she said. "If they were armed—"

"We'd both be dead," he said. "No thanks."

"Rico, have you forgotten what our job is? To protect and—"

"Don't lecture me," he said. "Our job is not to get shot, breaking up boxing matches between kids who won't live to twenty. If they enjoy punching each other's faces in, I say, let 'em."

"That's ridiculous!" She jumped in front of him. "Just because they're gang members doesn't mean they don't deserve—"

"I say it does!" He tried to step around her, but couldn't. "I'm not willing to get killed supporting one of your social causes. Show me an innocent victim and sure, I'm all over it. But I'm not rushing into the middle of a gang war, or a broken-down tenement, just because a big, mean dude is beating up some other big, mean dude!" He pushed past her, his shoulder bumping her backward.

"For God's sake, Rico," Val said, walking behind him. "You can't go judging which victim is worth protecting just because you don't think they'll outlive you!" Her voice shook, but she kept her volume low, noticing that they'd caught the attention of a few onlookers.

"The hell I can't," he said over his shoulder. "You don't like it, report me." He strode on up the street.

She pushed through a few pedestrians, catching up to him at the corner, and again blocked his progress, arms wide. "I need to know that you have my back," she said. "We're a team, remember?"

"Bad news, Dawes," Rico said. "I *don't* have your back in those situations. Do you know why? Because you don't have mine."

Val opened her mouth to object, but Rico cut her off.

"Oh, don't look so surprised," he said. "Think about it. In the past six months, we've had three cops shot in Clayton. You were at the scene every single time. Two of them were your partners. Do I need to spell it out any clearer than that?"

"Let *me* spell this out for *you*," she said, her volume rising. "Of those three officers, two of them were *your* partners at the time. One of the two got shot *before I arrived on the scene.* You, meanwhile, were conked out in the back room. And *I* got the sonofabitch who shot him off the streets. So if you want to argue over who gets whose partner shot, you'd better have your facts straight!"

"Get out of my goddamned way!" He pushed her to one side. She lost her balance, falling head-first toward the pavement.

At that point, Val's instincts and training kicked in. She grabbed his still-outstretched arm and turned, pulling his body under hers. The momentum kept her upright, but a very surprised Rico landed on the sidewalk at her feet, the air rushing out of him with a loud "Oof." He laid there on his back, struggling to regain his breath.

"Damn!" someone said behind her. "Did ya'll catch that?"

Val glanced around, and to her dismay, a crowd of onlookers gawked at her. Some of them held cell phones in the unmistakable pose of amateur videographers, recording everything.

***

Val and Rico cowered under Travis's massive frame, towering over them in the sergeant's cramped office. The video of the two of them arguing on MLK Boulevard played on the sergeant's computer screen for the fourteenth time, this time with the sound off. Travis had apparently put it on an endless loop before they'd walked in the door.

"What in the hell were you two thinking yesterday?" Travis yelled, waving his arms and stomping around them. His gray eyes blazed, and his sweaty, silver curls stuck to his forehead, flushed beet-red with anger. Val pulled her feet out of the way just in time to avoid getting them trampled by Travis's size-14 shoes.

Rico grimaced at Val, as if to say, *This is your baby.* She pretended not to see him.

"I mean, for God's sake. It's bad enough that people in these neighborhoods think we ignore them," Travis said, lowering his volume a notch. "But to fight about it—*literally* fight about it *in their presence*—gives a whole new meaning to stupid! Did you think they wouldn't have cell phones? This goddamn thing has already gone viral!"

"I can explain, about the physical stuff," Rico said. "I was trying to move past her, and didn't realize—"

"That you outweigh her by seventy pounds and could easily knock her down?" Travis leaned his bear-like frame into Rico's face. "Want me to show you how that works, Lopez?"

"I shouldn't have reacted like that," Val said. "I didn't realize—"

"That you could kill him seventeen ways from Sunday with your bare hands?" Travis shouted. "So you thought you'd give us a demonstration?"

Val bowed her head. "We were arguing, and things spiraled a bit," she said.

"A *bit*?" Travis threw up his hands. "Understatement of the year. Fuck." He shook his head. "Listen. I get it. Partners quarrel. But pay attention to where you are, okay? You guys want to piss all over each other, fine, but Jesus, not in public."

"Of course, we should have held our discussion in private," Val said. "That was a foolish mistake."

"You *think*?" Travis glared at both of them and sat on the edge of his desk. "And *what* you say matters, too." He pointed at Rico. "Lopez, for fuck's sake, saying we should just let them kill each other. *In public.* Is there any way you thought this would not get you suspended?"

"We should have been more discreet," Rico said in a low voice.

"Not just more discreet," Travis said. "More *smart*. More, I don't know, not-as-dumb-as-a-rock."

Rico bowed his head and nodded. "I'm sorry, sir."

"Sir," Val said, "it's not entirely Rico's fault. I should have—"

"I never said it was only his fault," Travis shouted back. "Just that what he said was *more* stupid. Your comments about a Clayton peace officer deciding who to protect or not—and then slamming his body to the ground—wasn't exactly public relations genius, either."

Val took a deep breath and gazed at her feet.

Travis circled his desk and plopped down in his chair, which somehow didn't break. "So, here's how this is playing. The public sees a big, brawny cop attacking his small, female partner...and getting his ass kicked. So, so much wrong with that." He sighed.

"I know, this looks worse than it probably is. But optics matter. So, Lopez, you're suspended with pay, pending investigation. Call your union rep and get your defense together. This shit's going to be on the six o'clock news, and we need to tell the press that you're already being disciplined."

Rico growled, then nodded, his head bowed.

"Dawes," Travis went on, "you'll get a reprimand in your file—'Conduct Unbecoming.' For tonight you're on desk duty. Which works out, because the mayor has another research job for you. Like we can afford to pay cops to write fucking term papers. Go on, scram, both of you." He turned his computer screen around toward his side of the desk.

Val led Rico out the door. Once outside, she faced him. "I'm sorry, partner," she said. "I shouldn't have confronted you."

"No, you shouldn't," he said. "And I shouldn't have said what I did. Now I get to pay for my mistake." He started past her, then stopped. "Do me one favor."

She nodded. "Anything. If you need me to testify—"

"Stop calling me 'partner.'" He strode past her, eyes blazing.

***

Val spent the next hour glued to a computer screen in the noisy, stuffy Bullpen, wishing she were anywhere else. An old-timer in the cubicle beside her, apparently hard of hearing, shouted random half-sentences into his phone. A team of thirty-something veterans stood nearby, arguing about baseball, and the unwelcome odors of somebody's onion-heavy dinner wafted in from the break room down the hall. She put earbuds in to drown out some of the noise, but focusing on her work remained difficult—and not only because of the distractions.

Most of the mayor's questions centered around comparing Clayton's statistics to national figures for the incidence and conviction rates on domestic abuse, rape, and other crimes of violence against women. In short, Clayton didn't come off well. In fact, the results left her even more depressed than the fight with Rico and their chewing out by Travis Blake. She'd started her summary memo, but hadn't gotten past the first paragraph when Dispatch transferred a call to her desk.

"Sum it up for me in fifty words or less," Michael Kim said after identifying himself. "I have to brief Megan in ten minutes, so I can't wait for the formal writeup."

"Megan?"

"The mayor," Kim said. "We're very informal over here."

"Noted." Val rifled through her notes, scribbled all over a legal pad. "Here's what I've got: 300,000 reported cases of domestic abuse in the U.S., almost ninety percent against women," she said. "That equates to 1 out of every 500, every year. One in five women gets abused over their lifetime. For Clayton, that translates into two to three cases per week, and our local numbers are a little higher. Nationally, it's one case every nine seconds."

Kim let out a low whistle. "That must keep the DA busy. What's our conviction rate?"

Val laughed, a bitter bark devoid of humor. "That's the most depressing part. Less than one percent—and most don't even get to trial. Ninety percent of reported rapes and assaults against women get plea-bargained down to misdemeanors—or the charges get dropped altogether. Most go right back home to their partners without missing a meal." She sighed. Repeating her findings only made her feel worse.

"So, if a guy rapes a gal, he has only a one in ten chance of going to prison?" Kim asked, incredulous.

"Less," Val said. "Three-quarters of rape victims never report it to police. One report in five leads to arrest. Most never get prosecuted."

"That's...that's crazy," Kim said. Keyboard-tapping sounds filled a brief silence. "Go ahead and send the report," he said. "What's your availability look like today? I may need to pull you into this meeting."

Val groaned. Not another damned briefing with politicians. "Sorry," she said. "We're, uh, short-staffed. And didn't you say the meeting starts in ten? It takes twenty-five minutes to get there. Time better spent writing this up for you, don't you think?"

Her cell phone buzzed on the desk, a number she didn't recognize. "Gotta go. Good luck in the meeting." She hung up before he could reply and answered her cell. "Dawes here."

"Valorie?" The male voice on the other end sounded familiar. "I mean, uh, Officer Dawes?"

"That's me," she said. "Who's this?"

"Diego Collier," the man said. "From the bridge? Where you found that girl in the river?"

"Oh, yes." Val had forgotten about giving him her card. "Did you remember something else about the crime scene?"

"Not exactly," he said. "What I was calling about, actually, was...I wondered if we could, you know, meet. For, like, coffee, or something."

Val pulled the phone away from her ear and stared at it. If she understood him correctly, a good-looking man had just asked her out. And, unlike most of the jerks who'd hit on her since college, he had actually been polite about it.

"Diego, that's very sweet of you," she said. "I'm not sure if that's a good idea, since we're both potential witnesses to the Olivia Lambert case. Lawyers might suspect collusion, or something." She had no idea if that were true, but it sounded reasonable, and gave her an excuse to say no.

"Actually, the prosecutor said I wouldn't be called, since I don't really know anything," he said. "And I wasn't much help to you that day. I thought I should, you know...make it up to you. You like coffee, right? I mean, all cops like coffee, right?" He laughed, a nervous chuckle. "Sorry, that's probably a stupid thing to say. Maybe we could go for a run together instead?"

She smiled. His nervousness charmed her a bit. How long had Beth been after her to go on a real date? At least to meet the occasional guy, have a conversation with a man who didn't wear a gun and a badge. She could count her dates—all of them, for her entire life—on both hands, with fingers left over. Beth was right. Time to change that.

She drew in a deep breath and held it for a long moment. "How about an early brunch? Claytown Café at 9:00 on Monday?"

"I love that place," he said in a rush of air. "I'll see you there!"

She hung up, her heart pounding. What had she just done?

Chapter Five

Curtis Iverson rode the elevator to the top floor of the sixteen-story glass high-rise that housed Constitution Finance and Equity, the largest privately held investment firm in Hartford's financial district. Over 1,000 employees reported to Curtis in his role as Vice President of Investment Operations. That included LeeAnn Schofield, the latest in a string of pretty young women who traded below-market salaries for the prestige, perks, and privileges afforded executive secretaries in large financial firms. He sometimes experienced a pang of guilt about low-balling LeeAnn on their salary negotiation ten months before and vowed to make it up to her on her next annual review. If she lasted that long, unlike her four predecessors.

LeeAnn greeted him with a cheerful smile when he entered the executive suite. She stood to hand him a yellow 9x12" sealed envelope with the word "CONFIDENTIAL" stamped across it in red block letters. "This came for you by private courier while you were at lunch," she said. "Oh, and your 1:15 meeting with Accounting was moved back to 2:00. I had to reschedule your appointment with the Pratt and Whitney team to Monday at 8:00 a.m. I hope that's okay."

"You're amazing, LeeAnn." *In so many ways.*

Her pale white skin blushed red, a stark contrast to her shoulder-length platinum-blonde locks. "Thank you, Mr. Iverson," she said, her bright blue eyes downcast.

"Please, call me Curt." When she handed him the envelope, her hand brushed against his. He inhaled a quick breath and his gaze fell to her body's ample curves. Yes, LeeAnn needed to stay on. Maybe he'd give her that raise sooner—with a promotion, perhaps. Into a role that kept her...closer. "I'd like to review the notes from last month's Accounting meeting," he said. "Could you print a copy and bring them in to me?"

"I could email them to you faster," she said, returning to her desk.

"I'd rather see them on paper," he said. "Apologies to the trees I'm killing. Please, don't tell my wife." He smiled, but chided himself for mentioning Megan and ruining the moment.

"Of course, Mr. Iv—uh, *Curt*." LeeAnn's fingers clicked on her keyboard, and moments later, her printer whirred.

Curtis hurried into his office and shut the door. The sender had not included a return address. He frowned and shook the envelope. It contained something stiff, like card stock. He slit open the flap and emptied it onto his desk. A short stack of documents, paper-clipped together, landed face-up with a brief, typewritten note on top.

Mr. Iverson,

Is there any reason that the attached should not go viral sometime between now and election day next year?

Perhaps you'd prefer to discuss this privately, rather than at a news conference. Call me at 2:15, or I call the *Hartford Courant* at 2:20.

No signature, just a typed phone number. Curtis stared at the note, his heart pounding. What did the mysterious sender know that would embarrass his wife and derail her candidacy? Many possibilities came to mind. *Associations* of a particular type, with certain *individuals,* of which and of whom Megan might not approve.

His breathing grew shallow. With shaking hands, he unclipped the letter from the rest of the packet. He slid the page aside, revealing a stack of 8x10" photographs. The top one showed Megan giving the kickoff speech at a recent read-to-poor-kids event at a local school, where he also volunteered once a month. Nothing sinister there. In the next, he posed with the other volunteers, his arms wrapped around the two youths on either side of him. Another showed a similar scene, this one with Megan. Nothing nefarious jumped out at him. He relaxed.

Until he uncovered a 4x6" portrait of a teenage girl with shoulder-length blonde hair, a wide smile, and dark eyes. A familiar face, and one that had splashed across newspapers and TV screens in recent days. The next photo showed him with the girl, entering the lobby of a well-lit building with his hand on her back. Black and white, this one appeared grainy and not quite in focus. The kind of image created by pulling a still shot from, say, a private security camera. In a building he knew quite well...and his wife did not.

Dammit!

He examined the pictures again with more care. Sure enough, in each image, the girl's brooding visage appeared.

Someone, somewhere, had connected him—and Megan, and her climbing political ambitions—with the late Olivia Lambert. His photos, in particular, looked incriminating, or at least embarrassing.

But how much did they really know? And who were "they"?

Curtis checked the note again, its implied threat, and the demand for the 2:15 call. A call he couldn't miss.

A quick knock on the door startled him, and he hid the photos under the yellow envelope. LeeAnn pushed open the door moments later, carrying a printout loaded with numbers and graphs. "Here's that accounting report you requested," she said. "I'm sorry, Curt—did I interrupt something?"

"No, no." He rested his elbows on the envelope. "Listen, I need to postpone that 2:00 meeting. Can we push it back to, say, 2:30?"

LeeAnn shot him a puzzled look. "Is something wrong?" she said.

"Nothing wrong, no," he said. "I just need to, uh, take care of something. Something urgent."

She glanced at the envelope and her expression grew suspicious. Dammit! He needed a diversion—one that would buy her loyalty, in case anyone came around asking questions. Questions that, if answered, would lead to politically damaging conclusions.

And if they asked the wrong people—people not sufficiently motivated to keep quiet—those answers might be forthcoming.

"This actually involves you," he said. "Would you please close the door and have a seat?"

Surprise replaced suspicion in her expression—good!—and she did as he'd asked. "What's this about?" she said.

"Ms. Schofield," he said, licking his lips, "let's talk about your future at Constitution Finance."

***

Travis kept Val on desk duty all weekend, but transitioned her to the swing shift where they needed more help. On the one hand, the high volume of calls helped the time pass. But sitting for long hours in the department's lousy desk chairs left her stiff and sore by the end of her Sunday shift.

A late-night run would remedy that.

After clocking out that evening, Val changed into running clothes and headed toward the rear exit of the precinct station. A well-lit running trail passed close by the back gate of the parking lot, one that afforded both security and privacy. It also presented a physical challenge with its occasional sharp, uphill grades. A steady rain fell outside, so she began her stretching regimen in the dingy, musty hallway. Halfway through a set of walking lunges, Rico Lopez turned the corner and headed her way.

Val took a deep breath, and not just because of the exertion. Their eyes locked, his full of intensity.

Shit. She averted her gaze. Maybe he'd let her pass without—

Rico stopped a few feet away from her and shoved his hands in his pockets, waiting until she glanced back at him before he spoke. "Dawes," he said, "can we talk?"

She paused in her lunges, glancing around the dark, empty corridor. "Here?"

He gazed at her for a moment, a frown forming on his face. "If that's okay."

She sighed and rested one leg on a chair, putting weight on it to stretch out her hamstrings. "I was about to go for a run," she said. "How about tomorrow?"

He edged closer, and lowered his voice. "For reasons I don't want to get into here...I can't tomorrow."

She dropped her leg to the floor, hands on hips. She took in his slumping posture, his downcast eyes, the solemn line of his lips. After nine hours of desk duty, she really needed some exercise.

But the relationship with her partner came first.

"Okay," she said. She sat in the chair, and as if on cue, the rain outside intensified, pounding the windows with mesmerizing regularity. Rico leaned against the wall across from her, arms folded. She waited several moments in silence while he pulled his thoughts together. Every so often he started to speak, then stopped. Finally, his gaze met hers.

"First, I wanted to apologize for being such an ass the

other day," he said in a hoarse voice. "And for getting you in trouble. I talked to Gibson and explained that I was the one who started the argument. I don't know what got into me, but I was out of line, and I'm sorry."

"Thanks, Rico. Apology accepted. I shouldn't have said what I did, either," she said. "It was childish and disrespectful."

"For what it's worth, Gibson agrees with both of us," Rico said with a sour grin. "I also told him, just so you know, that I do trust you, and I do have your back. All that crap was just my anger talking." He stared at his feet and took a few heavy breaths.

"I hear ya," Val said. "Been there, done that."

He surrendered a quick, sad smile and glanced up at her. The hall seemed to grow darker. Outside, the rain mixed with hail, pelting the windows like an angry drummer. Whatever else might come of this conversation, Rico had done her a favor, saving her from a solid drenching.

"So," she said after another long pause, "does this mean we're still partners?"

"That's the second thing." He turned away, stared down the dark hallway for a few seconds, then looked at her sideways. "Gibson is taking me off patrol for a while. Says I need to return to counseling before he can put me back on the streets. So, you're flying solo for a while."

"Aw, crap." Val hung her head. "He's totally overreacting. I'll talk to him—"

"No," Rico said, his sharp tone silencing her. He stared upward, and let out a long stream of air with puffed lips. "I'm...not in the right frame of mind to be out there. Ever since Samuels got shot, I've been a mess. Angry, jittery, half the time afraid to go into a situation that might get a little messy. The other half of the time I can't wait to shoot the first motherfucker who opens the door when I knock. Then I partner with Pops, and he gets it from the same dude. And don't even get me started with Gil."

"Hey, take it easy on yourself," she said. "You weren't even there for that one. But you were right, earlier: I *was* there, for all three. At the very least, I'm bad luck." Her voice caught as the reality of her words struck her. Three cops down in one year, all attached to her. Who'd ever want to partner with her?

"Tell me something," he said. "Has this screwed up your sleep at all? Because I'm a damned wreck."

Val nodded. "Yeah, but I've never been a sound sleeper anyway." She shuddered. No need to share why. Stay present, girl. "The images are hard to shake."

"I'm lucky to get two hours," Rico said. "On a good night."

"And on a bad one?" she asked.

"Most nights," he said, his voice raspy, "I lay awake all night, wondering how I could have stopped my partners from getting cut down by that fucker. In the end, I have to admit, I flat-out wasn't up to it." He met her gaze again. "Only you were able to take that asshole down. And I owe you for it."

Val swallowed hard. "Thanks," she said, her voice dry. A familiar pang tightened her gut. Yes, she remained proud of stopping serial rapist Richard Harkins after a long manhunt. But the memory of pulling her weapon, aiming, firing at another human being...watching him fall, and bleed, and writhe on the pavement...those memories still haunted her.

But so did other memories: seeing his young victims after the fact, bruised and broken, emotionally scarred...

And memories of another large, powerful man, hovering over her, pinning Val to her bed—

"How about you?" he asked. "What's a bad night look like for you?"

She looked away. "On a bad night," she said, "I dream."

***

Val spotted Diego waiting outside The Claytown Café on Monday morning, five minutes early and holding a newspaper over his head to shield himself from the steady drizzle. He smiled and extended a hand toward her when she approached. At first she shuddered, thinking he wanted to hug her *already*. Ugh. Then she noticed the pink rose in his hand. She couldn't remember what that color rose signified, but it struck her as sweet. Innocent, even.

"Thanks," she said, accepting the flower. She couldn't recall a guy giving her flowers before. "Shall we get out of the rain?"

Diego grinned, and his dark eyes seemed to glisten. Or was that the rain? He had a warm smile, perfect light-brown skin, and a gentle demeanor about him. So unexpected from such a handsome, athletic guy, and so welcome after too many experiences with aggressive jocks who only wanted one thing.

A tall, slender woman of about twenty, with shaggy pink hair streaked with black, greeted them inside the café's glass door. "Val-Pal!" Pinkie crushed Val in tattoo-covered arms before she could escape. "It's, like, so boss to see you. Who's this, the new boy toy? Hi, I'm Alexa, but everyone calls me Pinkie for some reason." She let go of Val and enveloped Diego in a hug of equal magnitude.

"This is Diego," Val said. "Diego, this is, er, *Alexa*, my favorite barista."

"Aw, you're too cool for school." Pinkie grinned, revealing a gold tongue piercing—new since Val's last visit—that matched the ones in her nose and lip. "Hey, did you hear? The cook added something to the menu for you. I totally hope you order it. The Hero's Gyro. Get it? I named it myself!" She guided Diego by the hand past the eight or ten tiny Formica-topped tables to a booth and slapped down a pair of menus.

"Some 'cinos for you two?" Pinkie continued as they sat. "Or are you more of a latté lad?"

Diego laughed, and his eyes sparkled again. "Whatever you do best here." He grinned at Val and mouthed: "She's awesome!" Diego's foot bumped hers under the table, and she resisted the urge to yank her leg away. Give him a chance, here.

"Cappuccino for me." Val laughed after Pinkie scooted back behind the service counter. "She's a Category Five hurricane, that one."

"Cool that they named a sandwich for you," he said. "You're a celebrity around here, eh?"

"Meh," Val said. "Pinkie likes me."

"No, I Googled you," Diego said. "You're amazing." He coughed into his fist. "I mean, you've got quite the story."

"Don't believe what you read, especially on that shitty Clayton Copwatch blog." Val's skin grew warm. He'd Googled her?

"No, really," Diego said. "You shot that rapist dude, and that gang leader. That takes balls, man."

Val smirked and glanced down at her lap. "Apparently not."

Diego's face fell. "Sorry, that was rude," he said. "I'm sounding like Kent now."

"Kent?"

"My running buddy. On the bridge?"

"Oh, yeah. I'd forgotten about him. On purpose." Val kept an eye on Diego to see how he'd react. Defend his friend's wolfish behavior, or kiss up to her on their first date?

Neither. "I'm glad," he said with a grin. "I was pretty embarrassed by how he acted there. Please don't hold it against me."

"You, no. Him, yes," she said, smiling. "So, you know my story. What's yours?"

"I'm a senior in pre-med at Western New England," he said, "going to UConn Medical in the fall. I hope...and so do my parents."

"Are they local?" Val said.

Diego's smile faded. "Mom is. They divorced when I was twelve, and my mom moved us kids—I have an older brother and a younger sister—to Clayton from Providence. Dad's still in Rhode Island."

"You didn't go to Liberty Heights High," Val said, "I'd have remembered you." She blushed, realizing what she'd just admitted: he had a seriously handsome face.

"Nope," he said, brightening. "Southside, class of 2015. I'm a Wildcat."

A year behind her, then. "Any sports?"

"Track—I ran the 440 and the half-mile," he said. "One year of football. But I'm not into the NFL or anything. Pro sports on TV are boring. You?"

"Track and soccer—high school and college. And jiu jitsu."

"Like, martial arts fighting?" he asked.

"Not 'fighting' per se. Non-violent self-defense," she said. "But not so much lately. Work keeps me too busy."

"I bet."

A moment or two passed, neither of them knowing quite how to continue. Val went back over what he'd told her. "Uh...why medicine? Why not law, or, say, astrophysics?"

"It's kind of the family business," Diego said. "Mom's an OB/GYN, and Dad's a clinical researcher for Metcalf. I even have an uncle who's a dentist."

"Yet the sight of a body makes you puke," Val said with a laugh. "I'd have thought that'd be old hat for you."

"We're doctors, not morticians," Diego said.

Val blushed. "Sorry," she said, not knowing what else to say.

He grinned. "I'm just messing with ya. Yeah, I've got a weak stomach. Med school's gonna be a trip."

"If you have a weak stomach, you're in the wrong place," Pinkie said, arriving with their beverages. She laughed. "Just kidding. The cook here's totally boss. What can I get you?"

"I'll do the Hero's Gyro," Diego said, "in Valorie's honor."

"Same," Val said. "How can I resist?"

Pinkie gathered up the menus, making wide eyes at Val and giving Diego a quick but approving smile. He lowered his gaze, and his foot nudged hers again. This time, she didn't move her leg away. His touch, even if accidental, spooked her less with each passing moment.

Diego cleared his throat and smiled at her. "So, why'd you become a cop?" he asked.

Val took a deep breath. "That's a long story," she said, "but the short version is, I always wanted to be a detective. Find bad guys who hurt people and put them behind bars."

"Like your uncle," he said.

She nodded. "My role model."

"A good one," he said. "I mean, except for him getting killed and all."

Another awkward pause ensued. Val chided herself. She'd gone on few dates, even in college, and had never developed any skill at making small talk. Apparently, neither had Diego. They exchanged smiles and sipped their coffees again.

"Excellent coffee," he said.

"The best." Val's ears burned. Say. Something. Anything.

"So, how often do you run at the river?" Diego asked after an eternity.

"Four or five nights a week," she said. "You?"

"I used to run there a lot," Diego said. "But since coming across Oliv—er, that girl's body, I've kind of, ah—"

"Wait," Val said. "You knew her?"

"I knew *of* her," Diego said. "Kind of."

"What do you mean, *kind of?*" Suspicion rose in Val's chest. She recalled Uncle Val's dictum when he'd served as a Clayton PD detective: There are no coincidences.

"I hadn't ever met her," he said. "I didn't know it was her, so—"

"Why would you think you should have recognized her?" Val said, tension creeping into her voice. "What's your connection to her?"

"None, really," he said. "But I guess Kent had dated her a few times—"

"Wait, what? How? Olivia was sixteen! Kent's what, twenty-four, twenty-five?"

"Twenty-one," Diego said. "Their families know each other somehow. I don't know how, you'll have to ask him."

"Why didn't either of you tell this to the investigators?" Val said, no longer hiding her frustration.

Diego grimaced. "Again, we didn't know it was her. And Kent never came down off the bridge, remember? Which, come to think of it, is kind of weird."

Val reached across the table and grabbed Diego's wrist. "You need to put me in touch with Kent," she said, "and I mean now."

Diego's eyes widened. "He just flew off to Florida for spring break. But I can give you his cell."

"Thanks. I'll need that ASAP." Val sighed. Another blanket of silence settled over them, this time borne out of tension and disappointment rather than awkwardness. They exchanged comments about the intensifying rainstorm, and how they, maybe, could run together sometime. But Val's heart was no longer in it. They ate quickly, declined Pinkie's suggestion of dessert, and split the bill without debating it. She left the restaurant minutes later with Kent's number in her pocket. Ah, the irony—ending a date by getting his friend's number...for work reasons.

The awkwardness of their date disappointed her, and Val doubted she'd see Diego again. But the unexpected link to Olivia Lambert's murder filled her with excitement—and a new sense of purpose.

Chapter Six

An hour after leaving the café, Val pushed through the wide glass doors at Clayton police headquarters, a concrete block of a building right out of the Stalin school of architecture. She rushed through the cavernous marble and granite lobby, pausing for a moment at the Wall of Remembrance to gaze with reverence at the photo of her uncle. She took the stairs to the third floor, and took a seat in the office of her friend and mentor, Detective Shannon O'Reilly.

"So, how is it you know this Kent Mercer, anyway?" Shannon asked after setting Val up with lukewarm coffee. The detective relaxed her tall, slender frame behind an oversized wooden desk, her long blonde hair tied up in a bun. "Friend of yours?"

"Friend of a friend." Val sipped the coffee. "Kent and another guy, Diego Collier, were running behind me when I found Olivia Lambert's body. Your team interviewed them, but with no ID of the victim at the scene, nobody connected Kent to her before now."

"Olivia's parents never mentioned any boyfriend," Shannon said. "But I checked him out after you called. He attends UConn at the Hartford campus, which must be how they met. Olivia took dual credit classes there. Kent worked as a lab assistant to one of her science profs. But he's clean as a whistle. No record, not even a traffic ticket."

"Diego thought their families knew each other somehow," Val said. "Does that check out?"

"Let's find out." Shannon waved Val closer and put her phone on speaker, then dialed. A woman answered.

"Mrs. Lambert, this is Detective O'Reilly with Clayton Police," Shannon said. "Sorry to bother you again. How are you feeling today?"

A long pause ensued before the woman's heavy voice responded. "I'm managing," Mrs. Lambert said. "How can I help you?"

"We're following up on a matter related to Olivia," Shannon said. "Do you know a guy named Kent Mercer?"

"He's a fine young man," Mrs. Lambert said. "His mother and I are friends, and I was Kent's first-grade teacher."

"Were you aware of the fact that he and Olivia may have been seeing each other?" Shannon asked.

Mrs. Lambert paused. "Livvy and Kent weren't dating. I'm certain of it."

Shannon and Val exchanged wary glances. Shannon took a deep breath. "A friend of Kent's informed us otherwise," Shannon said. "Diego Collier. He—"

"I don't know anyone named Diego," Mrs. Lambert said, irritation in her voice. "But I know Livvy. We talked every day. If she had a boyfriend, I'd have known about it."

"With all due respect, Mrs. Lambert," Shannon said, "teenagers don't always tell their parents every—"

"Are you calling my daughter a liar?" Mrs. Lambert said, her voice rising. "How dare you. Calling me to accuse her of this, while our family is grieving her loss! How heartless can you be?" She broke down, and loud sobs replaced her angry voice over the line.

"I'm sorry, Mrs. Lambert. I didn't mean it that way." Shannon shuddered out the last few words, her face clouded with guilt and worry.

The crying subsided, succeeded by sniffles. "If there's nothing else," Mrs. Lambert said, "I have a funeral to plan."

"Tomorrow," Shannon mouthed to Val. Into the phone, she added, "My sympathies once again, Mrs. Lambert. Thank you for your time."

The woman broke the connection without saying goodbye.

"Ouch," Val said. "I guess we touched a nerve."

"I'll have to assume that Mom also wasn't aware that Olivia was sexually active," Shannon said, shaking her head.

"Getting raped isn't the same as sexually active," Val said through gritted teeth.

"We need to bring Kent in, get his DNA tested, see if he's a match," Shannon said, oblivious to Val's testy tone. "Since you know him, can you help track him down?"

Val held her breath. "I don't really know him, but, sure," she said. "I may have burned my best bridge to him this morning. But I did get his number." She slid the scrap of napkin across the desk.

"Your date didn't end well?" Shannon said.

Val sighed. "My dates never end well."

***

Gibson assigned Val more desk work that afternoon, which included fielding overflow calls referred from Dispatch. Her first calls included four about loose and barking dogs, two from irate homeowners about suspicious men "walking while Black," and a purse-snatching two hours after the fact. But a mid-afternoon caller's seemingly innocuous complaint grabbed her attention.

"After he busted my fence," the woman complained, "he started creeping around my house at night. He looks in our windows all the time. I think he's trying to break in."

"How often has he done this, Mrs. Stapleton?" Val asked, typing notes into an online citizen complaint form. "And when did it begin?"

"Couple of times. He peeked in on my daughter last week when she was showering. I called 9-1-1 and you guys did *nothing*—like always. The girl's only sixteen, for God's sake!"

Val sat up and went on high alert. Another creeper stalking an underage girl—or, possibly, the same man. "Is he there now?" she asked.

"He's home, staring out the window right this second. He likes to look in her bedroom window while she's changing after school. Which is soon. Are you gonna get over here or what?"

Val took her name and address and promised a quick response. She found Travis in his office and explained the situation.

"Can you come out to the site with me?" she asked. "Gibson told me to respond to cases at my discretion, but I need a partner."

"We get calls like this every day. What's the big draw on this one?" Travis said, squinting up at her from his desk.

"He's stalking a kid," Val said. "What more do you need?"

"All right, let's go." They hustled to the parking lot. "Why didn't Dispatch send someone last time?" Travis asked, unlocking his cruiser with the remote. "That makes no sense."

"They probably heard a woman's voice and 'my neighbor's bugging me' and filed it under 'Who Cares?'" Val said.

Travis frowned. "A Peeping Tom with a perp still on scene ought to have been a Code 2. I'll kick some ass when we get back." He raced the cruiser out of the lot before Val had finished buckling in.

Fifteen minutes later, they arrived at Connie Stapleton's. The one-story cottage-style house had a mossy roof, with faded white paint on a patchwork of shake-siding shingles— at least, on the ones that hadn't fallen off. Grass grew in the multitude of cracks between concrete chunks that once comprised a sidewalk. Weeds choked most of the lawn.

Travis knocked on the front door and rang the bell. They

waited and listened. Silence. After Travis knocked again, Val glanced at the cedar-plank fence that divided the Stapleton property from the small, wood-sided Cape Cod next door. Its owner paid far closer attention to maintenance details than most other homes in the area. A wide gap toward the rear split the fence into two sections, both of which leaned at acute angles over Mrs. Stapleton's yard. The damaged fence Stapleton had complained about, Val assumed. An empty driveway ran along the fence.

Huffing with impatience, Travis knocked for the third time. "Did we get the address wrong?" he asked.

The door flew open, and a fragile-looking woman with hollow, deep-set eyes peered out at them. She wore a thick bathrobe and rubbed her straggly brown hair with a tattered towel. "Took you long enough," the woman said. "And you're too late. He left right after I called." She tried to close the door, but Travis stopped it with his foot.

"If you don't mind," he said, "we'd like to ask you a few questions, so we can—"

"I do mind," she said. "I got called in to work ten minutes ago. If I'm late, I lose the shift."

"Ma'am," Val said, "you called us. If you want us to stop your neighbor's stalking, we need your cooperation."

"You gonna stay and watch my daughter when she gets home?" Stapleton asked, her tone somewhere between skeptical and hostile.

"If what you tell us gives us cause, we can keep an eye out," Travis said.

"Fine. Ask me while I get ready." Stapleton glared at Travis and pointed at Val. "Her, not you." She disappeared into the shadows of the house, leaving the door ajar.

"I'll wait here for the daughter or the neighbor, whichever comes first," Travis said. He settled his massive frame into a metal folding chair by the door.

Val found Stapleton slipping into a plain blue dress in a rear bedroom, the door wide open. An unmade queen-sized mattress covered most of the floor, accompanied by a small wooden dresser stained dark cherry, and a white laminated makeup stand and mirror. The smell of mold competed with some sort of cheap perfume, enough to choke anyone who entered.

"I wait tables at the Jasper Street Diner," Connie said without facing Val. "Every shift they give me, I have to take it. I need the cash."

"Sure, I get that," Val said, scribbling on a small notepad. "What's your neighbor's name?"

"Boyd, Bobby, something like that," Stapleton said, strapping on a pair of flats. "A French last name of some sort."

"Is he new to the area?" Val asked.

Stapleton sat at a makeup table and applied foundation to her wrinkled skin. "He moved in over Christmas. He doesn't seem to have a job or anything." Her voice lowered to a conspiratorial whisper. "I think he's a fugitive, or maybe he's in witness protection. A lot of shady-looking guys come and go at all hours of the night. Probably a drug dealer."

Val peered out the bedroom windows. None faced the man's house. "Which room is your daughter's?"

Stapleton pointed toward the hallway and plugged in a hair dryer. "Second door on the left, next to the bathroom." She flicked on the dryer, which could have drowned out the noise of a 747.

Val checked the bathroom first. Sure enough, a small, curtainless window exposed the shower to the backyard. In the daughter's bedroom, two double-hung windows sported open blinds and faced the suspected neighbor's house. Stapleton's story seemed plausible enough.

She glanced around the bedroom. A twin bed tucked into the deepest corner of the room, and near it sat a small study desk. A half-dozen schoolbooks lay stacked next to the desk. A 4x6" photo of a much-younger Connie Stapleton smiled up from the back, holding an infant girl. Above it, on the wall, Sierra had mounted a framed 8x10" team photo, with gold letters emblazoned in fancy italics across the bottom:

Liberty High School – Varsity Volleyball, 2018-19

Val stepped closer to search the photo. Sure enough, the shy face of the late Olivia Lambert smiled back at her from the second row. A connection! Could the neighbor have known Olivia through Sierra?

"Who are you and what the fuck are you doing in my bedroom?" a girl's voice shouted behind Val.

Val spun around to face the speaker, a teenage girl close to six feet tall with long black hair tied back into a thick ponytail. She wore gym shorts, despite the frigid weather, and a "Liberty Lions" sweatshirt.

"Officer Dawes, Clayton PD. Your mother called us with a complaint about your neighbor. You must be Sierra."

"And you must be fucking crazy to listen to anything my mother says," Sierra said. "Bo's harmless. Which is more than I can say about her. Now would you mind? I need to change." She pointed to the door, and without waiting for Val to respond, yanked her sweatshirt over her head. She kicked off her shorts, revealing a white unitard, and glared at Val again. "Go on, you perv. Get out of here."

"If you could stay at least partially dressed for a second longer," Val said, reddening, "I want to ask you about...Bo, is it? Is that short for something?"

"Bowden Rousseau. Bo's an okay guy. He's not a stalker. Yeah, he looked in the window the other day, but I talked to him about it. I talk to him almost every day, actually. He's just worried about my mom and me, living alone." Sierra waited for Val, loud exhalations signaling that the interview had already gone on too long. "I'll give you his number, if it makes you feel any better. Right now I have to drive my mom to work and myself to practice, so could you please...?" She pulled jeans out of her dresser and waited, glaring, again.

Val sighed and exited to the living room, where Connie stood by the front door, holding her purse. "He just got home," Connie said, indicating the neighbor's house with a toss of her head. "May be a good time to go scare him a little, you think?"

"Mrs. Stapleton," Val said, "your daughter seems to think Mr. Rousseau poses no threat to you. Are you sure—"

"Oh, for Christ's sake," Stapleton said. "Typical cops, always taking the man's side. The sonofabitch is gaslighting her. I thought maybe as a woman you'd be more understanding. Guess that just goes to show." She fished a pack of cigarettes and a lighter from her purse and lit up, exhaling blue smoke toward the ceiling. "I don't know why I bother."

"I'm not saying who I believe," Val said. "Tell you what. We'll have a chat with Bo—"

"Oh, so now he's 'Bo' to you? You and him are old pals? Figures." Another massive cloud of blue.

"Connie, I—"

"Come on, Mom," Sierra said, rushing into the room and scooping car keys off an end table. "You're going to be late." She wore jeans and a button-down blouse, with her hair loose around her shoulders. In moments, she'd transformed from a rugged athlete to an elegant young woman. Her appearance couldn't have differed more from her mother's.

Stapleton opened the door and waved Val outside. As Val passed, Connie said in a low voice, "Stake out his house for a day, and you'll see. That creep is trouble, I tell you."

"Mom," Sierra said, "leave Bo alone."

Val stepped into the chilly March air to find the front stoop empty and an old Toyota Camry in the driveway. She waved to the Stapletons and promised to follow up, then trudged over to Bo Rousseau's house. Through the front window, she spotted Travis talking with a thin, curly-haired white man with leathery skin. The man punctuated his dialog with exaggerated waves of his hands and a nervous smile. Travis caught her eye and gave his head a tiny shake. She returned to the cruiser to wait.

Travis rejoined her several minutes later. "Mr. Rousseau claims to not know what Mrs. Stapleton is talking about," Travis said. "Says he's friends with the daughter. What'd you find?"

"Sierra agrees with him," Val said. "Mrs. Stapleton strikes me as a little unstable. But," she added, "it's all kind of creepy. Isn't he in his thirties or something?"

Travis nodded. "He's not exactly the model of stability and honesty, either. Kind of a shifty creep, if you ask me."

Val mulled that over. "Sierra and Olivia Lambert were teammates on volleyball. So he might have known her, too."

Travis considered it, then shook his head. "That's not enough of a connection to convince a judge to issue a warrant."

Val sighed. Perhaps not. But it was something. And it bugged her.

***

A knock sounded on Val's bedroom door early the next morning. "Val?" Beth said. "Don't you have to get ready for work?"

"Today's my day off." Val moaned into her pillow. So much for sleeping in.

The door popped open, and Beth entered, wearing shorts

and one of Josh's football jerseys. She held up a pair of steaming mugs of coffee, then sat on the edge of Val's bed.

Val sat up and accepted the offered brew. Beth never entered without an invitation. Something had to be wrong. "What's up?" she asked. "Where's Josh?"

"He…stayed at his place last night." Beth's expression grew somber. "I…wanted some alone time."

"You? Alone? In bed?" Val shook her head. "You alien bastard. Who are you, and what have you done with my friend?"

Beth laughed. Then worry clouded her face. "I had a reunion committee meeting, and then…I just needed to be away from him for a night. Is that bad?"

Val shrugged. "I may be the wrong person to ask, seeing as I've never needed more than a twin bed my entire life. But, hey, I'm sure everyone goes through this. Josh probably wanted a night off, too."

"He better not have!" Beth said, indignant. "I fully expect him to call any second, telling me how blue his balls are."

Val laughed and choked on her coffee, nearly spewing it all over her bed. "Did you *have* to say that when my mouth was full?"

Beth slid into bed next to Val, draping an arm over her shoulder. "I was hoping to spend some time with you last night, but you got home so late. When are you getting off this awful swing shift?"

Val's smile crumpled. "You shouldn't worry about me so much. Most days, my job is the most boring one in the world."

Beth scoffed. "Don't bullshit a bullshitter," she said. "Twice in the first six months, someone tried to kill you—that I know of."

"But they didn't." Val wished she could have summoned a more confident tone. "What brings this on, anyway? You've never worried about me before."

"You didn't used to find dead bodies of girls floating in the river before," Beth said, her voice quiet. "Please tell me you have a lead on this weirdo and are going to lock him up any day now. I have to admit, Val, this guy scares me, and a lot of other women I've talked to."

Val nodded. "He's a scary dude. But so far, we only know of the one victim for certain."

"Yeah. 'So far.' How reassuring." Beth snuggled down into the bed, dragging Val down with her.

"Something's wrong," Val said. "You don't usually let this stuff get to you."

Beth sighed. Val waited—Beth sometimes needed a few moments to gather up the right words. "I guess I'm kind of depressed about the wedding and all," Beth said after a long pause. "And Josh is no help. The jerk." She snorted and reached over the end table to grab her coffee.

"What'd he do?" Val said, careful not to add, "this time."

Beth drew another deep breath. "The night before last, one of his friends cracked a joke about…my body, thinking I couldn't hear it. A fucking fat joke! Josh not only didn't bust his ass," Beth went on in a rush of words, her voice breaking, "but he *laughed.*" Tears flowed down her face. "He fucking *laughed* at me, Val."

Val's heart ripped in half and she wrapped her arms tighter around her beautiful friend. She held her for a long minute, then whispered, "Men are pigs, aren't they?"

"Every damned one of them," Beth said, sniffling, then laughing. She wiggled out of Val's tight embrace and sat up again.

"Tell me he apologized, at least," Val said.

"The little shit practically got on his knees and begged forgiveness," Beth said, laughing out loud now. "But if he thinks that's enough, watch out. That boy's going to develop a serious case of rug burn before I let his sorry ass back in my bed."

Val laughed, imagining Josh's bony knees scraped raw on their apartment's cheap industrial carpet. "Imagine how much he'll save on shoes," she said with a wicked smile.

Beth snorted. "Speaking of guys," she said, "how'd your date go with that guy, what's his name? Dave?"

Val groaned and ducked her head. "*Diego.* It started out okay, but..." She sighed. "I don't think I should see him again."

"Val Dawes, tell me you didn't leave before dessert *again.*"

"Nobody has dessert at brunch." Val lowered her eyes again and sipped from her mug.

"Are you kidding? Sometimes I have *only* dessert at brunch. So what's the problem?"

Val sighed. "He's connected to the case. It...doesn't feel right to go any further."

Beth stared into the heavens. "It *never* feels right for you to 'go any further.' Good God, girl, give a guy a chance one of these days. When's the last time you had a second date?"

Val stared into her empty cup. "I'm not you, Beth. I just...can't. You know that."

A long moment passed. Beth rested her hand on Val's shoulder. "I'm sorry." She lifted Val's chin, forcing their eyes to meet. "Was he at least cute?"

Val nodded and smiled. "Yeah. Soft-spoken, athletic, an easy smile, kind eyes. Polite...respectful...smart, too."

"God, Val, he sounds perfect." Beth play-swooned over the bed, the back of her hand pressed against her forehead.

"Maybe I've forgiven Josh too soon. Come to me, Diego! Save me from marrying the wrong man!"

"Jeez, swoop right in, why don't you?" Val smacked Beth on the shoulder.

"I would never!" Beth straightened and cocked her head. "Are you sure you won't see him again?"

"I…don't think that's possible," Val said. "His friend may be a suspect, so—"

"Holy shit!" Beth laughed and slid off the bed. She mimed speaking into a mic like a sports announcer. "Winner of the gold medal, for the tenth year in a row…for creativity in finding the strangest possible guy to date…Miss Valorie Dawes!"

"Hey! Shut up!" Val swung her pillow at her, but Beth dodged it with ease.

"Strike one!" Beth said into her pretend mic.

"Cheater," Val said. "You know I won't hit you if it means spilling coffee all over my room."

Beth set her mug down on Val's end table and slid back into bed. She held Val in a tight hug. "I miss hanging out with you."

"Me, too," Val said, squeezing her back. "I'm going to miss it even more after you move out."

"*If* I move out. Fucking Josh!" Beth jumped up, ending the hug. "Since it's your day off, can we do something together tonight? Hit the gym or something?"

"I'd love that!" Val bounced out of bed, too. "You're sure? You aren't planning a night-long groveling session for your fiancé?"

Beth scoffed. "Let him suffer without me another night," she said. "Okay, I gotta get ready for work." She bounced out of the room, in as good a mood as Val had seen her in for months.

She pondered Beth's comments about Josh. Trouble in paradise, or a brief lover's quarrel? She harbored doubts about the guy, particularly whether he'd committed as fully to Beth as she had to him. She had never voiced her doubts to her friend. Not her place, she'd always thought. Beth could make her own choices.

But if Josh ever hurt Beth, Val vowed, he would rue the day.

Chapter Seven

A parade of black sedans with tinted glass pulled to a stop in front of the Nutmeg State Community Center. Tall, husky men with short hair and dark sunglasses—unnecessary in the drizzly, cold weather of late March—exited from every door of the front two and rear two cars. Like a precision drill, they fell into formation, a tunnel of dark suits leading up the walk to the center's entrance. The rear passenger door of the fifth car opened and a smiling Curtis Iverson emerged, wearing a gray suit and red tie. Megan Iverson slid out after him wearing a blue below-the-knee dress with a red sash. She smiled and waved to the TV cameras positioned behind burly bodyguards.

"Here's where we earn our OT," Travis Blake said to Val in a low voice.

Val followed Travis's lead, marching to the opening between the two lines of guards. They led the smiling, waving couple to the front door, with the dark-suited men forming a protective shield on either side.

The security detail seemed excessive to Val for a small-town mayor. The guards outnumbered the gathering of well-wishers, who clapped and yelled encouragement to Iverson. Several held "Iverson 2020" signs. Paid volunteers, Val guessed. Who else would wait outside in the rain?

Per protocol, they stopped in the tiny, dim foyer between the twin sets of double doors. Travis radioed the officers stationed inside: "We're ready." A voice radioed back: "On in two."

An amplified male voice inside the building pumped up what sounded like a much larger crowd, inciting them to cheer and chant: "Meg-*an*! Meg-*an*!" The cheering drowned out the emcee's garbled syllables, then morphed into rhythmic clapping and stomping of feet.

Travis's radio chirped static. He pushed open the door. "All right, Madam Mayor," he said. "The people await you."

Curtis hugged his wife and said something to her, and they followed a pair of security men inside. The remaining suits brought up the rear, two by two. Val and Travis entered and remained by the door.

The lobby of the community center had been set up with a stage at the far end, with a wide center aisle bisecting a few dozen rows of chairs. Cheering spectators covered in "Iverson 2020" and "I'm a Nut-4-Meg" stickers and buttons filled every seat. Piped-in music blared, and the crowd stood and accelerated its rhythmic clapping. As the mayor passed each row, a few smiling volunteers from each side joined the entourage, forming a massive parade of diverse faces—Black, white, young, old, and every conceivable gender identity.

"Clever," Val said. "It looks like a groundswell of support, growing as she reaches the stage."

Travis grunted. "Pure political theater," he said.

The crowd's cheers reached a crescendo when Iverson climbed onto the dais and shouted, "Thank you, Clayton!" The music amplified further, and blinking lights flooded the room—whether stage lighting or camera flashes, Val couldn't tell. The mayor blew kisses to the crowd and shook hands outstretched from the front row—VIP seating filled with big donors Gibson had advised them to watch with extra care.

"See anyone suspicious?" Val asked him.

"Besides the politicians, you mean?" Travis said with a smirk. "Not yet."

"Please welcome our next governor, Megan Iverson!" the emcee shouted into his mic. The crowd went wild again. The mayor approached center stage, smiling and waving into the cameras. Finally, the music faded, the cheering subsided, and Iverson opened her speech with a litany of thank-yous, acknowledgments, and claimed accomplishments before getting to the meat of her message.

"The great State of Connecticut has a proud history," she said, "of defending the rights and safety of our citizens. But today we face a crisis—and the most vulnerable among us are at a higher risk than ever before." The crowd's ebullient cheering quieted a bit, and the mayor's confident smile morphed into an expression of grim determination. "While official crime rates in our state have stabilized, this has not resulted in greater safety for many. Women, children, and people of color experience violent crime at levels of ten to fifty percent more than their white, male, adult counterparts. We need to fix this and *we need to fix it now*! Before another young girl dies at the hands of a predator!"

The crowd cheered even louder than before. "Black lives matter!" they chanted.

"Rape and domestic abuse are up in almost every city across the state," the mayor continued. "Here in Clayton, young women are being victimized at historically high rates. Young women don't feel safe walking alone at night. And who can blame them? Just ask Destiny Mathers! Ask the families of Olivia Lambert and Jaden King!"

"Take back the night! Take back the night!" the crowd roared.

Val shot Travis a puzzled frown. "Who's Jaden King?" she mouthed.

He held up a finger, pointed outside. He'd fill her in later.

"The problem is statewide, but solutions begin at home," Iverson said. "That is why I am announcing today that, under my authority as mayor, I am directing police chief Kevin MacMahon to appoint a special unit devoted to Women's Safety. I'm calling it the Women's Anti-Violence Emergency

Squad—in short, the WAVE Squad." The crowd responded with polite applause. "But the WAVE Squad won't be just another task force, lost in the bureaucracy," Iverson went on. "This unit will report *directly to me!*" The mayor paused to wait out a long, loud cheer, led by the women in the audience. Val maintained a poker face, but she had to admit, the idea intrigued her.

"WAVE is being charged with reducing rates of violent crime against women, children, and people of color by ten percent, *every year,*" the mayor said, to another round of raucous cheers. "A Citizen Advisory Board will oversee the work and report ongoing results to the public—that's *you*— *every month.* People, I want answers, and as the name suggests, I want to make—*waves*—*NOW!*"

More cheers. More chants. More loud clapping and stomping echoing off the cavernous walls of the lobby.

Val sighed. The mayor risked overselling the initiative with over-optimistic expectations. Like most people, she had no idea how actual policing works.

"When I am elected governor," Iverson said, her voice reaching top volume to stay above the din, "we'll bring the program statewide, to keep every woman and girl in the Nutmeg State safe from sexual predators!"

More cheers followed, and more loud music. Val gazed over the crowd in wonder, noting the emphasis of her pitch. Did people care that much about crime against women that the mayor could afford to make it the centerpiece of her campaign? Surely they'd done private polling to support that strategy. It didn't square with Val's own personal experience, before or since becoming a cop. But the mayor's commitment and energy made her doubt her cynicism. Maybe Megan Iverson *could* change things.

The mayor touched on a series of other bread-and-butter topics such as the budget, better roads, new parks, and improving the schools, but the crowd's enthusiasm waned. The energy returned when the speech wound to a close with a rousing call to action to clean up crime across the state.

"So if you want a safer, cleaner community—if you want to see our local successes in stopping violent sex offenders extend statewide—then join me in our march to the statehouse in 2020!" the mayor said.

More thunderous applause. The music resumed, and after several minutes of shaking hands, Iverson led her entourage off the stage and down the center aisle. Val and Travis escorted the group out the door, back to their waiting motorcade.

Once the mayor disappeared into her vehicle, Travis pulled Val aside. "All those statistics she cited...was that your research?" he asked, keeping his voice low.

Val frowned. "Sort of. Rape is up, but most of the other violent crime rates have gone down." She considered that another moment and fumed. The mayor's requests for Val to conduct research had come through official channels—not from the campaign. Taxpayers had paid for her work, burning hours she could have spent walking her beat. That, compounded by the mayor's misrepresentation of the facts, diminished the enthusiasm she'd felt a few minutes before.

"Is the chief aware of this?" Travis asked.

Val shrugged. She barely grasped office politics, much less the machinations of upper-level bureaucracy. "I'm interested in Jaden King. What can you tell me about her?"

Travis grunted. "Another drowning victim, from December. African-American girl, seventeen years old. Raped and drowned—oh, and get this." He leaned closer and lowered his voice to a whisper. "As with Olivia Lambert's case, this detail won't be in the papers, but she was barefoot, too."

"What the hell?" Val shook her head. "What's this guy

doing with their damned shoes?"

Travis shrugged, a hell-if-I-know expression sweeping his face. "I gotta check in with the crew. Give me a few." He sauntered off, mumbling into his radio.

"Valorie?" A female voice to Val's left caught her attention. A slender young Asian woman waved at her and ran toward her, arms outstretched.

"Amy?" Val recognized the woman as she drew near, an acquaintance from high school. She extended her hand for a shake, but Amy wrapped her in a hug anyway.

"It's so good to see you!" Amy said, releasing Val from the embrace. "Look at you, a policewoman! I read about you in the news last year. Are you working the event?"

"I am," Val said. Amy had always possessed a keen sense of the obvious. "What about you?"

"I'm an intern at WCLA-TV," she said. "Unpaid for now, but—wasn't that speech *amazing?*"

"It was...interesting," Val said. "Are you a supporter of the mayor?"

"Officially, I'm neutral, of course," Amy said. "But I have to admit, that proposal for the WAVE Squad was incredible! It's about time politicians focused on women's safety for a change, don't you think?"

"Sure," Val said, trying to keep the doubt out of her voice. "Look, I have to get back to work here, but—"

"Call me and we'll have coffee," Amy said, shoving a card into Val's hand. "Byeee!" She ran off to the WCLA-TV minivan parked across the street and disappeared inside.

Val gazed after Amy as Travis rejoined her. "I guess people really do get excited about this stuff," Val said.

"Whatever," Travis said. "Hey, I thought I should let you know. The shrink says Rico shouldn't return to patrol duty for at least another month or two. Sorry, Dawes, but you're stuck with desk duty and special events like this for a while."

Val sighed. If that meant doing research and security detail for a political candidate under the guise of public service, she'd be looking for a new assignment, and soon.

***

Megan Iverson waved one final time to the crowd of reporters and supporters outside the community center, then ducked into the back seat of the black sedan. Curt followed her in and side-hugged her before buckling up.

"You were splendid!" Curt hugged her again as the sedan pulled away from the rain-drenched curb. "The crowd loved you. And they loved the women's safety emphasis. It's a winner!" He patted her back, then pulled loose of her embrace.

"Thanks, honey," Megan said. "But you're not an objective observer. We'll see what the media coverage brings." She imagined the headlines: *Mayor baffles crowd with surprise campaign yawner.* While proud of her accomplishments, she'd never earned high marks for impassioned public speaking.

"The polling is underway already," he said with what she read as false bravado. "Pre-announcement polls for a baseline, post-announcement to measure the bump. That'll keep the buzz going, too." He smiled, but tinges of worry in his voice belied his rah-rah enthusiasm.

She looked away. "What about the media? Is the WAVE Squad big enough? Or did I go 'too local' or 'too small' for a statewide run?"

Curtis drew back, as if studying her. He'd urged Megan to make it the centerpiece of the campaign, overcoming her doubts that it could mobilize women, minority, and anti-crime voting blocs. Combined with her base of social progressives, blue-collar workers, and fiscal conservatives, he'd argued it would give her a powerful, if unconventional, winning coalition. He'd also insisted that it would open up some huge donor pocketbooks, like Emily's List and BlackPAC—money the cash-strapped campaign desperately needed.

Still, she appreciated his enthusiasm—and needed it, to counter her private pessimism. Megan, for all of her confidence and for all that she'd accomplished, suffered from a nagging case of The Imposter Syndrome. No matter how much she achieved or how many elections she won, doubts always crept in during quiet moments. Doubts she relied on him to relieve.

"Crime, and protecting the vulnerable, are universal issues," he said with his most reassuring smile. "Statewide if not national—hell, global." Curt side-hugged her again. "Not that your ambitions run to that scale...yet."

"Curt, I've told you a thousand times. I'm not interested in the White House," she said, failing to keep the irritation out of her voice. However high she reached, he always pushed her to climb higher. "I'm only half-convinced that I should try for the statehouse. Without your support, I'd never even consider it. Sometimes I think you should be the one running."

He shook his head. "I don't have the stomach or the patience for it," he said, turning his gaze away from her. "But I'll do whatever I can to help you." He squeezed her hand. "In fact, I have an idea to raise the visibility of the WAVE Squad. One that proves you're serious."

"Raises it?" She chuckled. "If anything, we need to broaden our appeal with some bread-and-butter politics. Jobs, infrastructure, and education funding, for example."

"Of course, and we've issued position papers on all of those areas," he said. "But they're lousy TV. Crime, though—especially crimes against women, the largest and highest-turnout voting bloc—is sexy. Trust me. The polling shows it, with what's going on nationally right now—the 'Me Too' stuff, the 'Believe Her' stuff, all that. Here, check this out." He pulled a report out of his briefcase and handed it to her, labeled "CONFIDENTIAL—Iverson Polling Data."

Megan skimmed the report, and the data supported his claim. She bent forward and yanked her ridiculous 2-inch heels off those aching feet. "Okay, okay. So, what's your idea?"

Curt paused, licked his lips. Patted his lap. She grinned and slid a bare foot onto his leg. Moments later, relief flooded every muscle. Reflexology, her favorite of the applied sciences.

He smiled. "Feel good?"

"Mmmm. Keep going. But you haven't answered my question…oh, yeah, there. God, you have an amazing touch."

Curt squeezed the soft flesh under her instep, then resumed his magical massage strokes. "The Citizen Advisory Board for this new initiative," he said, in an almost offhand manner. "Have you thought about who should chair it?"

Megan leaned back and closed her eyes. "I've gathered some names, but haven't vetted them yet. Why? Do you have someone in mind?"

"I do," he said. Again, that forced nonchalance.

She returned her gaze to his. That look in his eyes—the intensity, the one that said, *I want this.* She'd seen it before. She smiled and shook her head. "Curt. You're already my campaign treasurer. I can't ask you to do more than that." She lay sideways on the seat to face him…and so he could reach her other leg.

"Nonsense," he said, starting work on instep number two. "I haven't done enough. And putting your own husband in charge of this initiative will show how serious you are about it. Not just to the media, either. To the Clayton PD as well."

Megan pursed her lips, considering it. He had a point. Her own convictions on the issues had made her too easy of a sell on the idea. And holy cow, his hands worked absolute magic on the balls of her feet in that moment.

She patted his knee. "I *am* that serious about it," she said. "But is the public ready?"

"You heard those cheers in there," he said. "It wasn't just the women. The men in this state want their wives, daughters, mothers, and sisters kept safe, too."

Megan nodded. She had heard the applause, had seen men joining women in the chants and cheers.

"Meg," he said in a soft voice, "do you trust me?"

"Of course I do. It's just that..." She managed a weak smile. "I don't know if I trust *me.*"

Curt laughed and let her feet drop to the floor so he could hold her hand. "Megan The Imposter again?"

Her smile widened. "She knows her stuff, doesn't she?"

"She's brilliant," he said, chuckling. "And so is the real Meg Iverson, the next governor of the Nutmeg State."

She leaned over and kissed him, a quick but forceful mashing of lips—her "power kiss," as he often called it. "Let's do it. In fact, I'll announce it at our next rally." She pulled her cell phone out of her purse and speed-dialed. "Jamie? Meg. I need you to work on a new speech for me."

She glanced over at her husband, who had leaned back in his seat, his keen mind already churning on some other issue. Curt, the master multi-tasker, a trait she always admired in him.

Still, she sensed that he was holding something back. He'd never profited financially from their connection, so far as she knew. He had his own reasons for everything, and they didn't always begin with helping Megan get elected. But what those reasons were in this case, he kept to himself.

She might need to change that.

***

The door to the doctor's office opened, and Val stood, shoving her phone into her purse. Moments later, Gil limped out on crutches into the small waiting area, dodging the short rows of uncomfortable metal-framed chairs with practiced ease.

"Doc says I'll live," Gil said with a wry grin, waving away Val's offer of help. "Unfortunately, I'll have to survive without painkillers for the foreseeable future. She's afraid I like them too much."

"Are you telling stories again?" said a forty-something Black woman in a white lab coat emerging from the exam room behind him. Her name tag read "Dr. Williamson." The doctor's gentle voice completed her kind-doctor persona, along with her broad smile and soft gait. "Ibuprofen, 600 milligrams, four times a day. That's more than enough to manage your pain."

"See? She's so mean to me." Gil grinned and gestured to the receptionist. "Betcha *she'd* give me some oxy if I asked nicely."

The receptionist, a round-faced brunette wearing too much makeup, widened her eyes and shook her head in protest. Dr. Williamson tsk'd and ushered Gil to the door, with Val following. "Don't you be getting my staff in trouble," the doctor said, grinning, "or I'll have to call the cops."

"Next week, then?" Gil said.

"Do your exercises," the doctor answered and waved goodbye.

"Is there ever a time you aren't teasing someone?" Val asked while helping Gil into his SUV.

"That depends," Gil said. "Shannon O'Reilly says you went out on a date. Are you going to tell me about it? If not, I plan to be merciless."

"That's different from normal in *what* way?" Val asked. "Besides, I'd rather talk about work."

"And *that's* different from normal, how?" he parroted back.

She shut the passenger-side door and stuck out her tongue at him. He laughed.

"So, what's the big deal at work that prevents you from divulging all of your private life secrets?" Gil asked once she maneuvered his Ford Explorer into traffic. "And it'd better be good, or else we're back to merciless teasing."

"I'm partnerless again," Val said. "Rico's off patrol while he undergoes PTSD counseling, and everyone else is paired up. So I'm stuck on desk duty, and it's making me crazy."

"They'll find someone," Gil said. "Somebody always comes available, sooner or later. Take a right, here."

"The only current openings are in a different precinct," Val said. "That would require a transfer. Which could be permanent." She slowed to a stop at a red light and sneaked a glance at him. "Which means, they might not put us back together when you return."

Gil growled. "Can't say I like the sound of that. Where would they put you?"

"South End," Val said. "Guarding million-dollar homes and golf courses. *Bor-ing!*"

Gil laughed. "You could always join the country club. We could go there for lunch. You could become my rich friend."

"Only if I went on the take, big time," she said. "I'd sooner claw my eyes out."

"So, tell them no," Gil said.

Val stared at him. "Can I do that?" she said. "I mean, do I have any say?"

Gil shrugged. "Not officially. But Gibson would hate to lose you, and if he sees that you want to stay, he'll fight for you. Gibby's a good guy and he likes your work."

She sighed. "But if I make enemies downtown, that's not exactly good for my career."

"Just how soon did you plan to make detective? Get in the left lane."

"I know the way," she said, rolling her eyes. "My goal? Five years, ten at the most."

"First off, nobody in Clayton has ever made it faster than seven," he said. "Second, ten years is a long time for downtown brass to hold a grudge. Hell, most of 'em will retire by then. So, don't worry about it. I never do, and look at me." He laughed. "I'm such a great role model. Still a patrol sergeant after all these years, and a gimp, to boot."

"You could have made lieutenant by now if you wanted, and you know it," Val said. "You just can't give up street work. Or is it me you'd miss?" Val smiled and blushed. Forget his flirtiness—she needed to get her own under control.

"Both," he said. "When you go for detective, so do I, partner." He fixed her with a level gaze, a half-smile dancing on his lips.

Her face warmed again. Damn, this guy could get right under her skin whenever he wanted.

"Unless you go off and get married," Gil said, "have babies, and quit on me. Is that your plan?"

"Hell, no!" Val glared at him and accidentally jerked the wheel, tossing them both in their seats a bit. "I can't even get a second date. Hell, I don't even *want* one. Not with anyone I've been out with lately."

"This Diego guy's not Mr. Right, then, huh?"

Val's jaw went slack. "How did you find out his name?"

Gil's eyebrow raised and lowered, and he spoke in an awful German accent. "I haff vays of knowink thinks."

"Yeah, and that makes me very nervous." She proved it by taking the next turn way too fast, nearly driving off the road.

"You drive like you shoot," he said. "Fast and furious. So, Diego—"

"He's a potential witness, and his friend is a person of interest, in the Olivia Lambert case," Val said. "It'd be, at best, awkward."

"Only if you make it so."

"Meaning?"

Gil shrugged. "If you were interested, you'd find a way. But you're not, and that's fine, Val. Really."

She pulled into Gil's driveway, a modest split-level ranch on a cul-de-sac in a working-class neighborhood, and turned off the engine. "Thank you. That means a lot, coming from you."

Gil held up his hand, and she clasped it, shook it. She gazed out over his front lawn, neatly mowed despite his injury. Knowing Gil, he'd hired some underprivileged kid and paid him too much.

"So, what do *you* think?" she said. "About the partner and transfer thing."

His eyes narrowed. "Follow your instincts," he said. "Which are always superb. Somehow, you find your way to the right place, every time. Where that is, I don't know yet. Nobody does. But it'll become clear soon." He laughed. "That goes for work, too."

"Too?"

He grinned. "I was talking about Diego and that long line of men wanting to jump your bones."

"Shut the hell up." She let go of his hand and smacked his shoulder. "Next time I hit you where it hurts."

"Promises, promises."

Val shook her head. "You're incorrigible." But the smile on her face wouldn't go away, and her eyes wouldn't leave his.

He held his gaze with her for a few more moments, then leaned toward her. His face grew near enough that she could smell peppermint on his breath. Almost taste it...His face hovered a few inches from hers for a moment. Then his lips brushed her cheek, and he drew back, still watching her.

She stared at him, frozen in place. The usual sick twisting in her gut when men tried to kiss her in the past...didn't come. No fear or revulsion. Just a soft tingling on her cheek where his dry lips had pressed against her skin, and the steady thumping of her heart in her chest.

"Val," he said, "when I say follow your instincts, I mean...follow your heart. Wherever it may lead you. Okay?"

She nodded, the numbness flowing out from her cheek to her entire body.

"Now, this is awkward," Gil said. He picked up a crutch and held it aloft. "I don't mean this in a bad way, but...would you mind walking me to my door?"

She laughed, pressed the button on the garage door remote, and got out of the car.

Chapter Eight

Val left cash on the Claytown Café service counter and scooped up her coffee-to-go, rewarding Pinkie's quick service with a dollar tip. She turned away from the counter and nearly crashed into Amy Yang, rushing in through the front door.

"Amy!" Val avoided her friend's crushing hug, using her coffee as a shield and grasping her hand instead. "I didn't know you came here."

"As of today, I do," Amy said, brushing long, dark hair out of her eyes. "I'm starting a new job as the local media liaison for Megan Iverson's campaign. The office is right around the corner. So sorry I haven't called—life's been crazy. Do you have time to chat now?"

"I have a few minutes," Val lied. She had, maybe, one. "What happened to the TV station?"

"Forget that working-for-free BS," Amy said. "This job pays! No benefits, but at least I can start paying down my student loans. So, what's good here?"

"Pinkie, please set up my friend with one of your famous cinnamon mochas. On me," she said, calculating her bank balance. When Amy protested, Val waved her off. "I insist. Congratulations on the new job!"

"Thanks," Amy said. They moved to one side so the short line of customers forming behind them could place their orders. "I'm so excited. My boss, Jamie Whitfield, is the PR director. She reports directly to Curtis Iverson. He's the one that actually offered me the job. Mr. Iverson is so nice—everyone there is."

"He seems...nice," Val said. Actually, Curtis struck her

as somewhat slimy. "What a great opportunity for you."

"I can hardly believe it," Amy said. "After the rally the other day, I couldn't stop thinking about what the mayor said, you know, about protecting women from rapists and abusers. Then I thought, why am I working for some big company, getting paid nothing, when I could maybe help change things? Then I saw they were hiring, and—do you know what Curtis said?"

"Let me guess," Val said. "Was it, 'Will you work for minimum wage?'"

"He said I was a *top talent.* In so many words!" Amy's voice reached a pitch somewhere north of *mezzo soprano.* "A man that rich and powerful, and he noticed *me!*" She placed a hand over her heart for dramatic effect.

Val chuckled, suppressing the urge to roll her eyes. "That's great, Amy. I'm really glad for you. Ah, here's your coffee." She dropped her last remaining cash on the counter. "Look, I have to get to work, so—"

"Thank you so much! Next one's on me, as soon as I get my first paycheck. Byeee!" Amy embraced Val without warning and rushed out the door.

"Like, that chick's a trip," Pinkie said, picking up the cash. "Friend of yours?"

"Kind of," Val said, then chided herself for her standoffishness. Amy was nice enough, and Val saw no harm in developing a new friendship with an old acquaintance.

No harm at all.

***

Val spent another frustrating shift on desk duty in The Bullpen, responding to random citizen complaints that made her wonder if people ever spoke face-to-face anymore. "Yes, Mr. Moncada, it's legal for your neighbor to install a chain-link fence, so long as the fence doesn't encroach upon your property and he has the proper permits... No, sir, that would be the Planning Department... Well, then, perhaps you should restrain your German Shepherd—hello? Hello?" She hung up, only to hear her phone chime again. Another neighbor, reporting the invasion of her neighborhood by tall, green-skinned, four-eyed aliens. With nose rings. She promised to send the Space Force to respond. As soon as the city formed one.

The next call brought a smile to her face. "Shannon!" she said. "How'd you get through to me? I don't even know my number here."

"Easy," Shannon said. "I told Dispatch I had a complaint about my neighbor's honeybee collection." But the detective's voice fell somber a moment later. "I have news on Kent Mercer's DNA test," she said. "It isn't good."

"Not good in a 'doesn't help the case' way, or a 'Kent's in deep shit' sort of way?" Val's heart rate quickened. She didn't care for Kent and barely knew him. But he was a friend of Diego's, who *seemed* like a good guy, and she still felt bad about ghosting him since their brunch date.

"The former," Shannon said. "The test was inconclusive."

"I didn't realize that was an option," Val said. "Either the DNA matches or it doesn't, right?"

"DNA matching is not an exact science," Shannon said. "As the report explains, it's a complex statistical model that predicts the probability of a sample being from a specific person—such as Kent—versus a 'random person.' But in this case, they couldn't prove it *wasn't* some random person's with enough confidence to warrant an arrest."

"So, why not take a new sample?" Val asked, unease growing.

"From Kent, you mean? Because his sample isn't the problem. It's the sample from Olivia."

"Oh, crap," Val said. Her unease escalated.

"The 'foreign' DNA," Shannon went on, "that is, the

sperm and skin cells from someone other than Olivia, had 'lost structural integrity.' It's practically useless." She exhaled a heavy sigh. "And there's more."

"Come on, don't leave me in suspense," Val said, her impatience rising.

"There may have been multiple men involved," Shannon said. "Or at least, multiple semen donors, so to speak."

Val's heart sank in disgust. "She was gang-raped?" she asked, her voice tight and far too loud. Other officers in the room glanced over to her cubicle.

"Not necessarily," Shannon said. "She may also have had consensual sex. In fact, the varying ages of the semen samples make it almost certain that, consensual or not, she almost certainly had another partner one to three days before."

Val shuddered out a sigh. That complicated things, and not only forensically. Any defense lawyer worth their salt would use that information to paint Olivia as a slut, casting doubt that a man would have had to rape her. Or that he had done anything at all.

Memories from her childhood flooded back: Are you sure he actually did that? What did you do to lead him on? Why were you so scantily dressed? What did you expect him to do, seeing you like that?

"So, where does that leave us?" she asked in a dull voice.

"Back to square one," Shannon said. "Without a suspect."

Val pressed her eyes shut and guided the phone's receiver back to its cradle. It rang again moments later, but she ignored its harsh peal. At that moment, she didn't want to talk to anyone, about anything.

***

An untimely accident clogged downtown Clayton traffic Wednesday afternoon, engulfing Curtis Iverson's black

Mercedes in unending delays. A light drizzle gave him the excuse to close his passenger side window, almost silencing the noise from an amateur percussionist banging makeshift drumsticks on a collection of orange five-gallon buckets under the awning of an abandoned storefront. He wished Megan would ban the practice, but she never found the opportunity to make it a priority. Like so many other things he wanted from her.

No matter. Curtis had much more enjoyable companionship for this cross-town trip. His new campaign assistant, Amy, had jumped at the chance to drive for him. He'd worried that his initial impulse—bring the Asian girl to a meeting with Chinese-American business leaders—would appear to be pandering, if not racist. But when he explained how her presence would put the donors at ease, her enthusiasm doubled, putting his doubts to rest.

A floral aroma, redolent of jasmine and rose, meandered through the air between them. He liked the scent. LeeAnn, his secretary at Constitution Finance, also favored it, or something like it. Maybe Amy had picked up on that somehow. She had proven herself an ambitious young woman, eager to learn—and to please him. And here they sat, alone in his car, only a few feet apart...

But the traffic jam threatened to spoil his opportunity to get closer to her. Though she didn't complain, she huffed in frustration, shoulders hunched and arms rigid on the wheel. Plus, her nervousness made him tense, too, which might throw him off his game.

That situation required intervention. In two steps.

First, he called ahead to alert their meeting organizer about the traffic problem, relieving Amy's stress by parroting aloud their reassurances of understanding. Then, step two. After hanging up, he smiled at her and spoke in a calming voice. "Don't fret the delay," he said. "In fact, based on that call, it may help us. If anything, it appears they're more eager to make this endorsement happen than we are."

"That's great!" Amy smiled and relaxed her shoulders a bit.

"Are you nervous?" Curtis asked with a comforting smile.

"A little." Her head bobbed. "I want to make a good impression and help the campaign and—"

"I find," he said, "that talking about a familiar topic can reduce stress."

"Familiar, how?" she asked after a brief pause.

"There's no topic more familiar than yourself," he said. "Tell me something about you."

"Okay," she said, uncertainty leaking into her voice. "What do you want to know?"

He laughed. "Somehow I seem to have made you even more nervous," he said. "Don't worry, I don't bite. Not hard, anyway."

Curtis laughed, and Amy relaxed her shoulders a little more. Good. "Okay," she said. "Let's see, I graduated from UConn in broadcast journalism last year, with a minor in theater. I was interning at WCLA-TV for the past nine months—"

"I've read your resumé," he said, waving her off. "I want to learn more about *you*. Where did you grow up? What do you do for fun? What books or movies do you like? That sort of thing."

"Oh." Amy bit her lip and inched the car forward, then stopped. "I grew up in Clayton—my parents moved here when I was five. I played volleyball and lacrosse but wasn't good enough to make the team at UConn." She grinned. "I sucked, really."

"I doubt that," Curtis said. "You look so athletic—I'm sorry. That's probably not the type of compliment a young woman prefers to hear. Especially one as smart and attractive as you.”

“Athletic is fine,” Amy said, blushing. “Thank you.”

A few quiet moments passed. Curtis frowned. He’d made her nervous again, dammit. “So, you grew up here in Clayton,” he said. “Do you still hang out with your classmates from high school, or did you make new friends in college?”

Amy cleared her throat and craned her neck to the left, as if checking the lines of traffic ahead. “School didn’t afford me a lot of time for a social life,” she said. “Neither did my job at the TV station. At least, that’s what my last boyfriend said when he broke up with me.”

“He’s a fool!” Curtis tried to keep his tone light, even as the revelation made his neck tingle. “Why, I know a dozen boys your age who would love to meet a girl like you.”

“You don’t need to do that,” Amy said, again rushing her words.

He faced out the passenger side window and frowned. He wasn’t having much luck relaxing her. If they could only get out of this damned congestion...

“Hey, take a right at this next corner,” he said. “I can show you a shortcut that might get us around this traffic.”

“Okay,” she said, her tone brightening. The car in front of them surged ahead, and a few seconds later, she squeezed by and turned onto the side street. “Now where?”

“Four blocks, then left,” he said.

“Oh, I know which way you’re going,” she said. “I should have thought of that.”

“You’re doing great,” Curtis said. “I think we might make it on time after all, thanks to you.”

Amy grinned and blushed again, said nothing. They progressed down the narrow one-way street, crowded on each side by parked cars in front of tiny neighborhood shops.

Only the soft hum of their car's engine and the splashing of rain off the tires filled the void between them.

"Theater minor, huh?" Curtis said after she made the turn. "What plays were you in at UConn? Did you do any Shakespeare?"

She shot him a shy smile. "I played Adriana in *The Comedy of Errors*," she said. "That was my only lead role. Mostly I focused on the tech side of things—lights, sound, stage management. I don't hunger for the limelight like a lot of theater people."

"That's a shame," Curtis said. "A girl with your...*talent*...should always take center stage."

Amy reddened and stared ahead. "Uh, thanks," she said.

"You're welcome," he said.

Another long moment of silence passed.

"Well," Curtis said, "I'm so pleased that we could bring you on board. I'm very impressed with your skills and experience. Jamie's great with strategy, but we've needed someone who can craft a message, particularly one that can reach younger voters."

She furrowed her brows and cocked her head. "Experience? All I've done is intern at a TV station."

Curtis dabbed sweat off his forehead with a hankie. "Jamie's shared your news release drafts with me," he said. "They demonstrate a high level of skill—very high. In fact, I'd like to use your talents more in the fund-raising area, writing appeals to donors. Would you be up for that?"

Amy's jaw dropped a moment, then she broke out into a wide grin. "I'd love to! Anything to help Megan get elected. I think she's amazing, don't you? Oh, of course you do, she's your wife!" She laughed and covered her mouth.

Curtis faked a laugh along with her. But inside, frustration mounted. Why did she have to mention his wife?

Spoiled the mood. Well, he had a few minutes left to set things back on track.

"Great," he said, forcing enthusiasm. "After this meeting's over, why don't we sit down and go over some messaging strategies? I have some ideas, but I'd love to hear yours."

"That would be awesome!" Amy bounced in her seat and tapped on the steering wheel. She continued with her loose grip while turning at the next corner, causing Curtis to blanch, but she didn't seem to notice. Her face fell a moment later. "Darn it. I just realized—Jamie wanted to discuss a press release with me when we get back to the office. Can we meet after?"

"Sure," Curtis said, working hard to mask his excitement. "But that'll keep us at the office rather late. Are you okay with that?"

"Like I said," Amy said, nodding, "I have no social life."

"Well, then, let's plan a working dinner," Curtis said. "Do you prefer steak or lobster?"

"I'm vegetarian," Amy said in a small voice. "Sorry."

"Italian?"

She brightened. "I love a good pesto."

Curtis patted her shoulder. "A girl after my own heart."

Amy shot him a cautious look, then bit her lip again, nodding. He let it lie. No need to press the matter at the moment. He had time. Lots of time.

***

Thursday morning, Val hurried into the large precinct meeting room, dubbed "The Corral" by the old-timers, moments before Lieutenant Gibson stood to address the standing-room-only gathering. All but a handful of the precinct's nearly 100 uniformed officers and detectives jammed the spartan space, with over a dozen officers standing behind ten rows of folding chairs. Val found a spot next to Rico in the corner that afforded her a view of the podium. Next to Gibson, a portable whiteboard displayed a hasty scribble of the meeting's agenda, only two items long: *Charlene Washington,* and *New WAVE Squad.* Sergeant Blake stood behind Gibson, arms folded across his barrel chest.

Gibson tapped the mic and spoke in a matter-of-fact tone. "We'll keep this brief," he said. "Two things. First, we pulled another body out of the river on Tuesday. A young girl, similar in profile to the one Dawes found a few weeks ago."

Val froze. She hadn't watched the news on her days off, and no one had clued her in. She glanced around and noticed all eyes in the room had turned to her, expecting her to say something.

"When you say, same profile," Val said, "you mean—"

"Teenage girl, drowned, signs of abuse, and no shoes," Gibson said. "Only difference is race. Charlene's Black."

Murmurs circulated around the room. The air, already stuffy, grew warmer. A wave of numbness swept over Val. She'd need to access the girl's files right after the meeting.

"Second, partly in response to this, and at the direction of the mayor and the chief," Gibson said, "we're forming a new city-wide special investigatory unit. The Women's Anti-Violence Emergency Squad, or WAVE Squad, will focus on women's safety and crimes against women. I'm proud to announce that our own Sergeant Brenda Petroni will lead this unit. Sergeant?" Gibson smiled and pointed with an open palm at the front row of officers, then stepped aside.

Petroni, a stocky woman in her forties with curly brown hair, stood, turned, and waved to the room, acknowledging the tepid applause with a wide smile.

This caught Val by surprise. Petroni, like Shannon O'Reilly, had taken Val under her wing as a mentor of sorts, and she counted them both among her few friends in the department. But she'd gotten no heads-up from either woman. Still, the news excited her. She grinned and pumped her fist, bumping Rico in the ribs. "Sorry," Val whispered. He waved it off.

Petroni took the podium and waited for the murmurs in the room to quiet. "Thanks, Lieutenant. I know everyone here has a lot of questions. Let me anticipate the biggest one: who will we assign to the WAVE Squad? The budget allows for eight positions, including myself. Detective Shannon O'Reilly will serve as my deputy."

Shannon stood, right next to the seat Petroni had just vacated. Her tall, slender form seemed to tower over Petroni's. She flashed a toothy smile at the room to polite applause, then resumed her seat.

"The other six spots are open," Petroni continued, "with spots for a few more detectives and some uniforms. Email me if you're interested. I hope to fill the remaining slots by the end of next week. We'll operate out of the downtown HQ building. In return for stepping up, you'll be rewarded with poor working conditions, long hours with no extra pay, and a great, big thank-you in your personnel file." She acknowledged the laughs emanating from the crowd with a wink and a chuckle of her own. "Seriously, it's a great opportunity for anyone looking to bust out of their old routine and pad the resumé. Anyone hoping to make detective someday ought to give it a look." She rested her eyes on Val.

Val's heart thumped in her chest. With great effort, she resisted the urge to dash out and email an immediate application for a spot on the WAVE Squad.

After an eternity, Petroni returned her gaze to the center of the room. "Questions?"

"Are the positions open to men?" someone muttered, and a few people snickered.

Petroni acknowledged the remark with a thin smile. "It's open to any male officer willing to reverse our ridiculously low arrest rates for crimes against women," she said. "So, no." A bigger laugh followed that barb.

"Seriously, though," Petroni went on, "we'll draw personnel from all three precincts and the detective squads. Plus, the mayor's tossing in some interns to help with the research end of things."

Val's heart sank. She excelled at research and had counted that among her competitive advantages in landing a spot on the squad.

"How will you choose people?" someone asked. "Is seniority a factor?"

"Does each precinct get two people?" asked someone else.

"Hold on, one question at a time," Petroni said with a grin. "The key factors are: level of interest, expertise, your record of performance, and yes, we need at least one from each precinct, and two more detectives total. Seniority's a tie-breaker."

Val's despondency deepened. She'd served on the force for less than a year, putting her near the bottom of the seniority list. With two former partners taken down by a criminal's bullets, her performance record might also work against her, despite her high-profile arrest of Richard Harkins.

"If I apply but my partner doesn't, how will that affect my chances?" an old-timer asked from the front of the room.

"It won't," Petroni said. "Either way. Everyone's evaluated on their own merits, and we'll reassign as needed. Next?"

Silence. No hands raised.

"If there are no more questions," Petroni said, "thanks. Meeting adjourned. I look forward to hearing from you." With those words, she stared once again at Val, locking eyes for a few seconds. *You want in?* she mouthed.

Val nodded.

Petroni mimed typing on a keyboard, then pointed at herself before leaving the podium.

This time, when the impulse to dash to the nearest available computer hit her, Val did not resist the urge.

Chapter Nine

Val dashed from the meeting to her cubicle in The Bullpen and clicked the link Brenda Petroni had provided. After a few minutes, a shadow fell over her shoulder and shaded her computer screen. She spun her chair around to find Rico staring down at her, wearing a glum expression.

"S'up, partner?" she said. "Or, whatever we are now."

"Applying to the WAVE Squad?" He sipped from a paper coffee cup, nonchalant.

Val nodded. "Sure beats answering phones and playing security guard at the mayor's speeches. Which is all they've allowed me to do since...you know." Her face reddened. She didn't actually know the official designation of Rico's status. "Want to proofread it for me when I'm done?"

He shrugged, sipped his coffee, and winced again. "I thought I'd save you the trouble." He glanced around, then ducked his head toward hers and spoke in a low voice. "You ran out of the room so fast, you probably didn't see what happened after."

"No, I didn't." Val's stomach fell. Rico's face telegraphed grim news. She swallowed hard. "What did I miss?"

"Half the precinct wants in, from the looks of things. Petroni expects over a hundred applications, including every female cop in the department." He rested his elbow on the cubicle divider. "The pitch about how much it'll help someone make detective is a sweet incentive. And everyone's more senior than you."

"But she said seniority's only a tie-breaker." Val tried to keep the disappointment and defensiveness out of her voice.

"Even so, a rookie's resume just isn't going to compete." Rico sighed. "I'm sorry, Dawes. Like it or not, it's political. I know Petroni's your friend, and she probably fully intended to pick you. But if you get picked ahead of a hundred ten-year guys, there'll be hell to pay."

Val's throat tightened. Rico's points made sense. The odds of Petroni choosing her over the department's more experienced officers—all 325 of them, including a few dozen women—ranged from slim to none.

But quitting wasn't part of her makeup. "It can't hurt to try, can it?" she said.

He shrugged again and straightened. "I suppose," he said. "But don't get your hopes up."

"About what?" boomed another male voice. Moments later, the hulking figure of Travis Blake towered over Rico's. The smaller man stepped aside to allow Travis to share the space of the cubicle's opening.

"Rico's giving me the grim Vegas odds of making Petroni's new squad," Val said. "And I'm learning again that reality sucks."

Travis harrumphed and glared at Rico. "You've got inside information that nobody else has, Lopez?"

Rico shook his head. "Just keeping my eyes and ears open. What do you think, Sarge?"

Travis frowned. "It's like the lottery. If you don't buy a ticket, your odds of winning are zero. If you do, your odds of winning are...still right around zero." He chuckled at Val's expression of horror. "Still, unlike the lottery, it doesn't cost you two bucks."

"But what *are* the odds?" Val asked. "Realistically."

He inhaled a noisy breath through his nose and screwed up his mouth, thinking. "If it were me, I'd jump at the chance to hire you," he said. "But that's easy to say. You already work for me." He smiled. "I don't want anyone else stealing you, either."

"Sounds like there's no downside to applying, then," Val said, turning back toward the keyboard. But something in Travis's expression stopped her. "What?" she asked. "What am I missing? Is there a downside?"

The two men exchanged glances. Travis drew another deep breath and cocked his head to one side. "It depends on how things go," he said. "If they crack a few big cases, like the Olivia Lambert or Charlene Washington murders, then it could be a big feather in your cap. But if months go by and nothing comes of it, they'll dissolve the unit, and everyone associated with it comes away looking bad."

"Or, worse," Rico said, "what's supposed to be a temporary assignment becomes a permanent black hole, and you get stuck there. Meanwhile everyone around you accumulates valuable on-the-street experience. You end up falling further behind."

Val straightened in her chair. "H-how do these things *usually* go?" she said, bracing for the worst.

Rico tsk'd and shrugged, but said nothing.

Travis held his palms up flat, like the scales of justice. "Some good, some bad. Hard to tell."

After a long, uneasy silence, Rico crossed his arms and leaned forward again. "Special units work when they're driven by genuine need—the kind that arise from within the department. Like your inter-city task force a few months ago, when you nailed Richard Harkins. But the ones dreamed up by politicians..." His voice trailed away, and his expression turned glum. "Those are doomed. The election comes and goes, and suddenly, there's a new bright-and-shiny issue for the politicians to focus on. What if a new mayor comes in with different priorities? Your special unit fades into the shadows, and resources start to disappear. Successes are harder to come by. Suddenly, it looks like a failure, and everyone on it does, too." He sighed and turned to Travis. "Did I forget anything?"

Travis frowned. "That's one scenario. One of many."

Val sank deep into her chair. The words on her computer screen blurred, her optimism seeming foolish now. Rico's comments made sense. This initiative *was* politically driven and seemed destined to fail. Even if it succeeded, her odds of getting assigned to it appeared nonexistent.

She pressed the "save" key and closed the application. "I guess there's no rush to apply," she said. "And they're expecting me over at dispatch." She pushed her way past the two men and rushed down the hall. After turning the corner, she glanced back at them. They wore sullen expressions and turned away from her.

That told her everything she needed to know about the hopelessness of her application.

***

"They're full of crap."

Gil's emphatic repudiation of her colleagues' comments startled Val so much, she nearly let his barbells slip out of her grip—a dangerous move for a spotter. Not only did she expect him to be at least as cynical as both Rico Lopez and Travis Blake, but Gil had often characterized Travis's political instincts as spot-on.

"Careful!" He wagged his blocky chin at the rack, and Val helped guide the barbell onto the U-shaped supports. He sat up and wiped his face with a towel. "Your turn." He slid down to the far end of the bench, and she held his arm while he stood and reached for his crutches. He stumbled for a moment, and he grabbed her forearm to steady himself. Val's arm tingled long after he pulled his hand away, but he acted as though nothing had happened.

And nothing had, she reminded herself. Stop overreacting. She inhaled a slow breath of warm, humid air, her nose wrinkling a bit at the ancient police gym's sweaty aroma. She'd looked forward to spending the morning with Gil before reporting in for her afternoon shift. Doing simple things with him, like running errands or working out at the gym, always marked the high point of her week. She swapped the heavier weights on the barbell for a lighter set and took his place on the bench, wiping away his sweat with a towel. "So, you think I should go for it?" she said, laying back and readying her grip on the bar.

"I didn't say that," he said. "I just don't agree that, A, it's doomed to fail, or B, that it would reflect badly on you. Wait for me, I'll spot you."

"Doc said no weight on your legs," she said, rolling her eyes. "Just relax. So, you think the WAVE Squad has a good chance at catching the perps who did Olivia and Charlene?"

"I think it's a great idea, whether or not you solve those particular cases." Gil sat in a folding chair next to the bench, his muscular chest still heaving from exertion. "It's long overdue, and as far as it being political, well, that's *always* the case, isn't it? The need's been there. The politicians are just catching up to that fact." He waved over another officer who'd just completed a set of leg presses. "Give her a spot?" The cop, a second-year African American man Val had never met, nodded and held up a digit. Wait one minute.

Val shook her head. Forget waiting. She lifted the bar and inched it downward toward her chest, then raised it again. "The Inter-City Task Force…wasn't political," she said, huffing out a breath. "That was…our idea…remember?" Another rep with the bar. A third.

"Exception proves the rule. Slow down your reps if you want to benefit from—"

"I *know*." Val sighed and shook her head, but slowed her pace. "Okay, so let's say...the WAVE Squad...does fail. You don't think...that'd hurt my career?" Her fourth rep took twice as long as her third. The strain in her arms, shoulders, and chest intensified.

"Nah. If things go south, nobody's going to blame a rookie." Gil winced and shifted in his seat, cursing under his breath.

"Is your hip bothering you?" she asked, pausing with her arms at full extension. Where had that spotter gone?

"No—ow! Okay, yes," he said. "Price? You coming, or what?" He waved at the young cop again and expelled a long, noisy breath through his teeth. "No offense. At calling you 'too junior,' I mean."

"None taken," Val said, not fully convinced of her own words. She lowered and lifted again. "Although Petroni wouldn't hire someone who doesn't accept their share of responsibility—for the work, or the blame. Assuming there *is* blame. Sorry about your hip. Maybe you should skip your next set." She finished her sixth rep and guided the bar back onto the rack. Price glanced her way and winced. *Sorry*, he mouthed.

"I'll be fine," Gil said, pushing his weight onto his crutches. "Anyway, it doesn't matter whether or not you blame yourself. Perception matters, and nobody points fingers at a first-year uniformed cop when an investigation comes up dry. Are you getting off that bench, or what?"

"Patience!" She sighed and slid off. Incorrigible. "So, there's no downside. I should apply."

"Not so fast." He let her help him over to the bench, then waited for her to reset the weights on the bar. "There are downsides."

"Such as?"

Gil glanced around, his gaze settling on Price, and lowered his voice. "These 'special units' have a tendency to employ old-school tactics. Things that you and I disagree with." He nodded in Price's direction. "Like profiling."

"Racial profiling, you mean?"

Gil nodded, his face glum. "Think New York's 'Violent Crime' Unit. They've earned a pretty bad rep for targeting young Black men. You don't want to get painted with that brush."

"Forget the hit on my reputation," she said, her breathing returning to normal. "I wouldn't want any part of that. But would Petroni engage in that? Gibson's hand-picked leader of the unit?"

He shrugged and turned away, looking through the large, metal-framed windows that comprised the exterior wall of the gym.

Silence reigned for several seconds. Val followed his gaze out the window. Dark clouds rolled in from the southwest, pregnant with rain. A big electrical storm, one that might last all day. No doubt they'd get soaked on the slow trek to the car afterwards, with Gil still unsteady on his crutches. Maybe they should cut the workout short, get out while the weather still held.

"The timing is a problem, too," he said, still facing away from her.

"How so?"

He turned toward her, frowning. "The assignment is at least six months, but probably longer—we both know that. Right?"

"End of September the earliest, but probably into next spring or summer," she agreed. "So?"

He paused for a shallow breath. "What happens *four* months from now?"

Val held up her hands, shrugged. "Kids go back to school? Hell, I don't know, what?"

Disappointment filled his eyes. "You've already lost track, huh?" Gil blinked and bit his lip. "Barring any setbacks, my scheduled return date is August 1." He kept his steady gaze upon her, his eyes filling with moisture.

Realization dawned on her, and with it, a dull ache settled in her chest. "I'll still be on assignment when you return. Which makes it less likely that we'd be reassigned as partners."

Gil nodded and his gaze fell to his lap. The outside air grew dark, and a heavy raindrop splattered the windows, followed by a half-dozen more. "I mean, that's not a good reason not to do it," he said. "Hell, they'll stick me on desk duty anyway for the first few months."

"Maybe you can get assigned to the unit, too," she said. "We'll need people at HQ, coordinating—"

"Petroni and O'Reilly will coordinate everything and don't need my dead weight," he said. "I'm not mobile enough for the type of work you'll be doing." Dull tones of disappointment dripped from his voice.

Val gripped the barbell, searching for an answer. The thick drops fell with greater intensity on the giant windows, blurring her view of the grass-lined parking lot. At least, her vision got blurry. Somehow. Because she was *not crying, dammit, no, she would not cry about this*—

"Can't you come back sooner?" she said, her throat tightening. "If you're just doing desk work, anyhow, why not start now? I could stay put, and we could be partners—"

"No way." Gil shook his head. "My doctor would never clear it. August 1 is the best date I could negotiate. Even that's optimistic."

The clouds opened up, and rain mixed with hail pelted the windows loud enough to force her to shout. "I'll ask for reassignment as soon as you return!" Val dropped her hands off the bar, folding them across her stomach. Suddenly she had no strength for lifting.

"Don't be ridiculous." Somehow his quiet voice cut through the cacophony of the storm. "You have to do it. I'll—*we'll* figure something out." He rested his hand on hers. "If not at work, then in the real world. Okay?"

Warmth spread from her fingers, all the way up to her neck, her face, her chest. She folded his hands into hers, then sat up and glanced around. The gym had emptied, save for Price, who'd moved to the elliptical trainer, farther away, his gaze locked on TV monitors, headphones covering his ears.

Otherwise, Val and Gil had the spacious facility to themselves. The only sounds were the thrashing of the rising storm and the whirring of Price's elliptical.

Somehow, Gil managed to join her on the bench without her assistance. His hand rested on the small of her back. They stared out the window, watching the rain fall, and the lightning flash, and listened to the roll of thunder echoing off the distant hills. Her head found its way to his shoulder. His free hand caressed her face, and the confusion of the cold, gray world melted away.

***

Being stuck on desk duty afforded Val one luxury she wouldn't have enjoyed walking a beat: the opportunity to research the Charlene Washington case. While she lacked access to the official case files, internet searches of online news articles filled in substantial detail about the young woman's accomplished resumé.

Like Olivia Lambert, Charlene attended Liberty Heights High School, where she excelled in both academics and sports. Nominated for a Scholar Athlete Award, she'd lettered in varsity soccer, volleyball, and track while earning a near-perfect 3.96 GPA. She also contributed as a photographer to both the school newspaper, the *Liberty High Ledger*, and the school yearbook. She and her mother volunteered often at the food bank founded by her father, a pastor at the Clayton Church of God in Christ. She also somehow found time to serve as treasurer of the school's business club, the Association of Future Entrepreneurs.

Val shuddered at the last finding. When she'd attended Liberty Heights, the AFE had earned a reputation for being a bastion of white male arrogance—rich kids with a superiority complex. "Born on third base," Uncle Val used to quip, "and they think they've hit a triple." But according to the *Ledger's* online publication, the group had morphed into an organization promoting service, scholarship, and open opportunity, often finding internships for Liberty Heights students in the business community.

Including Olivia Lambert.

Val's pulse quickened. Olivia's and Charlene's lives had intersected on multiple fronts—classmates, volleyball teammates, and the internship program. One or more of those common interests could lead to their other shared trait: their violent deaths at the hands of a rapist. Possibly even the same one.

She moved her mouse to the "close" button on her browser, but her finger froze a moment before clicking. A photo on the AFE page caught her eye—one of Olivia accepting her internship at Constitution Finance. To Olivia's side stood the AFE's elected leaders, including Charlene. A middle-aged man Val didn't recognize stood on the other side of Olivia, grinning and handing her a certificate. Behind him stood past recipients of the award from the company.

One of those faces, a curly-haired white man in his early twenties, looked familiar. She zoomed in on the photo and glanced closer...and confirmed his identity. No doubt about it. Kent Mercer, Diego's running buddy, knew both Olivia Lambert and Charlene Washington.

***

The next Tuesday afternoon, Val exited the county courthouse in a deep funk after providing grand jury testimony on the Destiny Mathers assault case. The prosecutor had assured her they'd have enough to indict and convict the perp, but the process left her a little disoriented. Not knowing what other evidence he'd gathered, she had difficulty imagining a coherent narrative that would lock the accused up for the rest of his miserable life—an outcome she fervently desired.

A blast of exhaust from a city bus roaring by interrupted her musings. She glanced at the number on its rear display panel, growing smaller by the second, and cursed. She'd walked right past her stop and now had missed the damned bus! The next one wouldn't come along for at least another half hour. Growling epithets at herself, she popped into a small café to shake off both the late-afternoon chill and her grumpy mood.

The shop's layout required patrons to weave through four tiny stand-up tables to a service counter, staffed by a bored pair of twenty-something baristas, one male and one female. Nondescript pop music squeaked from speakers hung from an open, industrial ceiling, interspersed among wood-bladed fans circulating the shop's warm humidity at a lazy pace. Twin lines of booths occupied the long, thin dining area past the service counter.

One of the baristas waved her over. Halfway to the counter, a familiar voice called Val's name. She spotted its source, and a mix of affection and guilt flashed over her.

"Val!" Diego Collier hurried over, spreading his long, lean arms for a hug. Val grabbed his outstretched hand in both of hers. His face fell, but only for a moment, and he held on for several seconds.

"Hey, there," she said in a weak voice, forcing a smile. She peeked at the two companions he'd left behind at a nearby booth—a curly-haired man wearing an Adidas jacket, and a woman with straight black hair that hung below her shoulders. The pair sat close together with their backs to her, giggling and whispering to each other. The remaining dozen or so tables sat empty.

Diego's nervous agitation commanded her immediate attention, however. "What brings you here?" he asked, pulling her by the arm toward the coffee counter.

"Work," she said. "And, um, coffee. You?"

Diego grinned. "I'm volunteering for the Iverson campaign, and we're meeting with her staff to discuss our duties. 'Go Nuts for Meg', right?" He waved back at his two companions. Val gazed past him and her jaw dropped when she recognized both faces, now turned toward her.

"Kent?" she said. "And...*Amy*?"

"Wow," he said. "How do you know Amy?"

"Val!" Amy squealed with delight and rushed over to her. Preoccupied with the shock of seeing Amy with Kent, Val couldn't dodge the crushing hug her friend offered. She pretended not to notice the hurt look on Diego's face and broke the embrace after a few seconds.

"You're recruiting these two guys?" Val said in a teasing tone. "Iverson must be desperate." She locked eyes with Kent against her own will, and he winced.

"Are you kidding? These guys are great!" Amy pulled Kent away from the table. "They signed up for phone-banking *and* neighborhood canvassing. How do you know these guys?"

"We met briefly," Kent said, interrupting a surprised Diego. "Good to see you again, *Officer* Dawes." He extended his hand.

Struck dumb, Val accepted his limp handshake. "A pleasure, *Mister* Mercer." Back to Amy, she continued, "We met while running one day. Diego and I have, um, had coffee once or twice since."

"Once," Diego said. "Unless you're counting right now. Join us!"

"I don't want to interrupt official campaign business." Val reddened and edged toward the exit.

"It's okay. We were about to take a break to get more coffee," Diego said. "Right, guys?"

"I'm good," Kent said.

"Me, too," Amy said. "You two go ahead." She and Kent returned to their table and, once again, sat close together in the booth. Practically on each other's laps.

Diego smiled. "What do you want? I'll buy."

"That's not necessary," Val said. "I was going to get mine to go, so I don't miss my bus."

"I can give you a lift wherever you want to go," Diego said. That silly smile would not leave his face.

Val considered it. She'd get home in minutes by car, over an hour if by bus. And Diego *was* awfully cute...

Kent's laugh resounded over the low buzz of conversation in the cafe, followed by Amy's high-pitched giggles. Oy. But perhaps if she joined them, she could learn a bit more about Kent's history with Olivia Lambert and Charlene Washington.

"Okay," she said, smiling at Diego. "Cinnamon cappuccino, double shot. Thanks."

After he ordered, they stood at arm's length near the service counter, exchanging an occasional glance. After a minute had passed, she broke the silence. "I'm sorry I haven't returned your calls since the last time we went out," she said. "I just felt a little awkward, and, uh..." Her voice trailed off.

Words seemed so inadequate, especially with the hurt welling in Diego's eyes.

"That's okay," he said in a dull tone. "I understand."

"That's gracious of you," Val said. "I don't know if I would be so forgiving."

Diego shrugged. "It's my nature, I guess. But you *could* make it up to me."

Val's heart skipped a beat. "How?"

He grinned and leaned closer. "Give me a second chance?"

Their coffees came, rescuing her for the moment. Val grabbed them off the counter and strode over to Amy and Kent's booth, sitting across from them. "Have you solved the world's problems yet, you two?" she said, her tone light.

Amy's head jerked up and she scooted a few inches away from Kent. "We were just chatting about people we know in common," she said, blushing. "Did you guys know that Kent works for Curtis at Constitution Finance? *My* boss is *his* boss! Small world, huh?" She grinned at Kent, who blushed and ducked his head.

"That is a small world," Val said, her mind buzzing. Something about this connection seemed less than coincidental. "When did you start your internship, Kent?"

"Last summer, between junior and senior year," Kent said, his voice gaining confidence. "I was a Business Finance major, and still hadn't decided whether to go to law school."

"I bet old Curtis was a real ball-buster," Diego said, laughing.

"Actually, he treated me really well," Kent said. "In fact, that experience convinced me to sign up for Megan's campaign. I didn't realize they'd have such awesome staff working for them." He glanced at Amy and she blushed.

"Was that how you met Olivia Lambert?" Val asked.

The table went silent. Diego's eyes grew as large as his coffee mug, and Kent sat frozen, his coffee cup inches from his lips.

"The girl that died in the river?" Amy said, covering her mouth with one hand. "You knew her?"

"We've met," Kent said.

Diego's eyebrows furrowed. "Didn't your moms know each other or something?"

Kent glared at Diego, then cleared his throat. "Yes, but I actually got to know Livvy at school, last fall," he said. "She was taking advanced credit classes, and I was a lab assistant."

Val's ears perked up at his use of the nickname "Livvy" for Olivia. "Science lab? I thought you were a business major."

"I'm minoring in biology," Kent said, mumbling. "That's how Diego and I became friends, too—in BioChem class, junior year."

"Were you and Olivia dating?" Val asked.

"No, no," Kent said. "She's much younger, and I don't— didn't—know her well." Kent glared at Val. "I told all this to the detectives."

Diego's eyes grew wide, but he said nothing.

"So, you two never socialized?" Val asked. "Even, say, like this—a group of friends out for coffee?"

"Definitely not," Kent said, confident again.

"It's such a small world!" Amy said.

Val detected not a shred of doubt or worry in her voice. "What about Charlene Washington?" she asked, her eyes burning a hole in Kent's.

His mouth fell open for a moment. "Wh-who?" he said after too much time had passed. "I've never met her."

"Are you sure?" Val said. "Not even at the Association of Future Entrepreneurs award ceremony?"

Kent stared at her, confusion on his face.

"I saw a photo of Charlene's presentation ceremony." Val's voice took on a steely edge. "You were there."

"Kent?" Amy said, concerned. "Did you really know both of those girls?"

"No!" Kent said, his voice rising. "You know, there are so many of those stupid photo ops. They always were marching us interns in to fill the room. We were nothing but props for their PR shoots. I swear, I didn't know her."

A long silence filled the air. Val kept her eyes locked on Kent, who stared, frozen, at his empty coffee mug.

Finally, Amy broke the silence. "I believe you, Kent," she said. Turning to Val, she added, "Kent's a very honest guy. Why, when we paid for our coffee, do you know what happened? The barista gave him too much change? And he gave it back? And then added a thirty percent tip!" Her eyes grew wide and she scooted closer to Kent again.

"Thank you, Amy," Kent said.

Val glanced at each of them, then at Diego, who'd remained oddly quiet. "Well," she said, "I ought to get going."

"Me, too," Diego said. To Amy's concerned expression, he explained, "I promised Val a ride home. I'll definitely be there tomorrow night for my volunteer shift. Six o'clock, right?"

"You're ditching me?" Kent said with feigned annoyance that sounded more like relief. He turned to Amy. "Diego's my ride home, too."

"I'll drive you," Amy said, her voice dropping a register. "But I need to stop by the shoe store on the way home."

"Cool," Kent said in a rush of air. "I mean, that's...fine."

Amy turned to Val, eyes wide. "He even likes shoe shopping!" she whispered, fanning her face with an open palm. She turned back to Kent, smiling.

Yuck. Val rolled her eyes and slid out of the booth. "Dude," Val said when she and Diego made it outside. "I think we got away just in time. If we stayed any longer, they might've started making out right in front of us."

"I don't know how he does it," Diego said, shaking his head. "Every woman he meets wants to jump his bones." His face fell. "Wait, I didn't mean—"

"No worries," Val said, laughing. "I get what you mean. But when you say *every* woman...does that include Olivia Lambert?"

Diego coughed out a gust of air, almost a laugh. "If I can believe one-tenth of what that guy tells me, then yes. Even though I guess Olivia wasn't technically a woman...yet." He winced. "Sorry. Too soon?"

Val sighed. "She was under the age of consent. And he's what, twenty-one? So, was Kent telling the truth about their, er, *friendship*? Or did that extend beyond mentoring?"

Diego pointed to his car, a late-model Subaru WRX, and pressed the Unlock button on his key fob. "Kent helped get her into the advanced credit program."

Val nodded. That squared with what Olivia Lambert's mother had said—that the families had known each other for years. She paused with the passenger door still open, staring across the hood at Diego. "Was he telling the truth about Charlene Washington?" she asked.

"It's possible they met when she interned at Constitution Finance," he said. "But don't quote me on that."

Val blinked. Constitution Finance was a well-known bastion of testosterone. The two girls could have met any number of horny, wealthy men there. Men who might think nothing of flashing enough money around to impress an ambitious, underage teen—and keep her quiet about it, until it was too late.

"I've changed my mind," she said to Diego. "Could you drive me to police headquarters? It's less than a mile away."

He grinned. "You never take a day off, do you? Okay, sure. Maybe by the time we get there, I'll have you talked into a second date."

Val turned away so that he couldn't see her grimace. Gil's smiling face flashed through her mind, and the way his broad physique looked, even in sweaty gym clothes. His deep baritone voice when he imparted kind wisdom and patient instruction during her training. The admiration in his eyes whenever she mastered a new skill.

By contrast, Diego's good looks seemed boyish, his puppy-dog excitement immature, his glances more lustful than friendly. While intelligent and well-spoken, he also seemed naive, even gullible at times.

Or was Val judging him too harshly? Had she let their superficial differences prejudice her? His youth, his family's money, his dark complexion? Her neck and face warmed with guilt. Objectively, he was far closer to her in age than Gil, and it seemed unfair to compare his maturity level to a man a decade his senior. He had education and good manners, and treated people with respect. And, for God's sake, he did seem to like her.

His connection to creepy Kent Mercer—she cringed at yet another judgmental thought—bothered her. But she'd gathered some interesting clues about the Lambert and Washington cases through that association. Clues that might prove valuable.

Diego smiled at her, chattering away about a Katy Perry song playing on the radio. She hadn't noticed his dimples before, nor the sparkle in his big brown eyes.

Val exhaled a long, contented breath. If listening to the flirtations of a handsome boy was the price of expediting her investigation, it was one she could well afford to pay.

Chapter Ten

The short drive to police headquarters didn't give Diego much time to pitch his idea for a second date with Val. She escaped with a noncommittal "I'll get back to you" and a handshake rather than a hug goodbye. Thank God for restrictive seat belts. She scooted inside the ancient brick-and-concrete building as heavy, cold raindrops pelted her unprotected head.

Minutes later, she entered the WAVE Squad office on the fourth floor. A large open-air room occupied most of the space, with pairs of desks pushed back-to-back in small clusters around the room. A long table and chairs, set up for meetings, filled one end of the room, and a whiteboard, already gray from overuse, covered most of the adjacent wall. Heavy wooden doors with opaque glass windows led to three private offices and a small meeting room on the room's exterior. The scent of disinfectant didn't quite cover the musty aromas ubiquitous throughout the ancient structure.

To her surprise, the hulking figure of her precinct boss, Lieutenant Gibson, greeted her before she'd closed the door behind her.

"Dawes! What the hell brings you here?" he said, scratching the bald spot on his ebony scalp.

Before Val could answer, Shannon O'Reilly emerged from the meeting room and bounded toward her, squeezing her in a side-arm hug. "Val! Did you get my email?"

"What email?" Val said.

"You didn't? So, you just happened by?" Shannon asked, laughing.

"Er...kind of," Val said. "I had grand jury testimony today, and I came across some information related to the Olivia Lambert and Charlene Washington cases, so I thought—"

"You 'happened' to discover clues to a murder case? What, do people walk up to you and start testifying?" Gibson said, grinning at Shannon.

"Sort of." Val glanced from Gibson to Shannon, feeling a bit under the microscope. "It seems that both girls interned at Constitution Finance. I thought that might generate some leads."

"We're already on it," Gibson said. "Any specific names?"

"N-no," Val said. Dammit. Of course they already knew. How presumptuous of her to assume otherwise. "None that we don't already have, I mean."

Shannon and Gibson exchanged knowing glances. Val's face grew warm. Great. They must think her an idiot.

"Okay, well, that's all I had," she said. "Now, what's this email about?"

"Oh, good, you're all here," said another voice. Brenda Petroni appeared in her private office doorway. "We might as well chat now. In here."

Val followed Shannon into Petroni's office. A rectangular blacktop table with a half-dozen desk chairs filled most of the room. A gunmetal desk sat in the corner, neat and organized, with photos of Brenda's husband and family. The wall behind her desk consisted almost entirely of windows. An empty whiteboard occupied the opposite wall. "What's this all about, anyway?"

Gibson shut the door behind them and took a seat next to Val, across from Shannon and Petroni. "Your future," he said.

"We want to steal you from Liberty Heights," Shannon said with a sly smile.

"On the special unit?" Val's voice broke with excitement. "Really?"

Petroni's smile matched Shannon's. "The WAVE Squad. A limited term assignment. Renewable upon mutual agreement with the precinct. Right, Lieutenant?"

Gibson's dour expression softened. "I must be crazy, letting Downtown steal two of my best people." He glared at Petroni. "But it's only *temporary*."

"I'm the crazy one," Petroni said, eyes twinkling. "I'm burning a personnel spot on someone who clearly would do the work for free. Isn't this your day off, Dawes?"

Val expelled a blast of air, suddenly realizing she'd been holding her breath. "Kind of, but..." Rushing over to share her tiny scraps of knowledge on the case seemed foolish now.

"You'd be partnering with me," Shannon said. "A mix of street and office work."

"I'm counting on your research skills and your prior knowledge of the Lambert case," Petroni said. "We'll be looking at the Charlene Washington case, too, and others. We have a pretty broad mandate."

Val's heart leaped at the offer. She couldn't imagine a better partner than Shannon.

Other than Gil, of course. With that thought, her spirits fell. She didn't want to miss out on the opportunity here, yet she hated to miss the chance to reunite with Gil upon his return.

"You do want this, don't you?" Petroni asked after a few moments of silence. "I mean, you submitted an application."

"Yes, yes, of course I did," Val said. "It's just so...unexpected, and so fast."

"Like I said, we want our best people on this unit," Gibson said.

"Is *that* what you said?" Petroni said with a smirk.

"But we understand," Gibson said. "It's a big decision. You have tomorrow off too, right? Take a day and think it over. If you decide you can't leave us behind at Liberty Heights, nobody will hold it against you."

Petroni frowned. "But don't wait any longer than that," she said. "A lot of people want this opportunity. I *thought* you did, too, but..."

"I do," Val said. "But I appreciate the chance to think on it for a day. What else can you tell me about the assignment?"

They went over the details and logistics. She'd work at the headquarters building. She would get no salary increase, other than a bump in overtime pay. The experience would amount to on-the-job detective training. All that, plus the opportunity to partner with her friend, Shannon O'Reilly...the chance to work on a high-profile special unit, focused on an area of passion for her—it all seemed too good to be true.

Her Uncle Valentin's repeated warnings came to mind: "When something seems too good to be true, it probably is."

"One last thing," Gibson said before the meeting broke up. He glanced at Shannon and Petroni, then cast his eyes downward. "The, uh, mayor's office specifically requested that we assign you to this unit. Not that you can't refuse," he added, "but...well..."

"You can't refuse," Shannon said, laughing.

"Your refusal might get refused," Petroni said.

"More to the point," Gibson said, "we can't refuse. But you could...if it's not what you want."

Val bit her lip. The mayor's heavy-handed "request" gave her further pause. Rico's warnings echoed in her ears. Megan Iverson had twisted and politicized her prior work on the case, and the prospect of more of the same dampened her enthusiasm for what was otherwise a dream job. The prospect of losing the chance to reunite with Gil as a partner compounded her unease, twisting her insides into a knot of indecision.

"So, you'll let us know in twenty-four hours?" Petroni checked her watch. "Okay, it's late, so…thirty-six hours. Start of your Thursday shift. Deal?"

Val shook herself back into the present. "Yes, sir," she said. She tried to focus on the positives of the offer. But that tight feeling in her gut wouldn't go away.

***

A late afternoon run, twice around Clayton's three-mile riverfront loop, failed to deliver the clarity Val hoped for regarding the WAVE Squad assignment. The lure of helping to bring closure to the Olivia Lambert case excited her, as did the potential for fast-tracking it to detective. That prospect loomed so close, she could taste it.

But Rico's and Travis's warnings overshadowed the positives and grew larger with every footstep that pounded the pavement. The risks of failure, with such an understaffed effort. The politicization, already underway with Mayor Iverson's hard campaigning on the issue, and her husband's early intrusions into their affairs. Their interference with staff selection, even on Val's behalf, opened the door to future meddling, which could doom an otherwise promising venture. Gil's reassurances notwithstanding, she remained doubtful by the time she stopped at a park bench to begin her cooling-down routine.

While stretching her legs, her phone beeped. A text from Beth. *Happy hour?*

Her whole body felt lighter. *Yes, but I'm pretty dank—just finished a run.* Val smiled. That ought to quash any notions Beth might have of fixing her up with some new guy, a habit her friend seemed unable to break.

Clay Pigeon? Beth texted back. *It's warm, we can sit outside.*

Val laughed. Knowing Beth, that meant she already had an outside table.

Sure enough, Beth waved to her from a shaded seat on the sidewalk a few minutes later as Val approached the downtown watering hole. The Pigeon, as the locals called it, was one of Clayton's oldest bars, having opened minutes after Prohibition ended—or years before that, if one believed local folklore. Young, fit wait staff in tight jeans and form-fitting T-shirts bearing the cartoon image of the pub's mascot—a sassy, pudgy pigeon—hustled between tiny tables jammed with thirsty patrons, none of whom appeared a day over thirty.

"Hope you're hungry," Beth said after wrapping Val up in a bear hug. "I ordered us some low-carb apps. And that red wine is yours."

Val nodded, hoping the nosh included some protein. "Starved. All I've had since breakfast is a cappuccino."

"I thought this was your day off," Beth said.

Val sipped her wine. "I testified before a grand jury today on an assault case against a young woman. It...was tough." She went quiet for a moment, shivering in the sudden chill of the outdoor air.

"It is tough, isn't it?" Beth said in a soft voice. She leaned closer and rested her hand on Val's shoulder. "Bad memories...er, associations, whatever the right word is. I'm sorry."

Val blasted air between her teeth. "It's something I have to come to terms with, sooner or later. Sooner, if I'm going to get anywhere in life." She sighed. "Especially at work. They offered me a chance to join a new task force focused on violence against women. We've had a new spate of rape-murder cases against teenage girls, and the mayor wants to throw a pile of money and bodies at it."

"Yeah, other peoples' bodies," Beth said. "I don't like the sound of that. It seems dangerous."

"No more than walking a beat," Val said. "Less, probably."

"Chasing serial killers doesn't sound all that safe to me," Beth said. "Look what happened when you got assigned to that special team last year. You nearly got killed. He kidnapped your niece and sister-in-law, for God's sake!"

"True," Val said. Chill air washed over her, raising goosebumps on her skin. She rubbed her arms and gazed around the crowded outdoor space of the old tavern. The pub's now-bright decor failed to mask the tavern's history as a speakeasy. Reputedly, the town's criminal organizations once congregated here with corrupt politicians and cops on the take, cutting deals to decide who lived, died, suffered, and prospered. How similar was it to the mayor's task force—flashy window dressing, hiding its more insidious, unsavory basis?

The appetizers Beth ordered arrived—strawberry bruschetta, figs stuffed with goat cheese, and braised Brussels sprouts with balsamic vinegar. The eclectic mix amused Val and broke her out of her sour reverie. She grabbed a stuffed fig and dove in with relish.

"Career-wise, though, I have to admit, the special unit assignment sounds perfect for you," Beth said. "But isn't there any other way to stay involved and keep your career on track?"

"Yeah," Val said. "The slow way. Pay my dues, wait my turn, and hope the glass ceiling doesn't turn to steel in the meantime."

Beth frowned. "It is kind of an old-boys' club, isn't it? And you've always said you wanted to make detective by the time you're twenty-five. But does this special unit make that much of a difference?"

"It's a fast track," Val said. "And having found the body of one of the victims gives me a bit of a running start."

"Plus, you get the chance to help take another serial rapist off the streets," Beth said. "Permanently, I hope."

"Jeez, Beth, it's not like they're asking me to execute him." Val shuddered. The image of Richard Harkins bleeding on the sidewalk came to mind again.

"That's not what I meant. Please, Val—"

"I know, I know," Val said. "I guess I'm just a little sensitive about that still."

Beth's face grew sullen, heavy with concern. She set down a half-eaten slice of bruschetta and leaned over the table, her voice low. "Tell me straight, Val. Would this assignment put you in another situation where you have to confront this weirdo killer, and..." Her voice trailed off, but her lips turned down in a deep, sad frown.

Val took a deep breath, weighing her response. "It's impossible to say," she said. "But it's not likely. Detective work is mostly after-the-fact. Lots of digging around, asking witnesses what they know, putting things together into some sort of logical narrative. Seriously, walking the beat puts me at greater risk."

Beth reached out and took Val's hand in hers. "Which, you will recall, I also tried to talk you out of."

Val chuckled. "You tried talking me out of being a cop altogether."

Beth nodded, her eyes moist. "I still wish I'd succeeded sometimes."

"But you didn't," Val said. "And now, I need to decide what to do next in my career."

Beth took a deep, unsteady breath. "Valorie," she said, "you know damn well you won't say no to this. It's too important for you and your career. And the women of Clayton need you."

Val smiled, her throat tightening. Good old Beth. "Love you, girl," she said.

"Love you too." Beth let go of Val's hands and turned away. "Just...be safe out there, okay?"

"I will," Val said. "I promise."

She wondered, deep down, if she had it in her power to keep that promise.

***

At 7:53 a.m. Thursday morning, Val stepped off the downtown bus in front of police headquarters, face-first into a blast of wind and icy rain. She pulled the hood of her raincoat over her service cap and held it tight against the top of her uniform as a second gust whipped a stray lock of hair into her eyes. She whisked past the coffee cart that, despite the weather, commanded a long line of uniformed officers seeking a better shot of caffeine than the one awaiting them in the break room. Val marched on. On her budget, bad, free coffee beat expensive good stuff, especially since she'd be living alone soon. She reminded herself to post an ad on Craigslist for a new roommate, composing the wording in her head as she pushed through the heavy double doors at the building's entrance. *Roommate wanted. Female only, no pets, must love rookie cops with serious hang-ups about men, particularly rapists. Lifelong friend preferred.*

She hustled up the stairs to the fourth floor and slipped into the WAVE Squad office, not wanting to interrupt the loud conversation she'd overheard during her approach. Sergeant Petroni stood inside her office, door open, facing off against a tall, barrel-shaped white man with wavy, salt-and-pepper hair, wearing an ill-fitting gray suit. He continued his angry rant at Petroni, who gave Val a curt nod without taking her eyes off of him. Val took a seat at the desk farthest from Petroni's office and tried to look invisible.

"But that doesn't make sense!" the man yelled. "I have the *most* experience of anyone hunting down these creeps. Seven sexual assault collars in the last two years, and none of them walked. Not one! Who the hell are you gonna find with a better record than me?"

"I'm not arguing with your record," Petroni said. "I only have so many slots to fill, that's all. It's just numbers."

"But what about *my* numbers?" the man shouted. He shook a sheaf of papers at her. "Look at these. Unmatched in the department. I kick ass and you know it."

"Not denying that at all," Petroni said, using her body to edge him out the door of her office. "Really. I've committed all of our positions already. We just don't have a slot for you."

"Bullshit!" The man slapped the papers down on Petroni's desk and threw his hands up in the air. "It's politics, isn't it? Bunch of boot-lickers coming in here flaunting their connections, am I right? Huh? Deny it if I'm wrong. Go ahead. I dare you!" He followed Petroni into the Bullpen area and scanned the room. After a moment, he spotted Val.

"You!" he said. "Dawes, right? Valentin's kid? Did you land a spot on this task force?"

Val cleared her throat. "Valentin was my uncle, and I—"

"Leave her out of this," Petroni said. "Look, Mickey, you're doing good work down in South Precinct. I just—"

"*Great* work," Mickey interrupted. "Fucking fantastic work, if you ask me."

Petroni rolled her eyes. "Fine. Fantastic work. But if I took you out of South, your boss would cook my ass on that giant smoker of his and serve me over polenta at his next barbecue. Besides, like I said. The detective jobs are filled. There's nothing I can do."

"Fucking ridiculous! You got room for goddamned rookies," Mickey said, waving an arm at Val, "but not for the top violent crime detective outside of homicide. Makes no fucking sense." He stomped toward the door, stopping when he reached Val. "Congratulations, Dawes," he said. "Looks like you're in and I'm out. Who'd you blow to get your slot, eh? Or whatever the hell you lezzies do to each other. Fucking libtard politics!" He thudded into the hall, slamming the door behind him.

"Something I said?" Val stood and let out a long, heavy breath.

"Don't mind Mulroney," Petroni said. "He doesn't take rejection well. And that last little outburst tells you everything you need to know about why I didn't choose him. But I confess, I'm very pleased to see you here this morning. Is this a harbinger of good news?"

"I hope so," Val said. "I've decided to accept your offer to join the unit…if it's still good, that is."

"Damn straight it is," Petroni said. "Welcome aboard!" She offered a handshake.

Val accepted it and glanced over her shoulder. "What about you being all filled up?" she asked.

Petroni laughed. "We'd be too full for Mulroney, no matter how many empty chairs you see here," she said. "Anyway, he'd wanted a detective slot, and those are full. I've kept one uniform spot open, waiting for your answer. Now we're staffed up across the board."

"Great!" Relief flooded over Val. "Where should I begin?"

"Take a seat," Petroni said. "Shannon is due in at 8:30. In the meantime, fill me in on a few things. You found Olivia Lambert's body, right? How'd you happen to be there at that lucky moment?"

"I'd hesitate to call it lucky," Val said. "I was out for an evening run. The body just floated up at the right time, I guess."

"Floated, eh? That's what's weird," Petroni said. "Why didn't the killer weigh the body down, I wonder, and let the bass and perch do their work on the corpse?"

Val shrugged. "Must have been in a hurry to dump the body, I guess. I thought she might still be alive, so I just went in after her." She shuddered. "I hope I didn't screw up by doing that."

"No." Petroni smiled at her. "You were right to follow your instincts. The off chance of saving her life is worth any risk of crime scene contamination."

Val gasped. "Did I—? I mean, is that the actual place where—? He raped her on the riverbank, you think?"

"No, no. Poor choice of words," Petroni said. "We haven't figured out the location yet. But if it had been the crime scene...then we'd hope you'd take a little more care to preserve evidence."

Val's neck burned. Petroni was being generous, and they both knew it. "What should I have done in that case?" she said.

Petroni waved the question off. "It's moot. I'm more concerned that you're aware of the risks to your own safety in those and similar situations. Did you check around for the perp, for example, in case he was still nearby?"

The heat in Val's neck rose to her face and ears. "No," she said. "I just tried to recover the girl from the water. It didn't occur to me that a killer might still be there, watching."

"Unlikely, but you have to consider it." Petroni smiled and patted her arm. "You're a valuable asset to the team, and to the department, Dawes. I don't want to lose you for a lack of caution."

"I guess I have a lot to learn from you and Shannon," Val said.

"That's *Detective* O'Reilly to you, rookie," a voice said behind her. A familiar laugh followed the stern rebuke.

"S'matter, kid? Don't you know how to address your senior officers while on duty?"

Val spun in her chair. A tall, willowy blonde in an ocean blue roll-sleeve blazer, matching pants, and a cream blouse stood in the doorway, grinning at her.

"Great news," Petroni said. "Dawes is joining the team. Starting today, I hope?"

"If you'll have me," Val said.

"I'll call Lieutenant Gibson right now," Petroni said. "Shannon, it's time to start Val's training as this department's next great detective.

PART TWO

WAVE Squad

Chapter Eleven

To Val's delight, Petroni kept her promise to partner her with Shannon O'Reilly.

"You won't be walking a beat on this job," Shannon told her. They took seats at their respective desks, pushed nose-to-nose against each other in the corner of the WAVE Squad's bullpen. "But it's not all desk work, either. We'll be on the street plenty. In fact, my first goal for today is to follow up with friends and neighbors of Charlene Washington. What do you know about her case?"

"Drowning victim, African American, sixteen years old, signs of rape pre-mortem," Val recited from memory. "Body recovered four days ago, nicely dressed, and, like Olivia Lambert, no shoes. Deceased about two days when discovered. What have I missed?"

"Rape is almost certain," Shannon said in a glum voice. "Multiple partners. DNA tests are still being run and will be compared to Lambert's. Last seen by friends mere hours before time of death. There are other similarities to the first case, too: same high school, active in sports and after-school activities, and no boyfriend."

"Couple of geeks," Val said with a wan smile. "Like I was."

"Me too," Shannon said. "What else do we have?"

"Geeks aren't popular—at least, they weren't in my day," Val said. "Outsiders, with few friends their own age. Maybe attracted to older, more mature guys." Gil's image appeared in Val's mind, and her face reddened.

"Good thinking," Shannon said, jumping up to scribble notes on a whiteboard. She wrote "OL" on one side and "CW" on the other, listing Val's observations on a third column in the center. "What else?"

"Ambitious. All those academic activities were geared toward building a good resume for college scholarships," Val said. "What was Charlene's GPA?"

"Close to perfect, like Olivia's," Shannon said, nodding, and adding it to the list. "Good, good. Keep going!"

"Family," Val said. "Olivia, the oldest of three girls. Charlene had a younger sister, and an older brother—Gunther—who moved out years ago."

Shannon nodded. "He has a short rap sheet—a car break-in, vandalism, some petty theft, drug possession. We'll need to track him down. What else?" She wrote "Gunther-brother" in the "CW" column.

"Race, obviously." Val's face flushed, recalling Gil's warning about the detective unit's predilection toward racial profiling.

But Shannon didn't dwell on it. "And neighborhood of residence." Shannon noted it on the whiteboard and continued on. "Household income, pretty much the same—both middle class, from what I gather."

"Although," Val noted, "in Olivia's case, only her father works outside the home. Charlene's dad is a minister, her mother a librarian."

Shannon wrote "Both parents work" in Charlene's column. "Other differences?"

After a few seconds of silence, Val shook her head. "Not aware of any."

"Okay. Back to what they had in common," Shannon said.

Val pondered what other factors made the girls vulnerable. So many things. "Neither had driver's licenses yet...might have needed a ride somewhere, could have gotten into someone's car," she said. "Should we include that on our list?"

"Of course," Shannon said. "They're both smart—sorry, *were* both smart—so I doubt they'd accept a ride from just anyone. Someone they knew, perhaps?"

"Probably," Val said. "Trusted, too. The key question behind that is, who would they know in common?" She left unspoken the question: who would violate their innocent trust? She'd trusted "Uncle" Milt once, too.

"Teachers, coaches, and some fellow students, at least," Shannon said.

"Authority figures, taking advantage," Val said. "But which ones?"

Shannon smiled. "Answering that," she said, "is the heart of detective work. Not glamorous, but it's how we earn our pay. So, are we ready to roll? Charlene's parents are expecting us at 9:00 a.m." She whipped out her cell phone and snapped a picture of the white board.

Val exhaled tension out of her body. They'd avoided any overt racial profiling, although they'd skated right on the edge. Whether that persisted after their interview with the Washingtons remained an open question—one that weighed on her during their drive to visit Charlene's grieving parents.

***

Natalie Washington, a thin, forty-something Black woman wearing oversized red-framed glasses, opened the door of her 1980s-era Cape Cod-style home and offered a tired smile at Val and Shannon. Her trim, salt-and-pepper flat-top showed hints of amber on the sides, and her smooth skin remained unblemished by age spots or wrinkles. She wore a silky, light blue Caftan dress that draped almost to her ankles, and white wedge sandals. "Come in, officers," she said, stepping back and holding open the door. "Would you like something to drink?"

"Black coffee would be wonderful," Shannon said.

"Water, thank you," Val said. She wasn't thirsty, but Shannon had coached her to accept whatever hospitality a victim's family might offer. It helped "normalize" an otherwise awkward situation and gave them a renewed sense of control over their lives.

They followed Charlene's mother into the cramped living room, a rectangle broken up by wide arched doorways that led to an updated kitchen and a long hallway. Natalie offered them seats on a worn leather sofa. "I'll be right with you. My husband had an early meeting at the church this morning, but he should be home soon."

While Mrs. Washington prepared their drinks, Val's eyes wandered around the room. The Washingtons' taste in furnishings reminded Val of her father's. Lots of leather and brass, a recliner that almost matched the sofa facing a 40-inch flat-screen TV mounted to the wall, and a low bookshelf dominated by a component-based stereo with fake wooden speakers. No Playstation or XBox system here. Framed portraits of Jesus, Martin Luther King Jr., and Barack Obama occupied center stage on the wall opposite the room's large picture window. Other frames contained brief inspirational quotes or Bible verses. Two, she recognized: John 3:16 and Psalm 23. One she didn't recognize, from Jeremiah: "'For I know the plans I have for you,' declares the Lord, 'plans to prosper you and not to harm you, plans to give you hope and a future."

A lump formed in her throat. The Washingtons, no doubt, had made plans for Charlene to prosper without harm. Jeremiah's verse rang hollow, a mere platitude in the violent world of the twenty-first century.

Her gaze wandered to a family photo gallery in the hallway. The nearest set showed Charlene at various ages, including her most recent yearbook photo, and traced her maturation back to first grade or kindergarten. Another set featured Charlene's younger sister, Alysha, who could have passed for her twin if not for their two-year age gap. The photos next to those captured the entire family—Natalie, a man whom Val recognized from her research as Reverend Daryl Washington, the two girls, and the glowering face of a man of about twenty. Val guessed him to be her brother, Gunther.

Something about Gunther looked familiar. She stood and took a few steps toward the hallway to get a closer look. Two gold earrings dangled from the young man's right ear.

"Val, what are you doing?" Shannon hissed.

Before Val could answer, Mrs. Washington reappeared, holding a tray of drinks. "Here you go, officers—oh, I see you've found our 'rogue's gallery.' I really should take our wedding photos down! That one, of all of us, was the last time we were all together at Thanksgiving. That's Alysha's eighth-grade graduation, and...that picture of Char..." Natalie choked up, unable to continue. She dropped the tray on a low coffee table with a clatter and covered her tearing eyes with a delicate hand. "I'm sorry," she said. "I'll get a towel to clean up that mess."

"I'll get it," Shannon said, shooting to her feet and hurrying past her toward the kitchen. She mouthed at Val: "Help her!"

Val stood, helpless, in front of the crying woman. No doubt Shannon meant she should embrace the poor woman, but her anxiety over being touched by strangers kicked in, rendering her motionless. "How about...we sit, Mrs. Washington?" she said after too many uncomfortable seconds ticked by.

"Call me Natalie, please. And I'm...fine," Natalie said, waving her hands in front of her face. "Shoot, I really hadn't wanted to cry here this morning!" She picked up a half-dry napkin from the tray and dabbed away her tears. She sniffled and glanced back at the hallway. "What I was trying to say a moment ago was, we have more recent pictures of Charlene, if that would help."

"It would," Val said, and guided Natalie by the elbow to a chair perched perpendicular to the sofa. "I am curious, too, about the young man in the family photos. Is that her brother?"

"Gunther? Yes. Well..." Natalie gazed into Val's eyes, blinking away fresh tears. "I'm glad you asked before my husband came home. Daryl and the boy have a...difficult relationship." She blew her nose and paused another moment. "You see, Gunther's biological father isn't...in the picture. Daryl adopted Gunther after we married, and, well...Gunny always resented him a little."

"That's not unusual for a young boy who loves his mother and misses his father," Val said.

"Gunther never knew his father," Natalie said. "Daryl always loved him like his own son, but...Gunny's always been a handful."

Shannon returned with towels and blotted up the spills. "Was Charlene close to Gunner?" she asked.

Val winced. "Gun-*ther*," she whispered.

Natalie smiled. "Gunner works, too. That's what his friends call him. It came from Charlene—she couldn't say 'Gunther' as a little girl." She emitted a tiny, sad laugh. "Char worshipped her big brother. If only he'd have stayed closer to home and kept out of trouble..." She shook her head and pressed her eyes shut.

Gunner. In that instant, Val realized why his picture looked familiar. She took a deep breath and caught Shannon's eye, interrupting her partner's next question. "Mrs. Washington," Val said, "is your son involved in any gang activity, to your knowledge?"

Shannon's pained expression told Val she might have made a mistake, asking such a taboo question. But Natalie Washington's reaction reassured her otherwise.

"Unfortunately," she said in a steely voice. "That's how he got into so much trouble—street fights, drugs, and he even went to jail for stealing from a convenience store once."

Val winced. Her then-partner, "Pops," had made that arrest. Gunner went free after video footage showed he hadn't stolen anything.

"But Char had somehow gotten to him in recent weeks," Natalie continued, "and he'd hung out with those boys less and less lately. Thanks to her, I thought he'd turned the corner." Tears flowed down her cheeks again. "Now, I don't know."

Val sat next to Natalie and spoke in a soft voice. "His gang. Are they called The Disciples?"

"You know them?" Natalie said, matching Val's gaze.

"I've met Gunner," Val said, making eye contact with Shannon again. Her partner's lips curled up into a knowing smile, followed by a quick, approving nod. "I've always thought he was a pretty good kid."

"He was, once," said a booming male voice, entering from the kitchen. A tall, white-haired man with wisps of curly whiskers covering his chin removed a black fedora and raincoat and extended a long, bony hand. "Daryl Washington, Charlene's father."

Shannon stood and accepted the handshake. "Detective O'Reilly. This is my partner—"

"Valorie Dawes," Washington said, again in that cannon of a voice. "I recognize you from the newspapers. You shot that rapist a few months back."

Val stood and swallowed hard. "I returned fire in self—"

"Normally, I disapprove of violence," the Reverend said. "But—and I pray the good Lord will forgive me—that man had it coming. I hope that when you find whoever took my daughter from us, you'll show no greater mercy. Even if I burn in hell for saying so." He tossed his hat and coat to the floor in a flourish.

"Daryl!" Natalie said with a gasp.

Shannon cleared her throat. "Everyone in the Clayton Police Department wants to find and apprehend the perpetrator as much as—"

"Bull-turkey!" the Reverend shouted. "Excuse my French. I mean no disrespect, Detective. But nobody, and I mean nobody, on this planet wants that man caught and punished as much as we do. That said, I'm pleased to see that you have the right woman on the job." He smiled at Val. "I knew your uncle, Miss Dawes," he said. "Valentin was a fine man and an honorable servant of the law, and I'm pleased that you have followed in his footsteps."

"Thank you, Reverend," Val said.

"I apologize for my tardiness," the Reverend said. "Please, continue with your interview." He sat in the recliner, leaning forward. Val and Shannon resumed their seats on the couch.

"When did you last see Charlene?" Shannon asked.

"In the morning, before school, on the day she was..." Natalie's breath shuddered out of her. "Taken."

Shannon nodded. "Did she have activities after school? Sports, yearbook, something personal?"

"Yearbook," Natalie said. "She also had volleyball practice scheduled, but she never made it."

"We assumed that she'd gotten held up at the yearbook committee meeting," the Reverend said. "Char was quite the photographer, and we thought maybe she had a last-minute assignment."

"But the yearbook faculty adviser said she left the meeting early," Natalie said. "Without her camera."

"Which was odd," Reverend Washington said. "She never went anywhere without it."

Val scribbled notes on a pad and put a giant asterisk next to "camera." Perhaps it contained images of someone, or something, that could help the case. She opened her mouth to speak—

"Was she dating anyone?" Shannon asked.

"No!" the Reverend said. "Absolutely not."

"Char has only been on a few dates," Natalie explained. "She liked this one boy for a while, but…things didn't work out."

"He was only after one thing," Reverend Washington said. "Char wasn't interested in that."

Natalie's eyes widened and she looked away. Shannon puckered her lips, as if suppressing a smirk, something her glowing eyes confirmed.

"Do you have the boy's contact information?" Val asked.

"I can get it for you," Natalie said.

"How about people at school?" Shannon said. "Any names that come up a lot? Teachers, teammates, classmates, anyone involved in her extracurriculars?"

"She mentioned someone from AFE. That's her business club," Natalie said.

"Association of Future Entrepreneurs," Val said to Shannon's puzzled look. "What's that person's name, Mrs. Washington?" Her heart pounded, anticipating the name of Kent Mercer to fall from Natalie's red lips.

"It was a boy, an older boy," Natalie said. "We were very pleased, actually—"

"I wasn't pleased," the Reverend said. "The kid was twenty-one years old. You can't tell me he was just interested in being friends."

"He seemed nice," Natalie said, holding her husband's hand. "Very mature."

"He was a grown man!" the Reverend said.

"His name, though?" Shannon said. "Please?"

Natalie sighed and met Shannon's eye, then pointed to Val's notepad. Val readied her pen.

"His name," Natalie said, "was Diego Collier."

***

Val's head spun. Charlene knew Diego? More to the point, Diego knew Charlene, and he hadn't once mentioned this in their many encounters. And he knew Olivia Lambert, through Kent. He'd pretended to defend his friend's associations with the two girls, while hiding his own behind a veneer of sensitivity and kindness. Val fumed, angry at herself for not seeing through him sooner.

Preoccupied with her self-chastisement, she missed Shannon's next question. Reverend Washington's haughty laugh brought her back to the present.

"Tattoos? Of course not," he scoffed. "We don't permit our children to mutilate their bodies with such nonsense. She hasn't even had her ears pierced." He waved his hands at them, as if shooing the two officers away for their foolishness.

Beside him, Natalie Washington's eyes widened, and she turned her face to the side, covering her mouth.

"Mrs. Washington?" Val set her pen and paper aside. "I mean, Natalie. Do you agree with your husband's statement?"

Natalie glanced at her husband, who glared back at her. Neither answered Val's question.

"Mrs. Washington?" Shannon repeated.

Natalie grasped her husband's hand and took a deep breath. "It's true we've never given Char permission to do such things," she said. "But children often need to explore their own paths and make their own mistakes—"

"Natalie!" The Reverend pulled her hand in close. "Are you saying—"

"Daryl, stop!" Natalie winced. "You're hurting me."

The Reverend loosened his grasp on his wife's hand and hung his head. "I apologize," he said. "Forgive me."

Natalie glared at him, nodded once, and turned back toward the officers. "I discovered pierced earrings—simple posts—in Char's bedroom a few weeks ago," she said. "She has never worn anything except clip-ons in our presence, so one night last week, I checked on her while she slept." She blinked tears out of her eyes and wiped them away with her free hand, still refusing to face her glowering husband. "Both ears. I'm sorry, Daryl, for not telling you." Her voice faded to a whisper.

The Reverend stared at her, shaking his head. "I thought we agreed, Natty. She's still too young," he said in a hoarse voice.

"And tattoos?" Shannon asked again after a tense moment of silence. "Particularly on her legs or feet?"

Val tried to catch Shannon's eye, but her partner's focus remained on their interview subjects. Val searched her memory of Olivia Lambert's file, recalling nothing about tattoos. She'd noticed the girl's bare feet when she pulled her out of the river, but didn't recall seeing any body art. What was Shannon driving at?

"Not that I've seen," Natalie said, sniffling. "She's only sixteen. Wouldn't she have needed our permission?"

"Legally, yes," Shannon said. "But unscrupulous shops abound, as do fake IDs."

"What are you trying to imply, Officer?" Reverend Washington stood and towered over Shannon, pointing a long, angry finger in her face. "That our daughter is a liar and a fraud? That she is to blame for getting abducted and killed, because she's some sort of loose woman?" His shouts hurt Val's ears, and clearly his wife's, as she covered them with her hands.

Not Shannon's. She stood, reestablishing her bearing, but retreated a step from the Reverend's angry face. "I am not saying that at all," she said, and with a discreet wave, signaled Val to stand also. Val complied, and Shannon continued in a soft voice. "But unscrupulous tattoo artists have ways of getting around such regulations and are happy to take money from innocent and impressionable teenagers. It's not her fault, or yours, that she was attacked. As women who have to put up with unwelcome harassment from men every day of our lives, we would never insinuate as much. Please, Reverend Washington, accept my apology if I gave that impression."

Shannon's words and soothing tone seemed to calm the Reverend, and he bowed his head again. "No, I apologize for raising my voice, Officer," he said. "I let my emotions rule me for a moment. Of course you're right. Forgive me."

Val and Shannon left a few minutes later, with promises on each side to keep the other informed. Once inside the cruiser, Val turned to Shannon. "What was all that about the tattoo?" she said.

Shannon frowned and turned the key in the ignition. "Sorry, I thought you knew," she said. "The autopsies of both girls revealed a similar tattoo on the lower calf, upper-ankle area. We've held that detail back from the public. Along with the barefoot thing, it's a strong clue that the cases could be linked."

"What's the tat?" Val asked. "Something unusual?"

Shannon shrugged. "It's a drawing of a super-buff Rosie the Riveter, flexing her bicep, with the word *'Chingona'* inscribed on her upper arm. I'm not even sure what that means. Is it Japanese or something?"

"Chingona?" Val laughed. "It's Hispanic street slang for 'Bad-ass Woman.' But neither Charlene nor Olivia Lambert were Latina, so it's a curious mark for either of them to have."

"So why would they?" Shannon said, steering the cruiser away from the curb.

Val shrugged. "It could be a fad. In my senior year, everyone wore pajamas to school…for about a week. But why wouldn't their parents have noticed?"

"Because," Shannon said after a deep breath, "the autopsy report also showed that both of the tats were fresh—probably applied within twenty-four hours prior to their deaths."

Chapter Twelve

Val remained quiet for several minutes, absorbing the new information they'd gathered. Tattoos, piercings, the connection to Gunner, and most surprising, that Charlene knew Diego. It all made her head spin.

When city traffic stopped their progress across town, Shannon spoke up. "That 'older' guy Charlene's parents mentioned," she said. "Diego Collier. Isn't he a friend of yours?"

"Sort of," Val said. "We went out for brunch once. He let on that his buddy Kent Mercer was a friend of Olivia Lambert's, so I thought it best to cool things off right away."

"We're still watching Mercer," Shannon said. "Sounds like we might want to question Diego, too. Where can we find him?"

"He's a senior at Western New England, up in Springfield," Val said. "It's about an hour's drive. Shall we go?"

Shannon shook her head. "To do anything official across state lines, we'd have to clear it with the higher-ups. He'd be gone before we got permission. Does he live in Clayton?"

Val nodded. "With his mom, although he often visits his dad in Rhode Island on weekends. Let me check." She texted him: *Will you be home this afternoon?*

"Diego's not a tattoo artist by any chance, is he?" Shannon asked with a grin.

Val's stomach convulsed, imagining Diego somehow capable of doing much more horrible things than body art to Olivia and Charlene. "I don't even know if he has one," she said.

Her phone beeped. Diego had responded. *Going to Dads in RI after class. Pizza or movie Sunday night?* She told Shannon.

"Tell him yes," Shannon said. "We'll make it a threesome."

Val shuddered. "Ew."

"A threesome, not a three-*way*," Shannon said, laughing. "In the meantime, find out everything you can about this guy, and about where a gal might get a *Chingona* tattoo. I'll follow the leads on her teachers and faculty advisers."

Back in the WAVE office ten minutes later, Val returned the "favor" Diego had paid her and conducted an in-depth search of his on-line presence. She confirmed most of what he'd already shared: his parents' successful careers in the medical field, his occasional track victories in high school and college, and his volunteer work with AFE. But she found no further connection to either of the murder victims. Not even a religious affiliation. She sighed. Any further progress on that front would have to wait until Sunday evening.

She logged into the active cases database to review the two girls' files, and in particular, to snag a glimpse at the tattoo image they shared. Shot by a person whose expertise in forensics far exceeded their skill at photography, Charlene's tat photo suffered from overexposure and poor focus. Olivia's was too dark and taken at a tough angle. But they gave her enough to go on: a line drawing of a thin, 1940s-era brunette with muscular arms, a blue scarf in her hair, a white tank top, and a determined expression. At least the artist refrained from depicting a pinup girl with big boobs. More brawn than bra, she noted. Probably a woman's design, then.

Next she scanned Yelp and Google for tattoo shops that might offer a *Chingona* or even a simple Rosie the Riveter ink job, and found nothing. Or, rather, she found too much.

Clayton, a town of 120,000 people—about half between the prime inking ages of eighteen and forty-five—had some three dozen tattoo and piercing shops. About a dozen of them claimed to specialize in tats for empowered, "woke" women. Having never opted for body art of her own, she had no idea which ones could back up their claims and which were blowing smoke.

But she knew someone who would.

Val dialed one of the few numbers in her cell phone's Favorites list and grinned with relief when her roommate answered on the second ring.

"This is a rare treat," Beth said without a hello. "A midday call from my BFF! What's up? Is Chad's wife preggers again? Or did you already find someone to sublet my room and need me to move out?"

"None of those," Val said. "I have a question for you. When you snuck your sister in to get her inked for her eighth-grade graduation present, where did you go?"

"What the—? Valorie Dawes, are you finally breaking down and adding some art to that perfect skin of yours?" Beth said. "Oh. Em. Gee."

"No, no," Val said. "I'm working a case. I need to find a place that, um, doesn't look too carefully at the technicalities of the law when booking new clients."

"You're not going to bust him, are you?" Beth said. "Luis is a good dude, and I wouldn't—"

"No, I promise," Val said. "I just need to talk to him, get a feel for where an underage girl would go for this type of thing."

"Hold on, I have a customer." Beth's phone went silent. Val groaned. Beth worked at Macy's in women's wear, and shoppers could absorb anywhere from seconds to hours of a store associate's time, without warning. She hung up and texted: *Just send me Luis's info. Please?*

While she waited, she queried the crime database for all homicides in western Connecticut for the past two years involving underage girls with tattoos. To her horror, the list filled the screen. She narrowed the search, adding another keyword: *barefoot.* The list shortened to twelve.

Val perused the first file, a case involving an underage prostitute with dozens of tats. She discarded that one, along with two murder-suicides, perpetrated by family members. Four were drive-by shootings, blamed on gangs. Two girls died from blunt trauma injuries, linked to muggings. By the time Val's messenger app pinged with Beth's reluctant divulging of Luis's contact data, three cases stood out as worth pursuing. All three underage girls had not only been sexually assaulted in the Clayton vicinity in the past year, but also shared two other key attributes with Olivia and Charlene.

First, each would be described, as Beth would put it, as "outside the norm of conventional beauty." A little curvy, or even chunky, her brother-with-the-perfect-wife might say.

Second, each had a Rosie the Riveter tattoo on her lower left leg. One tat, on a young Latina, included the word *Chingona.*

Val stared at her computer screen, sickened and numb. Some sick fuck was out there, finding and killing intelligent young women with body-image issues...and branding them with tattoos associated with female empowerment.

Even worse: that sick fuck might be Diego Collier.

***

Brenda Petroni interrupted Val's research early Friday morning with a shout-out to the Bullpen area. "All-hands meeting in fifteen!" she announced. "Be ready to take notes. Who's out and who's in right now?"

"Three uniforms here, plus Grimes, me, and you," Shannon said, emerging from the small meeting room.

"What's up?" She paused in the doorway, notepad and pen in hand, a pair of black-rimmed reading glasses perched atop her bun of strawberry blonde hair.

"Mayor Iverson has an announcement for us. She's bringing people. Let's set up for a briefing. Come on, folks, move it!"

Val closed her browser and helped clear away files and notes scattered across the large meeting table. Meanwhile, Detective Grimes and his partner, Dion Woodson, set up a laptop and projector. "The mayor has a slideshow for us," Shannon explained with a roll of her eyes. "I'm sure it'll be captivating."

Moments later, the office door burst open. Michael Kim, the mayor's Police Department Liaison, led a small entourage into the office. The mayor strode in behind them, wearing a bright red skirt suit and a broad smile, confidence oozing with every step. She extended a handshake to Val. "Officer Dawes, always a pleasure." She shook hands and introduced herself to every officer in the room, then asked, "Is Sergeant Petroni ready?"

"Coming, Your Honor," Petroni called from her office.

Val frowned. Petroni didn't stand much for formalities, but keeping the mayor waiting struck Val as a terrible miscalculation. "Shall we close the door?" she asked Kim, placing briefing packets in front of every seat.

"Not so fast," came a booming, familiar voice from the hallway.

Moments later, Curtis Iverson appeared, pausing as if waiting for all eyes to light upon him. He flashed a toothy smile and adjusted the lapels of his blue suit jacket. Then he entered the room as if he owned it, smiling down upon all mortals fortunate enough to gaze upon him.

"Sorry for my tardiness," he said, not sounding the least bit sorry. "Traffic. Have I missed anything?"

"What the hell is he doing here?" someone whispered on the other side of the room—not quiet enough.

"How could you have missed anything," Mayor Iverson said, "when the show is all about you? Sergeant, are we ready to begin?"

"We're ready, Your Honor," Petroni said, strolling in. "Team, take your seats. Madam Mayor, the floor is yours."

Val sank into a seat in the rear, her eyes fixed on Curtis Iverson, chatting in a low voice with his wife. She wondered what about: the task force? Personal business? The campaign? Could they even tell the difference anymore?

Something about his presence here stunk.

No, not something. *Everything.*

***

Megan Iverson cleared her throat and gazed out over the room. Sergeant Petroni had telegraphed her disapproval of the sudden intrusion with her late entry and terse introduction. The officers in the room no doubt had picked up on her displeasure. She needed to deliver what most of them would consider unwelcome news, but first she needed to win back the crowd.

Fortunately, with over a decade in public service under her belt, she'd learned to always prepare for potential hostile audiences.

"Thank you, Sergeant," she said, offering her most saccharine smile to the unit chief. "I have two announcements to share with you today. The first is not mentioned in your briefing packet."

Papers rustled across the room, the sound of patrol officers and detectives closing their printed documents after being caught peeking ahead. As expected, all eyes now trained on her, like wolves hunting prey. Curt shot her a questioning look, a little wounded. She shrugged it off. He's a big boy. He could share the glory for a moment.

"I just received word that City Council will approve my special appropriations request to add $200,000 to the budget of the WAVE Squad." Megan kept her eyes on Petroni, whose surprise registered all over her round, pudgy face. The sergeant smiled and applauded. Good. Later, Petroni and her superiors would complain about being cut out of the loop, about not hearing the news ahead of this "public" announcement. At which point the mayor's staff would school them on how government works while apologizing for the "oversight," and, as always, holding her blameless.

"The funds," Megan continued when the applause petered out, "will be used for technology improvements, public information efforts, and to fund the activities of the Citizens Advisory Board." She smiled and stole another peek at Petroni, whose eyes narrowed even as she applauded a second time. She hadn't fooled the crafty old sergeant one bit. The Citizens Advisory Board, or CAB, was the real focus of this meeting. At least on this count, the police brass couldn't complain about being blindsided, as this briefing would precede the public statement by several hours, timed for the evening news cycle.

"That brings us to the second announcement," she said. "The CAB will begin its oversight role of this task force on Monday. Some of the community's leading lights have volunteered to ensure that the important work you are doing aligns with the needs of our citizens." Megan scanned the room again. Skepticism showed on the faces of every officer, including the rookie Valorie Dawes, despite Megan's careful backdoor phrasing of the CAB's true purpose. Nobody "aligns" citizen needs with anything. If anyone needed monitoring, it was the armed, sworn bureaucrats in front of her.

"Now, some of you may be wondering how adding another layer of government will help you accomplish your mission," she said. "I would be the last person to argue with you about that. I assure you, the CAB's role is purely advisory. They won't tell you how to do your jobs. Their job is to advise me of the ways we can best deploy the WAVE Squad to improve safety for women in the community." And, she added to herself, to keep the unit responsive to *her* priorities.

Arms crossed and scowls deepened in her audience. A tough sell, this group. A drop of perspiration trickled down her neck. Time to cut this short before she lost the room again.

"To this end, I have appointed my closest adviser to serve as liaison among the three entities. A man with great standing in the community. A lifelong resident who cares deeply about the safety of women in Clayton. My husband, Curtis Iverson." She stood, taking Curt by the elbow to encourage him to stand with her. He did, and Megan led the room in applause. The loudest applause came from her staff. The police officers could have been clapping at the ninth hole of a golf tournament.

"Thank you, Megan," Curt said. "I'm proud to serve you and the courageous, talented peace officers of the Clayton Police Department in keeping the women in our community safe. I look forward to chatting with each of you, and every member of the Advisory Board, about the best ways to achieve this critically important mission."

"Question?" A hand raised in the back. Megan recognized the man as Detective Grimes, a balding, twenty-five-year veteran of the department. "How, uh, *hands-on* do you expect this CAB to be? And, if you don't mind my asking, same question about your own role, Mr. Iverson."

Curt glanced at Meg. They'd anticipated the question and rehearsed a response. With a quick nod, she signaled him to field the inquiry himself.

"As a results-oriented guy," Curt said, "I set high standards for myself and for those who work for me. I also have a thirst for data and details. Once we've set our goals and have established strategies to achieve them, I expect that your operations will be so well-managed, you won't even notice that I'm here."

"So we're fucked," someone muttered. Laughter followed.

Megan scowled at the disrespect. She couldn't let that stand—

"On the contrary," Curt said before she could cut in. "I see us working together very well. Sure, for the next few weeks, while we get to know each other and establish new protocols—"

"We *have* protocols," Grimes said. "We don't need new ones. What we need is to keep the public off of our backs until—"

"What the detective means," Petroni said, signaling Grimes to stand down, "is that advisory committees often think of themselves as auditors and find it hard to restrain themselves from interfering with operations. How will you spare us from that, Mr. Iverson?"

"I'll make sure of it myself," Megan said, her hand on Curt's arm. "The success of this unit is the top priority of my administration." And of the campaign, she wanted to add. "The goal here is to allocate resources to make you more effective, not less. The minute this new Board gets in the way of that, I'll disband it myself." Which would never happen. Not before the election.

An unintelligible mumble in the back of the room generated a fresh round of laughter. Megan gritted her teeth, already regretting the moment she let Curt talk her into giving him the liaison role. She'd need him to proceed with a soft touch, to build trust rather than raise suspicions.

And Curtis was good at that.

Chapter Thirteen

Over a quick lunch of Thai takeout, Val briefed Shannon on the three unsolved cases she'd linked to the Olivia Lambert and Charlene Washington murders. "All drowned in the Torrington River since September of last year," she said, savoring the flavor of her spicy chicken curry.

"All smart girls with impressive service resumés," Shannon said, shaking her head. "And fresh tattoos. Why that, I wonder?"

"Marking his territory?" Val said.

"I remember the Hannah Brinkman case," Shannon said. "I thought we closed that one."

Val shook her head. "We detained a suspect, but his alibi held up. He's currently serving time in New York on a drug charge. He was in jail when Jaden King and Yolanda Garcia were murdered." She finished her meal and washed it down with a long swig of bottled water. "So, what's next?"

"I'll ask Grimes to follow up," Shannon said. "He worked the Brinkman case. For now, you and I need to find Luis."

With Shannon driving, as usual, they crossed the Torrington River and headed to the east end of town. They found Luis's tattoo shop in the Alphabet Soup neighborhood, so-called because the early settlers had named the north-south streets alphabetically for varieties of trees and wildflowers that no longer graced the broken-down sidewalks and parks in the area.

"There it is," Val said, pointing ahead to a tiny doorway wedged between a nail salon and a barber shop. A blinking neon sign read, "Heats Ink." A printed, letter-sized sheet of white paper pasted to the window next to the door added: "First-timers 20% off."

Shannon pulled the cruiser up to the curb one door down and glanced back at the shop. "We have to go in there?" she said. "I'm glad I've had my shots."

"This isn't the ritzy South End, that's for sure," Val said, rolling her eyes. "Come on, Princess."

Shannon grinned and smacked her shoulder. "When are you ever going to learn to respect your elders?"

Val laughed. "When they show signs of aging, which for you might be twenty years from now. So, how do we play this? Does one of us have to get inked or something and then pump him for his secret client list? Or do we just threaten to call the health department right away?"

"Watch and learn, young Jedi," Shannon said.

The inside of the cramped, dark shop carried aromas of bleach, musk, floral soap, and a chemical she assumed was ink. A cushioned metal stool sat near a faux-leather recliner, with a portable massage table folded up and leaning against a wall. Thin strips of shelving held various inks, disinfectants, and bleach-white towels. Posters and photos of various clients' designs, from elaborate dragons and warriors in battle to simple flowers and phrases, obscured mirrored walls on either side. A cheap wooden desk with a closed laptop sat by the pastel-blue, concrete block rear wall, next to a closed, heavy metal door.

"Anybody home?" Shannon called out.

The door burst open, and a burly, thirty-something Latino with wavy dark hair, a wispy goatee, and black-rimmed glasses rushed into the room. He wore a white cook's apron over jeans and a faded tank top from a heavy-metal concert tour. Colorful renditions of dragons, hawks, and scantily clad female warriors covered his arms, neck, and shoulders. His dark eyes flamed with excitement—or anger, perhaps, at seeing a uniformed and plain-clothes cop filling his salon, rather than a paying customer.

"Luis Morales?" Shannon said. "Detective O'Reilly. This is Officer Dawes. Do you have a moment to ans—"

"What's this about?" Luis said. Val detected a slight accent and no small amount of hostility. Luis pushed past them and wiped down the recliner with a white rag. "If this is about my business license fee, I paid it last week. Late, but so what? And I haven't violated my parole, so…"

Val recalled Luis's short rap sheet: he had served half of a three-year sentence on a narcotics possession charge.

"Do you recognize this girl?" Shannon held out a picture of Olivia Lambert. "Was she a customer?"

"No," Luis said. "I don't think so. But maybe, you know? I get lots of white blonde girls."

"What about her?" Shannon asked, holding up a photo of Charlene Washington.

Luis squinted at the photo. "Nope. She's too young, anyways."

"She's sixteen. Legal if her parents accompany her," Val said. "Can you look again?"

Luis shrugged. "I don't know her." He gave the same answer for the other three victims.

Shannon pointed to his laptop. "Perhaps you can check your records. It would have been in the past week—"

"I'm telling you, no way," he said. "Anyways, I've been closed most of the last week. I had the flu or something." He coughed into his elbow, as if for emphasis. "And nobody's been in here with their parents for over a month."

"You keep a customer sign-in log, right?" Shannon said. "Per city code. Can we see it?"

Luis glared at her. "You got a warrant?"

"*Señor* Morales," Shannon said, "you aren't the subject of any investigation. We're not here to close you down or give you a hard time. We're trying to track down someone who may have come into the shop with these girls. Can't you help us out?"

Meanwhile, Val drifted toward his desk at the back of the store.

His eyes darted from one cop to the other. "What's in it for me?"

Shannon crossed her arms. "Maybe I'll put in a good word for you on your next parole review hearing."

He scowled at them. "*Maybe*? That's bullshit. No way."

"Found it," Val said, grabbing the ledger off of his desk.

"Hey! You can't—"

"It's public record, isn't it?" Shannon said. "Look, you either show us now, or we get that warrant and it disappears into our evidence locker—for good. What's it going to be, Luis?"

He exhaled a noisy breath, defeated. "Okay, you can look, for one minute." He pointed at Val, his face flushed. "No taking pictures!"

Shannon nodded. "No photos," she said.

Val set the book on the desk and opened to the last entry, then scanned backwards through the pages. Most of the signatures were unreadable, though she could make out the printed names well enough. Mostly Latinx names, and as he'd asserted, no entries were dated on the day of Charlene's disappearance, nor for several days before.

Meanwhile, Shannon continued to question him. "Ever apply one of these?" she said, showing him a small card with the *Chingona* tattoo.

Luis glanced at the image. "Nah. Never seen that design before. Anyways, that's not my style." He pointed to the photos and posters on the walls. "I do more, how would you call it, *realistic* designs. A hundred percent custom work—

nothing from a catalog." He laughed. "Especially not something so fucking stupid as that."

Val grimaced. In her opinion, all tattoos were stupid.

"Let's say," Shannon said, "I wanted to get this particular tattoo, and I wanted to be...*discreet*."

Luis whooped with glee. "You mean you want it on your ass? Or on your boobies?" He laughed. "Let's make an appointment, *Señorita*."

"*Señora*, if you don't mind," Shannon said. "And no, thanks. Say, on my leg, where my slacks would hide it. Where should I go? If not you, which of your competitors might help me out with this?"

He shook his head. "I'm not ratting anybody out," he said. "Anyways, something like that, anybody could do it. You could practically buy it on Amazon." Val snickered at the joke, but Shannon didn't even break a smile.

Val closed the ledger, caught Shannon's eye, and shook her head. The ledger showed no sign that any of the victims— including the three she'd culled from her case search—had signed in, as required, for a session at Heats Ink.

"I see," Shannon said with a heavy sigh. "Well, *Señor* Morales, thank you for your time. If you happen to remember anything in the future..." She handed him a business card. "Let's go, Dawes."

Val set the ledger down, but before she walked away, a piece of mail on the desk caught her eye. The hand-inscribed envelope had been mailed to Heats Ink at a different address, on a residential street on her old beat in Liberty Heights. She committed the address to her memory and followed Shannon to the door.

Val turned back before exiting. "*Señor*," she said. "How often do you work from home?"

Shannon, already out the door, halted and stepped closer, putting Morales in her line of sight.

"*Perdone?*" Confusion and surprise filled his broad face.

"How often do you see clients at your house on Woodland Avenue, instead of here?" she said.

"I, uh...I don't," he said, his face reddening and his eyes lowering. "A long time ago I did. Nowadays, all my work is in the shop."

"I see," Val said. "Is that true of your competitors, as well?"

He took a breath, elbows bent, his hands held palms-up. "I...don't know," he said. "You'd have to ask them."

She smiled at him, her eyes narrowing to slits. "I see." She let her gaze linger, noted his body language: biting his lip, eyes darting, feet shifting. "Just curious."

"Nice catch," Shannon said once she'd restarted the engine. "Give me the address. Time for a home visit."

They arrived at Morales's cottage-style house within twenty minutes. The home needed some painting and loose roof shingles replaced, but nothing serious. A kid's bike and a tricycle guarded each side of the tiny concrete porch. Two young children played on the hard-scrabble lawn. They froze in place and stared once the cruiser halted in front of the property. "Mama, mama!" one of them yelled. "*Policià!*" They threw down their toys and ran inside.

Shannon sighed. "So much for the element of surprise." They strolled toward the front door, taking in the surroundings. Density-sized lots, about fifty feet wide. Each hosted 1980s-era or earlier single-family homes, duplexes, and triplexes, all in roughly the same level of repair as the Morales'. No driveways—people parked their Nissans, VWs, and Fords on the street.

A plump, dark-haired woman in a house dress emerged before they reached the door and smiled at them. "*Bienvenidos,*" she said. "How may I help you officers today?"

Shannon signaled for Val to wait. "Is *Señor* Morales at home?"

Val hid a smile behind her hand. Shannon knew better, but she played innocent like a pro.

"No, he is at work," the woman said. "I am his wife. Is there something I can do to help you? Can I get you some tea or coffee?"

"Coffee would be terrific," Shannon said, and smiled.

"One minute." *Señora* Morales bustled inside, leaving the door open. Shannon followed her in, Val right behind. They stood inside the door, surveying the living room. They saw the usual sights one sees in a house with kids: a flat-screen TV, a lumpy sofa, a few toys and a coloring book with crayons on the floor, and family pictures everywhere. Not the kids, though. Val guessed that *Señora* Morales had banished them to their bedrooms, just in case.

She returned with steaming mugs in each hand. "Would you like cream and sugar?"

"Black's fine for me," Shannon said.

"Cream, please," Val said. This time she meant to drink it. She ignored Shannon's exasperation and, once *Señora* Morales exited, shuffled into the hallway that led to the bedrooms. A bathroom at the end of the hall and three shut doors—bedrooms and a closet, Val guessed. And an open door—the one closest to the living room.

Shannon cleared her throat, alarm in her eyes. Val waved her off and peeked inside the open door.

The chemical-and-antiseptic smells confirmed it before her eyes did: Morales used the third bedroom as a home studio. The room contained a stool, recliner, and two tables, one of them filled with inks and a few tattoo pens.

She hurried back in time to give Shannon a thumbs-up before the *Señora* returned. They accepted her offer of a seat.

Shannon ran the same spiel with Morales's wife as she did with Luis: showed her pictures, asked if she recognized any faces or names. Every time, they received the same answer: No, no. And her husband no longer practiced his art at home.

"Never?" Shannon said.

"No, no," she insisted. Her voice wavered.

"You're sure?" Shannon said. "So if we were to search the premises, we wouldn't find any evidence of tattoos—"

"For a friend, sometimes," *Señora* Morales said with a rush of air. "Not for a long time. One year, or more. Two years. Yes. A very long time."

"Such as, say, this girl?" Val showed her a picture of Yolanda Garcia, the young Latina victim she'd unearthed in the database.

Señora Morales glanced at the picture, shaking her head. "No, no," she said. "I have never seen her."

"Now what?" Val asked when they returned outdoors.

"Now we canvass the neighbors, see if they recognize either of them," Shannon said. "You go left, I'll go right. Meet back here in an hour."

That produced more of the same: nothing. The few people that answered the door denied ever seeing any of the victims, and nobody *ever*, swear to God, saw anyone resembling a customer enter or leave the Morales residence.

"You know what that means," Shannon said when they regrouped at the car.

Val nodded. "Yeah. Nobody in this neighborhood talks to the police. So, what do we do?"

Shannon held up the car keys. "We go to a different neighborhood, of course. You said you knew how to find Gunner Washington?"

Val grinned. "Him, or someone else who can. Let's go downtown!"

***

Shannon steered the squad car along Martin Luther King Jr. Boulevard until Val signaled her to pull over a few blocks before their destination—the parking lot of an abandoned theater on the corner of Albany Street. "Gil trained me to approach The Disciples on foot," Val said. "If we pull the car into the lot, they'll disappear."

"And they're always there?" Shannon asked, turning off the engine.

"Someone is," Val said, "and they'll know how to find Gunner."

The two women walked at a brisk pace toward the theater. The weather had turned warm with little humidity, a beautiful spring day that made Val miss walking her beat. Many of the shops they passed had planted flowers in window boxes and planters, perfuming the air with floral aromas and bright colors. With every step, the sound of rhythmic drumming got louder. When the lot came into view, they spotted a small group of Black teens, sitting in a circle, rapping on a variety of overturned plastic buckets, metal trash can lids, and crates with their hands or wooden rods. Shannon grinned and clapped along, even dancing a little as they walked.

"Hot damn, girl," Val said, laughing. "You gonna bust a move?"

"Gotta find the fun in this job wherever you can," Shannon said, bumping Val's hip with her own.

"You never cease to surprise me," Val said, but she got into the rhythm for the final fifty feet of their stroll, too.

The drumming reached a crescendo when they got within five yards of the nearest drummer. Val whipped out a couple of one-dollar bills, tossing them into an open suitcase that held mostly loose change.

Shannon whooped and clapped her hands. "Thank you, guys!" she said. "That was great!"

The drummers and their friends stared at her, wide-eyed. "Thanks," said a tall kid of about seventeen with a temp fade haircut and a single gold earring dangling from his right ear. Val recognized him—he went by Pip, and must have recently earned the earring, a sign of rank within The Disciples. He wore a "Black Lives Matter" T-shirt and baggy shorts that hung several inches below the knee. "Didn't know you were such a connoisseur of street tunes, Copette," he said to Val. "Who's Officer Barbie here? New boss?"

Shannon added a few dollars to the suitcase and waved at the group. "I'm her partner, Detective O'Reilly. How's it hanging, guys?"

Several of the guys responded to her greeting with shrieks of laughter. "Long and hard, Officer Barbie," one of them quipped, and they laughed again, harder.

Val reddened. Shannon had a big heart, but not the best social skills. Still, she seemed nonplussed by the Barbie dig. "Don't stop playing on our account," Val said, scanning the group. "We're looking to talk with Gunner. You've heard about his sister?"

A solemn silence overtook the lot. A few gang members stepped back toward the assortment of broken-down bicycles and garbage dumpsters adjacent to the old, abandoned theater. Pip eased forward into the center of the circle, arms crossed. "We ain't seen him in a coupla days," he said. "Dude's grieving, you dig?"

Val nodded. "As are we. My partner and I are investigating Charlene's murder, and we were hoping—"

"It's aight," said a voice emerging from a crowded array of abandoned cars in the corner of the lot. A shorter, stocky youth of about twenty strolled toward them. Two gold earrings dangled from each ear. Gunner. "I didn't have nothing to do with Char's, um..." He stopped and covered his mouth with his fist, his eyes clenched shut.

"Understood," Val said, paying no mind to Shannon's frowning face. "We spoke to your parents this morning. We were hoping you might have seen her before she disappeared. Who she was hanging out with, or if she said anything..."

Gunner stared at them for a moment, then nodded and strolled back to the cluster of dead cars. Val and Shannon followed him, passing too many discarded needles and used condoms along the way. When they reached a distance that put them out of earshot of the group, Gunner faced them again.

"I saw her the weekend before, uh..." Gunner paused, collecting himself. "Char and me, we meet up—sorry, used to meet up—Saturday afternoons for a coke or something and hang out. Sometimes we'd listen to music on her phone or something." He shuddered out a deep breath. "I don't know why anyone would want to hurt that girl. She was good people, man." He gazed off into the distance, tears forming in the corners of his eyes.

"I don't either, Gunner," Val said. "That's what we're trying to figure out. Did she mention some new friends, a boyfriend maybe, that she wouldn't have shared with your parents? Any new people in her life?"

Gunner thought a moment, shook his head. "Char wasn't into, like, dating or nothing," he said. "This dude Jamal asked her out once or twice. He was like this jock sort of dude, not too smart. I told him not to get any ideas about getting in her panties and all, and poof, he gone." He allowed a tiny smile. "I mighta scared him off or something."

Val glanced at Shannon, who mouthed "tat" to her. Val nodded, taking the cue: keep taking the lead. "As far as you know, did she recently get a tattoo, or did she talk about getting one with you?"

"Hell, no," Gunner said, laughing. "The Rev woulda killed her if she ever came home with ink on her. Dude expected her to stay a virgin her whole life, I 'spect." He laughed. "Fucking Daryl."

"That Saturday, did she talk about any new interests or hobbies?" Val asked.

Gunner leaned against the hood of an old, rusted-out Buick and folded his arms across his chest. After a few moments' thought, he held up one finger. "She said something about this club she's in at school. Got some kinda award or scholarship or something."

"Association of Future Entrepreneurs?" Shannon asked.

"That's it!" Gunner clapped once and pointed at Shannon. "She said she'd be getting this new job out of the deal, 'cept for no pay. I told her she's crazy to work for nothing. She goes, 'It's an internship. That's how it works.' Pfft. Slavery, if you ask me."

Shannon jumped in again, excitement edging her voice. "Did she say anything about having to meet with anyone, or having to get the money, or—"

"Yeah, yeah," Gunner said. "She had to talk with some college dudes about her ideas and shit. She was gonna do that last week or something. Don't know if she ever did, 'cause like I said, I haven't seen her since that Saturday."

Shannon and Val exchanged knowing glances. Val's heart grew heavy, but she needed to ask. "Did you catch the name of those college guys? Either of them?"

"Naw," Gunner said. "I told her it sounded like a scam, like some white dudes trying to steal her award money. She said, naw, it's legit. Anyway, I guess one of 'em's Black, so, you know. Less likely. Sorry, I don't mean nothing by that, Copette."

"No worries," Val said. "Could I try to jog your memory, though, about these guys? Was one of them by chance named Kent?"

"Kent? Hmm." Gunner's face lit up. "Yeah, Kent, Carter, Kevin, something like that." He snapped his fingers. "Colin, maybe."

Val's chest grew heavier and she couldn't keep the dread out of her voice. "And the other...was it Diego?"

Gunner pondered, then shrugged. "I don't think she said both dudes' names. Sorry."

"That's okay," Shannon said. "Mr. Washington, you've been very helpful. We appreciate it."

Gunner's face soured. "My name ain't Washington," he said. "That's The Rev's name. He ain't never became my daddy."

"Sorry," Shannon said. "I assumed—"

"Just call me Gunner." He pushed away from the Buick and took a few steps, then glanced back. "In fact, don't call me at all, unless you got the name of the dude what got my sister." He sneered. "But you ain't gonna do that, are you now, Officer Barbie?" He sauntered away, hands stuffed into his pockets.

Shannon signaled to Val, and they departed in the opposite direction.

"Guess I screwed up there," Shannon said. "I should've let you continue taking the lead. Are you sure you can find him again if we need him?"

Val nodded. "If he wants to be found." She fell silent again.

"At least we got a lead, back to those college guys," Shannon said. "Our Sunday evening chat with Mr. Collier ought to be interesting."

Val took a deep breath. Diego's puppy-dog charm and irrepressible enthusiasm for dating her seemed like a big act now. She felt used, and a little sad. She'd found him fun and attractive, and as awkward as their time together had been so far, she'd enjoyed his attention, if only to feed her ego. That hadn't happened often in her life.

Interesting, indeed.

Chapter Fourteen

Val knocked for the third time on the front door to Gil's house the next morning and once again got no answer. He hadn't answered her multiple calls or texts, all sent within the last hour, including two on the one-mile walk from her apartment. She couldn't imagine that he'd forgotten their planned get-together. They hadn't missed a Saturday morning together since he'd come home from the hospital.

She glanced around. Nothing seemed out of order: lawn mowed, flowers watered, walkway swept, garden hose wrapped around its caddy hanging near the spigot. His Ford Explorer sat in the driveway, as always. All signs of him being home.

Val knocked and rang the bell again, then listened with her ear to the door. Nothing.

She checked the time on her cell phone—8:50 a.m., making her ten minutes early—and for messages. None. Shannon had agreed to a noontime start to their workday out of respect for her time with Gil. "Give him a hug for me," Shannon had said late Friday afternoon when they'd quit for the day.

"Friend of Gil's?" A bent, white-haired Latino waved from the porch of a neat, two-story bungalow next door. A lit cigarette dangled from the man's free hand, its acrid scent reaching Val in the gentle morning breeze. His other hand held a wooden cane, which seemed to support most of the lithe man's weight. An orange tabby jumped down from the broad, flat porch rail, startled by the man's sudden activity.

"I'm his former partner," Val said. "Have you seen him this morning?"

The old man took another drag on his cigarette and shook his head, then exploded into a mad coughing fit that lasted fifteen or twenty agonizing seconds. He waved the cigarette at her again. "Nope," he said in a raspy voice. "Not since lunchtime yesterday."

Val glanced around the neighborhood, a dense collection of modest mid-century homes on fifty-foot lots decorated with tiny patches of grass and flower gardens. A few other neighbors paused their outdoor chores to eavesdrop.

Val banged on the door again. "Gil?" she called out, fighting to keep the anxiety out of her voice. "Are you in there?"

"Try the back door," the man said. "There's a light on in the kitchen. I think it's been on all night."

Her heart pounding, Val dashed the short distance toward him and around the side of the house—only to discover her path blocked by a six-foot-tall cedar fence.

"The gate's on the other side," the neighbor said, wheezing. "Past the garage."

Val sprinted across the front lawn. As she spun around Gil's SUV, a bare light bulb shone through the row of small windows on the garage door. She scrambled over and peered inside. The bulb did little to illuminate the space, crammed with boxes, power tools, a washer/dryer set, and laundry supplies. Everything that the typical American keeps in garages, except a car.

Then she spied a foot. A man's foot, wearing a gray gym sock, sticking out of a pair of sweats, behind a set of boxes near the rear of the space.

Val rapped on the window. "Gil!" she shouted. "Are you all right?"

No response. No movement. Nothing.

She banged again. More of the same.

Val scanned the front step area. Where would Gil keep a spare key? Not where a crook would find it—no cop would do that. She searched the hedges, under the downspout tray, along the fence, through the gate. No key.

Her heart raced. How long had Gil been down? Was he breathing? Was he—

She cleared the panicky thoughts from her head, took a deep breath. Spied Gil's SUV again. Recalled the little black garage door opener clipped onto the visor on the driver's side, with three gray buttons. She ran to the car—locked. Dammit!

But Gil always had a Plan B, C, and D. And never an obvious one.

Val scooted to the back of the SUV, felt around the passenger's side. Bingo! She found the small, metallic case, stuck inside the rear bumper with a magnet. Moments later, the spare key fob it held blipped open the car door.

She jumped in, pushed the largest gray button. Nothing. Of course. Gil would never do anything so damned straightforward as to use the easiest button on the damned opener. She pushed each of the smaller buttons in succession.

With a bump and a rumble, the garage door clanged up on its track. She reached the body moments later and pushed away the boxes that had tumbled onto his torso. Confirmed that it was Gil.

"Gil! Are you okay?"

No answer. Val knelt beside him and checked his pulse—good. Breathing—yes! Alive, but unconscious. His head lolled to one side. An ugly red gash appeared on his exposed cheek, and a dark bruise covered half of his forehead. She spotted a utility sink next to the washer and soaked one end of a towel with cool water. After dabbing at the cut, she applied the wet portion to the unbruised side of his face.

"Gil, wake up," she said, shaking his shoulder again. "Please! Come on!"

"Mmmph." The non-syllable tumbled from his mouth, and one eye slid open. "Ufff," he said. "Utt da ffu?"

"You're hurt," she said, but her voice betrayed her relief. She slid closer to his side, and her knee bumped his hip.

"AAAGH!" Gil's eyes bulged open and he pushed her away with one hand. "Jesus H. Christ, Val, be careful!"

"Sorry!" Horrified, Val raised herself to a crouching position, realizing with horror that she'd bumped his fractured hip. She whipped out her phone. "I'll call 9-1-1. What happened?"

"No, no, just help me up—AAAGH!" He grabbed his leg, just below the hip, and winced. "Fuck, that hurts."

"What happened?" Val asked. "Did you fall, or—"

"No, I fucking jumped. What do you think?" He tried to sit up, winced again, and sucked in air through his teeth. "I was moving boxes, and my hip gave out. I guess I bumped my head...shit, just about everything hurts." His breath came in loud bursts, and he gritted his teeth.

"I don't dare try to move you," she said. "You need an ambulance."

Gil started to object, but instead of words, a loud cry of pain came out. After a few more moments of heavy breathing, he nodded. "Yeah, I guess you're right." He sucked in a deep breath. Then his eyes rolled back, and his body fell limp onto the floor.

***

Val leaned forward in the metal-framed waiting room chair, her chin heavy in her hands, her body drained of energy. Men and women dressed in scrubs scurried by, speaking words that ought to make sense. The aroma of disinfectant swirled around her, stinging her eyes.

Somewhere nearby a machine beeped, doors closed, and phones rang.

She checked voice-mail. No messages. Over two hours had passed since she'd placed that call to 9-1-1. Or had she? Maybe the neighbor had called. Val couldn't recall saying anything to the dispatcher, or hearing anything back. Except she'd shouted "Hurry!" or something like that. Something useless and unhelpful and one hundred percent necessary.

It must have worked, because sirens wailed in the distance, and grew closer, closer, so damned close, so loud. A man and a woman in scrubs had yanked her away from Gil. Karate-chopped her arms to force her to let go. Another guy, a firefighter, wrapped his burly arms around her and escorted her to the front porch, asking her questions. Endless questions. She didn't remember what she'd answered. Or how.

They'd loaded Gil onto a gurney and lifted him into the back of the ambulance. Somehow Val ended up next to him, holding his hand. The female paramedic monitored Gil's condition on some machines, mumbling things to Val about how great he was doing, how lucky he was. Blah, blah.

She considered calling someone, but whom? His ex-fiancée, down in New York? Val had met the woman, but didn't know how to reach her. Gil's younger brother, who lived in New Jersey or some such? She didn't even remember his first name. In the end, she'd called Shannon, who passed the word on to HQ, who'd have Gil's emergency contact info. But nobody knew what to tell them yet. Val hadn't heard squat since they'd arrived. Soon, she'd have to go to work, leave him here.

No. Screw that. Val wouldn't let Gil wake up in a hospital room alone. She'd miss a day's work if it came to that.

"Dawes."

Val sat up straight, and the dark, sweaty face of Lieutenant Gibson smiled down at her. Dressed in a Clayton PD sweatshirt and green, baggy painter's pants, he looked like he'd just finished mowing the lawn. She stood and nearly fell into him, steadying herself with a palm against his burly chest. "Sorry, sir, I—"

"No worries. I just got word from the medic about Kryzinski. Thought I'd update you." He patted her back. "How are you doing?"

"I'm fine. Just tell me!" She caught herself, cleared her throat. "Um...sir."

Gibson rolled his eyes and pushed her back into her chair. "Let's not get all hung up on protocol today, okay? Here's what I know." He sat next to her and paused, taking in a deep breath. "Gil refractured his hip in the fall and suffered a concussion when his head hit the concrete. He's stable, but on heavy meds. He'll be fine after surgery, but this set back his recovery by, well, almost completely."

Val slumped into her seat, allowing her head to loll around on her shoulders. Tears filled the corners of both eyes. "All that work in PT...he was so hopeful to come back by the end of summer." She shuddered and wiped the first few tears away with the back of her hand. "Dammit all to hell."

"Yeah." Gibson grimaced again. "There's no timetable yet, except for the surgery, which will be tomorrow or Monday. The OR is backed up at the moment, I guess. The sedatives will keep the pain down, but also will keep him pretty out of it."

"Can I see him?" Val asked.

Gibson laughed. "Could wild horses keep you away? Let's go make it happen."

***

Val arrived at Gil's bedside some twenty minutes later. Gibson found an excuse to leave them alone, which Val appreciated. When she took Gil's hand in hers, his eyes cracked open.

"You're late," he said with a faint smile. "You were supposed to make me breakfast at nine."

"I lost my recipe for Eggs Benedict," she said, choking on her words. "So I thought I'd smack your head with a frying pan."

"Explains a lot," he said in a breathy voice. "But pancakes would've been a better option."

Laughter burst out of her, too loud, too sudden. Inappropriate. "Sorry, I—"

"Meh." Gil squeezed her hand. "The doc said I fell somehow."

"You don't remember?"

Gil shook his head. "All I remember is looking in the garage for my waffle iron. The next thing I know, I'm lying on the garage floor, feeling like someone yanked my leg out of its socket with no anesthesia." He winced, then took a calming breath. "Good thing you figured out how to break into my house. I'll be filing a B&E complaint, by the way." He chuckled and winced again.

"I'm so sorry, Gil, I—"

"Not your fault. You rescued me, for God's sake."

Val shook her head. "It's my fault you're in this condition. If I hadn't been so stupid, you never would have gotten shot, and—"

"We've been over this a hundred times." Gil's voice took on a sharp edge. "It's not. Your. Fault."

Val swallowed hard. He could be so stubborn. "How long were you down? When did you fall, I mean? This morning, last night—"

"This morning, about six or six-thirty," he said. "I only writhed in pain for a few hours. Which isn't too bad. Most princesses have to wait years for a white knight to rescue them."

"Yeah, women have it a lot rougher than men." Val grinned along with him for a moment. "Seriously, though. The waffle iron could have waited."

He shook his head. "Not if I wanted to have breakfast waiting for you."

"Gil. I said I'd make you breakfast. You need to let me help you, okay?"

"I won't be waited on like an invalid."

"You *are* an invalid...temporarily. Unless you keep this crap up. Then I'll make it permanent." Val smiled, but the smile faded in the heat of his dark scowl. Oops. That one hit too close to home. "Sorry. But come on, man. I've been trying to protect you from things like this. Why don't you let me?"

He glanced at her, then looked away. "I don't need protection."

"We all need protection sometimes," she said. "I should know. I'm the worst. You've said it yourself, I don't protect myself very well. Which I need to learn how to do. Protect myself, and you, and when you get better, you'll pro—"

"That is such horseshit!" Gil gripped her hand with surprising strength and locked eyes with her. "Val, you're right—we both take stupid chances sometimes. Physically, anyway. But the answer to that isn't to lock ourselves down, the way we do—both of us do—emotionally."

Val's interruption caught in her throat. Gil had never spoken so directly about their shared tendency to bury their feelings. Maybe the drugs had loosened his inhibitions.

"You don't need to shut down, Val." Emotion rose in Gil's voice. "If anything, we both need to open up more. Be more vulnerable. Give people hugs. Visit family. Tell people you love them. Hell, go on a damned date once in a while. What's that kid's name, the runner?"

Caught off guard, Val spit out the name. "Diego."

"Right. Next time Diego asks you to dinner, say yes," Gil said. "Find out if you really like him. If not, try another guy. But stop living your life like love is the worst thing that can happen to you. Because it's not, Val. It's the greatest thing. Once you experience it, you'll agree with me. I promise."

Val stared at him, a long breath escaping from her open mouth. She replayed his words in her head, and they stunned her again. "I can't believe you just told me to date another guy. A suspect, no less!"

Gil laughed, a gentle sound that emerged from deep within his chest. "Must be the drugs." He waved his free hand over his prostrate form. "Besides, I can't do much for you right now."

Val gulped. "Do you mean as partners, or...?"

"Both." He made an ugly face, full of disgust. "I know the score here, Val. I'm out of action at least through the end of the year, probably longer. Your career can't wait for me, and neither can your personal life."

Her throat tightened, and tears gathered in the corners of her eyes. "This sucks. It's...not how this was supposed to happen."

He nodded. "You know what they say. Man plans, God laughs."

Val squeezed his hand, smiling at him. Uncle Val used to say that.

Gil sighed, and his face softened. "As much as I'd like for things to be different, they're not. I love you too much as a friend and as a partner to even think about holding you back. Don't wait for me. Go slay some dragons, catch some bad guys and nail their asses, and hell, while you're at it..." He grinned and winked. "Nail the asses of a few good guys, too."

Val blushed, first at the bluntness of Gil's advice, then at the message buried deep within his torrent of words. She gripped his hand in both of hers and met his eyes. "What you said...about loving me as a friend and as a partner." She drew a deep breath. She'd never told any man this, not since losing her uncle. And not in the way she meant it in this moment. "Yeah. I, uh...me too."

He nodded in that knowing way of his, and she stood by his bedside, holding his hand for a long, long time.

***

Val's bus ride from the hospital to WAVE headquarters included a transfer near Macy's, where Beth worked. After a quick exchange of text messages, the two met for an early lunch at a noisy downtown deli.

"I'm so sorry about Gil," Beth said while munching on a Caesar salad. She'd grown attentive to calorie-counting for the first time in her life as the day drew near for choosing a wedding dress. Josh's laughing at the "fat joke" probably played a role, too. "Will he walk again?"

"The doctor says yes. Soon, in fact," Val said. "Maybe within a week after surgery. But he has to start rehab all over. It really screws up his return to work."

"That so sucks." Beth rested a hand on Val's arm. "How are *you* feeling?"

"I'm...fine." Val choked on her quinoa pear salad, finding it hard to swallow. "Gil's the one who's hurt."

"Mmm-hmm." Beth shook her head. "It's okay for you to feel sad, too, my dear."

Val exhaled a long, heavy breath. "Yeah. Okay, I am sad. For him." She took another nibble of her salad. So bland, almost tasteless.

Beth picked at her plate. "Sorry. I know how much you care about him. He seems like a great guy."

"The best." Val picked up her fork, stared at it a moment, and set it down. "It's not fair."

"No, it's not." Beth squeezed her shoulder and gave her a sad look. "You've had a rough first year on this job."

"It's more than that," Val said. "Gil was the one guy on the force I could really talk to. I trusted him. I'm not so sure about the others, yet."

"The old male bastion still giving you grief for not having a penis?" Beth said with a half-smile.

"Fortunately, my boss and partner believe in me," Val said. "Still, I'm walking on eggshells all the time. The mayor asked me to be on this WAVE Squad over a lot of more experienced guys. It feels like all eyes are watching me. Like I'm not allowed to make any mistakes, you know?"

"You're human. Of course you'll make mistakes. So do they. So do I, in my job."

"Easy for you to say," Val said. "But mistakes in my job don't just cost money. They could cost lives. And even minor ones might hurt my career."

"I thought the whole WAVE Squad thing would be a real career-booster for you," Beth said. "Fast-track to detective, and all that."

"Yeah." Val's tone belied her frustration, and she chose her words so as not to reveal anything too sensitive. "We're just not making the progress I'd hoped for. For instance, that tattoo shop you told me about? Complete dead end."

"What's it been, two days?" Beth laughed. "You used to be a lot more patient, my friend. Come on, eat your lunch. You haven't eaten all day."

Val pushed her plate aside. "I don't have much of an appetite."

"Me either." Beth replaced the plastic lid on her salad and sealed it. "Hey, are you still running regularly?"

Val shrugged. "Not as often as I'd like. You want to join me next time?"

Beth mimed running, pumping her arms in playful slo-mo. "If I won't slow you down too much, Miss Track Star."

"I can go before work tomorrow...early. Can you break away from sleeping at Josh's for the night?"

Beth grimaced. "The boy toy is hanging out with his friends from college tonight. On a *Saturday!* Which I just found out this morning."

"That boy's in the doghouse again?" Val said with a sad smile.

"He's there so often, he ought to move in," Beth said. "So, let's do it. Three times a week, starting tomorrow. On the waterfront. You game?"

"You got it," Val said, and took another forkful of quinoa. With the prospect of spending more time with Beth on a regular basis, everything felt right again.

Chapter Fifteen

Even after her morale-boosting lunch with Beth, focusing on work that afternoon took all of Val's strength and discipline. Sergeant Petroni suggested she take the weekend off, and Shannon suggested she go home multiple times, but Val insisted that she needed the distraction. "If I go home, I'll just mope and worry about Gil," she explained. "Give me something useful to do."

"Let's talk about the other victims, then." Shannon spread printed summaries of the three cold cases across the large meeting table in the WAVE Squad office. "Starting with the tattoos. They're not consistent." She arranged photos from their files into a row. "Yolanda Garcia's is similar to Olivia's and Charlene's, but Hannah Brinkman's and Jaden King's lack the '*Chingona*' label. On Jaden, the woman is facing the other direction, and Hannah's is a silhouette figure."

"Hannah's was also the only tattoo that wasn't fresh," Val said. "Her case is the oldest. It makes me wonder whether hers gave the perp the idea to ink the others, as his trademark."

"Interesting theory." Shannon pored over the summaries again, then tapped on two of them. "Look at the dates," she said. "We found Hannah in September. Then Jaden, in early December. Ruled a suicide at first, later changed to 'undetermined.'" She shivered. "A barefoot drowning victim in the middle of winter. That should have gotten more attention."

"Yolanda died in early February," Val said, studying her case summary. She hustled to the whiteboard and scribbled the victims' names in chronological order along with the dates of their murders. "The window between each case gets shorter and shorter. Three months, two months, one month, three weeks." A river of ice flowed down her spine. "Holy shit. If that trend continues—"

"The next one could happen any day now," Shannon said in a hushed voice. "Crap."

Another realization struck Val. She strode over to a calendar and flipped through the pages, confirming the math she'd completed in her head. She faced Shannon again. "Not *any* day," she said. "Check this out." She added a column to the white board, labeled "DOW," and wrote entries for each victim. She stepped aside so Shannon could see what she'd written.

"Jesus," Shannon said. "Every single one of them died on a Sunday or Monday."

"Our next victim," Val said, "might have only a day or two to live. The question is, who will she be?"

***

Val and Shannon briefed Petroni and the other WAVE Squad members on their findings. The group then brainstormed a victim profile based on what they knew. After several hours of intermittent bouts of intense research and debate, Petroni stood in front of the group, pointing to the most pertinent facts on the whiteboard.

"So, this is what we've got," she said. "All five vics were high school juniors or seniors, ages sixteen to eighteen."

"How many public school juniors and seniors are there in Clayton?" Shannon asked.

Val checked her spreadsheet, already open on her laptop. "About two thousand. We can narrow it down, though. All five ranked in the top ten percent of their class," she said. "All are active in clubs and after-school activities. College bound, for sure. That gets our number down to about two hundred."

"Race and ethnicity?" Petroni said.

"Not factors," Val said. "They're all over the map."

"Income and wealth?" Petroni asked.

"None were rich," Val said. "All of them needed scholarships or financial aid of some sort to pay for college."

"Right," Shannon said. "All active in sports, though not all through school." She wrote "city leagues" next to Hannah's and Yolanda's names. "Religion?"

"All belonged to some sort of Christian church—all five different," Val said. "But none attended Central Catholic High. Each attended a public high school, and we've had at least one from each, with the last two from Liberty Heights."

"What does that give us so far, for numbers?" Petroni asked.

Val updated her spreadsheet. "Twenty girls in Clayton fit that profile. About one percent of the total."

Shannon grinned. "That's amazing!"

"Yeah, good stuff," said Detective Grimes, a paunchy, middle-aged white guy at the far end of the table. "That really narrows it down."

Val's chest swelled for a moment. It felt good to contribute.

Petroni nodded. "Yeah, but which twenty?"

Deflated, Val pushed the laptop aside. "That's the problem. This is raw data, from a macro level. Finding the individual girls is like the proverbial needle in a haystack."

"Not for the killer," Petroni said. "If he can do it, so can we. Plus, he doesn't know that we know all of this."

"Also," Shannon said, "we know he prefers Sundays and Mondays, works at night, and likes to drown the victims in the river. We can patrol the area on each side for the next two evenings. If he strikes again, we can catch him."

Grimes scoffed. "That's great for finding him after the fact, but I thought the goal was to stop him *before* he kills another teen. We need to work on preventative steps."

"We could put the word out to the high schools," Val said. "Feed the principals our profile and ask them to warn the girls who fit."

"To do what?" Grimes said. "Stay home for a couple of days? Avoid creepy guys in tattoo shops?" He shook his head. "Until we know more about the guy doing it, we can't say who we're warning them away from."

"I agree," Petroni said. "I don't want to start a panic. What we can do is stake out the schools, starting in late afternoons. I'll ask the chief for some uniformed help as soon as we're done here. So, what else *do* we know about the perp? Besides that he somehow met all five girls?"

Silence greeted that question, and Petroni grew agitated. "Well, folks," she said, "that's a problem, now, isn't it?" She slapped the white board marker into its tray and thrust her hands out in an impatient wave. "We'd better learn something fast," she said, "or come Monday, we might be pulling another shoeless schoolgirl from the Torrington River."

***

The next morning, Val reached the ramp to the Torrington River Bridge and slowed from a running pace to a slow jog, breathing hard in the warm spring air. Forty yards behind her, Beth huffed along the path, waving at Val in acknowledgment. Or perhaps it meant she should keep going across the river. She jogged in place, waiting. She didn't want to lose momentum, and, more to the point, she recalled the ugly scene she'd encountered last time she crossed the bridge alone.

Val shook off the mental image of Olivia Lambert's floating body and scanned the east bank. She had to squint into the low-hanging sun, which put the row of brick and concrete buildings along the waterfront in shadow. Still, the 20/13 vision that helped earn her top marksmanship awards at police academy enabled her to make out key details in the distance: A few men loped onto the far side of the bridge toward her. Neither looked familiar, but she wanted to imprint their faces into her memory, just in case. A hundred yards behind them, a young couple pushed a baby carriage and tugged a toddler by the hand. Another runner, a middle-aged white woman, trudged southbound. A few bicyclists zigged and zagged around the pedestrians in either direction. She shrugged them off—they didn't fit the profile.

"You...didn't...have to wait," Beth said, slowing to a stop behind her. She leaned on the railing, painted the color of oxidized copper, the same hue the city slathered on all of its outdoor metal inventory. "I'd have...caught up...eventually."

Val nodded and bit her lip to keep from laughing. Still jogging in place, she felt the endorphins flowing and work stress evaporating with each steamy breath. She turned to admire the view over the water and give Beth a chance to catch her breath. The bridge's steel cables and towers reflected in the river's blue, smooth surface and created the impression of a caged tunnel connecting the two riverbanks. She wished she'd brought a camera.

"Shall we turn back, or go on around?" Val asked.

"Onward, Christian soldier," Beth said, and dashed off ahead of her, laughing. "Last one across buys donuts!"

"Cheater!" Val howled in surprise, but she laughed, too. For good sport, she let Beth gain a thirty-yard lead on her before turning on the jets. Halfway across, the two men passed going the opposite direction, and she slowed to study their faces: a pair of out-of-shape men in their forties or fifties, judging by their thinning silver hair and thick waists. Neither had invested in new running shoes in years. A couple of weekend warriors, renewing their commitments to losing their beer bellies. Too old to be suspects. Sixteen-year-old girls interested in older men had their limits.

She closed the gap behind Beth to a few steps long before reaching the opposite end of the half-mile crossing, but didn't have the heart to pass her. Had it been Gil, or her brother, she would have raced ahead and run straight past the donut shop. Unfortunately, by losing, she might have to endure Beth's less-healthy choice for breakfast.

"Winner, winner, chicken dinner!" Beth shouted when she reached the east side ramp. "And I want to collect now." She jogged onward and Val caught up to her, running side-by-side, silent other than Beth's heavy breathing. "Here we are," Beth said, plopping down into a seat at a sidewalk café. "Beignets all around!"

Val glanced at the name and insignia on the storefront windows. "Boudreaux's N'Awlins Style Treats," the gold-and-black script read. "Try our coffee with chickory!"

"So healthy," Val said, shaking her head.

"And delicious," Beth said.

The server arrived, and they placed their orders for the cafe's Louisiana-based specialties. When he disappeared inside, Beth pointed to a shop across the street. "The other reason to come here," she said, "is to show you that place."

Val squinted, again into the sun. "Rat-a-Tat Tats," read a small, black-and-white illuminated sign hanging above a dark doorway. She shot Beth an inquisitive glance. "Luis's competition?"

Beth snickered. "Luis is Mr. Rogers compared to this place." She leaned forward and said in a low voice, "Josh got his first ink here, on a dare when he was fifteen."

"I've never seen Josh's tattoo," Val said before she could stop herself.

"And you never will!" Beth laughed and covered her mouth. "Not if I have anything to do with it."

Val blushed. "I can only imagine."

"No, you can't," Beth said, laughing louder. "At least, I hope not."

"Okay, now you *have* to tell me," Val said, unable to suppress a grin. "Come on, I can keep a secret."

The server came with their coffees and treats, and Beth, with a wicked grin, dipped her powdery confection straight into her coffee before shoving half of it into her mouth. "Mmm, so good," she mumbled, chewing.

Val sipped her coffee, puckering a bit at the unexpected bitterness of the chicory flavoring.

"Dip the donut in," Beth said, demonstrating again. "To sweeten it."

Val complied, and to her delight, Beth's advice proved spot-on. The coffee soaked into the airy dough, softening its crispy crust, and absorbed the thick layer of powdered sugar across the top. The combination created a symphony of deliciousness in her mouth. "Oh my God," she said.

"I'd never steer you wrong," Beth said.

Val washed the donut down with bitter coffee. "So, Josh's tat?" she asked.

Beth tossed her head and fanned her face in mock-dramatic fashion. "You're going to *force* me?"

"At gunpoint, if need be." Another bite and Val could feel the pounds piling onto her hips.

"Ooo-kay." Beth leaned forward. "You know he's into Dungeons and Dragons, right?"

"The role-playing thing, with the crazy dice?" Val said. "Still?"

Beth rolled her eyes and nodded. "His design is this elaborate fire-breathing dragon—huge—like from here to here." She dragged a finger from one side of her waistline to the other.

Val shook her head. "I've seen him shirtless," she said. "There's no visible ink on his stomach."

"Not on his belly, dodo," Beth said. "From here," and again she pointed to her waistline, "*south,* if you catch my meaning."

Val laugh-snorted coffee out of her nose. "Omigod," she said. "All over his—"

"A 'welcome mat,' they call it," Beth said. "And the dragon's fire-breathing snout is his you-know-what." She leaned closer and whispered through devilish giggles, "He even dyed his pubes orange to make it look like fire. He's a fire crotch!"

After a loud gasp, Val howled so hard, she doubled over, and her forehead knocked her half-full coffee mug to the ground, shattering it on the sidewalk. That only made both women roar even harder. The server scampered over, insisting that he'd bring them both refills and promising to clean it up right away, but Val waved him off, still unable to speak.

Spent from laughing, Val straightened in her chair, caught Beth's eye, and cracked up all over again.

"The point is," Beth said when she could finally speak, "is that he was underage, and very drunk."

"No doubt," Val said. "And a shop that would cater to that clientele..." She let her words hang, and Beth nodded.

Val waved her debit card at the server, who snatched it away and scurried inside. Then she snapped a photo of Rat-a-Tat Tats with her cell phone.

"Please don't go over there right now," Beth said, eyes wide. "Josh would kill me."

Val sighed. The shop didn't appear open, and Shannon would want to join her anyway. "Deal. Now, let's go run off a few hundred more of these calories!"

***

The man followed the two women in his car, sometimes stopping for a minute or more at a time to let them run past, then passing them again. A game of cat and mouse, where only the cat knew the rules. Valorie Dawes, his person of interest at the start of this sunny Sunday morning, stopped at the bridge ramp to wait for her companion. Then the taller woman, by far the more attractive of the two in every way, ran ahead of her wiry little friend.

He pulled over right before the bridge, following them with his eyes as they crossed. He timed his pursuit so they'd have to turn before he reached the other side. They ran abreast until they reached a tiny sidewalk café. The larger woman flopped down into a seat at one of the sidewalk tables. Dawes, though she'd barely broken a sweat from their short morning jog, joined her a moment later. The man drove a few blocks past them, circled the block, and parked a half-block away from the café, facing them.

Watching them.

The original plan had been to follow the cop. He'd expected her to visit her friend in the hospital again, but she surprised him with the morning run. And now...coffee and donuts? Weird choice for such a health nut.

By reputation, Dawes never went "off duty." All work, no play, even in her off hours. But here she sat, laughing with her friend over fancy coffee, like she hadn't a care in the world. Like she never obsessed about the barefoot girls they'd pulled from the river. Girls with feminine, curvy bodies, the way God intended. Not like skinny little Valorie Dawes.

More like her curvaceous friend in the skin-tight yoga pants and tank top.

He'd need to learn more about her friend.

Unexpected movement at their table caught his eye. The waiter buzzed around them, fussing about something on the ground. The women shooed him away. From his vantage point, he couldn't tell what had happened, but Dawes no longer had a coffee cup. Getting more, or all done? He needed to get ready to move, in case they walked his way. He couldn't afford for them to spot him.

Going forward, too, he'd need some help—some eyes and ears on the ground. Someone discreet, whose presence Dawes would never suspect.

More movement. Dawes held up her cell phone, aimed it at the tattoo shop across the street. As if to take a picture.

His spine turned to ice. If they'd picked up on the tattoo detail, it was only a matter of time before they found him.

He needed a diversion. Some way to change their focus, or muddy the waters, at least.

He smiled. He knew a way.

Chapter Sixteen

V al pushed open the heavy wooden door to Paisano's Pizza and inhaled the delicious scents of baking bread, spicy garlic, and roasted tomatoes. Her stomach growled in angry protest at the tempting aromas. She'd skipped lunch in favor of an intense gym session to work off the beignet breakfast with Beth. Her appetite would likely go unrewarded once again, if this went as expected.

She scanned the room, searching for Diego. Customers occupied only about half of the two dozen booths and tables, a slow Sunday night for the neighborhood establishment. Neon signs in the all-glass wall in front advertised the pub's national and local beer offerings, adding a harsh glare to the room's irregular lighting.

At the same moment she spotted him, Diego, reading alone in a corner booth, looked up at her. He set the book aside and returned her wave with a huge grin. He slid to the end of the booth as if to stand and got tangled up in the red-and-white-checked tablecloth that hung over on all sides. A tall glass of ice water teetered in front of him. He saved it from tipping just in time, but bumped a second full tumbler, dousing the candle that might otherwise have provided a romantic atmosphere, and drenching the bench opposite him.

Just as well. When Shannon entered behind her, his eyes widened and his entire face twisted in confusion.

"What's going on?" he asked when they arrived at the table. He scooted out and mopped up half of the spill with a handful of paper napkins. "I thought…"

"We need to talk," Val said, her mouth dry. She could only imagine how ambushed he must have felt, and she hated herself for it.

"What about?" Diego said. "Why is *she* here?" He grabbed his book and shoved it into his backpack.

A restaurant employee popped up with a mop and a bar rag and pushed them into an open, C-shaped corner booth in the back. That gave Val time to rethink her opening. She waited for Diego to sit, then took her seat opposite him. Shannon slid in next to him, blocking any thoughts of his escape.

"I apologize for not telling you I invited Detective O'Reilly along," she said. "I know you envisioned this as a date." She glanced down at her clothes and second-guessed the decision to wear flare pants and a pastel yellow blouse instead of a uniform. Date clothes. Shannon had argued it would put him at ease. Diego's fearful expression showed otherwise.

Val cleared her throat and continued on. "W-we met with Charlene Washington's parents."

Diego glanced from Val to Shannon and back again. "And?"

Val took an even breath, her eyes like lasers on Diego's. She'd half-hoped he'd deny knowing her, but he dropped his gaze and licked his lips. Val snuck a glance at Shannon, who gave her head a quick shake: *Wait.*

"I guess they told you I met with her," Diego said. Tears welled in his eyes, and he wiped them away with the back of his hand. "About her AFE scholarship."

Val waited, half to draw him out further, and half because she was too nervous to think of what to say.

"Go on," Shannon said, startling Val by speaking for the first time.

"I'm what they call an AFE Ambassador," Diego said. "Those of us who have been through the program and gotten scholarships give back by helping up-and-coming members with their applications, advice about colleges, stuff like that."

"When did you meet with her?" Val asked.

Diego chewed his lower lip. "We talked by phone a few weeks ago." He picked up a napkin and twisted it in his fingers. The server returned with fresh glasses of water and menus. Shannon shooed him away, saying they'd need a few minutes.

"When else?" Val asked him.

Diego blew out a noisy breath. Looking away, he took his time in replying. "Three—no, four weeks ago. That's the only time I met her in person."

Val did the math in her head. Charlene had disappeared three weeks before. That extra week made all the difference. "Can you verify that?" Val asked.

Diego shrugged and picked up his phone. A few taps later, he showed them his calendar, open to the Monday before Charlene's death. A 4:00 p.m. entry showed "AFE—C. Washington. Claytown Cafe." Val made a mental note to check back with Pinkie—then remembered their coffee "date" there. The barista hadn't recognized him. "Did Pinkie wait on you?" she asked.

He scrunched up his face. "Not sure."

Val cocked her head, heat rising in her voice. "Pink hair, lots of piercings, talks like a 1980s Valley Girl...and you're not sure?"

"Okay, she definitely didn't," Diego said, his words rushed and breathy. "Some guy did. I haven't seen him there since."

"Can I see your calendar again?" Shannon asked, reaching toward him.

Diego snatched the phone away and held it close. "What do you want to know?"

Shannon smiled, like a big sister giving advice. "I'm curious as to what's on your calendar for the following Monday."

"Nothing!" He stuffed the phone into his back pocket. "I was studying that day."

Shannon started to ask something else, but Val cut her off. "No matter," she said. "If I understand the rules, AFE requires students to log all mentor appointments with their faculty adviser. We'll see if, and with whom, she met that day."

Diego cast desperate glances at both women and seemed primed for flight, but the two cops had him trapped. That feeling showed on his face as well.

"Okay!" He threw his hands up into the air. "I was *supposed* to meet with her again on that Monday. She never showed."

"Did you report that to AFE?" Shannon asked.

Diego shook his head. "No-shows aren't that uncommon, especially with girls like Charlene, who are involved in so many other activities. It's a voluntary thing. I figured she'd either found another adviser, or had a conflict."

"You didn't call her?" Val asked.

Diego scoffed. "Charlene's the one that didn't show. It's her responsibility to—I mean, it *was* her responsibility..." His voice weakened and faded out. "If I'd have known, of course I would have called someone."

The server appeared and asked if he could take their order.

"I'm not hungry." Diego slid one arm through his backpack and slid toward Shannon. "Excuse me, I'd like to leave."

"Not yet," Shannon said, reaching out to grab him. Diego squirmed away and her hand snagged the loose flap of his backpack. The bag unzipped and its contents spilled onto the seat and floor under the table.

"Hey!" he shouted. "What the hell?" He leaned toward Val, his face inches from hers. "Jesus, Valorie. Am I under arrest or something?"

"I don't know," Val said. "Should you be?"

"No!" He slid into the corner of the booth and stuffed his belongings into his pack. "I didn't do anything to her, or—or anyone." He zipped up the bag and faced her again. "So, if you're not arresting me, and you're not interested in having dinner with me...would you mind moving out of my way?"

Val took Shannon's tiny nod as her cue and slid out of the booth. Diego pushed past her and headed toward the exit.

"Don't leave town," Shannon called after him. "And keep your phone on."

Diego spun around, shot them the finger, and ran out the door.

"He has to leave town to attend classes," Val said, sliding back into the booth. Her foot bumped something solid on the floor. She ducked her head under the table and picked a stray book off the floor that Diego had somehow missed. She set it on the table and gasped.

The cover featured a cartoonish image of Rosie the Riveter, flexing her bicep and making a fist. Much like the *Chingona* tattoo.

"Well, lookie what Diego's reading," Shannon said. "*Female Empowerment: Every Woman's Guide to Overthrowing the Patriarchy.* What do you suppose gave him the idea to research that topic?"

Anxiety crashed over Val like an avalanche. "I don't suppose it's assigned reading for his biochemistry class," she said in a tight voice. On impulse, she opened it and glanced at the inside cover. Many students wrote their contact info there in case they lost them. Sure enough, she found a name, email address, and phone number on the upper left.

But not Diego's.

It was Kent Mercer's.

***

Rat-a-Tat Tats opened at 9:00 a.m. Monday morning. Val and Shannon parked outside Boudreaux's beignet shop at 8:45. The sun peeked over the top of the three- and four-story brick buildings lining the narrow street. The morning glow lent a touch of brightness to the drab corridor of stone, long ago darkened by the exhaust of slow-moving automobiles and now-extinct factories.

"While we wait," Shannon said, blowing into her hands to ward off the morning chill, "go grab us some coffee." She handed Val a ten. "Go on, and don't look at me like that. I love you dearly, but you're still a rookie."

Val rolled her eyes, but did as ordered. This time, skipping the beignets for dipping, she added twice as much sugar to the bitter brews. She stepped back outside just as Shannon disappeared inside the tattoo parlor.

"Thanks for waiting," she grumbled. Annoyed, she crossed mid-block and nearly got plowed by a silver VW Jetta zipping around the corner. The driver, yet another bearded guy about Val's age, sped off without so much as a wave of apology. Passersby stared at her, and one said something about the irony of cops jaywalking. She ducked her head and hurried ahead, pushing the tattoo shop's door open with her foot.

Shannon had already started the interview with the shop owner, a sandy-haired, wiry white guy in his twenties. He sported a soul patch on his chin and a silver casing on his left front tooth. The man looked emaciated, with deep-set eyes and angry red pimples on his face and neck. His sleeveless shirt revealed that he, like Luis, supported his industry with regular visits.

Unlike Heats Ink, poster-sized photos of past clients plastered the walls of this shop. A woman's back revealed a bright red she-devil. Snakes wrapped around a man's legs, nearly reaching his crotch. Several others featured Samurai soldiers and Asian lettering. The most unusual was a Native American man's neck, face, and bald head covered in dark blue geometric shapes.

"I never seen none of those girls," the inker said, his breath redolent of stale tobacco. "You can check my log, but trust me, anybody you'd be looking for ain't signing their real names."

"Don't mind if we do," Shannon said. Val handed her a coffee and set down her own cup next to a sign-in book on the counter, already open to the most recent signature page. She leafed backward through the names, scanning each page.

Meanwhile, Shannon showed him more photos. "So, Jacoby," she said, "ever apply one of these designs?"

The tat artist craned his neck to look closer at them. "Sure," he said. "Lots of times."

Val froze and stared at him, but Shannon remained cool. "Lots, as in, five or six? A dozen? A hundred?"

"Whoa, dude." Jacoby laughed. "I ain't done a hundred of anything. Yo, maybe a half-dozen. That's a lot, in this business. Most people want something unique, you know?"

"Can you supply names of those clients?" Shannon asked in a casual tone, taking a huge slug of her coffee.

He frowned and shook his head. "I don't track that. Bookkeeping's not my thing, man. I only take pictures of the cool stuff, you know?" He pointed at the enlargements tacked to the wall behind him, then tapped the *Chingona* photos.

"Something cheap like that, it's so simple, I wouldn't *want* to remember."

Val sighed and returned her attention to the ledger. None of the five victims' names appeared. Given what Jacoby had told them, it didn't surprise her. What did, though, were two signatures she hadn't expected.

One was Sierra Stapleton, the teenager whose mother had complained about their neighbor's window-peeping weeks before. Connie Stapleton's signature, required for an underage tattoo, did not appear alongside Sierra's.

Another name did, however. The name of an adult, claiming on the form to be her father. Bo Rousseau—the creepy next-door neighbor.

"What tattoo did this girl get?" Val asked, showing the book to the inker.

He studied the register and sniffed. "No fucking idea. I don't even remember what she looked like."

"Tall, skinny white girl, long dark hair, very athletic," Val said. "Ring any bells?"

Jacoby smiled. "Oh, yeah, kind of," he said. "Pretty girl. Came in with her dad." He thought a moment longer, then his grin turned lascivious. "She got some strange Japanese saying on her ass. That was a fun one." He chuckled. "Weird thing? Fucking Daddy stood there and watched."

Val's stomach turned, and she couldn't keep the anger out of her voice. "It didn't occur to you he might not have been her actual father?"

"Hey, he had ID!" The guy backed away, hands raised in self-defense. "What am I supposed to do, get a fucking DNA test?"

Shannon shook her head and signaled for Val to continue checking the ledger. "What did the Japanese lcttcring say?" she asked.

"Fuck if I know. Victory, or Perseverance, some such shit." His face curled in disgust. "Frigging shame no one can see that one."

Val seethed, but Shannon caught her eye before she exploded at the dodgy bastard. She took a deep breath and returned to the book while Shannon grilled him further, getting nowhere.

Val scanned the customer ledger back to the previous September, the month of Hannah Brinkman's death. More of the same: random names, some illegible. Shannon continued to question him, so Val turned the ledger back to August. At that point, one very familiar name jumped off the page at her.

Diego Collier.

***

Shannon started up the cruiser but paused before pulling out into traffic. "Sorry to say, we need to bring your friend Diego in for formal questioning," she said. "His name keeps coming up in all the wrong places."

Val nodded, her throat tight with regret. "I agree. But so far all we have on him is that he knew Charlene, his buddy Kent knew Olivia, and he got tattooed by an artist familiar with the *Chingona* design. Not exactly a smoking gun."

"Plenty of smoke nonetheless," Shannon said.

Their radio crackled with the central dispatcher's voice. "Unit R-3, please report your 10-20," the dispatcher said at high-blast volume.

"Unit R-3 located at 2200 block of East Fir Street," Val said into the mic. "Do you copy?"

"Roger R-3," Dispatch said. "Please report to base at once for further instructions."

Val and Shannon exchanged puzzled glances. Shannon grabbed the mic. "Negative, Dispatch," she said. "We have a 10-17 up north involving a suspect—"

"Negatory," Dispatch said. "Your 10-17 is at headquarters. Please comply immediately."

"What '10-17' do we have at either location?" Val asked Shannon. A 10-17 meant "urgent business," and so far as she knew, they had nothing of the sort.

"Doesn't Diego have classes this morning?" Shannon said. "If we're going to bring him in—"

"Please confirm, R-3," Dispatch repeated.

Shannon shrugged and spoke into the mic. "10-4, Dispatch. We'll be there in ten minutes." She clipped the mic onto the dash with a little too much force, startling Val. "Something is rotten in Denmark," she said. "I've worked with Petroni for over a decade, and she's never once shoved an order like this down anyone's throat."

A few minutes later, Val's phone buzzed in her pocket. A message from Beth—"*WTF?*" She tapped on the attached link, which opened to a blog post on *Clayton Copwatch*, written by the notorious anti-police muckraker Paul Peterson. Her stomach turned. She knew him well. Six months before, Peterson's self-congratulatory blogs had emboldened serial rapist Richard Harkins and hampered efforts to apprehend him.

A quick glance at the blog's headline explained the urgency of their recall to base. Val read it aloud to Shannon:

"Shoeless Slut Slayer" Savages City
By Paul Peterson

Mayor Megan Iverson's new "WAVE Squad" is in hot pursuit of a serial sex offender who has raped and murdered several teenage girls over the past year.

The perpetrator, nicknamed by insiders as the "Shoeless Slut Slayer," has victimized at least three and as many as a dozen young women, ranging from 16 to 20 years old.

"A dozen?" Shannon laughed. "What does he know that we don't?"

Val read on:

> The victims are linked by several common traits, not least of which is that they were all found barefoot, even in the coldest months of winter. Other traits include their age and body type, described as "athletic to chunky" by insiders, who spoke to *Copwatch* on condition of anonymity.
>
> Clayton Police have not identified or arrested a suspect in any of these murders.
>
> Neither Police Chief Kevin MacMahon nor Sgt. Brenda Petroni, the commander of the WAVE Squad, could be reached for comment.
>
> Suffice it to say, the WAVE Squad has done nothing to alleviate the very real fears of Clayton's young women and their families. The killer is likely to strike again and again with impunity. When, and where, is anybody's guess.

"That son of a bitch!" Val gripped her phone so hard, she thought the screen might crack. "Really? 'Shoeless Sluts?' And how dare he reveal information about the killer's profile? Hasn't he learned anything about how dangerous that is?"

Shannon waved that off. "He'll always write whatever garbage he gets," she said. "My question is, who the hell leaked that to him? And what else that he hasn't yet published?"

"But tipping off the killer that we know his M.O. is going to make our jobs even harder!" Val shouted.

Shannon covered one ear, cringing, and nodded. "He knows. He just doesn't care. Besides, that's not always true." She turned the radio down, whose continued chatter and static made it hard to hear at normal speaking volume. "Some serial killers get off on the notoriety, and sometimes they're not even conscious of little tics like removing their victims' shoes until it's pointed out to them. It might make him even more likely to continue leaving those types of clues."

"It could lead to copycats," Val said. "And calling them sluts, as if it's their fault—he's disgusting."

"True. Hopefully the regular press doesn't copy that." Shannon thought for a few seconds. "Interesting that the tattoo detail didn't leak. That could help us sort this out, if we do get copycats."

Val sank into glum silence in her seat. That stupid Paul Peterson. He'd ragged on her from the moment of her appointment to the force, claiming she'd gotten the job through nepotism. Never mind that a dead uncle can't pull any strings. Then he'd mocked them over their struggles to catch Harkins, all the while lauding the man's cleverness and elusiveness. Now he was leaking details useful to copycats. Fucking jerk.

Plus, all of this discussion assumed that the killer would strike again. And, as Peterson pointed out, she and her colleagues had no idea of where, when, or whom.

Chapter Seventeen

The door to the WAVE Squad office burst open, interrupting Curtis Iverson's carefully crafted rant over the information leaked to that insipid anti-cop blog. He hated tardiness and hated interruptions more. When he recognized the two *prima donnas* entering several minutes late, his face, already warm and probably as red as a ripe strawberry, grew hotter. The wiry uniformed brunette with hazel eyes was Valorie Dawes, his wife's current favorite employee in the city's sprawling, bloated bureaucracy. The other, a tall, willowy blonde, he'd met a few days before when Megan had introduced him to the group. Sergeant Riley or something. Not bad looking, either of them, although both too skinny for his taste.

Kind of like Megan.

He shook off that distracting thought and cursed under his breath. He'd have to repeat much of what he'd already said. His hands curled into fists, crinkling the printout of the blogger's post into a mangled tube. He turned his questioning glare to Petroni, daring her to force yet another interruption.

"That's everyone," the sergeant said in a calm voice. Dawes and the blonde took the last two empty seats at the table—the ones closest to him on each side. "We can *formally* begin the meeting now," Petroni added. She turned toward the newcomers. "In case you're not aware, we've had some sensitive material leaked to a member of the press—"

"Which must stop immediately," Curtis said. "As chairman of the Citizens Advisory Board overseeing this unit, I want everyone in this room to provide a detailed list of whom they've spoken to about this case, when, and where." He tried hard not to shout. "When I say detailed, I mean verbatim, or close to it. And I need it no later than noon today. Understood?"

A moment of silence passed. The cops exchanged wary glances, as if waiting for someone else to speak first. After an eternity, Petroni rose to her feet at a snail's pace, her own gaze fastened on Curtis's. For several seconds, the only sound in the room was the sergeant's heavy, angry breaths.

"Mr. Iverson," she said, her voice full of spite. "With all due respect, *sir*. I'm in charge of this unit, and I alone give orders to my staff. As for your Board's *request*, I will take it under consideration, once you have submitted it in writing, through proper channels. *Sir.*"

Curtis's blood boiled. Insolent bitch couldn't distinguish a request from an order. She needed an education, then. He whipped out his cell phone, tapped on Megan's personal cell number, then held the phone out, facing the room. Its speaker burped out the long, unmistakable tones of ringing, followed by the tinny voice of his wife.

"Curt?" she said. "How'd your briefing go?"

"You're on speaker, Meg," he said in a loud voice. "To the WAVE Squad. Please tell them what you told me half an hour ago about our plan to plug the leaks."

A loud sigh sounded on the other end. Dammit, Meg! Not the reaction he wanted. He almost put the phone away, but she spoke before he could hang up. "Please take me *off* speaker and hand the phone to Sergeant Petroni," she said.

He grimaced, turned speaker mode off, and slid it down the length of the table. Petroni picked up the phone, covered the mic with her palm, and gave Curtis the dirtiest look he had ever seen from a mid-level bureaucrat. Then she strode into her office and slammed the door behind her.

Curtis started when the door slammed, and hoped nobody noticed. He hated when people saw him get ruffled. No doubt Megan heard it, too, and would deal with the rebuke.

Cheered by that prospect, he regrouped and sneered at the silent officers around the table. "Who's the second in command here?" he asked, scanning the room. One of the men, no doubt.

"That would be me," the tall blonde said, raising her hand. "Detective O'Reilly."

Jesus. Except for the laugh lines around her eyes, she looked even younger than Dawes. "You're in charge now," he said. "Relay my orders to your team."

O'Reilly chuckled. "No, sir."

Curtis's face blasted heat again. "*What?*"

"Mr. Iverson," O'Reilly said, "I don't report to you. None of us here do. My commanding officer is still in charge until I receive other orders from *her* CO."

Curtis barked out a hollow laugh. He had to give her credit. She had balls. But not smarts. Time to show these idiots how the private sector handles these situations. "You don't know how this works, do you, Detective? Apparently you want to join your dear sergeant in the unemployment line. Fine. Who's your number three?"

No hands raised for several seconds. Then, a balding white guy seated next to Dawes, Detective Grimes, cleared his throat. "Mr. Iverson, you're going to get the same response from everyone in the room, all the way down to our newest rookie." He indicated Dawes with a jerk of his thumb. "So, unless you want to fire the entire staff of your wife's own special task force—which you have no authority to do—and create a media shitstorm in the middle of a serial murder investigation, I suggest we defer further discussion until Sergeant Petroni returns."

Curtis's blood pressure rose with each word Grimes uttered. The insolence of the man, speaking to a well-connected civic leader, with oversight authority over them all! He glared at the detective, searching for words, finding none that wouldn't alienate them further.

And alienate them, he had. Which was not his goal. He needed their cooperation and loyalty—willing, preferably. Forced, if need be.

He opted for strategic retreat and lowered his voice a few notches. "Fine," he said. "We'll see who prevails here." He sat in his chair with a thud.

Moments later, Petroni's door flew open. Her feet pounded the carpet until she reached Curtis. She held his cell phone out toward him. When he reached for it, though, she dropped it onto the table with a clatter. "Oops," she said. She marched to her seat and remained standing. He checked the phone for damage. Nothing apparent, yet. Fucking cretin.

"I'll need everyone's contact sheets by noon today," Petroni said, her face flushed. "That includes any conversations you've had within the department, and, of course, anyone in the press. Understood? Good. *Dismissed.*"

She spun on her heel and strode back into her office, slamming the door shut behind her. The remaining officers remained frozen in their seats.

Curtis grinned. Good old Megan, backing him up once again. No doubt she'd chew him out later for putting her on the spot. But he'd repay her loyalty a dozen times over, and she knew it. "Now," he said in the calm voice of authority, "You all have your orders. The Citizens' Advisory Board looks forward to reviewing the information you provide. I promise that whoever is responsible for the leaks to the press *will be fired.* Don't think that your precious police union can protect you, either. Oh, and one thing your sergeant forgot to mention: we'll need those reports updated daily."

The officers all stared at Curtis, as if dumbstruck. Idiots! "Are you all deaf?" he shouted. "Get to work!"

O'Reilly stood and strolled to Curtis, stopping less than a foot from him. Her eyes, nearly level with his, flashed icy blue in the room's flickering fluorescent glare. "Excuse me," she said. "I need to get past you to meet with my commanding officer."

He swallowed hard and backed up a step—and collided with Grimes, who had snuck up behind him. Grimes nudged him back toward O'Reilly, who swung him around by his shoulders 180 degrees and steered him toward the door. In a moment, all the other officers formed twin walls of blue on either side of him, leaving him only one path—toward the exit.

"Have a good day, sir," O'Reilly said, all saccharine. Dawes, closest to the exit, opened the door, bowed like a servant of the royal court, and gestured for him to leave.

Curtis straightened, shook off the insult, and strode out the door. It slammed shut behind him. He whirled around and gave a moment's thought to charging back in there and showing them who the real boss was. But with his hand resting on the doorknob, he changed his mind. He'd show them another way, using the levers of power already bestowed. They'd beg for a chance to kiss his ass next time they met. Especially that smug broomstick of a blonde, O'Reilly.

***

After slamming the door on Curtis Iverson, Val pored through her case notes and created the contact list he'd demanded. Like the others in the room, the task annoyed her. Not only because it duplicated work they'd already done, but also that it felt so counterproductive.

"If the point is to prevent leaks," Dion Woodson groused, pecking away at his laptop, "why are we sending our data to an outside citizens group?"

"Political fucking grandstanding," said Grimes.

Val paused in her typing. "There is a silver lining to all this," she said. "At least we'll have all the contact info in one place now." Petroni had insisted that they log all notes into the central case file.

"You can quit kissing ass, Dawes," Grimes shot back. "The boss can't hear you when she's hiding in her office."

Val's face burned, and she returned to her typing. After a few more minutes, Shannon emerged from Petroni's office. If they'd discussed the source of the leak, she gave no sign.

"If your lists are done, let's all go hit some more tattoo shops," Shannon said to the group. She passed out a marked-up assignment list of shops to the other detectives. "Then we stake out the high schools from two o'clock until four today. Riverfront from four till nine. Late night tonight, everyone."

"Don't we need to follow up with Diego Collier?" Val asked.

Shannon shook her head. "Springfield police have him under surveillance until he returns here, then we'll pick up his trail. Petroni doesn't think we have enough for a warrant yet."

"What about Kent Mercer?" Val said.

"Same," Shannon said. "The truth is, we don't have much on anyone. The uncertain times of death and disappearances make it hard to pin them down for alibis, and there's no physical evidence attaching either guy to any of the victims. We can't arrest everyone who happens to know one of them."

"So what do we do?" Val asked.

Shannon sighed. "Detective work, Dawes," she said. "Which is a fancy way of saying, a whole lot of poking around and waiting for someone to make a mistake."

Poking around and waiting summed up the rest of their day. They interviewed four more tattoo shop owners, got nothing. They munched takeout while watching the parking lot of Liberty Heights High empty out from 2:00 until 4:00 p.m. Other teams scouted the remaining high schools, and nobody reported any suspicious characters hanging around.

Once the last after-school clubs quit for the day, the teams spread out around the city. Val and Shannon cruised the downtown streets, a mix of aging and decaying retail storefronts, vacant housing projects, and struggling start-ups. Only the bars and fast-food restaurants seemed to be thriving, yet traffic still went nowhere. They moved on to the waterfront area, featuring gleaming new high-rises built on the ashes of long-abandoned industrial sites, thanks to an influx of federal urban development grants.

"I need air," Val said after an hour of sitting. Shannon dropped her off at the police gym and continued to cruise adjacent streets while Val changed clothes. She jogged the three-mile waterfront loop, joining dozens of other Claytonians who blew off steam through an evening endorphin rush. She grimaced when she passed the site where she'd found Olivia's body, but otherwise studied faces of male runners. None seemed nervous, even with her "Property of Clayton PD" sweatshirt advertising her police presence. During her second lap, the skies darkened and heavy rains fell. In minutes, the cloudburst transformed the loop from a busy downtown park to an ominous, abandoned urban core, driving away both potential killers and victims.

At 9:00 p.m. they ended their thirteen-hour day with nothing to show for it except frustration and exhaustion.

"The good news is, nobody got abducted, at least not from the waterfront," Val said while Shannon drove her home. "Maybe we prevented a crime, for a change."

Shannon grinned. "There's always tomorrow."

"Hey, Miss Sunshine. You must be a big hit at parties," Val said.

"I'm a cop," Shannon said. "Nobody invites me to parties. Not the fun ones, anyway." She pulled her car to a halt in front of Val's apartment. "All right, hot shot. Try to get some sleep tonight. We have another big day of tattoo shop research ahead of us tomorrow."

Val splashed through the puddles on the uneven sidewalk leading up to her apartment building. Like a kid. Hell, if being a cop meant she wouldn't get invited to parties anymore, she had to find her fun somewhere.

She inserted her key into the door of her building and looked up at the sound of an oncoming vehicle. A small silver sedan pulled away from the curb, pausing for a moment abreast of her. Suspicious, she squinted to identify the driver, but the car pulled away before she could make out any details.

She rushed inside and slammed the door behind her, suddenly short of breath.

***

The man hovered over her, his whiskey-laden breath gagging her every time she inhaled. A dim light behind him put his face in shade, but she could tell he was older, and large—well over six feet, and 250 pounds or more. The darkness made it hard to identify their familiar location, other than it was indoors, and cold. She tried wiggling free, but she couldn't move her arms—he'd bound her to the bed, somehow, and his considerable weight pinned her legs apart.

He reached for her, grabbing at her shirt. No, not a shirt—a pajama top. He lifted her one-handed, and cold air washed over her feet. He tossed her back onto the bed, and her head slammed into the wall. She saw stars for a moment and only vaguely realized that he'd hiked the left leg of her pajama bottom up to her knee. Moments later, searing pain stabbed her on the left calf, just above the ankle. She screamed and flailed at him—

***

Val woke, screaming and clutching her left leg, her heart racing. She flicked on the light and checked for a tattoo, or the burn from a brand, which was how it felt in the dream. Nothing. She exhaled, long and hard, and relaxed against the wall, hugging both legs to her chest. She hoped she hadn't woken Beth, then remembered her roommate had gone to Josh's, their engagement back to all-systems-go. So, nobody woke up...and, she had no one to talk to about it. Again.

Val knew the identity of the man in the dream, though she couldn't see his face. "Uncle" Milt, the family "friend" who'd raped her weeks before her thirteenth birthday. She'd had similar dreams countless times since that awful night, though none in the past few weeks. This time, too, he'd taken on more of the character of Richard Harkins, the serial child molester she'd pursued and who'd put Gil in the hospital—

Gil!

Her heart sank, and tears threatened to wet her face. His surgery had been scheduled for—she checked the clock—noon, fourteen hours before. Val had gotten so wrapped up in her case, and the shock of Curtis Iverson's belligerent attempt to micromanage the WAVE Squad, that she'd clean forgotten. She was the worst friend ever. She grabbed her phone and entered a reminder to call the hospital before work that day. Not that he'd take her call after what she'd done.

Fuck!

She sank back into her bed and gazed about the room. Depressingly plain. Val had done little to make it feel like home, to personalize it or provide comforting memories. No posters or art on the walls—just some basic, generic furniture. The necessities. Her only decorations, if one could call them that, were a handful of photos on her dresser: her uncle, her brother with Ali, and an ancient family photo taken before her mother abandoned them. Before Milt. Innocent times she'd long ago left behind.

The dream—how lame, that she kept reliving that scene from a decade before, one that put her through three years of formal therapy and seven more years of self-loathing. A scene that she could have—should have—avoided, in retrospect. Milt had telegraphed his perverted interest in her for months, and she'd left her bedroom door unbarricaded the night her parents left them alone in their house. His leering comments about how much of a "young lady" she was becoming. The creepy personal questions. The staring. The gifts. Of *course* he'd take the next step and try to have his way with her. She should have done something to stop him.

Then Val cursed herself out for the hundredth time. She'd gone over all of that in therapy. How it wasn't her fault, and she couldn't have done anything to prevent it. Milt had used his power over her and abused her parents' trust in him. Milt bore all responsibility for his horrible crime, even though he'd never been brought to justice.

It's not my fault. It's not my fault. It's not—

As it had in the dream, Milt's face morphed into the haggard, jowled visage of serial rapist Richard Harkins. Harkins had stood over her, gun drawn, threatening to repeat Milt's crime against her before ending her life. She'd let Harkins get away multiple times, allowing him to victimize several young girls all across the state. He'd nearly added Val's sister-in-law and five-year-old niece to the notches on his bed. Had she only paid attention to the clues right in front of her, she could have taken him off the streets and prevented almost all of them. Prevented Gil's near-fatal shooting, and the wounding of "Pops" Papadopoulos. All of those events *were* her fault. How could anyone take her seriously as a potential detective?

And here it was, playing itself out again, with a new serial rapist—and killer. One who left a trail of identifying clues, who operated, somehow, within her own circle of acquaintances, without giving himself away. Surely he spent each evening laughing at her and the rest of the "WAVE Squad." Maybe Curtis Iverson was right about them needing a kick in the ass from his Citizens Board.

Val grabbed a notepad off her desk and scribbled notes on it. Nothing of any consequence, just a stream of consciousness to get the angry thoughts out of her head. Names, dates, places: Olivia Lambert. Charlene Washington. Hannah, Yolanda, Jaden. Torrington River Bridge. Diego. Kent. Luis. Liberty High. Heats Ink. Rat-a-Tat Tats.

Then, out of nowhere: Sierra Stapleton and Bo Rousseau. Those names stared back at her, particularly Bo's. Something—a lot—about him bothered her. She scribbled another note below his name: *Could he be the one?*

And, more chillingly, under Sierra's: *Could she be next?*

She turned off the light and lay down, but her guilt and suspicions nagged at her. She knew without a doubt that she'd get no more sleep that night.

Chapter Eighteen

A double-shot cappuccino and a cinnamon granola bar from the Claytown Café did a half-assed job of recharging Val's batteries after a fitful night's sleep. The longer-than-expected line risked making her late for work, and cold, heavy raindrops dotted the sidewalk, so she spent twelve bucks on an Uber Express. The driver, a dark-haired man about her age with a trimmed beard, jumped out and held open the passenger side door of his silver Volkswagen. "Are you Valorie?" he said. His deep-set brown eyes flashed once with what felt like recognition, then glanced away.

Suspicion flared up inside her, then subsided. Of course he recognized her—from the picture on her Uber account.

"I didn't expect a cop," he said, and smiled, displaying dimples above the dark line of his beard. "Don't they issue cars to you guys?"

She wiped rain off her face before sliding into the passenger seat. "Once I'm on shift, yeah," she said. In no mood to chat with strangers—was she ever?—she gazed out the window for the ten-minute ride to the precinct. They passed a mix of nail salons, liquor stores, darkened bars, and ethnic takeout restaurants, interspersed among boarded-up shops and abandoned gas stations. Val spotted more burnt-out street lights than working ones, rendering the traffic-clogged streets dismal and dark in the morning's sudden downpour.

"Was this a five-star ride?" the driver asked when he dropped her off. "I know it was short, but I'm new, and I could really use the reviews."

"Sure. Whatever." She hurried into the building and barged into the office at exactly eight o'clock. She shook rain off her Clayton PD jacket and slipped it onto the back of a chair. She sat in it like a wheelbarrow dumping a load of bricks.

"You, too?" Shannon said, greeting her with a sleepy smile. "Damn, we're going to need something exciting to happen to get us jazzed up today."

"Careful what you wish for," Grimes said from across the room. "I like the quiet days. Nothing depresses a crime wave like a three-day New England rainstorm."

"Not sure if this counts as exciting," Brenda Petroni said, entering from her private office, "but we got an answer back from the AFE faculty adviser." She handed a printout to Shannon. The detective's face curled into a dissatisfied frown.

"Bad news?" Val asked.

Shannon lifted a shoulder, let it drop. "Depends on your point of view. Corroboration for Diego's alibi on the date of Charlene's disappearance. Ditto for Kent Mercer and Olivia Lambert. Each of them had verified attendance at other appointments that afternoon with AFE scholarship applicants."

"That leaves a lot of time unaccounted for later in the evening," Grimes said.

"Not for Mercer," Petroni said. "He worked late at Constitution Finance. Curtis Iverson himself confirmed it, as did his secretary."

"Not Diego Collier?" Val asked in a dull tone.

"Not that night, but..." Petroni ducked back into her office a moment and returned with a printout in her hands. "The night of Jaden's death he was in Rhode Island, and on Hannah's, he was..." She stopped, puzzled. "Also confirmed to be working at Constitution Finance."

"Iverson again?" Val asked.

Petroni shook her head. "His assistant, LeeAnn Schofield. Still, something about that connection bothers me."

"You think Iverson's protecting those two boys?" Grimes asked.

"I don't know," Petroni said. "But three of the girls had internships there, too. That's too big of a coincidence."

"There are no coincidences," Shannon said. "Not in this line of work." She moved toward the whiteboard and picked up a marker. Before she wrote anything, her desk phone rang.

"WAVE Squad, O'Reilly here." She grimaced and scribbled notes onto a small notepad. "Where?...Got it. What time did they—? Okay. Any body markings? Uh, huh. And who—? What's the first name again? Constance. Got it. We'll be right there." She hung up and sighed. "Something's gone very wrong in this town."

"Why? What's up?" Val said.

Shannon's gaze fell. "We've got another body." She added another column onto the victims' profile chart on the whiteboard. "Another teenage girl...with tattoos, and no shoes."

"And her name was Constance?" Val asked, her heart pounding. "What's her last name?"

"Constance wasn't the victim," Shannon said, striding toward the door. "That was her mother's name. She goes by Connie. The daughter's name is..." She paused and checked her notepad.

Val stood and braced herself against the table. Please, please don't let it be—

"Sierra Stapleton."

Val's heart fell, and the world spun in dark circles around her.

***

Shannon drove, and Val caught her up on her previous encounter with Connie and Sierra Stapleton on the way. Shannon parked the unmarked SUV behind a black-and-white police cruiser, and the two women fell silent for a moment. The weeds had grown taller since Val and Travis Blake had visited, and the Stapletons' Toyota sat in the driveway. The raindrops on the windshield hadn't been swiped by wipers in the last several hours. Val touched the hood to confirm. Cold.

They approached the house. The paint on the siding of the Stapleton home had begun to bubble and flake off. The wooden planks underneath soaked up the rain that continued to fall, on and off, amid gusts of icy wind blowing in from the north.

"You ready for this?" Shannon asked Val.

Val sighed. "I can't believe it. We just talked a week ago. Sierra practically kicked me out and told me to mind my beeswax. Said her mother was nuts for complaining about the guy." She pointed to the house next door. "That's where Bo lives. Should we start there?"

Shannon shook her head. "We'll start with the mom, find out what she knows, who else she names as strong leads. I'll send the uniforms over there to make sure Bo doesn't go anywhere, assuming he's home." She clicked open her door. After a moment, Val followed suit, and they strode side by side to the front door, which sat ajar about a foot.

"Detective O'Reilly with Officer Dawes, on scene," she called in through the opening. A moment later she pushed through, Val following. They entered a dark room, with only the light of a single shadeless lamp illuminating the space. A ring of used tissues littered the floor around Connie Stapleton, sitting on the sofa. A uniformed officer stood in silence nearby. Tall, male, nondescript.

Despite the intrusion, Connie didn't get up from the sofa, didn't look up, didn't move. She wore bright polyester slacks and a white cardigan over a print blouse. Tears flowed from swollen eyes, her cheeks red and smeared with dark mascara. Sadness gripped Val's heart, seeing her. Nobody faked grief like that.

"I'll give you the room," the uniformed officer said.

"Make sure the neighbor doesn't go anywhere," Shannon said, waving him outside. He nodded and exited through the front door.

"Mrs. Stapleton? I'm Detective O'Reilly." Shannon took a knee in front of the grieving woman and spoke in a soft voice. "I need to ask you a few questions."

"I told that cop everything. I don't know nothing else," Stapleton answered, her voice hoarse.

Shannon glanced at Val for a moment, eyebrows raised. "Yes, I'm sorry," she said. "We have a few more questions. We want to find the person who did this to your daughter and make sure he doesn't do this to anyone else, ever again. Don't you want that?"

"It was Bo Rousseau!" Stapleton pointed at Val. "I told you that last time. Did you do anything to stop him? No! And now my daughter's gone!" She broke down again and covered her face in her hands. "Useless, all of you! Useless!"

Shannon motioned Val closer. "Sergeant Blake spoke with Mr. Rousseau last time," Val said, "and we plan to again today. If he's responsible—"

"Responsible? Hah! He's the most irresponsible piece of shit you'll ever meet," Stapleton said, spittle flying from her lips. "But could Sierra see that? No. What she saw in him, I'll never know. Ain't hard to guess what he wanted. Lousy perv, chasing underage girls!"

After a brief pause, Shannon asked, "When did you last see your daughter?"

Stapleton gazed at Shannon, as if seeing her for the first time, then blinked. "Uh...yesterday. In the morning, before school. I had the breakfast shift at the restaurant, so she had to take the bus to school. I was going to pick her up after, but my boss asked me to work a double, and we need the money, so..." Her voice trailed off. "My baby," she said in a whisper.

Val searched her memory for details of her run-in with Sierra. "Did your daughter have volleyball practice after school?" she asked. "Or some other—"

"Hell if I know," Stapleton said. "Girl's always lying to me, anyways. Why she doesn't trust me, I'll—I mean, *didn't* trust me...oh, Christ," she said, breaking down again.

"Do you mind if I look around in her room?" Val said.

"I don't give a fuck what you do," Stapleton said, blowing her nose into a crumpled tissue. Shannon nodded at Val, waved her on.

Val slipped down the hallway to the girl's bedroom. Shannon's voice remained audible, as did Connie's. "Do you know if she planned to meet with anyone—in particular, a man, or a boy her own age?" Shannon asked.

"I told you, I got no idea what she does with her time," Connie said, then cried out in grief. "*Did* with her time," she added, sobbing again.

Val scanned the bedroom. Not much had changed since last time. Bed unmade, volleyball team photo and unplugged phone charger cable on the dresser, a few clothes on the floor...including her shorts, team jersey, and sweats. No volleyball practice, then.

No purse visible. Her school backpack lay against the bottom of the dresser, with Sierra's student ID clipped to one of the straps. Val slipped on a pair of latex gloves and unzipped the backpack, revealing a laptop, a spiral-bound notebook, and a couple of textbooks. It appeared she'd dropped the pack on the floor, changed clothes in a hurry, and went out.

The top drawer lay open an inch. Val slid it open halfway. Underwear and ankle-height socks, rolled into balls, filled most of the drawer. One ball of socks, though, looked...wrong. Like it consisted of more than just cotton fabric. She touched it. It contained something solid...no, paper. Rolled-up paper. She took a photo of the drawer with her cell phone, then peeled back the outer layer of sock a few inches. Enough to expose its contents.

Cash. A roll of bills, thirty or forty at least. Judging by the bill on the outside, a twenty, it held several hundred dollars, maybe a few thousand. A lot of money for a high school girl. Why?

Val moved to the girl's closet, tried the door—locked. The handle had a keyhole. Not the little holes often found on bedroom or bathroom doors—a real key slot, like an exterior door. She glanced around, listened. Shannon's muffled voice drifted in, interrupted by Connie's angry retorts, also unintelligible. So they couldn't hear her, either.

She fished a credit card out of her wallet and, with a little wiggling of the latch and the handle, she popped the lock open in under a minute.

The closet contained all the usual items she'd expected to find. Blouses, pants, and skirts hung on the rod, with shoes stacked onto shelves to one side. More dirty clothes lay in piles on the floor. She sifted through them, found nothing. The shelf over the rod contained more shoes, some shoe boxes, and a camera bag, the kind that held fancy SLR cameras and replacement lenses.

That last item surprised her: she hadn't seen any evidence that Sierra pursued photography as a hobby. She lowered the camera bag from the shelf. Something rattled inside, tiny objects against plastic. She unsnapped the top flap, and solved the mystery behind the cash in an instant.

The bag held some two or three dozen unlabeled pill bottles, several small bricks of white powder wrapped in plastic, and a half-dozen zip-lock baggies filled with green, sticky leaf.

***

Val returned to the living room, surprised to find Shannon sitting next to Connie Stapleton, consoling her. Somehow Shannon had won the woman over, or at least gained enough trust to allow her to hold her and speak in a low, sympathetic voice into her ear.

Val waited until Shannon glanced up, then signaled that they should chat outside. Shannon whispered something else to Connie, and the woman nodded, releasing her grip on Shannon's arm.

"What'd you find?" Shannon asked once they'd closed the door.

"Sierra was dealing," Val said, and outlined what she'd found. "I was careful not to disturb any evidence."

Shannon whistled. "Sounds like we've discovered what she and Bo Rousseau had in common," she said. "Let's go talk to him."

Shannon banged on Rousseau's front door, and he answered moments later, his weather-beaten face soaked with tears, his greasy hair a tangled mess. Dark smears stained his white ribbed tank top, and the knees of his faded jeans sported ragged tears. He wore no shoes or socks. "Did you find her killer?" he said, his voice filled with grief.

"Not yet," Shannon said. "We'd like to ask a few—"

"I'll tell you everything I know and help you any way I can!" He waved them inside.

They followed Rousseau into a small rectangular living room with arched doorways leading to the kitchen and a dark hallway. A threadbare sofa took up most of one wall, facing a 24-inch flat-screen TV and a stereo; no other furniture. A couple of heavy-metal concert posters hung from thumb-tacks on the smoke-stained white walls. Traces of gray ash lined the edges of the floor.

Rousseau brought an unpainted ladder-back chair from the kitchen and sat in it, facing the sofa. Val and Shannon sat across from him. The stench of stale tobacco smoke wafted from his sweaty body.

Shannon cleared her throat. "Mr. Rousseau—"

"Bo, please."

"Bo." Shannon smiled. "Thank you. When and where did you last see Sierra?"

"Sunday night," Bo said, wiping his nose with a tissue. "We was hanging out, watching the Celtics game…no, the Bruins. They was playing the Rangers, I think. She likes to come over—*liked*—when her Ma was working late."

"How late did she stay?" Shannon asked.

Bo shrugged. "Nine, ten o'clock. Till her Ma got home from work."

"Can anyone else verify that you were here?" Val asked, taking notes.

Rousseau shook his head. "Well, only her Ma. She yelled at Sierra to get her butt home when she pulled in."

"What about before?" Val asked. "Anyone?"

"Nuh-uh."

"Were you two…boyfriend and girlfriend?" Shannon asked.

Bo held out both hands. "No, no, no," he said, tearing up again. "Nothing like that. We was friends, you know? Sierra was like a little sister to me. I swear, I never even kissed her."

"Just friends," Shannon repeated, doubt in her voice.

"That's right," Bo said, smiling now.

"Not business associates?" Val said, unable to keep an accusatory tone out of her words.

Bo cocked his head, puzzlement overtaking his expression. "Business? No, we ain't in no business. I do construction and maintenance work. That's not the type of work fit for a girl. No offense."

"None taken," Shannon said. "Who's your employer?"

"Different people," he said. "I maintain my house and some others for my landlord for lower rent. I get other jobs here and there, wherever I can find them."

"Gig work?" Val said.

"Yeah, exactly," Bo said.

"How's that pay?" Shannon asked.

He grimaced. "Okay, when there's work. Enough to get by. No benefits though, like insurance, or paid vacation. This ain't no government job like you got." He grinned, revealing crooked teeth, and his breath reeked of whiskey and tobacco.

Shannon coughed and waved a hand in front of her face. "A little early in the day, isn't it, Mr. Rousseau?"

"I just lost my best friend!" He stood and pointed a gnarly index finger at them. "You ever been in my shoes, you'd know what it feels like!"

Val drew in a deep breath. "I have been in your shoes, unfortunately," she said, "and we do understand." She pushed an image of her alcoholic father, plastered after a daily breakfast of bourbon and cokes, out of her mind. He'd suffered as much as Val over the loss of his brother Valentin years before. "But we're concerned for your well-being. Have you had anything to eat today?"

He stared at her, his face screwed up in disbelief, but calmed and retook his seat. "I had some toast," he said. "I ain't got much of an appetite."

Shannon gave Val a thumbs-up and fidgeted in her seat. "Bo, you referred to Sierra just now as your 'best friend.' You know that she was only sixteen, and—"

"I told you, there weren't no funny business going on with us," he said. "I looked after her, is all. Her mother, she never paid Sierra any attention, and she lost her dad a long time back—I never even met him. I didn't want nothing bad to happen to her, so I…I looked in on her."

Val rolled her eyes. Looked into her windows, he meant. "When you two hung out, did you ever have a few drinks, maybe smoke a little?" She mimed taking a hit off of a joint, watching his eyes.

"No, no…well, I mean, *I* mighta had a beer or two sometimes," he said. "But she was a good girl. Never drank or did no drugs or nothing. Least, not when I was around."

"When you were 'hanging out,' did anyone else ever join you?" Val asked. "Any of your friends, or hers?"

Bo shook his head, then stopped, cocked his head. "Maybe a buddy might stop by, if he didn't know I already had company," he said.

"Can you give us their names?" Shannon asked. "When you get a minute."

"Sure, sure." He reached for her notepad and jotted down some names.

"What was the tattoo Sierra got over at Rat-a-Tat Tats a few weeks back?" Shannon asked.

Bo shrugged. "Did she get a tattoo? I never seen it."

"The shop owner says you did," Val said. "He says you stayed and watched."

Bo halted in his writing, eyes still fixed on the page. "Now that you mention it, I kind of remember," he said. "Some Japanese writing across her back. A whatayacallit, Tramp Stamp."

"On her back, or lower?" Val said.

Bo shrugged, a smile tugging at his lips. "I didn't watch closely. Just made sure he wasn't hurting her, you know?"

"What did the writing mean?" Shannon asked.

He paused again, tapping the pen on the page. "Something like, 'The harder the battle, the sweeter the victory.' Supposedly." He chuckled. "You never know what those bozos actually print on you."

Shannon nodded to Val again. Her turn.

"Were you aware that Sierra was dealing drugs?" Val asked.

Bo froze again, then lifted his head to match her gaze. "I never saw her do anything like that."

"I didn't ask if you saw her do it," Val said, although that would have been her next question. "I asked if you knew about it."

Bo pressed his lips together and pushed the notepad back to Shannon. "I guess it don't matter now," he said, his voice cracking. "Yeah, kinda."

"Kind of?" Shannon asked in a sharp tone. "Were you ever a customer?"

"No!" He stood and paced the room, rubbing his hands together. "I don't do drugs, and I tried to get her to stop, but she wouldn't listen to me, you know? Said I was just another dumb-fuck adult—sorry—telling her shit she didn't need to hear." He shook his head, rubbed his hands through his hair. "She was under all this pressure, you know? Get good grades. Win at sports. Join all these clubs so she could get into a good college. Hell, *pay* for college. So, yeah, she started using. Zoomers, coke, mollies, shit like that."

Val wrote "amphetamines, coke" on her notepad.

Rousseau continued. "And to pay for it, maybe she started dealing. Other kids at school, mostly, at first. Lately..." He sighed and hung his head. "I don't know who. Whoever would buy, I guess."

"But not you, or anyone you know?" Val asked.

Bo paused again, rubbing his hand over his mouth, breathing hard. Finally, he reached out to Shannon, and she handed the notepad back to him. He scribbled something on the pad and tossed it back to her. "I gotta use the john a minute, if that's okay," he said.

"Sure," Shannon said. "We'll wait."

Bo disappeared down the hall. Val leaned close to Shannon and said in a low voice, "I'm starting to feel that this one's not connected to the others. You?"

Shannon nodded. "I'd like to hear from the medical examiner, see if the other factors connect—the tattoo, rape, so on."

"Body type is wrong for the Slayer," Val said. "Sierra was tall and thin. The others were curvier. Plus, this one just screams 'drug deal gone bad' really—"

A toilet flushed down the hall, and Val straightened to ensure Bo wouldn't walk in and grow suspicious of their private chat. They waited several seconds, listening for the sound of water running. Instead, the toilet flushed again.

Shannon jumped up and dashed down the hall. "Open up!" she shouted through the bathroom door. Val caught up with her a moment later.

"I'm taking a crap," Bo said, his voice muffled. "Give me a minute."

"Bullshit," Shannon said. "Open up *now!*"

The toilet flushed a third time. Shannon swore and kicked the door next to the handle, hard. The door bounced open, and Bo howled in obvious pain. The door fluttered back toward the jam, but Shannon pushed her way in and tackled Bo into the bathtub. The shower curtain tore off the rod and covered them in pale yellow plastic. A few dozen oblong white capsules about the size of aspirin scattered across the tile floor. Val helped Shannon to her feet, then scooped a few pills into a tiny evidence bag and snapped a picture of the constellation of white dots covering the floor.

Shannon picked Bo up by the arm and forced him into a sitting position on the toilet. "Dumbass, we weren't here to bust you for possession," she said. "Now we have no choice. You have the right to remain silent—"

"I didn't kill her!" Bo said.

"Perhaps not," Shannon said, "but unless you want to do hard time, you'd better make plans to tell us a lot more of what you know about her."

Chapter Nineteen

Val led Bo Rousseau into a hot, concrete-block interview room down the hall from the WAVE Squad office. A one-way mirror dominated one wall, separating them from a tiny observation chamber. Under the watchful eye of a uniformed officer, Val cuffed Bo to an uncomfortable wooden chair bolted to the floor. She made sure the small table and the room's other two chairs remained out of his reach.

Afterwards, Shannon joined Val and the recording techs in the darkened observation chamber. "The medical examiner isn't done with his analysis, but the unofficial word is, no *Chingona* tattoo," Shannon told Val. "Sierra has the Asian lettering across her lower back, as advertised, and a few tiny flowers on her chest. Where a judge wouldn't see them, if you catch my drift. No news yet on signs of sexual abuse."

"Drugs in her system?" Val asked.

Shannon grimaced. "Too soon to tell. No needle marks. The blood work might take some time."

"So, how do we approach Bo?" Val asked. "Focus on Sierra, the drugs, or take a shotgun approach?"

"Start with what we've already got," Shannon said. "Drugs, and his connection to the young Ms. Stapleton. Leverage that into anything else he might know and go from there."

Unlike at home, Rousseau refused to talk without his lawyer present. That lawyer, a forty-something ambulance chaser named Lucas Glenn, showed up an hour later. He declared the search unlawful, no matter how many times

Shannon tried to explain "probable cause" to him, or that Bo had invited them in.

"Fine," Shannon said after another half hour of fruitless haggling. "We'll book Mr. Rousseau on possession with intent and obstruction, and let the courts sort it out. In the meantime, your boy's going to miss a few days of work."

Glenn scoffed and pushed gold-rimmed glasses up his long nose. His squinting eyes reminded Val of an angry weasel. "He'll be out on bail before you even file your paperwork, detective," he said, which elicited a sour grin from Rousseau. "Congratulations. You've silenced a key ally in the investigation of your murder case. I hope you're satisfied."

Shannon chuckled. "Most *allies* tell us what they know about a case," she said, "and don't destroy evidence."

"Allies usually get something in return for helping," Glenn said.

Shannon cocked her head and signaled to Val that she should park herself behind Rousseau. "A word outside, counselor?"

The lawyer smirked and patted Bo on the shoulder. "I'll be right back," he said. "Keep your mouth shut, understand?" He followed Shannon into the hallway. The door lock clicked into place behind them.

Val stood in silence behind Bo, hands folded. Rousseau picked at a fingernail for a few minutes, then tried to stretch, but the cuffs prevented that.

"Can you loosen these a little?" Bo asked. When Val didn't respond, he shook the chains at her. "Come on, I ain't gonna try to escape or nothing."

Val stepped over beside him and held the keys in front of her. "Maybe," she said.

"Maybe what?" he said. "What I gotta do, show you my dick or something?"

Val strolled to the opposite side of the table and locked her gaze on him. Bo struck her as a petty criminal, an opportunist who would snatch a woman's purse or sell coke cut with baking soda to unsuspecting high school kids. A liar for sure, and sleazy enough to coerce sex from the underage Sierra. He might even kill someone in a fit of desperation—and Sierra seemed like a tough enough girl to make him desperate.

But a serial killer? Bo struck her as too pathetic, too submissive, and too stupid to carry off one murder, much less a half-dozen, without leaving a trail of evidence leading straight to his door. If he had killed Sierra, Val would expect to see more of his innate nervousness on display. His shifty demeanor spoke more to trying to beat the drug rap, and to not ratting out someone far more dangerous.

"Why didn't you help her?" Val asked without looking at him.

"Help who? Sierra?" Bo snorted. "I told you guys, I didn't do nothing. I ain't seen her in two days."

"I'm not saying you did," Val said, keeping her tone friendly. "You were her friend, right?"

"I am—hey, don't be trying to get me to talk," he said. "You heard what my lawyer said."

Val shrugged. "I'm not a detective. See this uniform? No chevrons, nothing. I'm just a rookie cop. They don't trust me with any of the moving parts yet."

Bo squinted at her for a second, then laughed. "Oh, I get it," he said. "Moving parts. You're funny, Dawes."

Val smiled at him. "Thanks. You're funny too, Bo. And smart. Kids her age need that." She chuckled. "Listen to me! I'm not so much older than her."

"Yeah. You look young."

Val laughed. "I get that a lot. So does my partner. Not Sierra, though, right? I pegged her for eighteen or twenty when I first met her. Remember when her mom called us on you?"

"Which time?" Bo struggled against his constraints. "Come on, man. Can't you let these chains out a little?"

Val fussed with the keys a moment, moved a step toward him, stopped. "Plus, Sierra was smart. Pretty. College-bound. Such a shame, what happened to her. She had big-time potential, am I right?"

Bo dropped his gaze, his eyes watering. "Yeah," he said. "She was a good kid. That's why I was looking out for her, you know?"

"Sure," Val said. "Like a big brother. God, I wish I had that when I was her age." She thought of Chad, who *had* been there for her until he went away to college, leaving Val alone with her alcoholic father. Her chest tightened, and her eyes grew as moist as Bo's. "But Sierra did have that. She had you. That's pretty cool, Bo."

Bo nodded, and tears trickled down his cheeks. "You got a tissue or something?"

Val sat on the edge of the table, facing him. "Here's what I don't get. You were looking after her, with her dad being gone and all. You knew she was getting in too deep with the drug dealing and all. Why didn't you say something to her? Wise her up a little? Warn her—"

"I *did* warn her," Bo said, almost a shout. "I told her to keep it close to home—friends and acquaintances only, you know? She wouldn't listen."

Val blew out a noisy breath, shaking her head. "Yeah. Kids—me, just a few years ago—we think we know everything."

"I told her not to trust that frigging guy," he said, more tears flowing. "Fucking college guys, rich kids, Dad's a doctor or something, said he could get her this high-end stuff. I said bullshit, right? What high school kid buys that boutiquey shit? But he talked about all the money she could make, and, man, she wouldn't fucking listen..." Bo's voice faded away, his body wracked with sobs, and his head drooped so low, Val feared he'd bang it on the table. Lucky for him, the cuffs stopped him before he made contact. His head bounced back up, and he yelled at Val, red-faced. "Would you *please* loosen up these goddamned chains?"

"Sure." Val circled behind him and rustled his cuffs a little. She couldn't loosen them, but she could make a show of it. "Let up a little! You're pulling too hard for me to do anything," she said.

Bo relaxed his arms and shoulders, sagging into his chair. Val rattled the chains a bit more. "How's that?" she said in a soft voice. "That's as far as it'll go."

Bo tugged at the cuffs again and shrugged. "S'fine, I guess. Thanks."

"Now, since I helped you." Val strolled back around the table, still facing away from him, certain she'd give away her charade if she looked his way. "Can you help me a little? Something that, you know, doesn't implicate you. Like, that college guy you mentioned. What's his name?"

Bo sneered. "I ain't telling you nothing until Lucas cuts me a deal on the possession thing."

Val nodded. "Okay, fair enough. No names. Maybe some way that we can find the guy on our own? Because, I'll be honest with you. Your lawyer's kind of a dick, and my partner can't stand him. So, he's not likely to get very far with her." She leaned closer and whispered, "But she trusts me. If I tell her you're a good guy, that you're helping Sierra—screw helping us, right? We don't deserve it. But Sierra does. Doesn't she?"

Bo stared at her. His lip twitched, but he said nothing.

"So if you were to tell us something that helped us track him down...he'd never be able to trace it back to you, because you didn't give him up, right? And if he hurt Sierra—killed her, or got her killed—"

"The dude's from out of state," Bo said in a low murmur. "That's all I got."

"You never met the guy?"

Bo shook his head.

Val licked her lips. "He lives out of state, or goes to college out of state, or—"

"Both, I think," Bo said. "He goes to some college up in Massachusetts."

"Lots of schools in Massachusetts," Val said. "Which one?"

Bo shrugged. "I could be wrong. There was something screwy about this dude. Like, she said he got his stuff from a lab in...I wanna say, Rhode Island?"

Val's blood chilled. She knew a guy who fit that description. A guy who, until recently, had expressed far too much interest in dating her.

***

As Val predicted, Lucas Glenn refused Shannon's deal, so they booked Bo on the drug charge, leaving the murder rap looming over him. "The guys in the observation room say you did some nice work in there," Shannon said to Val afterwards. "I wouldn't have pegged Diego as a dealer. Stealing from his mommy and daddy, eh?"

"Should we bring him in?" Val asked.

Shannon shrugged. "Petroni wants the team to brainstorm a stronger profile of the killer first," she said. "I don't blame her. I feel like we're flying blind a bit. We're at a body count of at least six, and if we don't come up with some answers, we may see victim number seven far too soon."

An hour later, the WAVE Squad convened in the large meeting room. "Okay, so what do we know about the Slayer?" Petroni asked, standing at the whiteboard.

"Start with the basics," Detective Grimes said. "Male, eighteen to thirty-five."

"Or older," Val said. All eyes in the room turned toward her, a mix of surprise and irritation on most of the faces.

"What makes you say that?" Petroni said.

"The victims all share a key trait: ambition," Val said. "They wanted to get ahead, and specifically, to earn scholarships to a top school. My theory is, they sought help from people with resources—who can shepherd them through the process, help them jump through hoops. People with money. *Men* with money. Most twenty-one-year-olds don't have it."

"A lot of them can get it," Grimes said. "Besides, some young men have money. Your jogger friends, for example. So I think your theory is…well, just a theory."

"And a good one," Shannon said. "We're talking tendencies here, right?"

Val breathed a sigh of relief and mouthed a "thank-you" to her partner. Shannon gave her a discreet nod.

After a moment of silence, Petroni wrote "M, 18-35+" on the board. "All right, what else?"

"Access to tattoos," said Dion Woodson, Grimes's partner.

"Fixation with shoes—or, rather, removing them," Petroni said, adding notes to the whiteboard. "Why?"

"Foot fetish," Grimes added. "The guy's obsessed."

"Trophies," Shannon said.

"Or to exert power and control over the victims," Val said.

"Keep 'em barefoot and in the kitchen, eh?" Grimes said with a laugh.

Petroni glared at him, but jotted down all three suggestions. "What else? What does the killer want?"

"Access to high school girls," Grimes said. "So, a teacher, guidance counselor…or mentor." He sniffed and glanced at Val. "Again, your jogger friends fit right in."

"Let's back up a moment," Val said, her neck growing warm. "The experts group serial killers into four groups: mission-oriented, visionaries, thrill seekers, and power-and-control seekers. Each one gives us insight into a potential killer profile. Broad brush, but it can help narrow the field a bit."

"I like it," Petroni said, writing the categories on the whiteboard. "Let's walk through them."

"We've seen no sign of any sort of mission, right?" Shannon said. "The victims aren't in any way the 'dregs of society,' so to speak. There's no controlled crime scene, and the only thing connecting them is the lack of shoes and the tattoos. That's hardly the stuff of a sociopath trying to 'clean up' society."

"Okay, let's remove that type for now," Petroni said, not sounding convinced, but she erased the category. "I'm also with you that it's not some weird, psychotic visionary on a mission from God. This guy's too organized for that." She erased "Visionary" as well.

"So that leaves Thrill Seekers and the Power-and-Control types," Grimes said. "The consistency of his method and markers, the rapes, the dumping of the bodies—all of that's consistent with the Thrill Seekers."

"Which means, our boy is collecting mementos of each kill," Shannon said. "The shoes."

"Possibly," Val said, nodding. "Still, we can't rule out the Power-and-Control type. In that case we'd look for someone with a more dominant personality, and with their own history of abuse. Someone who is or was on the path to success, like the girls. Someone whose ambitions got frustrated—perhaps, by a woman." She paused and leveled a somber gaze at Shannon. "A strong woman."

Dion Woodson cocked his head. "Doesn't Diego Collier fit that type?"

Val sighed. "He's shown no animosity at all toward women, never once has had anything bad to say about his parents...and he's too young to have been denied success in life. Besides, he lacks the confidence you'd expect of the Power-and-Control type."

"You're right about that," Grimes said. "He's kind of a pussy."

Val made a sour face, but said nothing.

Petroni did, though. "Not my favorite descriptor of sensitive men," she said, "but we get your point."

"Still, the *Chingona* tattoo fits the profile of a Thrill Seeker," Shannon said, "sending us messages with each kill, as does the shrinking time lapse between murders. Like a drug addiction, the high from each event wears off faster and faster. They're more opportunist, and the shoes could be their 'trophies'. I can't rule Diego Collier out of that profile."

Heads nodded around the table. Val weighed those arguments and had to agree. "Still," she said, "my gut tells me we're looking for someone on the higher end of the serial killer age demographic. Thirties, maybe even forties."

"Your tiny little rock-hard gut doesn't count as evidence," Grimes said, chuckling.

Petroni patted her own stomach. "Now, if mine did, we'd have an abundance of evidence." Modest laughter signaled a release of tension in the room. "All right, let's narrow this down some more," she went on. "What about race or ethnicity? Anything?"

"Eclectic taste in his victims," Grimes said. "That tells me, probably non-white."

"How so?" Val asked.

"Because white dudes go one way or the other—Black victims or white victims—and not both, in my experience," Grimes said. "Minorities spread it out a bit more."

Val struggled to find words to respond. In her frustration, coherence and clarity escaped her.

Not for Shannon. "Baloney," she said. "There's not a scrap of evidence supporting that claim. In fact, the vast majority of serial killers are white."

"Over half of all murders are committed by Blacks," Grimes shot back. "Look it up."

"Most of that is gang-related," Val said. "And gun-related. Most murders committed with any other weapon are committed by whites. Especially serial killers."

"We also have the rape factor at work here," Shannon said. "Most rapes are perpetrated by someone familiar with the victim."

"And three of the six victims are women of color," Grimes said, satisfaction rising in his voice. "Like it or not, whites hang out with whites, Blacks with Blacks, and so on."

"So we're back to how the victims all knew the perp," Petroni said. "Someone either into thrill-seeking, or power and control. Older than the girls, although we don't know by how much. Appears to have money. Given what we have on each suspect, where does that leave us? Let's start with the guy in lockup—Bo Rousseau. Is he good for it?"

"He's older, white, and knew Sierra Stapleton. No known connection to any of the others," Shannon said. "And dirt poor. Not a guy who brings a gal from rags to riches."

"Drug dealers have access to money," Dion Woodson said.

"I think the Stapleton case is an outlier," Val said. "Bo may be good for that one, but it doesn't seem to fit. The drug thing—"

"The bare feet, the tattoos," Grimes said, sounding irritated. "Come on. We can't rule it out."

"We don't have the ME's report on the body yet, so we can't confirm that she has the same tattoo, or whether she was sexually abused," Petroni said. "Let's mark Stapleton as a 'maybe.' How does Bo fit the profiles?"

"No 'trophies' found in a search of his house," Shannon said, "or any diaries or records. So, not a Thrill Seeker."

"Shows some signs of having been abused," Grimes said. "That fits the Power-and-Control profile."

"Unconfirmed, and he doesn't fit in other key ways," Shannon said. "Submissive personality and impulsive. Not a well-organized guy who has his act together."

"Okay, Bo's a weak fit," Petroni said. "What about that Mercer kid?"

"Upper-middle-class income parents, not 'wealthy,'" Grimes said.

"He was a mentor to at least two of the victims," Val said. "A position of perceived power and authority. Older than all of them."

"Appears organized and well-connected," Grimes said. "Any history of abuse in his past that might trigger him?"

"Unknown," Shannon said. "We should investigate that. And search his home."

"For a search, we need a warrant, and we're not getting one until we can narrow this down," Petroni said. "How about Diego Collier?"

"Same as Mercer, except for race," Shannon said.

"Disagree," Grimes said. "Collier's parents are wealthier—and divorced. Maybe there was abuse going on that led to them breaking up?"

"That's pure speculation," Val said. "We have no evidence of that."

"Sure we do," Shannon said. "The other night at the pizza place, I noticed some things about him. Any other guy getting ambushed on a date like that—"

"Wait, you're dating this guy?" Woodson said, his eyes wide.

"No!" Val said. "*He* thought it was a date, and—"

"I insisted on that little ruse. My bad," Shannon said. "Look, when we cornered and surrounded him, how did he react? He put up with it and let us push him around. That's a sign of having suffered from abuse."

Val sighed. She couldn't deny it. "And he puts up with crap from me, too," she said. "To be honest, I've been kind of leading him on, ever since I found out that his friend Kent knew Olivia Lambert. To keep my channels open, see if he reveals anything. And he has." She bowed her head. She felt awful, like she was selling out a friend.

"Let's bring Diego Collier in for a little chat," Petroni said.

"I think we should start with Kent Mercer," Val said. "He knows at least the last two victims, maybe more. He fits both profile types, except for his age, and his bullying personality makes up for it on the Power-and-Control type. And he disappeared so fast from the Olivia Lambert scene, I have to think he was trying to hide something."

"Okay, bring them both in," Petroni said. "To minimize bias—Grimes, you and Woodson take Diego Collier. O'Reilly, you and Dawes take Mercer. Let's sweat them both and see if either talks. Rock and roll, team!"

Chapter Twenty

Shannon pulled Val aside in the fourth-floor corridor outside the WAVE Squad office and folded her arms. "Are you okay, Val? You seem...disturbed."

Val dropped her gaze. "In my opinion, we're barking up the wrong tree, going after these two guys. Especially Diego."

Shannon leaned in. "You can't let personal feelings get in the way here."

"I'm not," Val said, backing away, her neck growing warm. She knew she sounded defensive and resented Shannon calling her out on this. "I agree that it looks bad for Diego. But I feel like we're jumping to conclusions. To me, the evidence is as strong against Kent as it is Diego, but..." She spread her arms, not sure if she should continue.

"What?" Shannon said. "What are you implying? That we're giving Kent a pass because he's white? I disagree. We're hauling his butt in here, too, remember."

"Not only Kent," Val said. "Everyone else. For instance, we haven't looked at a single family member, or—"

"In a serial murder? What are you saying? That Hannah Brinkman's father killed her, and then got a taste for it, or something?" Shannon shook her head. "Read the case files. We cleared family members of each victim. Hell, in Sierra's case, there *are* no brothers, no fathers, no uncles. Yolanda's as well. Talk about barking up the wrong tree!"

Val glanced around, noting other officers and bureaucrats popping in and out of offices. Walls could talk, and well-connected political types always seemed to be wandering the halls. "My point is, we aren't looking at...all possibilities."

"Okay, who else, then?"

Val lowered her voice and leaned closer. "Can we talk somewhere more private?"

Shannon studied her for several seconds, then grabbed Val by the arm and pulled her into a nearby women's restroom. As usual in the ancient building, the bathroom reeked, as if someone had poured ten gallons of bleach into a backed-up sewer pipe. One of the long fluorescent lights overhead flickered like an old-fashioned movie projector, and the other had burnt out. It felt—and smelled—like a dark alley behind a skanky bar.

Val checked all four stalls—empty—while Shannon turned on both faucets and locked the deadbolt of the entry door. Then she faced Val. "Okay. No one can hear us in here. What's on your mind?"

Val swallowed hard and, despite their secretive location, kept her voice low. "I didn't dare say this in the meeting...there's another guy, a little older, who fits the Power-and-Control type," she said. She wiped droplets of perspiration from her brow. "Someone who also knows several of the victims...and has gotten a lot closer to the investigation recently. If you know what I mean."

Shannon crossed her arms. "Don't pull punches. Explain it to me like I'm five."

Val's breath grew shallow, her voice shaky. "He's throwing his weight around. Using his influence with the mayor. Demanding all of our reports. Why do you think he's doing that?"

Shannon's mouth widened. "Curtis Iverson? You can't be serious."

"Sh!" Val patted the air with her hands. "Think about it. How does it make sense that he's so interested in this investigation? Plus, the guy's so...creepy."

"Dawes." Shannon put her arm around Val and drew her in, shoulder-to-shoulder. "That's crazy. The guy is anything but frustrated. Rich, accomplished, married well—the symbol of stability. He doesn't strike me as being a psychopath."

"But he *is* a control freak, as we just saw," Val said. "And he's...I don't know. Something's wrong with him."

Shannon grinned and shook Val's shoulder. "Yeah, I don't like him either. But I don't see him roaming around the city at night, picking up overachieving young girls and tattooing, raping, and killing them. If nothing else, his wife, Her Honor the Mayor, is a pretty perceptive gal. Don't you think she'd notice that?"

"If she did," Val said, "would she tell us?"

Shannon dropped her arm from Val's shoulders and groped for words. "No, but she'd damn sure tell *him*, and kick his ass to the curb. Talk about strong women! She's as tough as they come."

"Tough isn't the same as strong."

After a moment, Shannon nodded. "Fair point. But the Power-and-Control profile suggests a guy whose ambitions have been thwarted by a woman. Does that fit Curtis? I'd say no."

"Maybe he's jealous of her success," Val said, wishing she sounded more confident of that.

"He's made a fortune in business," Shannon said. "I'd expect—"

Someone knocked on the door. "Can a gal get some bladder relief?" a muffled woman's voice said.

"Out of order!" Shannon shouted back. "Use the third floor." Footsteps and the woman's voice, grumbling unintelligible complaints, faded down the hallway.

Shannon eyed Val again. "Look," she said. "Right now the evidence points to a couple of college guys, one of which we need to go lock in a hot room and tighten the thumbscrews on. I'm not saying we count out Curtis Iverson or anyone else. I'm saying we have to follow the leads we've got, hottest ones first. Okay?"

Val nodded and sighed. "You're the boss, boss." But down deep, she harbored serious doubts about the direction the team was going.

***

The plan to grill both boys at once hit snags the very next morning. First, Grimes reported that he couldn't find Diego. A visit to his mother's yielded an empty house, and a call to her office disclosed that she'd gone to the hospital on an emergency. She'd be unreachable for at least a few hours. Diego's father professed no knowledge of his whereabouts since Sunday afternoon. Grimes put out an all-points bulletin on Diego's car, but Val guessed that he'd returned to campus in Springfield and might not return until dinnertime.

Second, Brenda Petroni issued a private warning in her office to Val and Shannon about how to proceed with Kent. "We'll need a stronger than usual case for probable cause on Mercer before we lock him in a sweatbox," she said. "Mercer's family is already threatening to sue us for running a DNA test on him for Olivia Lambert, and that didn't produce any results."

"Dammit, Sarge, that's a Catch-22!" Shannon said, heat rising in her voice. "How are we going to get more evidence on Mercer if we can't talk to him?"

The verbal explosion startled Val. Petroni, however, appeared unperturbed by Shannon's uncharacteristic outburst. "I never said you shouldn't talk to him," she said. "I'm saying do some homework first. Have you talked to friends, professors, anyone else close to him? Do you even know where to find the guy?"

"The last part, I can answer," Val said. "He's in class at UConn's Hartford campus this morning."

"Perfect. That will give you a chance to talk to acquaintances before we haul him in." Petroni glanced at the clock. "You'd better hit the road. You'll be lucky to get there by lunchtime."

Approaching their vehicle, Val pulled Shannon aside and spoke in a low voice. "I understand the urgency of heading to Hartford, but can we stop by Mercy Hospital first? I want to check in on Gil. And I think he could help us."

Shannon smiled, a crinkly crease of her lips, accompanied by sad blue eyes. "Of course. I've been wondering about how his surgery went, too."

They found Gil in a drug-woozy state strapped into his bed in a semi-private room, watching sports talk on TV. The other bed lay vacant. "Look what the cat dragged in," Gil said, grinning and flicking off the TV. "About time you visited. I wondered if you were expecting me to walk to your place."

"Hey, you old grizzly bear," Val said. "I see the surgeon reconnected your grumpy bones. I was hoping they'd amputate those."

"They'd have to remove all 213," Gil said with a wider grin, "including both of my teeth. How're you doing, O'Reilly?"

"Not as good as you, apparently," she said. "Petroni saddled me with your old partner. You didn't warn me about how salty she can get."

"What?" Val said, mouth agape. "When have I ever—"

"Too late," Gil said, shaking his head. "You're stuck with her now. No returns, no refunds."

"You guys are both jerks," Val said. "Come on, Shannon. Let's go to Hartford."

"Not so fast." Gil waved her over. When she got close, he held out his hand. Val set hers in his palm, and he squeezed, engulfing her hand in warmth. "Good to see you, my friend. How's the case going?"

"Inching ahead," Val said, choking the words out. Damn, he knew exactly how to make her feel loved and useless at the same time. "Shannon and I are off to chase some leads. I was wondering," she said, "do you think your old Hartford pal Jalen Marshall might help us out? We need some local eyes on the ground there."

"My friends are your friends." Gil scribbled Jalen's number on a slip of paper. "Can I come along? I'd give anything to get out of this germ ward."

Val's heart leaped into her throat. Oh, if only... She loved Shannon, but nothing compared to having Gil by her side.

As a partner, she reminded herself. At *work*.

Gil tried to sit up, then gasped in pain and tapped the nurse-call button on the side of the bed. "Ow. Damn. Sorry, I'm overdue for my intravenous lunch."

Val flinched, her own body experiencing pain in sympathy for Gil. She sighed and signaled to Shannon with a shake of her head: time to leave.

"If Gil's calling for morphine," Val said when they'd reached the hallway, "you know he's suffering."

"Good call on hitting up Jalen Marshall," Shannon said. "Hartford stole a good one from us there. You worked with him on the Harkins case, didn't you?"

Val nodded. "And my uncle trained him. Unfortunately, his partner, Ben Peterson, is pretty useless. I attended Police Academy with him. Ben could never decide whether he wanted to murder me or marry me. Maybe both."

"I know the type," Shannon said. "Any relation to that blogger that ran the 'Shoeless Slut Slayer' story?"

"Cousins." Val grimaced. "Stupid and evil run in the family."

"Let's hope Jalen's found a new partner," Shannon said. "We don't need idiots like that getting in our way."

Val nodded, but the nagging, sinking feeling in her gut suggested that plenty of idiots remained in her future.

***

On the hour-long drive to Hartford, Val called Jalen Marshall, who agreed without hesitation to provide whatever local help they needed, including interrogation rooms and on-the-ground support.

"Tell Gil he's in trouble with me," Marshall said, laughing. "That SOB ain't allowed to wallow in a hospital without giving me a chance to humiliate his pansy ass. That bastard. Never misses an opportunity to let some nurse kiss his boo-boos."

Val ended the call and shook her head. "I may never understand men. They never miss a chance to kick a guy when he's down."

"Try raising teenagers," Shannon said. "It's all that, plus they stink to high heaven."

Val placed a second strategic call to another figure from her past. During Val's freshman year at UConn, Detective Tanisha Jordan investigated the abduction of the daughter of Val's friend Rhonda. They'd fallen out of touch in recent years, but Tanisha had invited her to call anytime she needed help.

"Dawes! So good to hear your voice," Tanisha said. "Please tell me you're looking for a job here in Storrs. We've had two spots vacant for over a year now."

"Tempting, but no," Val said. "Memory tells me you had a sister working in the UConn registrar's office. Do you think she could help me track down a student on the Hartford campus?"

"You've got a memory like an elephant," Tanisha said. "Awright, give me his deets and I'll see what I can do."

"Who don't you know?" Shannon said. "Geez, you're a damned rookie and an introvert, and your network is deeper than mine."

"Thank my uncle for that, I guess," Val said. "Everywhere I turn, people feel they owe his family a favor." But she allowed herself a small smile. It felt good to contribute.

Tanisha Jordan called back a few minutes before they reached the main Hartford UConn building, a four-story limestone structure occupying a long city block near the Connecticut River. "Bad news," Tanisha said. "Mercer's not in class today. At least, he's not in a class *room.*"

"The schedule he shared with us a few weeks ago showed him in classes all day on Wednesdays," Val said, her expression darkening.

"Technically, he's in a class, but it's his internship," Tanisha said. "Physically, he spends most of his day at Constitution Finance. It's not far from you."

"I know where it is," Shannon said. "Let's talk to his advisor first."

They parked in a public lot about a block away from the UConn building and found the director of the internship program in her office. Dr. Nicole Bray was a fiftyish, overworked soul with about an acre of frizzy red hair, an abundance of freckles, and even more energy. She bounced around her cluttered office, gesturing with reckless abandon as she answered their questions.

"One of your interns knew one of the victims," Shannon said after summarizing the case. "Kent Mercer. Do you know him?"

"Mercer? Good kid," Bray said. "Smart kid. Straight-A student, does the work—extra work, actually."

"Extra credit stuff?" Val asked.

"That, and he's a perpetual volunteer, especially if there are girls involved." Bray rolled her eyes. "Whatever motivates 'em, I'm not one to judge."

"Tell me more about that volunteer work," Shannon said. "Do you mean he tutors the incoming high school and freshman students?"

"Coaching, more than tutoring." Bray searched for something on her desk, tossing books and papers about in random piles, ignoring the items that fell to the floor. "Helping the newbies navigate the internship process, balancing work and school. He's good at it."

Val showed Bray the photo of Charlene's scholarship ceremony, the one that Kent was in. "So, this event would be part of those volunteer duties?"

Bray nodded and flashed a wicked grin. "The kid photographs well, you know what I'm saying?"

"Why does that matter?" Val said, trying not to roll her eyes.

"We do lots of PR—we have to. The program is funded almost entirely by private sector grants and scholarships."

"You mean," Val said, "corporate 'donors' pay for not only the interns, but the operation of the program? Your salary, for example?"

"You're a clever one," Bray said, cackling. "Yes. So we return the favor and create lots of press availabilities. Every time a new kid comes on, we do a big promo, invite the local paper of the kid's hometown, social media, the works. Any time we need a pretty male face to fill in, Kent's always one of the first to raise his hand." She paused a moment to think. "Sometimes I wonder how he always seems to know about these things before anyone else." She shrugged. "Whatevs. The kid's a pistol. He knows how to play the game. He'll go far."

"Does Kent get paid for his work at Constitution Finance?" Val asked.

"Sure," Bray said, resuming her search. "The kids do valuable work for these companies and we expect them to be fairly compensated. Part of their comp is experience," she added, "and networking. We have a super-high placement record. Almost a hundred per cent land market-wage jobs within three months of graduation."

"Dr. Bray," Shannon said, "we understand you keep a log of all mentor appointments with AFE students from the high schools. Do you have that handy?"

Bray paused her frenetic pawing of papers and peered at Shannon through her oversized glasses. "What do you need that for?"

"We need to know everyone the victims interacted with, especially on dates close to their deaths," Shannon said. "We think they knew their killers, and trusted them."

"Okaaay," she said, drawing out the word. She pushed another stack of papers aside, reached into the disorganized mess, and pulled out a purple file folder labeled "Mercer, K." She held it close to her chest. "You can look, but the file's got to stay here."

"I don't want to take up too much time," Shannon said. "Can we make a copy and—"

"You got a warrant?" Bray said. "Cuz that's private information. Confidential."

"We could get one," Shannon said, "but that'd mean going back to Clayton, writing it up for a judge, coming back, taking up more of your day...can't you help us out here?"

"Not without the kid's permission," Bray said.

"Just a glance, then?" Shannon said, her voice gentle. Bray nodded and gave her the folder. Shannon handed the file to Val, and held on an extra moment. She dipped her head with a knowing gaze. "You might want to call Jalen, tell him we'll be running late," Shannon said.

Val smiled, her heart rate accelerating. They had no appointment with Jalen. She guessed that Shannon wanted her to snap pictures of key pages while pretending to be on a call. That would violate search rules, and she didn't feel right about overstepping that line.

But Bray had okayed her looking. Val opened the file and scanned through the pages while Shannon questioned Dr. Bray.

"Has he had any complaints filed of any kind? Missed appointments or days of work? Pestered girls for dates, or been accused of harassment?" Shannon asked.

"None that I'm aware of," Bray said.

Val continued flipping through the file while Shannon peppered Bray with questions about the program. A canary-colored page stapled to the back, entitled "Interactions Sheet," detailed Kent's official meeting history with AFE participants and faculty. The list included candidate interviews, coaching sessions, and his regular work schedule. Most importantly, the sheet revealed mentorship appointments with two of the victims: Hannah Brinkman and Olivia Lambert. Not Charlene Washington, Yolanda Garcia, or Jaden King.

"Do you also keep files on the high school internship and scholarship applicants, particularly the AFE members?" Val asked.

"If they apply for our program, we track them," Bray said. "All of that's on the tracking system somewhere. Don't ask me where. I only print out the records of the college kids under my supervision."

"Might you be able to share what you have on Diego Collier?" Shannon asked.

"Collier? Name doesn't ring a bell. Let me look." Bray rummaged around on her desk some more. Val suppressed a laugh. Shannon knew damn well Diego didn't attend UConn and thus Bray wouldn't have any records on him. She was up to something.

Shannon confirmed it a moment later. She glared at Val. Do it! she mouthed, miming taking a picture.

Val hesitated, took a deep breath. Any evidence they obtained from snapping photos without permission would be inadmissible in court, as would any evidence it would lead to—as "fruit of the poisoned tree."

She turned away from them and held her phone above the page, without opening the camera app. Instead, she used her own memory—not quite photographic, but pretty reliable—while Shannon distracted Bray from Val's search.

"Who else does Mercer hang with?" Shannon asked. "Does he have any close friends in the program?"

"Other than the girls? Nah. But he gets along well with everyone, especially at Constitution," Bray said, searching her desk with greater intensity. "Curtis sure likes him."

"Curtis?" Shannon glanced at Val. "As in, Iverson?"

"You know him?" Bray said, halting her search, then nodding. "Of course. His wife's your mayor, right? Running for governor now, I heard. She any good?"

"She's a fine public servant," Shannon said in a monotone. "What's Kent's relationship with Curtis Iverson?"

"Curt's his sponsor," Bray said. "His boss, in a way, although most of the time, execs like him delegate day-to-day supervision of interns to underlings. But from what I can tell, Iverson has taken kind of a personal interest in this kid."

"Any idea why?" Shannon asked.

Bray shrugged. "The Iversons don't have kids of their own, right? I'm thinking he sees this young, bright kid as the son he never had. It's not the first time I've seen it and it won't be the last."

Val located a letter of praise in Kent's file from Curtis Iverson. Iverson lauded Kent's "natural ability" at financial analysis and customer relations. Another document, a memorandum to the file, outlined Kent's responsibilities, and instructed him to report to Curtis's personal assistant, a woman named LeeAnn Schofield.

Meanwhile, Bray collapsed into her chair, gripping a fistful of her abundant hair, as if using it to hold up her head. "I don't know what I did with Diego Collier's file," she said. "Are you sure he's in the program?"

Val closed the file, caught Shannon's eye, and gave her a curt nod.

"Maybe through another department," Shannon said. "If you find it, please let us know. In the meantime, we'll get out of your hair."

Val choked back a laugh. They could get lost in the woman's crazy mop.

"Dr. Bray, thank you," Shannon said. "You've been most helpful."

"Any time," Bray said. "Detectives, good luck on the case. I'm sure you'll find that Kent Mercer has had nothing to do with those girls' deaths. He's really a sweet kid."

Again, Val choked, this time in disagreement rather than laughter. "I hope you're right, Dr. Bray," she said. But she didn't believe it for a minute.

Chapter Twenty-One

The elevator door opened on the top floor of Constitution Tower, a gleaming sixteen story needle of metal-framed glass in Hartford's dense financial district. Val and Shannon stepped into the lobby of the executive suites of Constitution Finance, expecting to find a staid, antiseptic rendition of office space reproduced everywhere in corporate America. Instead, an expansive view of downtown high-rises, highways, and greenspaces rose to greet them behind a wide, achingly modern reception desk. Lush greenery in large pots filled every corner and windowsill.

"Nnnn I help yew?" intoned the petite, bob-cut blonde woman seated at the desk without looking up from her computer screen. Her red lipstick glowed in contrast to her alabaster skin. Painted-on eyebrows arched high across her forehead, and her face seemed incapable of hosting a smile.

Shannon flashed her badge. "Detective O'Reilly, Clayton PD. This is my partner, Officer Dawes. Is Kent Mercer available?"

The woman arched an eyebrow even higher—how, Val had no idea—and glanced at Shannon, then Val, then her screen again. A few clicks later: "Nnnnooo, he's in a meeting. Please have a seat—"

"Get him out of his meeting," Shannon said, her voice clipped and gaining volume. "Please."

"What's the problem, officers?" A familiar voice reached them from an office to their right. Curtis Iverson stood in the doorway, and a statuesque, long-haired blonde with porcelain-white skin peered around him. Like the receptionist, her lips sported the same bright red lipstick. As if the company, or at least Iverson's staff, followed some weird hair-and-makeup code.

Shannon straightened and smiled at him. "Good afternoon, Mr. Iverson. May we have a word with you?"

"What's this about?" he asked.

"Your intern, Kent Mercer," Shannon said.

Iverson blinked and turned to the woman behind him. "LeeAnn," he said, "could you help these officers?" He swiveled back to Shannon and Val. "Ms. Schofield supervises Mr. Mercer."

"How about we talk to both of you at once?" Val said. "Save us some time."

"I'm afraid that's not possible," Curtis said. "I have some urgent business to dispense with."

Val noted his choice of words. In her experience, people "dispensed" with trifling matters, not ones of high importance.

Shannon frowned, nodded. "Very well. Ms. Schofield?"

They followed Schofield into her office and took seats facing her desk. The space reflected a mind geared for practicality and efficiency. Her clean, glass-top desk contained only her computer, a desk phone, and a notepad and pen. A two-drawer filing cabinet lay within arm's reach of her desk chair, on top of which sat a photo of a white, thirty-ish man with brown hair. Her husband, Val guessed. No kids in the picture. Two nondescript prints hung on the wall—department-store art bin material. Spare and utilitarian.

"Ms. Schofield—may we call you LeeAnn?" Shannon readied her pen and notepad.

"You may call me Ms. Schofield, Detective."

Shannon blinked. "Ms. Schofield. What is your position here at Constitution Finance?"

Schofield smiled. "Office Manager of the Investments Division."

Shannon returned her smile. "That sounds like a job that would keep you very busy."

"Very." Schofield sat rigid, back straight, hands folded on her desk, ankles crossed under her chair. She seemed nervous to Val.

"Nevertheless, you got saddled with supervising Mr. Iverson's intern?" Shannon said in a commiserating tone.

"I wouldn't use the term 'saddled.' Mr. Mercer does an excellent job and works well independently." Her smile faded a touch, then returned. As if forced.

"How long has he worked for you?" Shannon asked.

"About ten months. He worked full-time last summer, part-time during the school year. His one-year appointment ends with his graduation, which I believe is at the end of May."

"I see. What does he do for you here?"

Schofield shifted in her seat, and her face grew more relaxed. No doubt, Shannon's intent with the softball questions, Val guessed. "Research and analysis to support investment decisions for various clients," LeeAnn said. "Market trends, specific instruments—"

"Stocks, bonds, things like that?" Val interjected.

"Exactly," Schofield said. "Lately, we've included him in a few customer face-to-face meetings to present his findings. He's very poised and professional, and it wouldn't surprise me to see him hired into a permanent position as an analyst."

"You say he works part-time," Val said. "How many hours per week?"

Schofield tapped on her keyboard. "Eight to twelve, depending on his academic workload. Wednesdays and Fridays, four to six hours each day."

"Not Mondays?" Val asked, taking notes.

Schofield shook her head. "He has classes on Monday."

Val scribbled on her notepad: No work alibi for Olivia, Char. Check class sched.

"So, he was not working on March 11 or April 1?" Val asked. "Or this past Monday?"

Schofield glared at her, a look of utter disdain. "If those are Mondays, then no."

"How many other interns do you supervise?" Shannon asked.

Schofield's mouth snapped shut, as if the question upset her. She cleared her throat. "At the moment, none. I was recently promoted into this position, and we reassigned supervision of interns to their respective departments. For continuity's sake, I kept the responsibility of supervising Mr. Mercer until the end of his appointment. After that, the responsibility for future Investment Division interns will pass to someone else."

"Your receptionist said Kent was in a meeting when we arrived," Shannon said. "Who with?"

Schofield's face screwed up into a puzzled frown. She clicked on a few more keys, tapped her mouse, and shook her head. "I'm not at liberty to say. Would you like me to call him in?"

"Yes, please," Shannon said. "Also, could you look up his schedule for some other dates? September 10 and December 9 of last year, and February 3?"

Schofield tapped the keyboard. "The last two dates are Sundays, also not work days. September 10...a Monday. No, he wouldn't have been scheduled."

Val and Shannon exchanged glances. Val wrote: *No work alibi for ANY vics.*

"Thank you," Shannon said. "Perhaps now would be—"

A double-rap on the half-open door behind them cut Shannon off. "Sorry to delay you," Curtis said, hustling into the room. He pulled up a chair next to Schofield's desk, facing the two cops, and crossed one leg over his other knee. "What have I missed?"

"Ms. Schofield filled us in on Mr. Mercer's schedule," Shannon said, "and on his duties. We were about to—"

"Did you have specific dates in mind?" Iverson said, folding his hands over his bent knee.

Shannon frowned. "Mr. Mercer apparently doesn't work Mondays, so—"

"He does occasionally, on special projects," Iverson said. "For example, a few weeks ago—April 1, I believe? No, April 8. He worked after-hours with me, here, at the office on a client presentation."

Val's scalp tingled. "Are you sure about that date?" She glanced at Schofield, who reddened and remained silent.

"I'm sure."

Val glanced at LeeAnn Schofield. Her alabaster skin flushed pink, and she'd sealed her red lips tight. "Ms. Schofield, when you checked the calendar—"

"I stand corrected. Mr. Iverson and Mr. Mercer both worked late that night. Their timesheets confirm it." She swiveled her screen toward them for a moment, a grid of numbers Val couldn't read.

Shannon widened her eyes, said nothing. Val pursed her lips. Computer records like that would stand up in court. "How about...March 11?"

Iverson gazed at the ceiling for a moment, rubbing his chin. "That would have been...yes, well, he and I attended a function together. A Young Entrepreneurs ceremony, or something of that sort?"

"Association of Future Entrepreneurs?" Val prompted.

"That's it!" He snapped his fingers. "A scholarship dinner. Afterwards, he and I and a few other scholarship recipients went out for ice cream—my treat. I believe I expensed that item, did I not, LeeAnn?"

"Yes you did, sir," Schofield said.

Dammit. Two alibis now. "And...February 17?" As a test, Val named a date not associated with any of the murders.

Iverson pondered that a moment. "No, I can't speak to that day," he said. "That was Valentine's Day weekend, and I didn't work that Monday. I took Megan to New York for a romantic weekend." He glanced away from Schofield, who nodded, as if to confirm his claim.

Shannon jumped in before Val could respond. "Could you provide a list of dates—specifically, Sundays and Mondays—where you and Mr. Mercer worked together on special projects? Time of day would also be helpful, if you can."

"What's this all about?" Curtis said, uncrossing his legs and leaning forward. "Does this have anything to do with the cases you're investigating on the WAVE Squad?"

"We're...pursuing leads related to those murders, yes," Shannon said. "Mr. Mercer may be able to share some useful information. As you have, sir."

"You're a little out of your jurisdiction," Iverson said. "And, I might add, way out in left field. Kent Mercer is a good kid—smart, polite—"

Val scoffed, unable to stop her reaction.

Iverson glared at her. "You have something to say about that, Ms. Dawes?"

"My experience with Kent Mercer is...different from yours, Mr. Iverson."

"Is it, now." Not a question. "Perhaps you are letting your personal relationship with Mr. Mercer cloud your judgment."

"Perhaps you are as well, sir."

Schofield gasped. Shannon clenched her jaw shut, an "oh, shit," expression on her face.

Iverson, after a moment's slow burn, said through gritted teeth, "That was impertinent. Please explain yourself, Ms. Dawes."

Val drew in a deep breath and held out a hand to stop Shannon from speaking for her. "It just seems that, given your position as chair of the Citizens Advisory Board overseeing our investigation, that your role here in protecting Mr. Mercer, providing alibis for him when you have inside information on the case—"

Iverson leaned forward, his face darkening, and pointed a finger at Val. "Are you accusing me of interfering with the investigation?" he said, his voice steely. "How dare you? You come all the way to Hartford, and barge into my corporate office, with no appointment and without warning—" He paused for breath, and his voice rose in volume. "*Demanding* an audience, throwing around accusations, and somehow *I'm* the one inserting myself into *your* investigation? The nerve of you!" He whirled to face Shannon. "Detective, have you forgotten who I am, and who *created* your task force? Are you fucking *serious*?"

Shannon held up her hands in surrender. "I apologize for my young partner's indiscretion," she said in a conciliatory tone. "Of course, we have no reason to believe that you'd ever obstruct our investigation of this or any other case. Please excuse Ms. Dawes's defensiveness. I'll be sure to provide corrective instruction to her to ensure this doesn't happen again."

Val stared at her, slack-jawed, fury rising within her. She couldn't believe Shannon had thrown her under the bus like that. She searched for words, but Iverson cut her off again before she could speak.

"Instruction, hell!" Iverson said, seething. "I insist you take proper *disciplinary* measures. As you know, Detective, I can and will follow up to make sure that happens!"

"Understood, sir."

"Now get the hell out of here!" Iverson waved his arm at both of them and half-turned away. When neither one moved, he stopped. "Well? Do I need to pursue a complaint against you as well, Detective?"

"No, sir," Shannon said. "However, we're not quite finished with our business here. We'd like to speak with Mr. Mercer."

"Not on my company's time, not on my dime, and not on my premises," Iverson said, spittle flying. "You want to talk to him, find him back in Clayton, or get yourself a damned warrant. You can figure out for yourselves which option will get you in less trouble with me—and which one will keep me breathing down your necks as chair of your oversight board. Now. Get. *OUT!*" He stood and pointed with a straight arm out the open door.

Shannon nodded, stood, and tugged Val by the arm out the door. They rode the elevator in tense silence, which held until they reached their vehicle.

"I know you're pissed," Shannon said, "but Val, you—"

"I can't believe you didn't have my back in there," Val said, fighting to keep her voice calm. "Again."

"Oh, I see. That's what you think this is about." Shannon frowned and started the engine, leaving the car in Park. "Val, you can't say things like that to people. Not unless you have evidence to back yourself up. And you don't."

"What evidence do I need?" Val said. "He's chair of the CAB. He's in our shorts, demanding detailed reports about our progress on the investigation. He's providing alibis for a person of interest. What part of that doesn't spell 'obstruction' to you?"

"The part where he's married to the mayor, for starters!" Shannon drummed hard on the wheel. "And the part where, as he said, we ambushed him in his workplace, when we had no need to. That's on me—I'm the senior partner here, and I made that call. So, don't worry, I'm not going to 'discipline' you. Still, this is a learning opportunity for you, Val. You won't get a lot of information from people if you go around accusing them of X, Y, or Z without being able to back it up. And you couldn't."

"Because you wouldn't let me!"

"Because if I did, you would lose your badge, and so would I!" Shannon gripped the wheel and shook it, growling out loud. "Val, he's not an ordinary Joe. He's the mayor's husband and chair of our oversight board. He's the last person we want to piss off, other than perhaps the mayor herself. Don't you get it? He can crack our ass any time he wants, and right now, he wants. So now we have to do damage control, and hope he cools off enough that this can blow over."

"That's what's important to you?" Val said. "The politics? Not solving the case?"

"Dawes. For God's sake. You have no right to say that to me." Shannon's face glowed bright red.

"But I—"

"God dammit Val. I'm not arguing with you about this any longer!" She pulled the car out into traffic, and Val sank deep into her seat for the long, silent drive back to Clayton.

***

Instead of a long drive, though, Shannon surprised Val and drove back to the UConn Hartford campus. This time, she parked in a metered spot in front of the building.

"What are we doing back here?" Val said.

"It's a college, right?" Shannon said with a grin. "So, watch and learn."

Val stared at her, grasping for words that wouldn't come. Shannon seemed chipper and upbeat, as if the contentious meeting with Iverson and their subsequent argument had never happened. Gil had once described her as unflappable—the understatement of the year, perhaps.

"Show me the pics you took of Mercer's file," Shannon said, out of the blue.

"I didn't take any," Val said. "Didn't need to. What do you want to know?"

Shannon cocked her head, frowning. "Didn't I tell you to—"

"We didn't have a warrant." Val met her partner's glare with one of her own. "I'm still a rookie, Shannon. You might get away with stuff like that. I can't—I'm still on probation. And, well...I want to do this the right way."

Shannon held her gaze, expression hardening. "Are you saying you disobeyed a direct order?"

Val scoffed. "First off, the 'order' was a little vague. Silent, in fact. You expect me to read your mind?"

"Don't pretend that you didn't—"

"And second, we didn't have permission. I'm not willing to risk having evidence get tossed on a technicality and watch a potential murderer walk because of it."

Shannon sighed, and her look of disapproval softened into bemusement. "You're being difficult today, you know that?"

"You've trained me well," Val said with a grin.

"Yeah, well, take notes, smart-ass, I'm training you some more," Shannon said. "While you were busy 'memorizing' his file, Bray let on that they'd scheduled their monthly check-in for later today." She pulled out a nail file and worked on a ragged cuticle.

A long, silent minute ticked by. Val fidgeted, still unsure of their plan. "So, what am I taking notes on?"

"What you need most," Shannon said. "Patience."

Val groaned, but couldn't argue that point.

After an hour of uneasy silence, Kent Mercer ambled up to the UConn building, dressed in a navy blazer, dark gray slacks, and white shirt with no tie. No overcoat, despite the chilly, damp weather. He had a backpack slung over one shoulder and a phone in his hand, the focus of his attention as he loped along down the sidewalk.

"Wait for me to get behind him, then stop him in his tracks," Shannon said. Moments before he reached the vehicle, she jumped out and circled around the car. Val exited the passenger side, blocking his path.

"We need a word with you," Val said, holding open the back door of the cruiser.

Kent's eyes widened and he paused, a fearful expression on his face. "I…have an appointment with—"

"That'll have to wait," Shannon said, maneuvering with Val to block any escape. Kent's only clear path was into the waiting vehicle. "We have some questions. It won't take long."

"My car—"

"We'll bring you back here when we're done," Shannon said. "We're not even leaving town. Come on, stop wasting our time. The sooner we start, the sooner we're done."

"I want my lawyer present!" he shouted. "You can't question me without him!"

"Sure we can," Val said. "You're not under arrest. We'd like you to help us find Olivia Lambert's killer. Don't you want to help us?"

"I've told you everything I know about her," he said. "I swear!"

"Then perhaps we should start by talking about Hannah Brinkman," Val said. "Whichever one you like."

Kent started to object again, then his face fell, and he clamped his mouth shut. Val spun him around, pushed his head down to prevent it from colliding with the roof of the vehicle, and shoved him into the back seat.

***

Jalen Marshall set them up with an interrogation room and a tech who recorded their questioning of Kent Mercer. Shannon offered Kent a bottle of water. He accepted and took a long swig.

"Let's start with some dates," Shannon said. "When did you last see Hannah Brinkman?"

"Only the one time," he said. "I helped her with the internship application. Like I've done with dozens of applicants."

"Six," Val said.

He stared, blank-faced. "Six?"

"Six applicants, four female," Val said. "According to your file."

Kent frowned, obvious puzzlement straining his expression. "What file?"

"Records we obtained from the University," Val said.

"Dr. Bray told you this?" He took another sip of water.

"Who's Dr. Bray?" Shannon said, winking at Val.

"My adviser," Kent said. "Look, I meet with lots of students. UConn only logs meetings with kids who formally apply to the program. As an AFE College Ambassador, I'm asked to help students from any AFE chapter, no matter what college they apply to."

"Any chapter meaning any high school?" Shannon asked.

Mercer nodded. Squirmed in his seat a little. Sipped his water bottle, a tiny amount.

"So when did you meet with Hannah?" Shannon said.

"September, I think? Or August. I'd have to check my calendar."

"Please do," Shannon said.

Kent opened the app on his phone. "August 26," he said. "Four o'clock."

"And you never met with her again?"

He shook his head. "I might have seen her around the internship office. We never spoke again."

"How about Yolanda Garcia?" Shannon kept her tone easy, conversational.

"Who?"

"Name doesn't ring a bell?"

Another shake of the head. "I don't know her." More squirming.

"Jaden King?"

Kent paused. "The name sounds familiar. What does she look like?"

Val slid a photo of Jaden onto the table in front of Kent. The girl's bright smile radiated confidence and trust, as if nothing bad could ever happen to her.

He squinted at the photo. "I...can't say whether I ever met her. Though she kind of looks familiar."

Val slid another photo onto the table. Charlene Washington.

"What's this, a test to see if I can tell Black girls apart?" He sneered at them. "I told you weeks ago that I knew Charlene. Not well."

"Where were you last Monday evening?" Shannon said, her tone growing sharp.

"Studying. In my room."

"All night?"

"Until ten or eleven, then I went to bed." Kent's tone grew defensive. "Alone."

"Can anyone vouch for you?" Val asked.

He shrugged. "My mom, I guess. I think she was home."

"We'll ask her," Val said. "When's the last time you saw this girl?" She set a photo of Sierra Stapleton onto the table.

"Never."

"Not once?" Val asked. "Even when you and Diego Collier made your drops?"

"My 'drops?' What the hell are you talking about?" Sweat gathered on his forehead. He wiped it away with his sleeve.

Val and Shannon exchanged glances. Kent's nervousness belied his protest. "When did you and Diego last hang out?" Val asked.

"What the hell?" he asked, his voice exploding. "I thought you said I wasn't a suspect!"

"I didn't say that," Shannon said. "I said you could help us find or identify the suspect. If that's you, then—"

"It isn't me! I didn't kill any of those girls!" He stopped short, as if he'd meant to say more.

"So, you recognize their names," Val said.

"Wh-whose names?" The tiniest sip of water.

"The victims," Shannon said. "Of rape, kidnapping, and murder. Was it you? Or was it Diego?"

"I don't know anything about all that!" Sweat beaded on Kent's forehead, plastering his light brown hair to his scalp. "And I didn't do it!"

"Of course not," Shannon said, her voice calm. "But you know these girls, so maybe you can help us find who else knows them. We need to find out who they all know in common so we can narrow down our list of suspects. Who else besides you fits that description, Kent?"

"Nobody! I mean—I don't know them. And I don't know who does." Sweat flowed down his round face, drops hanging from his jaw.

"Back to dates," Shannon said. "Tell me where you were and who you were with on September 10 of last year."

"No idea. Can I look it up?"

Shannon nodded at the phone. He tapped on the app. "AFE meeting at South Clayton High School."

"Where Hannah went," Shannon said.

Kent shrugged. "So did I. So? I didn't see her there."

"Records say she attended the meeting." Shannon leaned over him. "So did you. The same night she *died.*"

"I didn't see her! I swear!" He caught himself, took a few calming breaths. "We only met the one time. I didn't really know her."

"What about February 3?" Val said.

"I..." Kent checked his phone again, and a smug smile crossed his face. "Skiing at Okemo with a group of friends. I can give you their names."

"You skipped school that day?" Shannon said. "And your internship at Constitution Finance?"

"I took the day off. So what?" He turned away from Shannon.

"We'll want those names and contact info—your ski pals." Shannon nodded at Val.

Val picked up the questioning. "What about December 9?"

Tap, tap on the phone. "Studying again. I had a Finance final coming up."

"Alone again?"

"Yes. I usually study alone. And no, I don't remember if my mom was there or not that night." He shrank further into his chair. "Can I go to the bathroom?"

"Soon," Shannon said. "March 11?"

Kent checked his calendar again. "I worked late at Constitution Finance, helping Mr. Iverson prepare for a client meeting. We talked about this a month ago. Don't you remember, Detective?"

"I do," Shannon said, with a curt nod to Val. "And I remember being disappointed in what you told us."

"But it was true."

"And April 1?"

"Volunteering for the Iverson-for-Governor campaign." He cast another smug look at Val. "Amy Yang can vouch for me."

"We'll be sure to ask her," Shannon said. "So, Mr. Mercer, think hard. Besides you, who else knows all of these young women? Each from a different high school, but all smart, near the top of their class. All involved with sports, with AFE—" She stopped and stared at Val. "What's up, Dawes?"

Val's mouth hung open for a moment. "Kent, isn't there a city-wide coordinator that oversees all the various AFE chapters?"

"Not one individual," he said. "There is a Coordinating Council in each city, composed of the presidents of each chapter. They coordinate activities, elect representatives to the state and national boards, coordinate internship programs. I was on the Council, senior year...why are you looking at me like that?"

"Are there adult advisers to the Coordinating Council?" Val asked.

Kent nodded. "One teacher from Clayton schools, one college rep, and one private sector. They're not heavily involved. I don't remember them attending our meetings."

"They'd know who served on the Council, and they'd be aware of the top scholarship applicants, wouldn't they?"

Kent thought for a moment. "I guess so. The faculty do all the evaluations and scoring. Guys, I really, *really* need to pee."

"I'll get you a diaper," Shannon said. "When we're done."

"Come on!" Kent moaned and crossed his legs. "This is brutal."

"Give us their names," Shannon said. "Of the advisers. Then we'll think about your potty break."

"I don't know!" Kent said. "They rotate every two years, and I'm not involved anymore. But you can find out. Call the AFE office, or the school district."

Shannon whipped out her nail file again and worked on a ragged edge, as if she had all day. Kent wiggled in his seat, tears forming in the corners of his eyes.

"Let's give him a break," Val said. She moved closer to Shannon and lowered her voice. "So we can chat."

Shannon nodded and knocked twice on the door. Guards escorted him out of the room.

"Okay, so you're the 'good cop' today," Shannon said, grinning. "That's okay, I can play at being bad."

"It's not about that," Val said. "Kent's alibis are weak, but I still think the perp is older. What if it's one of the three advisers? They'd have access to each victim."

"Except Sierra. She wasn't in AFE," Shannon said.

"Right. Which supports my theory that hers is a copycat. Bo, or an up-line dealer."

"Theory supported mostly by speculation," Shannon said. "But, yeah, I admit, it fits. Okay, let's wrap up here and keep an eye on him, see if he makes any mistakes. In the meantime, let's follow up with these new leads he's given us."

"I'll take the ski pals and Amy Yang," Val said.

"Good. I'll grab the parents and locate the faculty advisers." Shannon slipped on a pair of plastic disposable gloves and shoved Kent's water bottle into her purse. "Just in case we need fresh prints or DNA." Her phone buzzed and she checked her messages. "Good timing to quit here anyway. Grimes has located Diego Collier."

Chapter Twenty-Two

When Val and Shannon arrived back at WAVE headquarters, they learned from Petroni that Grimes had still not returned with Diego Collier. "They located him," Petroni said, "but he saw them coming—and he ran. Springfield PD put out an APB on him and his car, but he hasn't turned up. Yet." Her face grew long. "It doesn't look good for your boyfriend, Dawes."

"He's not my damned boyfriend!" Val's face grew warm, and warmer still when Petroni and Shannon both burst into laughter.

"Your buttons are too easily pushed, Val," Shannon said. With a rueful smile, she added, "You remind me of myself at your age. If my experience is any indication, you'll get over it fast."

Her face still burning, Val trudged to her desk and got to work on verifying Kent's alibis.

She reached Amy Yang first. "Vaaalll!" Amy's squeal rose to a glass-shattering pitch in an instant. "It's sooo good to hear from you. Are you calling to help with the campaign?"

"Not exactly," Val said. "I wondered if you could verify something for me related to the WAVE investigation. Were you—"

"Ooh, it's so cool that you're on that case!" Amy said. "So exciting. You know, I told some of my former colleagues at the TV station—actually, more like former supervisors—and they were all like, 'Oh, could you get us an interview with her?' And I was like, well, I'll ask—"

"I'm the last person anyone would want to interview on the case," Val said. "My boss, Sergeant Petroni, would be the one to—"

"Not on the case, silly," Amy said. "The story is you, girlfriend! Rookie cop, local girl, shot that rapist dude last year, famous uncle, it's wicked juicy, you know what I mean?"

"Yeah...Maybe some other time." Val shuddered at the memories Amy referenced. She'd taken down Richard Harkins after a long chase, but only after he attacked Val's own family. She'd never forget how close he came to hurting Kendra and Ali.

"Back to the case real quick," Val said. "We spoke to Kent Mercer, who told us—"

"You spoke to Kent? What a coincidence! Kent and I were talking last night, and he thought we could all go somewhere together? Him and I, and we thought you and Diego, like a couples thing," she said. "Has he brought that up with you? I think Diego likes you, girl."

"No, he hasn't." An ache rose in Val's temples. "When did you say you spoke with Kent?"

"Last night," Amy said. "We've talked almost every day since we've met. He's awesome."

Val imagined Amy's body swooning to match the tone and cadence of her voice. "What time?"

"Around nine, till around ten...thirty, ten-forty-five," Amy said. "We lose track of time, sometimes."

"I see." Val rolled her eyes. She couldn't imagine feeling that type of infatuation for a boy her age. Or any age. "On what dates have you gotten together with him in person?"

"Not enough," Amy said. "Let's see, we were together this past Sunday...and Saturday...and before that, on Tuesday, when we saw you...and the day before, when we met. So, four times."

"Wait, you said you met last Monday? That would be, what...April 8?" Val's breath grew short, excitement building over capturing Kent in an outright lie.

"Yeah...I'll never forget that day," Amy said with a loud sigh. "He walked into the campaign office and smiled at me. I asked him if he wanted to volunteer, and he said yes...I knew right away that he was special."

"You're sure about that date?" Val said, double-checking her notes. "Not April 1?"

"Oh, no, definitely not," Amy said. "That would have been my first day—I know it wasn't then. Valorie," she said, getting serious, "is Kent in trouble?"

"That's what we're trying to figure out," Val said. "Thank you so much for your help." She hung up before Amy extolled Kent's virtues yet again.

She wrote in large letters on her notepad: "Mercer—No Alibi for Charlene/Apr 1. Lied!"

Energized, she called all three of his ski buddies, with far less success in busting open Kent's story. Each swore that they spent the entire long weekend skiing and partying with Kent at Okemo Ridge, over two hours' drive from Clayton. It was Kent's first alibi that checked out, and she had to admit feeling disappointed.

"I had much less luck," Shannon admitted a short time later when they debriefed at their adjacent desks. "Both of the AFE faculty advisers are women. Definitely not a fit for the profile, particularly with the finding of semen in the bodies of the first five victims."

"What about the private sector rep?" Val asked.

"Good news and bad," Shannon said. "The good news is, it's someone from Constitution Finance. A person we know."

Val's breath caught in her throat. Another link to Curtis Iverson!

"The bad news is, that rep is also female," Shannon said. "LeeAnn Schofield, the office manager."

"Might she be scouting potential victims, or inadvertently helping the perp?" Val asked.

"Something to explore," Shannon said. "But she didn't strike me as the type."

"Any luck reaching Kent's mother?"

Shannon nodded. "Mrs. Mercer vouches for him being at home all night on Monday, studying."

"Which Monday?" Val asked.

"All of them," Shannon said, rolling her eyes. "To say that her credibility may be compromised would be the height of understatement."

"His alibi for Yolanda's murder in January checks out," Val said in a dull voice. "And I'd have a hard time disconnecting her case from the others."

Shannon smiled. "At least now we can connect each of the victims to Constitution Finance."

"Except Sierra," Val said. "No internship, no AFE, no scholarship, and the drug connection just shouts out at me."

"I think you're right—Sierra's case doesn't fit with the others," Shannon said. "Oh, and her preliminary ME report came in. No signs of rape, and no *Chingona* tattoo. Just the tramp stamp."

"Which didn't get leaked to *Clayton Copwatch*, so we're looking at a possible copycat with the shoeless thing," Val said.

"If so, we'll treat it as a separate investigation," Shannon said. "Which means splitting the staff into discrete teams."

"That sucks!" Val said. "That'll slow down the investig—" Her jaw dropped as the realization came over her, and from the look in her partner's eyes, over Shannon as well.

"Say it," Shannon said. "Out loud. I know you're thinking it."

Val shuddered and hugged her elbows. "That...may be just what the serial killer wanted." She sank into a chair. A cold, numb feeling erupted in her chest and crept down her spine, and she repeated the words that chilled her.

"Just what the killer wanted."

***

Val and Shannon brought Petroni up to speed on their findings in the sergeant's private office.

"This is great work, in a short amount of time," Petroni said. "I know it's been a long day, and it's going to get a lot longer. Still, it's hard to believe that we only discovered the Stapleton girl's body yesterday morning."

"Ironic that her case is the one giving us more leverage on the other five than all the work done before this," Shannon said.

"Ironic, how?" Petroni said.

"We believe she's not connected to the serial killer," Val said.

Petroni waved that off. "I'm not convinced yet. Until I am, we treat her as Shoeless Number Six."

Val noted with satisfaction that she omitted the rest of Paul Peterson's ugly nickname for the perp. Which reminded her: "How has the press coverage gone, other than *Copwatch*?" she asked.

Petroni sighed and shook her head in disgust. "Bad. WCLA-TV did a noontime story on the 'when will it ever end' bullshit theme, as expected," she said. "The mayor piled on a bit, saying she's devoting 'every last cop and every last dollar' to the search, which is even more bullshit. The worst thing is, they repeated the details Paul Peterson revealed— barefoot girls and all. Payback, I imagine, for being scooped by a blogger. That's on me, for not feeding our usual beat reporters fast enough."

Her phone rang again, the double-ring of an outside line. "That's probably another one. My phone has rung off the hook today. From what I've been told, Sierra Stapleton will be the top story on all the local new programs again tonight."

"How can we help?" Shannon asked.

Petroni threw up her hands in frustration. "Arrest the fucker. How else? On that front, Grimes is less than half an hour away, with Diego Collier in tow. He's asked us to pull together some background to drive the interrogation. Get on it."

Val's role amounted to calling friends of the victims to establish their social circles, and in particular, to determine if they'd seen the girls with either Diego or Kent. The first, Emily Roberts, a classmate of Olivia Lambert's, cried for ten minutes before Val even asked a question.

"On the day she died," Emily said through choking sobs, "we were gonna hang out, do some studying and all. But...Livvy never showed."

"Did you hear from her at all?" Val asked.

"She texted me about an hour before we were to meet," Emily said. "She was gonna meet a couple of dudes about her scholarship thing."

"Did she mention their names?" Val asked.

"Nope. Sorry." She broke down crying again and was of no further help.

Val cursed. So close to providing a real clue, yet so far.

Ethan Stokes, a high school classmate of Yolanda's, provided a little more detail, but not much. "I thought I saw her that night at the downtown Starbucks," he said in a sad voice. "Around, I don't know, eight-ish? She was with two guys, like, college-age. One guy was def white, the other might've been Black, or Puerto Rican. I didn't recognize them."

"Could you identify them from a photograph?" she asked, getting excited.

After a long pause, he said, "Nah...I didn't get a good look at either guy. Sorry. Hey, I hope you nail this guy. Yolanda was a sweet girl."

Unlike Emily and Ethan, Niya Cole, a friend of Charlene's, seemed more angry than sad when Val reached her. "She totally stood me up that night. Said she had 'kind of' a date, and couldn't make it to the yearbook meeting. I'm like, 'Girl, you can't blow off yearbook! You made a commitment!' And she's like, 'Girl, it's the only time I can see him, and my parents would kill me, so you have to be cool and not snitch me out.' And I'm like, Girl, I don't snitch on people!"

"Did she say his name?" Val asked, taking furious notes.

"No. Some college dude," Niya said. "It wasn't Jamal, her ex-boyfriend, cuz I saw him later. He got pretty heated when he found out she was seeing someone else...I guess I kinda ratted her out a little."

Before she followed up with the next contact, Petroni called out to her. "Dawes? My office. Now." She whirled and went back inside. Only then did Val notice Shannon creeping to her desk from the vicinity of the sergeant's office, with a guilty expression on her face.

***

"What is it, Sergeant?" Val asked after taking a seat in Petroni's office. She fidgeted in her chair, zippering her fingers together to stop them from shaking.

"I got a call from the mayor's office. Seems you and her husband had a bit of a tense conversation." Petroni sat down across from Val, deep lines creasing across her forehead.

"Y-yes, ma'am. Detective O'Reilly already beat me up a bit about that."

"Well, I'm going to beat you up even more. You almost brought the house down on us here." Petroni rubbed her temples, closed her eyes. "Powerful people like Curtis Iverson are used to being treated with...deference. A fancy word for kissing their asses."

Val smiled. "I'm familiar with the term."

"What you did," Petroni said, "was verbally kick him in the balls. A direct attack on his testosterone-fueled toxic masculinity. I explained—I hope—that it was a case of youthful idealism run amok. But there's pressure coming down, and I mean a lot of it from a lot of places, to bust your ass pretty hard over this. Ranging from a formal writeup to a suspension or reassignment—or worse."

Val sunk into her chair. Dread flowed over her. Losing this assignment so soon would look even worse on her record than the doomsday scenarios Rico had painted. "What did you tell them?" she asked.

Petroni opened her eyes again, hooding them with her fingers. "I told them to go jump in the coldest part of the river, of course. *This* time." She paused, her mouth set in a line. "Next time..." She let her voice trail off.

"I get your message," Val said, relieved. "I have a question, though, Sergeant."

"Which is?"

Val took a moment to form words around her nervous thoughts, her eyes glued to her hands. "How would you prefer I handle similar situations when they arise in the future? A powerful, connected icon of the community who appears to be obstructing our investigation...or, you know...worse." She looked up, surprised to find a smile on her boss's face.

"You want my honest answer?" Petroni said.

Val nodded.

Petroni leaned in. "Kick him in the balls again," she said with a grin. "And be ready to take your punishment. I guarantee you, it'll be worth it."

"It won't end my career?" Val asked. She couldn't help but grin back.

"Nah," Petroni said. "I've done it a few times myself. Yeah, I'll never make Chief of Police. Otherwise it hasn't hurt me...much."

Val left Petroni's office feeling fifty pounds lighter. Petroni's perfunctory rebuke, paired with a not-so-subtle wink at Val's poke at the powers-that-be, suggested that, despite her doubts, she was on the right track. Detectives needed to get aggressive at times, even—or especially—with the rich and powerful. Pursue the truth at any cost, Petroni seemed to be saying. That message fell on welcome ears.

With renewed vigor, Val dove into the task of prepping Grimes for his questioning of Diego. She pored through the case files of each of the victims and created a chart, noting any connections he may have had with each victim. The result painted a picture of undeniable opportunity for a serial killer.

Diego had met Olivia Lambert, as she'd discovered, through Kent Mercer. He'd advised Jaden King and Charlene Washington through AFE. She suspected him of supplying drugs to Sierra Stapleton, though how they'd met, she hadn't yet figured out. That left holes only in his network for Hannah Brinkman and Yolanda Garcia. But both of them had also applied for AFE scholarships or internships.

As for Hannah, Kent had advised her, again through AFE. Diego had met Olivia through Kent—could he have met Hannah the same way? Kent, Diego, and Hannah had also attended South Clayton High School, though not all at the same time, and they knew some of the teachers and staff. A weak connection, but maybe enough for a serial killer.

Another idea struck her: all six girls, like Diego, were active in sports. Yolanda played city league co-ed softball in the summer. Val plugged the team name and league into her browser and, in moments, had a photo and roster of the prior summer's championship team on her screen. Both confirmed that Diego and Yolanda had been teammates.

Excited, she returned to the final empty slot on her page. Hannah, like Diego, ran track, and while their tenure hadn't overlapped, the coaching staff hadn't changed in over a decade. Val's track coach at Liberty Heights had encouraged grads attending nearby colleges to train with the varsity team on occasion, both to inspire the high school athletes and to build relationships with college programs. Maybe they did that at South Clayton High as well. It was worth a shot.

She dialed the head coach's office number, got voicemail, and as the greeting instructed, pressed "2" to forward the call to her cell. The coach, Ginnie Henderson, picked up on the third ring.

"Coach," Val said, "Officer Dawes, Clayton PD. I'm sorry to interrupt you during practice. I'm following up on the Hannah Brinkman murder case, and—"

"Have you found that son-of-a-bitch yet?" Henderson said. "Please tell me yes. I want to wrap my hands around that creep's neck personally and choke the life right out of him!"

"We're working on it," Val said. "Coach, while Hannah was on the team, did you ever invite alumni to come back and work out with the squad?"

"Sure," Henderson said. "All the time. You think one of them might have had something to do with it?"

"We're checking into that possibility," Val said. "Tell me, was Diego Collier one of those alums?"

"Diego...a boy? No, we wouldn't have let the guys run with the gals, for security reasons," Henderson said. "That doesn't mean they didn't mingle afterwards. Hold on, Officer. Let me ask the boys' coach. Hey, Murph! Did a kid named Diego Collier ever work out with you as an alum?"

From the muffled static filling Val's ear, she guessed that Henderson covered the phone to discuss it further with the boys' coach. "Yeah, he says they did," Henderson said. "Couple of times. He'll have to double-check and get back to you. How can I reach you, Officer?"

"Call the Clayton PD and ask for me," Val said. "Valorie Dawes, WAVE Squad—"

"Dawes? Not the same Val Dawes that kicked our asses in 400-meter hurdles at the All-City Meet three years running?" Henderson said.

"Yes, ma'am, that's me. It's been a while," Val said, glad the coach couldn't witness her proud grin.

"Damn, girl, if I'd known it was you, I'd have hung up," the coach said, laughing. "Kidding! Happy to help you out, Dawes. And I'm glad you're doing well. You don't really think Diego did it, though, do you?"

Val paused before answering. Deep down, she didn't think so. But staring at the chart in front of her, she had to admit, it looked really, really bad for him.

Chapter Twenty-Three

Cold pepperoni pizza and warm Cokes, courtesy of Brenda Petroni, awaited Val and Shannon in the observation room adjacent to the interrogation chamber where Diego Collier sat waiting in a metal-framed chair, hands folded on the table in front of him, head bowed. Through the one-way glass, Val took stock of Diego's condition. He slumped in his chair, fear and shame written in sweat all over his face. He looked exhausted and beaten down. She wondered how physical Grimes had gotten with him. A few steps behind him, the dark-haired, stocky figure of Officer Dion Woodson stood guard, silent and at attention. The interrogation room's bare, light-green concrete block walls emanated cold indifference, reflected in Woodson's dark aviators.

On the secure side of the glass, four tired bodies—Shannon, Val, Grimes, and the recording tech—squeezed into the cramped observation room. Dim lights shone on the desk built into the wall. A laptop and a couple of monitors displayed different angles of the interrogation room. Detective Grimes finished a final check-in with the tech and took a huge bite of a slice of pepperoni, addressing them with his mouth full. "Whatha got f'me?" he said, chewing.

"Lots of holes to fill, some gotchas to expose," Shannon said. She cracked open a Coke and waited for the foaming can to settle down before taking a sip. "What, no bourbon?"

"Text me if you think of anything else," Grimes said, leafing through their report. He chomped again on his pizza. "Mm, good stuff here."

Val's stomach growled and, not waiting for an invitation, she snagged a slice and took a bite. Bland, with not enough cheese or pepperoni and way too much dough. Whatever. Calories. She wolfed it down and grabbed another.

"How do you stay so skinny?" Shannon asked her.

"Fast metabolism, and I worry a lot," Val said. "Right now, I could eat this entire pizza and still lose five pounds."

"Nervous about your boy, eh?" Grimes said. "Don't worry, I won't rough up that pretty face of his…much." He laughed. "Save a slice or two for Woodson. Poor bastard hasn't eaten since breakfast." He walked out, licking his fingers and smacking his lips.

Val sat at the counter next to the recording tech, a forty-something uniformed white guy with a five o'clock shadow and a buzz cut, and Shannon sat next to her. "Let's roll 'em," the tech said, clicking a key on his laptop. The two monitors blurred a moment, then displayed closer views of Diego, focused down at his face from opposite angles. "I can zoom in whenever you want, with whichever camera you choose," he said. "They both record in sync with the audio, no matter what, so don't be shy. You can't break anything."

Grimes pushed his way into the room and glanced back at them—or at his reflection in the mirrored glass on his own side of the wall. He sauntered around the room, as if inspecting it for bugs. Diego shifted in his chair and followed Grimes with his eyes, but said nothing.

"Zoom in on the kid," Shannon said. The tech clicked and dragged his mouse, and Diego's sweaty face filled the screen.

"Too much," Val said, swallowing her last bite of pizza. "Show his body language." Shannon nodded at him, and he zoomed back out a bit.

"You know why you're here?" Grimes asked, off-camera, after an eternity. His voice sounded thin and metallic over the laptop's tiny speaker.

Diego stared at him, still saying nothing.

"A lot of high school girls have gotten hurt lately," Grimes said. "More than hurt. Murdered." He wandered into view on a second monitor and turned to face Diego head-on. "We thought you might help us find the killer."

Diego scoffed. "I wish I could."

Grimes smiled. "I hope you can. We don't want any more girls getting hurt. You don't either, do you, Diego?"

"No, sir, of course not. But I don't know anything—"

"Maybe you should check with your friend Kent Mercer on that," Grimes said.

Diego started, licked his lips.

"That's right," Grimes said. "We had a little chat with Kent this afternoon. He seemed to think you know some things."

"*I* do?" Diego said. "No, no. He's wrong. I don't."

"Why might he say that you would, then?" Grimes asked. Friendly. Conversational. Not accusing.

"Kent didn't say that," Val said under her breath to Shannon.

"Diego doesn't know that," Shannon said. "Sh. Listen."

"I don't know," Diego said. "Maybe to save his own skin."

"Why would he throw you under the bus, then?" Grimes asked. "Kent's your friend, isn't he?"

"Yeah, but—"

"How long have you guys known each other?" Grimes asked. Curious, as if they were chatting in a bar.

"Five or six years," Diego said. "We met in high school."

Val nudged Shannon. "That's not what he—"

"Sh!"

"High school?" Grimes said. "Huh. I thought you only met a few years ago...a biology class or something at UConn."

"I never said that," Diego said. "Is that what Kent told you?"

"Diego was there when Kent told me that," Val said to Shannon. "He sure didn't correct Kent's story then."

Shannon nodded and tapped a notepad in front of Val, mimed scribbling. Val nodded and jotted down some notes.

"Why don't you straighten us out, then?" Grimes said. "When did you two become friends?"

"We only recently started hanging out," Diego said. "We run together a couple of nights a week—or, used to, before all this stuff happened."

"Stuff?"

"The murders and all." Diego wiped sweat off his brow. "With exams and graduation coming up, I guess we both have gotten kind of busy."

"Exams." Grimes's voice grew flat, disbelieving. "You want me to believe that's what's keeping you busy."

"Studying for exams, I mean," Diego said, sweating more. "And term papers, and—"

"You're so busy studying for exams," Grimes said, "that you can't go running with your best friend?"

"I didn't say he was my *best* friend," Diego said. "Just *a* friend."

"Who is your best friend?" Grimes said. "What's his or her name?"

"I don't have a best friend," Diego said. "I'm not nine years old."

"Is that how long it's been since you had a close friend?" Grimes sat across from Diego. The tech clicked on a few keys, and Grimes's face filled one of the two monitors, Diego's the other, both close-up. "So, you're kind of a loner, then?"

"I didn't say that!"

"I'm just asking."

Diego wiped his brow again. "I have lots of friends."

"Good, good," Grimes said, pushing a pen and paper at him. "Write down their names and phone numbers."

"What?" Diego said in disbelief. "Right now?"

Grimes glanced around the room. "You got something better to do with your time?"

Diego's head drooped forward and he shook his head, facing the table. "I'd need my phone to look up their numbers."

"We'll get to that part later," Grimes said. "Just the names for now."

Diego scribbled on the page. After a moment, Grimes said, "Don't forget the girls."

Diego's face contorted with confusion. "What girls?"

"The girls you know. And *knew*." Grimes waited a moment. "Like, say, Hannah Brinkman."

Diego started to object, then paused, exhaled. "I...barely knew her, really."

"That's okay. We want a complete list. Anyone whose personal calendar we could look at, and find corroboration for what you're telling us."

"How could you—"

Grimes tapped the paper. "You write, I ask," he said, sharpness in his tone. "How'd you meet Hannah, by the way?"

"Kind of through Kent," Diego said.

"Kind of?"

"Bullshit!" Val said.

"Grimes has got this," Shannon said, smiling. "Watch."

Diego shrugged and paused in his writing. "Kent was her AFE adviser, and we'd run into each other now and again."

"She remembered you?"

Diego cocked his head. "Remembered me?"

Grimes lifted a shoulder, let it fall. "From track?"

"Track?"

"When you went back to South Clayton High and worked out with—"

"Oh, yeah. Right. I forgot about that." More sweating. "Yeah, she probably remembered me. Me, not so much—she's not really my type, and—"

"Your 'type'? What's your 'type'?" Grimes's sarcasm pierced the air, making Diego wince.

"I dunno…girls more my age, I guess," Diego said.

"Like Olivia Lambert? Yolanda Garcia?"

Diego shook his head. "I met Olivia through Kent. He was her AFE adviser, too, and they kind of socialized," Diego said.

"So, what, you tagged along on one of their dates?" Grimes said, disbelieving.

"N-no…I mean, I sometimes saw them together, and we'd say hello, and—"

"Olivia said hello, too?" Grimes asked. "Or did you ignore her?"

"No, I mean yes, she would," Diego said, licking his lips. "She was a friendly girl and all."

"She felt comfortable around you?"

"Yeah, I guess. Why wouldn't she?"

Grimes shrugged. "No reason. Tell me something, though. How is it you just happened to be running by when Officer Dawes pulled her body out of the river?"

Diego held both arms across his stomach. "I–I don't know. That was weird. If I'd have known, I'd have stayed home that day."

"Because you didn't want us to find her?"

"What? No, I–I have kind of a weak stomach, and—"

"You're in med school, and you can't stand the sight of a cadaver?" Grimes asked, incredulous.

"Pre-med. Yes. I know, it's hard to believe, but—"

"*Very* hard." No hiding Grimes's sarcasm now.

Diego's body lurched and he covered his mouth, as if trying not to vomit again. "I…I don't expect to become a surgeon…maybe pediatrics…"

"An OB/GYN, like your mother?"

"No, pediatrics, or adolescent medicine...I don't know. It's too—"

"You like young ones then, eh?" Grimes flashed a cruel smile at the camera. Val read his expression: *Gotcha!*

"What? No, no, all I meant is—"

"Let's stay on track, shall we?" Grimes stood and arched his back. The tech zoomed out the image, as if expecting the detective to move around again. "What about Yolanda Garcia? How did you meet her?"

Diego took deep breaths, calming himself. "Sports. I played on an Under-21 co-ed softball team with her. She's an outstanding player."

"Was."

Diego blew out a noisy breath, nodding. "Right. Was."

"Cute, too, eh?" Grimes smiled at him. "I mean, for her age."

Diego shrugged. "I guess."

"Kind of a powerhouse."

"Athletically, yes."

"Personality-wise, too, right?" Grimes moved closer to him, rested both hands flat on the table. "I interviewed some of her friends. They described her as a real firecracker."

Diego smiled. "She was outgoing, yes."

"A feminist, right? Kind of outspoken?"

Diego shrugged. "A lot of girls these days are. It's not like in your day." He smiled, apparently proud of himself for the age dig.

Grimes didn't blink. "A real *Chingona*, eh?"

"A...what?"

"*Chingona*. A 'badass woman.' You know some Spanish, don't you?"

"Not that term."

"Bullshit!" Grimes slammed the table with an open palm. "Don't fucking lie to me, son!"

"What? I'm not, I just don't—"

Grimes ran to the door, knocked on it. A moment later it opened, and someone handed him a book. Grimes rushed back to Diego and slammed the book onto the table. Diego startled out of his chair.

"Sit the fuck down!" Grimes grabbed Diego by the shoulders and forced him back into his chair. "You recognize that book?"

"That's my missing—"

Grimes shoved the book into Diego's face. "You recognize the *cover* of that book?"

"What the hell? It's for an ethics class—"

"Ever seen that image anywhere else besides your book cover?" Grimes slammed the book back onto the table. "Think hard. I want the truth this time, son."

Diego, shaking, stared at the book cover, his mouth wide, taking deep breaths. "I've seen it on the internet and stuff," Diego said. "Rosie the Riveter. World War Two. Right?"

Grimes stared at him, arms crossed. In a calm voice, he said, "Got any tattoos?"

Diego sat back in his seat. "A couple, yeah. Is that against the law?"

"Any place I can see them?"

Diego blew air out of his lips, tugged his shirt collar down. A cartoonish figure of two Hobbits appeared on his shoulder—Frodo and Samwise. "I'm a Lord of the Rings fan," he said. "And the other one..." He pushed his seat back a bit and raised his right pants leg, exposing dark ink on his calf. "It's Sanskrit," he said. "It means 'Savior of Lives,' a reference to my chosen profession."

Grimes cocked his head, waiting.

"Medicine," Diego said, exasperated. "I'm going to be—"

"Tell me about Charlene Washington," Grimes said.

Diego lay his hands on the table, one on top of the other, as if to keep them from shaking. "I...was her AFE mentor. That's...all."

"Her mentor."

"Yes," Diego said, his voice quiet.

"That's what you kids call it these days?"

"C-call w-what?" Diego's hands shook as hard as his voice.

"What we used to call 'dating.' Hooking up. Doing the nasty. *Fucking!*" Grimes leaned close, and the screens in front of Val and Shannon showed close-ups of both men's faces, inches apart, out of focus.

"No! No, I never—we never even—man, you gotta believe me!" Diego said. "Sh-she kind of had a crush on me. It happens a lot, okay? The girls in the program look up to us. We spend time paying attention to them, and sometimes they've never had someone really praise their abilities before. People who are not their parents or their parents' age, I mean, someone closer to their age. The boys around them, a lot of them are total jerks, you know? So they develop crushes on us. It doesn't go anywhere. At least not for me." He paused, a pleading expression on his face. "I guess for Kent and Olivia, maybe it did."

"So now it's all about Kent Mercer," Grimes said. "I suppose Kent killed Sierra Stapleton, too?"

Diego's eyes widened. "S-Sierra—St-Stapleton?" he said. "Wh-what happened t-to her?"

"You tell me," Grimes said. "Since you hang out in tattoo parlors together."

"What? No, no," Diego said. "I've met her, and yes, I told her about Rat-a-Tats, but we—"

"Apparently you know all about her," Grimes said. "I suppose you're going to tell me that somehow she's connected to your best friend—sorry, *good* friend—Kent, even though as far as we can tell, they've never met?"

"Sure they did," Diego said, tripping over his words. "Sierra and Olivia were teammates on volleyball. Kent probably attended a match, and—"

"How is it you know so much about Sierra?" Grimes said, his voice calm again. "You two friends? I know, not *best* friends, but maybe you should have written her name on this page." He snatched the paper away from Diego and scanned it. "Hmm. Not on here. Why not, I wonder?"

"We met the same way," Diego said. "Through Olivia and volleyball."

"Just the one time, then?" Grimes said.

Diego shrugged. "Maybe more than once. Through Kent and Olivia...until Olivia, you know..." He gulped and lowered his voice to a whisper. "Died."

"So, are you saying that Kent supplied Sierra Stapleton with the stolen pharmaceuticals she's been selling?" Grimes tossed the page into the air, let it flutter to the floor. "Go on. Say it, if it's so."

Tears etched down Diego's cheek. "I...I need to stop now. No more questions until I have a lawyer present."

Grimes laughed. "Watched a lot of TV, have you? Let me educate you on something." He folded his hands. "You think you have rights? You don't have shit. See, we haven't actually arrested you. You're here out of courtesy. We thank you for that, really we do. Now, if we charge you with something, then we have to read you your rights, and give you the chance to lawyer up, and if you did that, we'd have to say okay. Here, we're just talking. Trying to solve a murder. You think we give a shit about your little drug deals? For fuck's sake, kid, I don't care how you earn your beer money.

"I do care about those girls. Olivia, Hannah, Charlene, Yolanda, and Jaden. And Sierra. And all the other girls I don't

know about yet, who haven't been molested and murdered—
yet. So, help me figure that out, and we can all go home
tonight, okay? Sound good to you?"

Diego shook his head. "I'm not answering any—"

"Where were you Monday night this week?" Grimes said,
raising his voice.

"I—I said—"

"*Where?*" Grimes pounded the table.

Diego shuddered out a sigh, tears flowing. "I was...doing
my taxes. They were due at midnight, and I—"

"We'll check on that," Grimes said. "Two weeks before?
April 1?"

"As I told Valorie and her partner, I was at Claytown
Café—"

"You were with Officer Dawes? All day and all night?"
Grimes laughed. "She begs to differ."

"No...part of the day. I don't know, I need my calendar."

"Sunday, February 3?"

"Probably in Rhode Island, visiting my—"

"December 9?"

"Again, probably at my father's house, but—"

"September 10? That's a Monday night." Grimes arched
his back, as if stretching for a long workout.

Diego appeared relieved. "That's my Dad's birthday. I was
with him, watching Monday Night Football, at his house in
Newport. I remember, because the Jets won for a change,
and he said they gave him a birthday present. I didn't return
to Clayton until Tuesday morning."

Grimes stared at him for a long moment, then stood. "I
need a break," he said to Woodson. "Back in a few." He
knocked on the door and slipped through a moment later.

Val, watching in the observation room, let out a slow
breath. "Wow," she said. "That was intense."

Shannon nodded. "Imagine how Diego feels," she said.

Val shook her head. She couldn't imagine how he felt. But one thing she could imagine was Diego being guilty of murder.

***

"That kid's guilty as sin," Grimes said, bursting into the observation room a moment later. "He knows every one of those girls, his alibis suck, and he fits the profile to a T. I say we book him."

"So, what's his motive?" Val said.

"Deep-seated resentment over being rejected by girl after girl in his life, starting with his mother," Grimes said. "Most recently, by you, it appears."

"Fuck you, Grimes," Val said, heat rising under her collar. "You're not pinning this crap on me. And 'rejection' is bullshit. You didn't establish that, and even if you did, how does it fit the profile?"

"He could be striking back at women to assert his dominance," Shannon said. "A sick transference of revenge against all women for the perceived slights by a few. Not just you," she added. "Remember, this string of murders started a long time ago. I agree with Dawes, though, Grimes. You haven't established it."

"I have with his mother," Grimes said. "He called her to ask her to come down here with him. She was 'too busy' with patients. Fits the pattern of maternal neglect, leading to misogyny. I bet you a six-pack his dad fills his ears with poison about her every weekend, too. Another case of Coors says I'll find an ex-girlfriend from high school who dumped him and looks a lot like Olivia Lambert, right down to her bare feet. Any takers?"

Shannon held up both hands in surrender. "You know him best, Val," she said. "Does his story fit?"

"I don't know him well enough to say," she said. "But we should find out before we charge him with anything."

"Let's let him stew in there for a while," Grimes said. "I'll get a warrant to search his house, his phone, computer, whatever. We'll have this case wrapped up by morning."

"You want him to break, put him in a cell," Shannon said. "We can keep him 48 hours. That ought to give us plenty of time."

Minutes later, Dion Woodson marched a stunned and frightened Diego out of the interrogation room in handcuffs.

***

Val fell straight into bed that evening, pausing only long enough to brush her teeth and peel off the clothes she'd been wearing for over sixteen hours. Her heart ached over the Diego situation, and her head throbbed even more. She considered searching for some aspirin, but that would mean lifting her fifty-ton body up and opening her eyes. Turning on a light. Screw that.

She tossed and turned for an hour or two. Petroni's mild scolding that afternoon rolled through her mind, and with each reliving of it, her boss's tone grew harsher, more ominous. After ten or twelve times, she pictured Petroni standing over her, screaming, "You screwed up! One more mistake and you're *through*, Dawes! You hear me? *Through!*"

Val sat up, hugging her extra pillow, wishing it were Gil— and then feeling guilty about it. She and Gil were friends— nothing more. They'd made that clear a hundred times, if not a thousand. Romance would screw everything up—their friendship, their potential for becoming partners again, maybe their trust. She wouldn't risk it. Couldn't.

She tried to picture someone else, then. Someone who would provide comfort and warmth. Beth had filled that role growing up, but she'd moved on, met Josh, gotten engaged. Soon she'd not only be an absentee roommate, but gone altogether, starting her life with him. Beth had found her happiness. Good for her.

She wondered if she'd meet someone who could fill a similar role for her. Someone strong, kind, intelligent, patient...Diego's face sprang to mind, and she shut that down. He checked all those boxes, sure, but he may well be heading to the state penitentiary—for good reason. Even if he hadn't committed unspeakable violence against those girls, he had supplied drugs to high school kids. Not the type of guy she'd trust with her heart.

Val pictured him in prison, envisioning a boy turning into a hardened criminal. Or one abused, tortured, and beaten by his fellow inmates. Either way, a horrible fate.

Try as she might, she couldn't help blaming herself for it. Not for the drug-dealing, but for the suspicion of murder circling him. Had they never met, would he be in city lockup at that moment? No way.

Val stared at the ceiling, wondering what sights greeted Diego in his jail cell.

Chapter Twenty-Four

Grimes, true to his word, convinced a judge to issue a warrant at 7:00 a.m. for the search of Diego's residence. At 7:30, Shannon and Val met Grimes and Woodson at the curb in front of a sprawling Tudor-style home in Clayton's wealthy South End. The two-story, four-thousand-square-foot house appeared brand-new, as did the silver Mercedes E350 parked in the double-wide driveway. Climbing rose vines hugged the brick walls. Mature hydrangeas edged a golf-green-quality lawn. Hundred-year-old willow and Japanese maple trees lined the perimeter of the property. All of it spoke of decades worth of careful, expensive groundskeeping.

"This family's got money," Grimes said. "If we're looking for a sugar daddy for these girls, Diego fits that mold, too."

Grimes knocked and rang the bell, waited a few seconds, then repeated the routine. "Come on, get your ass out of bed, lady," he grumbled. Woodson smirked back at Shannon and Val, standing at the steps leading to the door. Val's heart jumped a moment later when the extra-wide wooden door swung inward. The blocky shape of an Asian Indian woman in her late forties appeared in the doorway. Her long, black hair framed her face and fell in loose waves over her shoulders. Large brown eyes squinted at them. A mix of suspicion, Val guessed, with the necessity of fighting off the morning sun shining into her eyes. She wore tan slacks and a simple pastel blue blouse, both crisply ironed. On her feet, ankle-high nylon socks.

Val peeked behind her. A row of shoes, men's and women's, lined the wall. She grimaced. The woman checked two boxes in the profile right off: thicker-than-average body type, no shoes.

"Detective Grimes, Clayton PD. We have a warrant to search the premises." He held it out to her. "Are you Mrs. Collier?"

"I'm Doctor Mangal," she said with a slight British accent. "My ex-husband's name is Collier. If that is whom you seek, you are in the wrong state." She began to swing the door shut.

Grimes stopped it with his foot. "Is this the residence of Diego Collier?" he said.

Her thin eyebrows rose and her head tilted back. "Is Diego in trouble?"

Grimes rolled his eyes at his companions. "You could say that. Did you notice he didn't come home last night?"

"I hadn't," Dr. Mangal said. "He's a late sleeper, and—" She glanced at the driveway and stared, mouth open. Val guessed she'd expected to see Diego's silver WRX parked next to hers.

Val peered closer at her. A light coat of makeup couldn't quite hide the dark circles under her eyes, and her slow-motion movement belied exhaustion. "Late night, Dr. Mangal?"

"Very," Mangal said. "I had a breach birth case, requiring a C-section...I didn't get home until after two." She blinked into the bright sun. "What's this all about?"

"It's all in the warrant," Grimes said, shaking it at her. She took it, scanned it again, and her face fell. "So, are you going to let us in?" Grimes added. "Or do we have to storm the place?"

"Of course, of course." Mangal waved them in, and they all donned gloves and slipped clear plastic booties over their shoes. Val brought up the rear, as Grimes had assigned her the task of baby-sitting Diego's mother while the others searched the premises. She stole a glance at the shoes lining the wall. A pair of white 2-inch heels, some flats, men's Adidas running shoes, a pair of men's sandals. None appeared likely fits for the Shoeless victims.

The team spread out through the house—Shannon in the kitchen, Woodson and Grimes up the wide, winding staircase to the second floor. Val followed Dr. Mangal into the spacious living room. Expensive-looking, impeccably clean, white leather furniture sank at least an inch into the plush wall-to-wall carpet.

Mangal stumbled to the sofa and sat, holding her head with one hand, as if fighting to maintain composure. Val took a seat in a nearby armchair. "I know this is upsetting," she said. "Can I get you some water?"

"No, thank you." Mangal glanced at Val. "I recognize you," she said. "From the newspapers."

Val sighed. Once again, her notoriety over shooting the child molester, and being the niece of Valentin Dawes, was coming home to roost. "Yes, ma'am."

"Diego mentioned you," Mangal said. "You're Valorie, aren't you?"

Val grew dizzy for a moment. "He talked about me?"

"He described you as very smart and beautiful," she said.

"Sorry to disappoint," Val said, reddening.

"Not at all," Mangal said. "In fact, I am quite relieved. I was afraid he'd developed another crush on a...much younger girl."

As in, a high school girl? "Does that happen often?" Val said. She wished the others hadn't already dispersed through the house. Someone should record this. *She* should record this.

"Oh, no," Dr. Mangal laughed. "He has had few girlfriends. I think you're his first police officer crush. However, we are not here to discuss my son's dating life."

Val's face must have given something away, because she added, "Are we?"

"Bingo!" Grimes shouted from upstairs. "O'Reilly, get up here. We've found the mother lode!"

"Mother lode of what?" Dr. Mangal's eyes widened, and she wet her lips several times. "I...don't understand. Where is Diego?"

"Dr. Mangal," Val said, "while you were helping your patient with the miracle of life, your son spent the night in city jail, on suspicion of narcotics distribution and murder."

"Murder? What do you mean? Diego wouldn't hurt anyone! Who was murdered? Why wasn't I notified?"

"Hasn't he called you?" Val asked.

"Like I said, I worked late...I haven't checked messages...oh, my lord." Mangal sank onto the sofa. "This can't be happening. My boy, my darling boy..."

Woodson appeared at the bottom of the stairs. "Dawes," he said. "You need to come up here."

"Excuse me a moment," Val said. "Officer Woodson will assist you." She widened her eyes at him. He scowled and shuffled into the room.

Val took the stairs two at a time and arrived in Diego's bedroom barely breathing hard. Shannon arrived moments later. Grimes turned toward her, wearing a dark expression, and pointed to a small, glass-and-metal desk in the corner behind him. On it sat a keyboard, monitor, and mouse. No computer. Val guessed he docked his laptop there when he studied at home. A few books lay stacked on one side, and a shelf above the desk stored about a dozen more.

Only after taking in all of those details did she notice the pictures tacked to the wall. A photo of a softball team showed Diego standing behind Yolanda, his hand on her shoulder. Another of the South High girls' track squad, with Diego grinning off to one side amidst a handful of coaches. Two AFE publicity shots—one with Jaden, another with Charlene. In the center of it all, a 6x8" framed picture, somewhat pixelated as if produced on an inkjet printer from a low-res image...of Valorie.

Not a recent one, though. He'd somehow found her high school yearbook photo and enshrined it on the wall behind his desk. In a place he'd see every day.

"Not your boyfriend, huh?" Grimes said.

Val, suddenly dizzy, steadied herself with a gloved hand on the desk. "Jesus," she said. "I had no idea."

"Get this." Grimes held out a quart-sized plastic bag of little white pills. "Found it in his underwear drawer. Not very original."

"Those look like the ones—"

"At Bo's and Sierra's," Shannon said. "The lab will tell us for sure, but they're dead ringers." She opened the closet door and clucked disapproval. "Damn, no women's shoe collection," she said. "That would have sealed it."

Val moved closer to the desk. A weekly calendar grid taped to the adjacent wall displayed Diego's schedule. "Ethics: Breaking Down Barriers" occupied the Monday, Wednesday, and Friday 10:00 a.m. slots. "That confirms his story about the textbook," she said. She pulled the page off the wall, revealing the prior semester's schedule underneath. No ethics course, much less the Breaking Down Barriers class.

"The *Chingona* tat didn't appear on a victim until February," Shannon said. "After the new semester started."

Val's heart sank. The facts kept stacking up against Diego, continuing to disprove her instincts—or biases— about him. "Does that warrant cover his computer, phone, all that?" she asked Grimes.

"That, and his DNA," he said. "They're swabbing him as we speak, and the techs have his data gadgets under scrutiny. They should have answers by noontime. Petroni's working on a warrant for his dad's house in Rhode Island. With what we have here, though, we have enough to charge him. Don't you agree, O'Reilly?"

Shannon nodded. "Sorry, Val. I know he's your friend."

Val winced. "We had coffee once or twice. It's not like we grew up together."

Grimes laughed. "I don't think that's what O'Reilly meant by 'friend'," he said, wiggling his eyebrows.

Val fumed in silence. But she had to acknowledge the disappointment welling inside her. It sure felt like she was turning on a friend.

But how could she be friends with a murderer?

***

"Madam Mayor?"

Michael Kim, Megan Iverson's liaison to the police department, stood in her doorway, holding a single sheet of paper in loose fingers. His trademark poker-faced optimism gave way to nervous fidgeting and rapid eye-blinking. Something had rattled the kid, enough for him to interrupt her busy morning—and to call her "Madam Mayor" instead of by her first name, their in-house custom.

Her concentration broken, Megan sighed, clicked "save" on the speech she'd been preparing, and slid her keyboard aside. Some days she regretted her open door policy. "Come in, Michael. What's on your mind?"

He crossed the spacious room, taking tiny, hesitant steps, and set the paper face-up on her desk. Still fidgeting, he sat in a guest chair opposite her. Sitting without invitation—breaking the office norm of making all meetings short, stand-up wherever possible—could only mean bad news. She cleared her throat and scanned the page.

"Shit," she said a moment later. "Have you emailed me this link?"

He nodded. "I wanted to make sure you saw it, so I—"

She waved him out, found the email, and clicked to the WCLA-TV site. The one-minute video clip appeared at the top of the screen. She ran it. A young male reporter holding a mic stood in front of police headquarters.

> *"Sources close to the Clayton Police Department have confirmed the identity of the body pulled from the Torrington River two days ago," the reporter said. "The girl, sixteen-year-old Sierra Stapleton, is likely the sixth victim of the so-called 'Shoeless Schoolgirl Slayer.' Stapleton, a junior at Liberty Heights High School, presented many of the same characteristics as five other victims found in the past eight months."*

"They released her *name*?" Megan said, incredulous. "Of a *kid*? What kind of idiot— "

The screen shifted to show a taped-off crime scene along the Torrington River.

> *"WCLA News has confirmed that Mayor Iverson's 'WAVE Squad,' formed to investigate this string of violent crimes against women, still has no suspect in custody," the reporter said. "Insiders blame infighting, disorganization, political meddling, and poor leadership for the failure."*

"Holy crap," Megan said, holding her aching head. "How in the hell—? There is so much wrong with this!"

> *"Unfortunately, key details of the murderer's methods and tactics have leaked, and bloggers have published the information online," the reporter continued. "This, sources said, may lead to copycat cases and could complicate the*

investigations further. Meanwhile, the crime spree continues."

The screen image filled with the face of the news anchor, a dark-haired woman in her thirties.

"Jason, we understand that those bloggers, rather than the police, have established some patterns of the killer's behavior. For instance, he attacks underage women of a certain body type, and only on specific days of the week. What more can you tell us about that?"

"Yes, Daniela, that seems to be true," the reporter said, taking over the screen again. "All these crimes occurred on a Sunday or a Monday, after dark. However, police have yet to issue any advisories to warn young women about these specific dangers, something critics are saying is a gross dereliction of duty."

"I have WAVE Squad commander Petroni holding on line two," Kim said.

"Get me the chief!" Megan said. "Oh, shit." She noticed another story on the WCLA-TV website and clicked it. A video of her leading opponent in the governor's race, incumbent Lieutenant Governor Bobby Finn, appeared over a headline: "Finn says Iverson's politicization of police foils murder investigation." Companion "color" stories about past serial killers dotted the rest of the page.

She waved Michael out and picked up line two. "Sergeant, have you seen the news?" she barked without saying hello.

"Yes, Your Honor," Petroni said. "We're looking into—"

"We spoke about this, what, two days ago?" Megan said. "You claimed to have procedures in place to prevent leaks of this sort. Do you know how bad this is?"

"Yes, Madam Mayor," Petroni said. "Unfortunately, some folks in the press felt betrayed by us, thinking *we* somehow fed the story to that Peterson guy, and it looks like they're taking retribution. We're working on—"

"Spare me," Megan said. "Just plug the damned leaks and fire whoever's responsible. Fire everyone and start over if you have to. Now, tell me, is it true that you don't yet have a suspect?"

"We do, but he hasn't been charged," Petroni said. "We're searching his house as we speak and we expect the DA will arraign him by tomorrow."

"Tomorrow is two days late," Megan said. "We lost another girl to this bastard on Tuesday. How many more victims will it take before you folks get serious about stopping this madness?"

"We're doing everything we can," Petroni said in a dull voice.

"Do more," Megan said. "And tell Chief MacMahon, if I don't hear from him within five minutes, tomorrow you'll both be working night security at the mall!" She slammed the phone down and rubbed her temples.

"Megan?"

She glanced up. Michael Kim again, appearing far less nervous than before. She smiled at him. "More bad news?"

He smiled back. "I hope not. Your husband, line three."

"You know," she said, "I have a secretary."

Michael blushed, and his gaze dropped to his feet. "He insisted I find you right away." A moment later, he slipped out of the room.

"Yes, darling," she said into the receiver once she'd caught her breath. "I take it you've seen the news?"

"Un-fucking-believable," Curt said. "I tell you, Megan, we need to tighten up our citizen oversight of the WAVE Squad. They're a mess!"

"How would that help?" she said. "Seems to me, we already have too many people sticking their fingers in that pie. How would adding more untrained civilians—"

"I'm not talking untrained civilians. I'm talking about me," he said. "A direct extension of you. Someone who can manage a complex operation, and who knows how to keep them focused. Did you know what that rookie cop you love and her ditzy partner did the other day? They held my intern in custody for several hours, throwing around a bunch of wild accusations. *My intern*, for Christ's sake!"

"No, I didn't know that," Megan said, anger growing. "Why the hell—"

"They've done nothing to educate the public about what they could do to protect themselves," Curtis went on. "The people need to be informed so they can take positive, concrete steps to keep themselves safe. Instead, we get leaks and half-truths from 'anonymous' sources. What a mess!"

"You're right, of course," she said. "I'll direct the police's public information officers to issue an update."

"Those idiots?" He laughed out loud. "They're part of the problem. No, we need an independent voice on this one."

"True," Megan said, her headache intensifying. "Would this be an appropriate role for the Citizens' Board?"

"I was hoping you'd say that," he said. "I've drafted a set of guidelines for the public, but I wanted to run it by you first...?"

"Send it," she said. "Curt, my love, where would I be without you?"

"Let's never think about that awful possibility," he said. "Because that means I'd be without you, and I never want to imagine that."

Her computer pinged, signaling she'd received a new email. Curt's. She clicked it open, scanned it. Solid information, giving away nothing that could help a copy-cat, with suggested actions: a 10:00 p.m. curfew—8:00 p.m. for those under eighteen—until the killer was in custody. Immediate replacement of broken streetlights throughout the city. Shutting down the running trail around the river at sunset. A toll-free number to report suspicious activity.

"Send it, and add my endorsement," she said. "Cc: my staff. Thank you, darling. You're too good to me."

"You're welcome, Governor," he said, and laughed. "Sorry. Premature? But I know how good you'll be in that job. I can't wait for that next level of success for you."

She hung up, a warm feeling welling up in her chest. So many times, Curt had raised doubts in her mind about his faithfulness and loyalty. Then days like this would come along, and it restored all her faith in his commitment to her.

The serial killer situation spelled potential trouble for her campaign, one based—at Curt's suggestion—on a message of law-and-order that would empower women. At times it felt like a risky choice. But he had great instincts and always seemed to know what to do, what to say, to salvage even the worst circumstances. Turning an embarrassing story about leaks and an unsolved murder into one about giving individual women the knowledge they needed to protect themselves, for example. That would play well in the press.

Once again, her trust in him looked like it was about to pay off.

Chapter Twenty-Five

Curtis Iverson rested his hand on his desk phone's receiver, still warm from his call to Megan moments before. The WAVE Squad's apparent mishandling of the investigation spelled trouble for his wife's campaign. But it also presented an opportunity—for both of them. If she demonstrated the calm leadership and critical problem-solving abilities that this moment required, she could vault herself ahead of the crowded field of candidates for the governor's mansion. And he could continue to help her do that.

For starters, he needed to take some decisive action of his own. He picked up the phone and dialed the number of his newest assistant on the campaign.

"Iverson for Governor, Amy speaking."

"This is Curt. Did you see what your old pals at WCLA-TV broadcast this morning?"

"I'm so sorry," Amy said. "I'm trying to track down what happened. I can't believe nobody called me first before they ran that!"

"What?" Curtis snarled. "Hold on a moment. Let me get this straight. Either you didn't use your connections at the TV station you worked at less than a month ago—or you did, and they ran it anyway. Neither reflects highly on you right now."

"I—I was only an intern there," Amy said. "I didn't have any pull—"

"In that case, why the hell did I hire you?" Curtis's voice rose, but he took care to keep his volume low enough so that LeeAnn couldn't hear in her adjacent office.

"Because I could help…with messaging?" Amy said, her voice breaking.

"Exactly. Part of messaging is to use your connections to prevent hit pieces like that."

"I try to, sir," Amy said in a whisper.

"How so? By leaking negative information to them? Is that how you stay on their good side? I should remind you who signs your paychecks now, young lady."

"I didn't leak that story!" Disbelief mixed with angry sobs made her words almost unintelligible.

"Best that I never find out you did," Curtis said in a menacing tone. "Now get to work repairing the damage. I'm going to send you a press release and I want you to get it out to every media outlet in the state. For God's sake, make sure WCLA's lead story tonight is a retraction of today's garbage. I want an explicit statement that they don't blame Megan for these murders, and in particular for this most recent victim. Are we clear?"

After a few uncertain gasps of breath, Amy said, "Mr. Iverson, I don't know for certain if I can—"

"Find out for certain!" Curtis slammed the phone down. Stupid kid. He had no patience for incompetence. He'd made his expectations clear when he hired her.

Most of them, anyway. He smiled. A pretty girl like that, she no doubt understood that there might be some other…expectations…attached to the major career boost he'd given her.

He buzzed LeeAnn's number. "Please cancel all of my afternoon appointments," he said. "I need to get over to Clayton, and I don't expect I'll be back today."

After a tense silence, LeeAnn said, "Mr. Iverson, as you no doubt recall, with my recent promotion, my duties no longer include managing your calendar and calls."

"Well, yes, of course." Curtis gritted his teeth. In truth, he had no idea what LeeAnn's new job responsibilities were, other than managing the interns.

Ah! The interns. "Yes, of course. I meant that perhaps one of your assistants could do this for me? As a favor from you." He coated his words with as much sugar as he dared.

"Yes, Mr. Iverson, I will arrange that. As a *favor*." LeeAnn's tone lightened. "By the way, interviews for filling my old position as your executive assistant begin tomorrow morning. Will you still be available to make those?"

"Yes, yes." He hung up and grabbed his coat off the rack, made sure his cell phone had enough juice, and whisked out of the office. Once in his car, he scrolled through his phone's favorites list and grimaced. He'd had to call Brenda Petroni far too often in recent days.

"*Another* all-hands meeting?" Petroni said in response to his request-that-wasn't-a-request. "Mr. Iverson, how do you expect WAVE to do any actual investigative work if our detectives are always attending citizen oversight meetings?"

"Just do it," he said. "I'll be there in one hour. I want a full briefing by everyone who knows anything. And I mean *full*." He hung up without waiting for a response. Stupid bureaucrat, always playing the cover-her-ass game.

Music would settle him down while he drove. He clicked on the radio. Too late, he noticed he'd left it tuned into the news channel. More coverage of how the latest murder might be the Slayer's sixth victim. He changed the station and shook his head. Idiots. It should be obvious that she wasn't one of the Shoeless Sluts.

That made him chuckle despite his angst. Regardless of what else anyone might say about this case, that nickname was genius. People would blame the victims for getting killed as much as or more than they'd blame Megan for not stopping the killer. So clever. The city ought to put the blogger on payroll.

That train of thought, combined with a terrific run of John Coltrane, Miles Davis, and Herbie Hancock on the classic jazz station, put him in high spirits by the time he pulled into the police headquarters lot in downtown Clayton.

That didn't last long.

"So, you have a suspect, but didn't feel it was important enough to inform the public?" he said, rage building, after the WAVE Squad had gathered. "You thought, 'Hey, let's let the public go on living in fear.' Doesn't that violate every policy and protocol known to western democracy?"

"The protocol applies to arrests and indictments," Petroni said, her voice calm. Detectives O'Reilly and Grimes flanked her on either side, with the uniformed officers—Dawes and Woodson—keeping a silent vigil next to their respective partners. "Mr. Collier is being held for questioning—for now," Petroni went on. "We're meeting with the District Attorney later this afternoon to determine whether we have sufficient evidence to charge him."

"Why not arrest and charge him on your own?" Curtis demanded. "You do it every day on other cases."

"This is a high-profile case, and we don't want to embolden our killer, if he's still out there, with a show of false confidence," Petroni said.

"Bullshit!" Curtis slapped the table with an open palm. Another classic cover-your-ass move. "Isn't there a greater risk of copycat killings so long as you haven't made an arrest?"

"Our killer has always struck on Sunday or Monday nights," O'Reilly said. "I don't think sitting on this for a few hours is going to change our killer's Thursday afternoon plans."

O'Reilly's observation caught Curtis by surprise. That part of the pattern had, so far, escaped his notice. But he couldn't reverse course now. "It's killing us in the press," he said, with much less force. "I have indications that WCLA will hit us hard in their five o'clock broadcast. The only way to get ahead of that story is to make a formal arrest *and* tell people about it."

Petroni took a deep breath, her lips set in a line. Silence weighed in the air for several seconds.

"Are we going to let press coverage dictate police strategy, then?"

All heads turned to face the source of that comment—the wiry young female cop, Valorie Dawes, who until then hadn't spoken a word the entire meeting.

Dawes drew herself up in her chair and took a long breath before continuing. "I mean, shouldn't proper police procedure—"

"That's enough, Dawes," Petroni said, her expression darkening.

"Who the hell do you think you are?" Curtis said, seething. "And who do you think you're talking to?"

Dawes turned to face him, hazel eyes blazing, ignoring her sergeant's command. "A citizen," she said. "A well-informed one, with an unusually acute interest in—"

"I said *enough*, Dawes!" Petroni's face turned purple with rage and she stood, leaning over the table and pointing at her.

Dawes paused with her mouth open, words in mid-formation. She closed her mouth and ducked her head.

"After this morning's search of his home, I'm confident we have enough to proceed with a formal arrest this afternoon," Petroni said. "His attorney is already at the courthouse, filing motions for his release, so it's best we act fast anyway. Detective Grimes will work with the Public

Information Officer to draft a press release. Will that satisfy the mayor, Mr. Iverson?"

Curtis fought to contain his elation. He'd expected to have to fight a lot harder than this to force their hand. He wondered what evidence they'd gathered in their morning raid on the kid's home. He'd have to pull whatever insights he could from his intern, Kent Mercer, the kid's running buddy.

For now, that would have to wait. "If you can make it stick, yes, it will," he said. "Do you think he's good for most, if not all, of the 'Shoeless' murders...?"

"That I'm not able to say until we meet with the DA," Petroni said. "We'll keep the Citizens Board and the mayor's office informed. That's the best that I can offer you at the moment."

"Obviously, I'd like more, but that will do for now," he said. "If you wouldn't mind copying me on your news release...?"

"We will, sir."

Curtis shook the sergeant's hand before leaving, a limp fish of a handshake he didn't recall from their meeting two days before. So, she was pissed at him. Fine. As long as she gave him what he needed.

On his way out, while the other officers gathered up their things to leave, he overheard Petroni direct Dawes into her office. Good. The smartass deserved a dressing-down. In the meantime, the public's opinion was already forming about this case and his wife's handling of it as mayor—and how she'd handle it as governor.

Which meant that Curtis still had a lot of work to do.

***

Val followed Sergeant Petroni into her private office and pulled out a chair to sit. Petroni stopped her.

"Don't bother sitting, Dawes. This won't take long." Petroni's tone carried venom and frustration, reflected also in her facial expression.

"If this is about my remarks to Mr. Iverson—"

"Of *course* it is! What the hell were you thinking? Have you forgotten what I told you less than twenty-four hours ago?"

Val's stomach churned, her ears burning. "Y-yes, Sergeant. You said if I faced the situation of a person like Mr. Iverson interfering with the investigation, I should stand up to him—"

"I used the phrase 'kick him in the balls,' I believe," Petroni said, her face softening.

"Right. And you said that I should go ahead and kick."

"And?"

Val sat back in her seat, surprised by Petroni's forceful tone. "And...I, uh..." Her face flushed. She drooped her head, blew out a loud breath. "Take my punishment."

"Exactly. This time, I have no choice. And the punishment needs to be real."

Frustration and dread settled over Val. Petroni had winked at Val's last "transgression," which, in fairness, had been worse. Why crack her ass this time?

Petroni went on, answering the "why" question. "It's too soon after the last incident. Twice in 24 hours. I can't let it pass."

What sort of punishment? Val wondered. They couldn't demote her—she held the lowest rank in the department. Other options sprang to mind: suspension without pay, removal from the task force—

"I have to write you up," Petroni said. "A formal reprimand. Conduct unbecoming an officer and failure to follow a direct order. It'll go on your record and will come up during your annual review."

Val stared at her. "A reprimand, Sergeant?"

"Yes. Why, what'd you expect? A commendation?"

"No, but—"

"It's the first step in our progressive disciplinary path," Petroni said in a softer tone. "You don't want to reach the second step, which is suspension, or, at the Chief's discretion, anything up to termination. Clear?"

"Yes, ma'am." Val had several questions, but thought it best not to antagonize Petroni at the moment.

"Good. Get out."

Val stumbled toward the door, stunned.

"Dawes?"

Val stopped with her hand on the doorknob and half-turned toward Petroni. "Sergeant?"

"When's the last time you slept?"

Val took a heavy breath. "I get four or five hours a night...most nights."

"Have you taken a day off since you started with us?"

"On WAVE? No, but..." Val cleared her throat. "I seem to recall you saying we wouldn't have days off."

"Yeah, that sounds like me." Petroni grimaced. "I'd like to think of that as hyperbole, but...anyway. Dawes, I know you're dedicated and want to learn, but you need to take care of yourself, too. You're no good to anyone if you burn out in the first two weeks."

Val nodded and forced her body to relax a little. She hadn't eaten a proper meal since she'd started on the WAVE Squad and hadn't exercised in days. Not since—

She shook her head in wonder. The run with Beth felt like eons ago. "It's hard to find the time," she said.

"Find it," Petroni said. "That's an order."

Val shuffled out of the office and found her partner waiting at her desk.

"How far up your ass did her foot go?" Shannon asked. "Should I get you some Preparation H to ease the pain?"

"A gallon of antacid, maybe," Val said. "She's writing me up. I expected worse."

"Me, too. She must like you. Well, you'll want even more heartburn meds after what I'm about to tell you." She handed Val a report, several sheets of paper stapled together with the letterhead of the forensics team.

Val scanned the report, and her heart sank. Diego's DNA matched a sample taken from Charlene Washington.

"This alone is enough to indict," Shannon said. "Grimes and I are heading over to the DA's office now. Sorry, not you," she said. "I need you to finish writing up our findings from this morning's search of his house. Can you bang that out in the next half hour? Email me as soon as you finish. I'll fill Grimes in on the drive over."

Shannon left her with a sad smile. Val trudged over to her desk, the weight of her mistakes bearing down on her bent shoulders. Petroni's mixed messages left her bewildered and rudderless. She'd encouraged Val to stand up to Curtis Iverson's bullying and interference, then punished her for doing so.

Well, next time, Petroni could stand up to Iverson herself. Though she probably wouldn't, dammit. Then how would they—

Her cell phone buzzed. She checked Caller ID. "Amy?"

"Valorie, I'm sorry if this is a bad time. I didn't know who else to call," Amy said, sniffling.

"What's wrong?" Val's head ached. The last thing she needed at that moment was the responsibility of consoling this drama queen.

"It's Curtis," Amy said. "He's blaming me for the bad coverage the mayor got today and insinuated that I'm responsible for leaking information to the press about your investigation.”

“Information about the Shoeless murders? Why?”

“Because WCLA ran that story today,” Amy said, moaning. “I’m afraid he’s going to fire me. What am I going to do?”

“Wait, slow down.” Val glanced around the room. Dion Woodson sat at his desk about fifteen feet away, staring at his computer screen, apparently oblivious to her. Still, Val lowered her voice. “Why does he think that? Have you talked to anyone at the TV station about it?”

“I don’t know!” Amy sobbed again. “He says I should have been able to stop them from running the story. I tried to explain I was only an intern, but—hold on a sec.” A rustling sound filled Val’s ears, as if Amy had tossed her phone into a bag of hair brushes. “Sorry, I’m back. I have to be careful about who hears me.”

“Are you at the campaign office?” Val asked, alarm bells ringing.

“Yes, but I’m on my cell,” Amy said. “Is that a problem?”

“Amy, if people suspect you of leaking information about the case, it’s probably best that you don’t call me,” Val said, irritation rising in her voice. Too loud. Woodson glanced over at her, eyebrows furrowed. Val reduced her volume to a whisper. “I’ve got to go. All I can tell you about Curtis is, he’s an equal opportunity harasser. He took us to the cleaners today, too, and I’m paying for it with a reprimand. Trust me, it’ll pass. Hang in there, okay?”

“I’m so sorry. I didn’t mean to get you in any trouble. I just...well, with Kent under investigation, I didn’t think I should call him. That’d look bad, you know? So I thought, who else knows him? Diego’s not answering his phone, and, well, I’ve known you the longest, and—”

"I really have to go, Amy," Val said. "Listen, I'm sure it'll be fine. Let's talk later tonight, okay? To check in."

"Thanks, Valorie. You're the best." Amy sniffled and hung up.

Val let out a slow breath, and once again caught Woodson eyeing her. His gaze snapped back to his computer, but his interest raised Val's eyebrows. She reviewed the conversation in her head and shook it off. She'd done nothing wrong. Accepted a call of distress from a friend on her personal cell phone and ended it quickly. Nothing at all to worry about.

Why, then, did it nag at her so much?

***

Writing the summary of the team's evidence against Diego made Val's heart sink again. The drugs found in his home matched Sierra's, and Grimes had confirmed they'd come from his father's research facility in Rhode Island—missing samples of new medications undergoing clinical trials. Another felony to add to the list. The photos of the victims in his room, as well as the "shrine" to Val, spoke to an obsessive personality, which fit the Thrill Seeker profile. The "Rosie the Riveter" textbook cover linked him to the *Chingona* tattoo. The no-shoes rule in his mother's house. The similarity in build of the first five victims to his mother, which Freud would say constituted his "ideal woman," if she remembered her Psych 101. All circumstantial, but damning.

Further, while Val suffered her chewing out with Petroni, Shannon had pressed Diego about the DNA match, and he admitted to having consensual sex with Charlene. He'd withheld that information earlier because it constituted statutory rape. He had no explanation for why he'd claimed not to have seen her on the day of her death.

Worse, his cell contained the numbers of three of the six victims: Charlene, Jaden, and Sierra. His call history showed that he'd spoken by phone with each in the days leading up to their deaths—AFE-related, he claimed, in Jaden's and Charlene's cases, and "personal business" in Sierra's. Drugs, Val assumed, with a bitter taste in her mouth.

His alibis didn't hold up well, either. Tech analysis of his laptop had confirmed his claim that he'd filed his taxes online Monday evening at 9:00 p.m. from his home Wi-Fi. That left plenty of room for him to meet up with and kill Sierra.

One fact in his favor: the DNA found in Sierra's body didn't match Diego's—it matched Bo's. Shannon had squeezed Diego to admit to selling drugs to her, but his lawyer advised him not to talk any further.

Regarding Charlene being a "no show" on April 1, staff at the Claytown Cafe told Grimes and Woodson that they'd seen Diego there only once—with Val. None of them recognized Charlene from a photo. Val grimaced. Maybe he was just confused.

Or he lied. That argument seemed more and more likely.

On the dates of Jaden's and Yolanda's deaths, Diego's father confirmed that he'd stayed the weekend in Rhode Island. But the time of departure left enough wiggle room to return to Clayton in time to commit the murders. Constructing a plausible narrative of how he'd met up with them might take some doing, however.

His father confirmed they'd spent the evening of Hannah Brinkman's murder together, watching Monday Night Football, but he returned to Clayton afterward. Again, the hour of Hannah's death, in the wee hours of the morning, left open the possibility of him making it home in time to do the deed.

On the night of Olivia Lambert's death, he'd met with Charlene Washington—until 6:00 p.m. The ME established Olivia's time of death at around 2:00 a.m. Plenty of time for rape and murder.

One thing gnawed at Val, though. All of those narrow windows of opportunity left open the question of when and how he'd have gotten each victim tattooed. He was no tattoo artist. An accomplice might have done it, but who? And when?

The other weak spot, in Val's estimation, was motive for the first four murders. She could concoct a reason in Sierra's case—a drug deal gone bad—and, in Charlene's case, jealousy over the guy Gunner had mentioned, Jamal. Or rejection, or some other humiliation arising out of the sex they'd had.

Thinking of Gunner, Val shook off that explanation. Pissing off a member of one of the city's most notorious crime gangs would rank as a Grade A stupid move. Diego didn't strike her as stupid.

Plus, Thrill Seekers liked to keep mementos, if not diaries, of their victims. They also loved to publicize their acts, to the point of taunting the police with notes or symbols at the crime scene. This killer had hidden his crime scenes, and the search had found no physical evidence linking Diego to the crimes.

But her job wasn't to prosecute the case—just gather and summarize evidence. She proofread the report, saved it, and sent it to Shannon.

Their meeting would take at least another hour, and until Shannon returned, she had little else to do. Sergeant Petroni's advice rang in her ears: *Take care of yourself, Dawes.* For Valorie, that meant one thing. She grabbed her workout bag from its semi-permanent place under her desk and headed to the gym.

Ninety minutes later, she emerged from the shower, exhausted, yet exhilarated from the rush of endorphins. She'd capped off a grueling weights session with twenty minutes of pounding a heavy bag. With every punch, she imagined the face of the Shoeless Slayer—starting with Diego's. For whatever reason, it morphed into a different face every few minutes. Kent Mercer's. Curtis Iverson's. Richard Harkins, the man she'd hunted down months before. Then her own childhood attacker, "Uncle" Milt. With each shift, her fists flew with greater speed and rage, threatening to tear the bag from its moorings. She stopped only when her forearms grew too sore to continue.

Dressing at her locker, her phone rang. "We got him," Shannon announced in as happy a voice as Val had ever heard from her. "The DA wants him on all six murders, plus the drugs and rapes. They're adding mutilation, even, over the tattoos. This kid's going away for life ten times over."

"Great," Val said, but her voice reflected her lack of enthusiasm. "Does that mean we've closed the cases?"

"Sure does," Shannon said. "We're going to celebrate at the Blue Line. Petroni's buying. You coming?"

"Sure," Val said. "See you there in a half hour." She buttoned up her blouse halfway, then stopped. She peeled it off, hung it back up, and pulled a fresh set of workout clothes out of the locker. Suddenly, she wasn't quite done pounding that bag.

Chapter Twenty-Six

The following morning, Val's ringing phone woke her far too early, reverberating in wine-soaked areas of her brain she didn't know she had. Weird—she'd put her phone in "Do Not Disturb" mode the night before. Only the few listings on her "VIP" list could get through: Dad, her brother Chad, Beth, Shannon…

And Gil.

Her eyes popped open and she sprang upright. Adrenaline pumped through her body, a rush ten times that of caffeine. She blinked at the screen. Shannon. She sighed in relief. At least it wasn't another Gil emergency. "H'lo?"

"Turn on the local news," Shannon said.

Val trudged out to the living room, flicked on the TV, and tuned the set to WCLA. She lowered the volume and watched in the dark.

"…have arrested a man in the Shoeless Schoolgirl Slayer murders," the fifty-something male anchor said, his somber face aimed straight at his viewers. "Authorities also charged the suspect, twenty-one-year-old Clayton resident Diego Collier, with drug trafficking and multiple counts of mutilation and rape. The District Attorney plans to bring an indictment in front of a grand jury later today.

"The arrest comes after weeks of intense pressure on the mayor and City Council to devote greater resources to hunting down the killer. Mayor Iverson responded by creating a so-called 'WAVE

*Squad' within Clayton PD, which, sources say, led
to the arrest."*

"I don't understand. What's the big deal?" Val said, glancing at the clock. 5:15 a.m.

"Keep listening," Shannon said. "I heard this segment earlier—it gets worse."

The image on-screen had shifted to a group of protesters, chanting and marching outside the county courthouse.

"...protested downtown late last night," the reporter said. "Group representatives, who declined to be interviewed on camera, complained that authorities blamed Mr. Collier, a Black man, for the crime despite compelling evidence pointing to a white suspect, who they released without bringing charges. Back to you, Dan."

The WCLA anchor moved on to national news, something about The Ukraine. Val muted the TV, rubbed her eyes, and sat on the sofa. "Whoa," she said. "How the hell did they get that information?"

"Yeah. Exactly," Shannon said. "Petroni's pissed. She thinks you might be responsible."

"Me?" Val shouted, forgetting the early hour. "I would never—"

"I told her the same thing, but she's got a bug up her butt, and you know how stubborn she can be." Shannon lowered her voice. "Still, I have to ask. Did you speak with anyone outside the department about the case? Anyone at all? Your brother, roommate—"

"No. No one. I haven't even seen anyone since before you met with the DA yest—" Her voice caught as she remembered Amy's distressful phone call.

"What?" Shannon said. "Val? When's the last time you spoke to someone outside the task force?"

"I didn't discuss the case," Val said. "The Iverson campaign's local media coordinator is an old high school acquaintance. She called me yesterday afternoon, looking for a shoulder to cry on. I put her off, because I needed to get that report out to you. Woodson overheard me talking to her. I wonder if he misconstrued something."

"How soon can you get into the office?" Shannon said.

"Thirty to forty minutes if I can get an Uber," Val said.

"I'll pick you up in ten."

Val hung up and rushed toward the bathroom. Beth's bedroom door swung open, and she stood in Val's path, wearing a Patriots jersey that hung to the middle of her thighs. "What the effing F, Valorie?"

"Sorry for waking you," Val said. "Work emergency. I need to jump in the shower and go. I'll explain later."

Beth harrumphed and beat her to the bathroom door. "Wait. I've got to pee. Damn, I had an awesome dream going." Her voice faded behind the closing door.

Val growled and stomped back into her bedroom. By the time Beth emerged from the bathroom, four of her ten available minutes had ticked off the clock. What part of "emergency" did Beth not understand? No time to shower now, so she settled for a quick hot-water sponge-off.

Shannon's horn blared outside before Val finished getting ready. She cursed and hurried into a pair of jeans, a long-sleeve T-shirt, and slip-on flats. She could change into her uniform at the station.

Once again, Beth blocked her way. "Isn't that the cute guy you went out with a few weeks ago?" she said, pointing the remote at the TV. Diego's mugshot filled the screen with the caption: "Shoeless Schoolgirl Slayer Suspect." Dammit, how many times would they run this story?

"Really, Beth," Val said. "I have to go—"

"Do you think he's the killer?" Beth asked, wide-eyed.

"You know I can't tell you anything about that," Val said, pulling on a jacket.

"Ooh, weird," Beth said. "Did he, like, act all stalky with you or anything? Damn, girl!"

"He seemed nice enough when we had coffee," Val said. Shannon's horn blared again. Great. The neighbors must love this.

"Please tell me you never brought him here," Beth said as Val scooted out the door. "So creepy!"

Val winced at the suggestion. She'd never endanger her friend's safety, but she understood Beth's point. Living with a cop had its downsides.

So did living with Beth. Because of the distraction, she'd left her coffee-to-go on the kitchen counter.

Shannon peeled away from the curb before Val could close the car door behind her. A steady rain splashed the windshield faster than her wipers could clear it. "Check this out," Shannon said, shoving her cell phone into Val's hand.

Val scanned the article on Shannon's screen. "Iverson Campaign Staff Shake-up," the headline blared. The article reported in breathless terms that the campaign, foundering in the polls, had reorganized and released several staffers, including their new local media assistant, Amy Yang.

"Poor Amy," Val said. "That's what upset her last night. And I forgot to call her back. Crap."

"Best that you didn't, for your career's sake," Shannon said. "Keep reading."

Val did. The article huffed:

Such a move, this early in the race, suggests a campaign in disarray, struggling to define a coherent message. Despite the mayor's well-publicized recent events highlighting her strong law-and-order stance, voters surveyed struggle to associate Iverson with any specific issue as central to her candidacy.

"My guess is that the campaign leaked the arrest," Shannon said, "and sacrificed your friend. The problem is, if they're blaming her, then the mayor's going to blame you."

"But I didn't—"

"I'm not talking about what's real," Shannon said. "I'm talking about what's perceived. And this sucks for you."

They arrived at police headquarters before 6:00 a.m., the building's official time for opening up to public access. They entered through a back door to avoid the press already gathered out front and rode the slow elevator to the fourth floor in silence. Val's heart pounded in anticipation of the confrontation awaiting her.

"Tell the truth, and you'll be fine," Shannon said. She led the way to the WAVE Squad office door and found it unlocked, lights shining through the top half of the door's semi-transparent acrylic panel.

"There she is." Sergeant Petroni rose from a sitting position against the edge of the long black table occupying the center of the room. Two fifty-ish men in black suits and crew cuts stood on either side of her, their expressions grim. One stood at least six-five, and both looked like they ate wild tigers for breakfast.

"I'm Inspector Blanchard, Internal Affairs," the taller of the two men said. "This is my partner, Inspector Finley. Can we have a few minutes of your time, Officer Dawes?"

Val nodded, tight-lipped, too nervous to speak. She glanced over to Shannon for support, but she had already turned to follow Petroni into the sergeant's office.

The two IA men escorted Val into a small meeting room and shut the door. Val sat at one end of the six-foot rectangular table. Finley stood near the door, leaning against the wall. Blanchard wandered the cramped, stuffy room. Chairs took up most of the space not occupied by the table. A whiteboard filled the wall opposite the door. Small framed posters spouted the department's Mission, Vision, and Goals statements and anti-discrimination policy—all of which, in Val's experience, were honored mostly in the breach.

"Sh-should I have a lawyer present, or a union rep, or something?" Val wrapped one hand around the other to keep them from shaking.

"If you'd like, sure," Blanchard said, smiling. "But things will go more smoothly for everyone if we can just talk a little."

"Sergeant Petroni assures us you wouldn't do anything to harm the investigation," Finley said. "On purpose, anyway."

Val glared at him, but said nothing.

"Think of this as tidying up some loose ends," Blanchard said.

"Filling in the gaps," Finley added.

Val's heart filled her throat. Her uncle had told her stories of how IA worked. "They're detectives, too," he'd said. "But instead of hunting down criminals, they hunt down bad cops. And in their eyes, all cops are bad cops."

Val glanced from one to the other, wishing she'd remembered to grab a cup of coffee before heading out with Shannon. After her initial rush of adrenaline, fatigue had returned, filling her mind with fog and confusion.

"We understand you spoke with a member of the Iverson campaign late yesterday afternoon," Blanchard said in a somber tone. "Would you care to fill us in on what you talked about?"

"We just want to know what happened," Finley said, his voice friendly. "Hey, it's early. I bet you could use some coffee, eh?"

"That would be awesome."

"Steve, go find us all a cuppa Joe." Blanchard smiled at Val. "Without my morning brew, I'm useless."

Val nodded. Finley, a solid block of a man with a ruddy face and short, white hair, grumped but slid out of the room.

"While we're waiting," Blanchard said, "tell me about Amy Yang. You guys went to school together, or something?"

Just tell the truth, Shannon had advised. And this question seemed harmless enough. "H-high school," Val said. "I don't know her well."

"She seems like a bright girl," Blanchard said.

Val nodded. "She's an intelligent woman."

Blanchard chuckled and tapped the side of his head. *Woman*. Right. I still get that wrong sometimes. I'm a, whattayacallit, a little old-school." He laughed. "Okay, I'm a chauvinist pig, according to my wife. But I'm working on it."

Val glanced at his left hand. Wedding ring. At least he hadn't lied about being married.

"So, you and Amy, you socialize sometimes?"

Val shook her head. "Not really."

"No?" Blanchard's face curled in confusion. "That's weird. She called you yesterday, right? I mean, we're not saying you called her, or anything."

"You're correct, Inspector. I didn't call her." Val chose her words carefully. "Is this meeting being recorded?"

"Call me Tony." He extended his hand and smiled.

"Tony." She didn't accept the handshake. "Again. Is this on the record?"

"Well, we're not into the formal part of anything yet," Blanchard said. "So there isn't any 'record' to speak of, at this point."

"I'll take that as a yes," Val said.

Blanchard waited, again not responding. Val remained quiet. Two could play this game.

"So, *she* called *you*, then?" Blanchard said after a long pause. "Does she do that often? Do you, say, go for drinks, or coffee, or go clubbing, stuff like that? 'Girls night' or whatever it's called?"

"We've had coffee once or twice."

"And you talked at Iverson campaign events, where you worked security detail?"

Val's breath caught in her throat. How in the hell—?

Before she could answer, Finley returned and set three black coffees on the table. Val grabbed one and took a much-needed sip. Bitter and acrid, but welcome. In an instant, it seemed, clarity inched back into her consciousness.

Blanchard sipped his coffee. "Amy's dating a guy, what's his name...?" He searched his memory, or pretended to. Val waited.

"Kenny," Finley said. "Kenny Mercer."

"Kent," Val said.

"Kent?" Finley repeated.

"Mercer. His name's Kent, not Kenny," Val said. Crap! Too late, she realized her mistake. They'd trapped her into admitting that she knew details about Amy's personal life. Their exchange of glances confirmed they'd caught it, too. Dread crept over her.

"Right, Kent Mercer," Blanchard said. "You know him, then?"

"You know that, or you wouldn't be asking," Val said. "I interrogated him Tuesday afternoon."

"You knew him before that, though, right?" Blanchard said. "Through Amy Yang."

"No. I mean, yes, we'd met, but not—" She stopped and took a deep breath. "It's time we brought in my union rep."

Finley sighed. "Sorry, the union rep doesn't start work until seven. That's a good hour-plus from now."

"I think we could get this whole thing over with in less than an hour," Blanchard said, again in a friendly tone of voice. "Far less. Ten, fifteen minutes."

"That's okay," Val said. "I can wait."

"Might be longer," Finley said. "Maybe seven-thirty, eight o'clock by the time he gets in, clears his schedule, gets over here."

"If at all," Blanchard said, nodding. "I've seen where they're already booked all day with other meetings. Meanwhile, we sit here, twiddling our thumbs."

"And all that time, the leaks continue," Finley said. "Where if we just talked, we could sort all of that out in no time."

"Of course, if you don't want to cooperate, that's your choice," Blanchard said.

"No skin off our nose," Finley said.

"Good," Val said. "Let's wait, then." She sipped her coffee, already getting cold.

Finley frowned at Blanchard, who swirled the coffee around in his cup, checked his watch.

"This is such a shame," Blanchard said. "A mess. I mean, all the buzz around here is about what a great cop you've been."

"Like your uncle," Finley said. "Here you are, following in his footsteps, becoming a detective."

Val rolled her eyes. So transparent, these two guys, trying to soften her up by praising her uncle. No way she'd fall for that.

"I hear you're an exceptional profiler," Blanchard said. "Petroni says your work on that really pushed the case forward."

Val shrugged, but the compliment made her feel better.

"Said you didn't think they should be looking at Collier," Finley said. "That they only like him 'cause he's Black."

Val started to object, stopped before taking the bait.

"Do you think we've got the wrong guy?" Finley asked. "Off the record. Come on, we all have opinions. I'm not so sure about it, myself, y'know?"

Val sipped her coffee, the slow burn in her gut twice as warm as the contents of her cup.

Seconds ticked by in silence. A minute. Two.

Blanchard stood, stretched, and sighed. "Okay, I get it. Well, I don't think we'll waste our time, sticking around here, waiting hours and hours for the union rep."

"Complete waste of time," Finley said, finishing his coffee and tossing the cup in the trash.

"We'll file our report with what we know, and move on," Blanchard said. "Want to recap it for us, Steve?"

"Sure," Finley said. "Amy Yang, Dawes's old high school friend, calls yesterday right before Dawes sends her evidence summary to the DA. Later that night, the news leaks about the arrest of Diego Collier, who you'd been dating—"

"That's not true!"

The two men paused, exchanged glances again. "Oh, yeah. You young people don't date anymore," Blanchard said.

"You 'hang out,' is the current phrase," Finley said.

"Diego and I don't 'hang out,' or date, or anything," Val said, then admonished herself: Shut up!

Blanchard smiled. "See, that's the type of thing we need cleared up," he said. "That's why we need you to cooperate. To correct those misperceptions."

"I'll share everything once my union rep—"

"Oh, screw this," Blanchard said, throwing his coffee cup toward the trash can. He hadn't finished, and coffee splashed the wall and floor. Unperturbed by this, he pointed his chin at the door. "Let's go, Finley. Wait here, Dawes."

The two men slipped out, leaving Val alone with her paranoid thoughts.

***

After a few long minutes passed, Shannon pushed the door open and sat catty-corner from her at the table. "You're toast," she said to Val. "What in the hell did you say to them?"

"What do you mean?" Val said. "I didn't tell them anything."

"Those two meatheads barged into Petroni's office, kicked me out, and closed the door," Shannon said. "They referred to you as Janelle Monáe, that protest rapper. Which, despite what my teenage kids think, isn't a compliment around here."

Hot tears stung Val's eyes. Her throat tightened, making speech difficult. "As in, I'm singing to the public?"

Shannon nodded, a grim expression on her face. "With a message that isn't very welcome in these halls."

Val collapsed into her chair, a heavy weight crushing her shoulders. "Shannon, I didn't do it. I swear." A moment later, panic struck, and her heart raced. "Is this going to splash back on you, as my partner?"

Shannon stared at her, saying nothing.

"Fuck," Val said in a whisper.

"Here's the problem," Shannon said. "It comes on top of too many other...*issues* that have come up lately. Things that make you look...less like a team player. It's going to make it hard to scrape you out of this."

"What issues?" Val sat upright, her face tense. This can't be happening. "I've worked my ass off on this case."

Shannon sighed. "Yeah. Well, things have...happened. I may or may not have informally shared some details with Petroni, who's been asking for updates on how you're coming along in your training, and—"

"*What?*" Val shrieked, the sound of it piercing her own skull like an icepick. "You've been blackballing me with the boss? Seriously?"

"Not blackballing," Shannon said. "Just...updating her. On, let's call them, your more teachable moments, and how I'm—"

"Ratting me out for my mistakes!"

Shannon paused, took a breath or two. "Petroni took a risk, bringing a rookie cop on board to the city's most visible and sensitive investig—"

"So now I'm a bad *risk*?" Val seethed, disbelief flowing over her. "Is that your professional opinion of me?"

"Val," Shannon said. "It's not like that. I tell her the good and the bad—and mostly it's good. You're a hell of a cop. I wish we had ten more like you."

"Sure," Val said, sarcasm lacing her words. "With ten of me, we'd be a much less *risky* bet. Makes *perfect* sense!"

"You're making it hard to help you right now," Shannon said. "Which I really want to do."

"Sure, sure," Val said. "With your help, I'll be well on my way to my new career in shopping mall security. Paula Blart the Second."

"Maybe it'd teach you to follow orders!" Shannon glared at Val.

"When have I not followed orders?" Val said, her tone more demanding than she intended. "Specifically?"

Shannon took a deep breath and met her gaze. "All right, I'll bite," she said. "When I wanted you to take pictures of Dr. Bray's file—"

"That was illegal!"

"No, it wasn't. You didn't just refuse—you were sneaky about it." Shannon's voice grew steely and cold. "Had I known you had a problem with it, I'd have done it myself. Now we don't have the data. And another thing. You went cowboy with Curtis Iverson—not once, but twice, even after I called you out on it. Put him on a rampage against us. How the hell does that help the team?"

"He was covering up—"

"Maybe. Maybe not. You don't get to decide that all by yourself, Val. We're a team—you and me, as partners, and the whole WAVE Squad. We need to work together. No rogue operators. Got it?"

Val, stunned by the uncharacteristic bluntness from her soft-spoken partner, opened her mouth to reply, but could form no words.

"The upshot," Shannon said, "is that you've created an image for yourself of being a solo operator—not a team player. Normally, that'd just be my problem, as your partner. As a mentor, I can deal with it by pointing out better ways of going about things. But when shit like this hits the fan...I can't defend you, Val. I'm sorry. It's not that I don't want to. I just can't."

Val stared at Shannon, long and hard. This woman she'd admired, had been thrilled one week before to get the chance to work with and learn from, transformed in front of her eyes into a scheming turncoat. Someone who Val had thought would have her back, but instead, sold her out to the suspicious, scapegoating bureaucracy.

"Get away from me," Val said in a hoarse whisper. "If you're going to sell me down the river, I'd rather drown alone than have you fit me for new cement shoes."

"Val, I—"

"I said get out!" Val tore her eyes away from her partner's sad face. She wasn't buying that remorseful act, not for a minute. She stared at the black tabletop until Shannon's footsteps sounded across the floor, followed by the slam of the door closing behind her.

When she looked up, Sergeant Petroni appeared, leaning her stout frame against the wall by the door.

"Sergeant, I didn't hear you come in."

"Of course you didn't," Petroni said. "You were too busy throwing out the only person who's been arguing your case for the past hour. You ever heard the phrase, 'don't bite the hand that feeds you,' Dawes?"

"Feeds me to the wolves, you mean," Val said. "Running to you with stories of every mistake I've made—"

"Dawes, stop it!" Petroni took two long strides and leaned over the table, her face reddening and towering over Val's. "She did nothing of the sort. I asked for her daily evaluations of how you're doing. Most of it was positive. Okay? So stop blaming Shannon for your problems. You brought this on yourself, and you need to own it."

Val let Petroni's words sink in, confirming that she was, in fact, in trouble. "So. IA says I'm the leak, and you believe it, because I'm not a 'team player,' is that it?"

"No. I don't believe it." Petroni's voice softened, and she sat across from Val. "But I can't do much about it. They don't work for me, Dawes. They work for the chief, and he works for the mayor. And guess who wants your ass on a plate?"

A fresh wave of fear, this one mixed with revulsion, washed over Val. "This is all political?"

"One. Hundred. Percent." Petroni held out her hands. "It's horrible, but that's how this works."

"So...what, then? I'm suspended? Or...fired?"

Petroni sighed. "Internal Affairs has enough data to put you under suspicion, so they say. Not enough to get you suspended, and a long, *long* way from fired. With the report they're filing, though, I can't keep you on the case. I just can't."

The weight of Petroni's words landed like sandbags on Val's shoulders. "So, I'm...off the WAVE Squad, then?"

Petroni nodded. "I'll let Lieutenant Gibson know. You'll be reassigned back to Liberty Heights. I suggest you take the rest of today off, because you haven't been off the clock since you started here, and show up there tomorrow morning." She straightened and stepped toward the door. "I'm sorry, Dawes."

Val nodded, an aching burn torching her throat. "Yeah," she said in a hoarse voice, "me too."

The door closed behind Petroni. The fluorescent lights, recessed into the ceiling, flickered and buzzed. After a few moments, both of the long, silvery tubes burned out, shrouding the room in chilly darkness.

PART THREE

GOING ROGUE

Chapter Twenty-Seven

Val followed Petroni's advice—advice that sounded more like orders—and clocked out, avoiding eye contact with Shannon, Dion Woodson, and Detective Grimes, each of whom busied themselves at their desks. She stuffed her few personal possessions into her gym bag and ran down all four flights of stairs and out of the building. She didn't even break a sweat. But the exertion made her light-headed, and reminded her that she hadn't eaten a single morsel all morning.

She checked the time: 6:20 a.m. She needed comforting, both from friends and from food. Too early to call Gil, so that left one option.

Claytown Café at 7? she texted.

To her joyous surprise, Beth answered her text in seconds: *See you there!* By the time Val hopped off the bus in front of the funky diner, Beth had already secured a private table in the back.

Pinkie greeted her with a grin and an attempted hug, which Val evaded by pretending to move out of the way of another customer entering the restaurant. Nonplussed, Pinkie grabbed Val by the arm and dragged her to Beth's table, chattering nonstop. "Val-Pal! It's been, like, forever and a half, girlio! I was beginning to think you'd found another barista," she said. "Cinnacino, right?"

"Missed you, too, Pin—er, Alexa," Val said. "Yes to the cinnamon cappuccino, with two percent milk."

"Regular coffee, plenty of cream, please," Beth said.

"Awesome! I'll get that going, pronto pony." Pinkie buzzed off, singing some Broadway tune in what sounded like perfect pitch, though Val couldn't tell with the café's awful acoustics.

"Thanks for coming, Beth," Val said once she'd taken a seat. Her dour mood lifted a little, a combination of Pinkie's goofiness and the comfort of seeing her lifelong friend. "So, Josh wasn't up for cooking you an early breakfast today?"

Beth shrugged. "He's still asleep. So, tell me, what's the 9-1-1? You never call before breakfast unless something big's going down, and even then…nope, never." Her eyes narrowed, and she grabbed Val's arm. "Spill."

Val sighed. "I…got kicked off the WAVE Squad this morning. For a bullshit charge of leaking that story we saw on TV."

"What? That's crazy!" Beth sat back in the booth, shaking her head. "You'd never do that."

"Thanks. I wish they'd take your word for it."

"Want me to go down and kick a few butts?" Beth said, making a fist.

Val laughed. "Yes! I'll give you a list of names." Her mood lifted a little. If nothing else, she'd always have Beth in her corner.

"I stayed up and watched the news when you dashed out this morning," Beth said after Pinkie delivered their coffees. "What a picture they painted of him! Weird, because he sounded like a decent guy, from what you told me."

Val sighed. "I thought so, too, at first," she said. "Part of me still thinks so."

"Is he getting a bum rap, then?" Beth said.

"I'm…not sure." Val glanced around to make sure no one could overhear. "Let's just say, I have doubts."

Pinkie returned, and they ordered breakfast—scrambled egg whites and a fruit cup for Beth, a Mediterranean omelet for Val. When Pinkie had moved out of earshot, Beth leaned in and lowered her voice. "So, how did the story leak, then? What's your theory?"

"You remember Amy Yang from high school? She works for the Iverson campaign."

"Sure," Beth said. "What's she doing, getting mixed up in politics? Amy seemed smarter and more innocent than that."

"She called me the other day. The next thing you know, her old boss at WCLA-TV is running this big exposé on how we only arrested Diego because he's Black. I didn't tell her a thing, but this entire episode makes me wonder who I can trust anymore."

"What kind of rat would pull a stunt like that?" Beth said. "Girlfriend, I don't blame you for being mad. This person who complained—is it someone who you confided in?"

"It's not just one person," Val said. "Sergeant Petroni went along with the Internal Affairs creeps, and my new partner, on a number of occasions, didn't have my back— including this time. The mayor's husband seems to have it in for me, and you know how things ended with Rico. And Pops, before him. The only guy I can fully trust in the department these days is Gil, and because of me, he's in the hospital."

"You can't keep blaming yourself for Gil's situation," Beth said. "I know how much you care about him, but he put himself back in the ER, not you."

Val shook her head, moping. "He wouldn't have gotten shot in the first place if not for me."

"Valorie." Beth cast an admonishing glare over her coffee cup. "You'd have taken a bullet for him, right? So let him take one for you."

Val sighed. Beth didn't understand. "Gil can't do anything for me now. Not from a hospital bed. Besides, he's no better at office politics than I am."

"I thought politics benefited you, in this case," Beth said. "Didn't the mayor ask you to be on this task force?"

"Insisted on it," Val said, her tone dour. "But her husband hates me."

"How'd you piss Curtis Iverson off?" Beth said. "He's a dangerous enemy to have, especially with Megan on the rise."

"A few of the victims interned at his firm," Val said. "Shannon and I started asking questions, and boom! The hammer comes crashing down, and he blames me. And…he's a bully. Inserts himself into our investigation, shouts to get his way when his mealy-mouthed 'charm' doesn't work, and plays the 'mayor's husband' card whenever someone pushes back on him. He's an asshole."

Beth shook her head. "It sounds to me like you just don't like the man."

"And you do?" Val's mood soured. She'd expected more support from Beth. She missed the days when Beth would have her back, no questions asked—finishing her sentences, if not her unspoken thoughts. Why all this pushback?

"Alexa?" Beth said to the approaching barista. "Could I please get a warm-up on my coffee?"

"Sure. Call me Pinkie," the barista said, setting their plates on the table. "Everyone does."

Val, noticing the tiny smattering of egg whites on her plate, swapped dishes with Beth.

"Oh, so sorreee!" Pinkie said, hands pressed to her cheeks. "I totally got that backwards, didn't I?"

"Don't worry about it," Beth said, laughing. "Everybody thinks Val must eat like a bird to stay so skinny, but I'm the one that has to fit into a size 10 wedding dress in August."

Pinkie's mouth gaped wide. "Really? Oh, that's cooler than a school full of jewels!" She raced around behind Beth and wrapped her in a suffocating hug. Beth laughed and pulled Pinkie closer in an awkward, backward embrace.

Val had grown accustomed to Pinkie's oddball expressiveness. Even so, this one surprised her. She scooped a chunk of Greek omelet onto her fork. But the manners her father had pounded into her forbade her from taking a bite until Beth could, too. Instead, she stared at her plate, then at her cappuccino, then at the two women again.

How different they were—from each other, and from Val. Pinkie, the free spirit, said whatever popped into her mind, and seemed to have no ambition beyond making friends with every customer who entered her shop. Beth, the boy-crazy, loyal friend, craved her material possessions and found bliss in everything suburban and middle-class. And Val…what was she? How did she come across to them, and to her colleagues? Like a crusader, she guessed. Too serious about everything. Passionate only about her work, blind to the other pleasures in life. Guarded. Even a little angry, perhaps.

Val shook herself out of that train of thought. She had her virtues. Intelligence, loyalty as fierce as Beth's, intuition, and perceptiveness. Like right now, seeing the differences between the two hugging women. Beth, curvy, with a wide smile and perfect, tanned skin, lending her a sexy beauty that attracted all those boys she was crazy about. Pinkie, with her pale, skinny body decorated with piercings and colorful tattoos of all kinds—

Tattoos!

"Pinkie," Val said, "I was wondering. Where do you get your work done?" Val indicated her own arms and neck, whose counterparts on Pinkie were ninety percent inked in colorful, elaborate designs.

"Oh, I love my artist," Pinkie said. "Remind me before you go and I'll get you his name. Topher's the best!" She wiggled away to another table, whose impatient patrons seemed about ready to leave without paying.

Val dug into her omelet while Beth picked at her egg whites. "I'd starve if I only ate such a small amount," Val said. "How do you do it?"

"I need to drop two dress sizes by August," Beth said. "You do what you have to do for love and vanity. And hey, it's working. I already lost enough to fit into my old prom dress."

"Why would you even know that?" Val asked. Since she'd never attended a prom, she had no gown to fit back into.

"Because I'm wearing it to the reunion next Friday," Beth said. "What are you wearing?"

"What reunion?" Val said.

"Our five-year, silly," Beth said. "I know you got the invitation. I'm on the committee."

Val rolled her eyes and took another bite of omelet. The savory flavors of fresh feta cheese, sun-dried tomato, spinach, and black olives blended into salty perfection in her mouth. "Must've slipped my mind. I have to work—uh, well. Maybe not anymore."

"Please come!" Beth said. "It'll be fun, and you need a change of scenery. Josh can find you a date—"

"No!" Val said, waving her arms in front of her face. "No more blind dates with his friends. That last guy, Mr. Octopus, is lucky he only went home with crushed testicles."

"Don't remind me," Beth said. "Josh almost broke up with me over that."

"It was your first date!"

"Was it?" Beth said in a dreamy voice. "Time flies when you're in love."

"Yuck."

"Don't like the eggs?" Beth smirked.

"I'm not bringing a date."

"Stag is fine," Beth said. "There are a few guys coming alone, too. Remember that guy Nicky from English class?"

"Nicky who?"

"Evans. Never mind, he's not your type. We'll hook up with all the old gang and make it a group thing," Beth said. "Come on, Val. You need this more than anybody."

Val sighed. A change of pace might be just the thing, as a matter of fact.

***

Val waved goodbye to Beth outside Claytown Café and headed toward their apartment at a brisk pace. Beth offered to drive her, but Val begged off. "You'll be late for work, and I could use the walk," she said. The crisp air, freshened by an overnight rain, felt good inside her lungs. Moments later, the sun peeked out behind the dark gray clouds enough to take the edge off the chill. She yearned for a talk with Gil, but 8:00 a.m. still seemed too early. Perhaps after a nice, hot shower—

Her cell phone buzzed in her pocket. She checked Caller ID and groaned. She considered sending the call straight to voicemail, then resisted the impulse. Amy wouldn't call this early without a good reason. Besides, Val had a few things to say to her, too.

"Valorie!" Amy said between sobs. "It happened, like I said it would. Curtis fired me!"

Val sighed. When had she become Amy's crying shoulder? "I'm sorry to hear that, Amy," she said. "Did he say why?"

"He didn't have to say," Amy said. "I know why."

"The BS about the leaks?" Val asked.

"That's the official reason," Amy said. "Not the real one."

Val stopped at a "Don't Walk" signal and caught her breath. She hadn't paid attention to how fast she'd been walking. Her frustration with Amy's melodrama had led to an unnecessary quickening of her pace. "So, what's the real reason?"

"I shouldn't tell you over the phone," Amy said. "It's…sensitive. Can we meet somewhere and talk?"

The "Walk" signal blinked at her, but Val stayed rooted in her spot, undecided on how to proceed. "Are you sure I'm the right person to talk to?" she said. "What about Kent? Aren't you two still dating?"

"Kent's at class, with his phone off," Amy said, crying again. "And he still works for Curtis, both at Constitution Finance, and at the campaign. I don't want to put him in a tough spot, and truthfully, I'm not sure if I can trust him."

"Amy, I have to confess," Val said. "I'm a little hesitant. Your calling me at work yesterday got me in a lot of trouble. They think I leaked the story—to you."

"What? That's so crazy! Oh, Valorie, I'm sooo sorry!" Amy burst into tears again, sending pangs of guilt through Val's heart.

Val sighed. Hearing Amy's story might shed some light on whether and why Curtis Iverson had set them both up for this. "Okay. Come to my place. I'll brew us up some tea."

Val texted her the address and changed her mind about walking. She needed to straighten up the apartment before Amy arrived. Her Uber app showed a car a few blocks away. She climbed into a silver VW Jetta a minute later.

"Hey, I've gotten a ride from you before," she said to the driver, a bearded twenty-something with dark eyes. The tips of his dark brown hair peeked out from under his knit cap.

"Did you give me five stars?" he asked, smiling. "I'd remember you if you did."

"I promise I will, this time," Val said. "If you hurry."

He did, driving in silence through the busy city streets. She caught him eying her a few times. Damned creepy Uber drivers. She avoided eye contact for the rest of the ride. So much for five damned stars.

Twenty minutes later, Amy curled up on Val's couch, sipping green tea from a giant ceramic mug. Val sat across from her, hands wrapped around a matching blue mug. Beth's stuff, like the modern art prints on the walls and the TV—hell, the sofa itself. All stuff she'd have to replace when Beth moved out in a few months.

"So, you said Curtis had a—how should I say this? An ulterior motive for firing you?" Val asked.

Amy nodded and wiped fresh tears away from her cheeks. "Last night, after I called you," she said in a halting voice, "Curtis came to the campaign office. I was working late, trying to limit the damage from the press leaks. I was on the phone with my former boss at WCLA when he arrived." She took another sip of her tea and fell silent.

"And?" Val said, patience already eroding.

"Curtis waved me into his office," Amy said. "I...thought maybe his mood had improved. He smiled at me, even gave me a 'thumbs-up' when he realized what I was up to."

"That wasn't the case?"

"Well...kind of." Amy dipped her head and took a deep breath, then met Val's gaze. "When I stepped inside his office, before I could say a word, he said I needed to drive him somewhere. He said not to worry about anything—the leaks, I guess he meant—and that we'd work it all out. I was so happy, I almost cried."

"Where did he want you to take him?" Val said, trying to move the narrative along.

"He didn't say, at first," Amy said, tears welling again. "He asked me if I'd had dinner. I said no, and he said we should 'fix' that. That confused me, because I thought he needed to go somewhere specific, right away, and this seemed...out of the way, you know?"

"So, where did you go?" Val said.

"I thought maybe he had a dinner meeting with a campaign donor. I'd driven him to one of those meetings before. A steak place on Hartford Avenue. I headed in that direction, but he gave me directions to that new condo building on the waterfront."

"Trillium Towers? The one with that fancy Italian place on the first floor?" Val asked. A place she'd never tried—too pricey.

"That's the one," Amy said, and set down her empty mug. "But instead of going in to dinner, he headed straight to the elevator. He said he'd get 'room service,' and laughed, like it was a joke, like we were in a fancy hotel or something. I didn't understand what was going on, so I sort of laughed too, and rode up to the fifteenth floor with him."

"A residential floor."

"He asked me what I wanted for dinner. I was nervous...I asked for a salad. He laughed and said, 'Oh, that's how you stay so skinny. You should have some pasta, get some meat on those bones.' So...weird, you know?"

Val nodded, already growing suspicious. "You went inside with him?"

Amy sipped her tea, seeming to struggle with her explanation. "I'd...been there once before. With Kent. Our, uh, first time." She blushed. "I thought the room was Kent's. He had seemed so comfortable in the space. Then Kent explained it was 'a friend's' place—a 'work-from-home office.' He didn't elaborate. I never imagined it was Curtis Iverson's."

Val stared open-mouthed at Amy. "How freaky! Did Curtis know that you and Kent had, ah, been there together before?"

"If he did, he didn't show it," Amy said. "At first, I thought it couldn't be Curtis's, either. I asked him whose place it was, and he gave me a funny look. 'Do I strike you as a man who would bring you to another man's home?' he said. At that point, I was so embarrassed, I kind of missed what he meant by 'bring me home.'" Amy set down her tea, curled into a ball on the couch, and buried her face in her hands. Tears slid down her nose and wet her chin.

Val fidgeted, waiting. A good friend would sit by Amy's side, hold her, tell her everything would turn out all right. Tell her she's not an idiot for "going home" with Curtis and expecting an innocent evening of talking politics.

But Val and Amy had never been close friends. And Val was no hugger, no soft shoulder to cry on. She'd never developed that skill, or never got the Good Friend gene in her DNA. Even with Beth.

She could feel Amy's pain and identify with it. Like nearly every woman she knew, Val had her own tale of victimization at the hands of a more powerful man. A tale she shared with very few people. So few, she could count them on the fingers of one hand.

And where had that gotten her? Had carrying that pain around inside of her made her a healthier, happier person? Tougher, perhaps. More resilient, maybe.

Or perhaps what she'd always counted as one of her strengths actually weakened her. Weighed her down. Made her slower to understand other people's needs. The needs of friendship, connection...and love.

She wiped away a tear.

Wait. A *tear*? She was *crying*? Over one of the most annoying people she'd ever met?

Damn.

She slid across the narrow gap between them and rested her hand on Amy's side. "Hey, Amy," she said. "Take your time. I'm...I'm here for you."

In a flash, Amy sat up and threw her arms around Val's neck, crushing her in a tight hug. "Thank you, Valorie," she said. "You're such a good friend." She squeezed Val again and rocked her body side to side. "It means so much to me that you're taking the time to listen. Thank you, thank you." Another tight squeeze, followed by a series of calming, heavy breaths.

Val patted Amy's back and pulled out of the embrace. Her body shook, as if *she'd* suffered the trauma instead of Amy. "What happened inside the condo?" she asked when Amy's breathing calmed.

"It was…kind of weird," Amy said. "Curtis asked me to…take off my shoes. Kent had asked me the same thing. With Kent it kind of made sense, it being someone else's apartment, with white carpet and all. With Curtis it felt…kind of creepy."

"No doubt," Val said, shuddering. "Then what?" When Amy paused, Val panicked a bit and rushed her words. "If you don't feel comfortable telling me—"

"No, no, it's all right. I want to," Amy said. "I left my shoes by the door. Curtis gave me a tour of the place, and he kept…*touching* me. At first it seemed accidental—his hand brushed my arm or my back, and I'd move away, and nothing happened. It felt weird, because I'd spent half the night there about a week before. I didn't tell him that, in case Kent would get in trouble. Then he wanted to show me the bedroom." Amy pressed her clenched hands against her cheeks. "I didn't want to go in there, so I said, 'What about the dinner with your clients?' He laughed and said we had plenty of time. Stupid me, I *still* trusted him."

"I take it you never got dinner," Val said.

"He put his hand on my waist and guided me into the 'office space,' which turned out to be another bedroom," Amy said, dropping her hands. "I tried to stop him. He kind of pushed me in with his body. Like, he put his body right up against mine. Not in any sort of *accidental* way. In a…" Amy gagged. "Sexual way. I could feel his…*thing*, you know, pressing into me. Then he put both arms around me from behind and tried to kiss me. I—I broke free and moved away from him. It was an enormous bedroom, so I got a good ten or fifteen feet away. I said, 'Curtis, I have a boyfriend. I hope I didn't give you the wrong idea.' He said it wasn't the wrong idea, it was a great idea—something like that. He chased after me, grabbed at me. Somehow I got away. I couldn't get to the door, but I hid in the big walk-in closet and locked the door behind me. He said something like 'I like this game!' Valorie, it terrified me."

"I bet," Val said. She'd hung on Amy's every word, her own sense of terror rising, imagining herself in the same situation. The dreadful memory of being assaulted by a large, powerful man flooded over her. But Amy had one advantage that twelve-year-old Val hadn't had: the opportunity to escape. "Were you able to…fend him off?" Val asked.

"Better than that," Amy said. "I discovered it was a walk-through to the master bathroom. It took me a minute to get out of there because I stumbled over some shoes on the floor. Curtis caught up to me out in the main corridor, near the elevator. That's when he fired me."

"Just like that?" Val asked. "That's outrageous!"

"Not exactly," Amy said. "First, he tried to get me back into the condo. I threatened to scream, and he changed his whole demeanor. He apologized for coming on to me, said he 'misread my signals' and that it wouldn't happen again. That he had canceled his client meeting, because he needed to talk to me, which of course I didn't believe. He said he was concerned about the leaks, and that he couldn't trust me anymore," Amy said. "He said he'd hoped we could have worked it out, but with what had just happened, he didn't see how we could. Then we heard people coming, and he got nervous, you know? He let me leave. Then he texted me, saying it'd be best if I resigned—better for my career than getting fired."

"That's a textbook case of sexual harassment!" Val said, taking Amy's hand. "Amy, you can fight this. You can't let him get away with it."

Amy shook her head. "I want nothing to do with him, or that campaign," Amy said. "I'd rather put it behind me and move on. Besides, even if I wanted to fight him, I'd never win. He's so powerful and well-connected."

"That's how people like him stay powerful!" Val caught herself, took the sting out of her tone. "What about the next young woman he hires? You don't want him to victimize her, do you?"

"How would I prove it? We were alone…I went there willingly…he could paint this as me having cold feet at the last minute. I'd be dragged through the mud. No, thank you." Amy pulled away from Val and folded her arms across her chest.

Val sighed. She couldn't argue with Amy's characterization of the incident, or of how Curtis might frame it. Still, she couldn't quite give up yet. "Mr. Iverson was your boss," she said. "He'd told you it was a business meeting, and he used his power to trap you. Any halfway decent lawyer could make that case."

"Yeah, one I can't afford," Amy said. "No thanks."

Val clenched her teeth in frustration. "So, what sort of help are you asking for here?"

"Can't you, like, arrest him or something?"

Val smiled, a weak one constrained by her sadness and frustration. "Not unless you file a complaint. Even then, I doubt my bosses would back me up, for the same reasons you're reluctant to fight him."

"Didn't he break the law?" Amy said.

Val sighed. "We have to prove it," she said. "That starts with you."

Amy folded her legs against her body and wrapped her arms around them. "I'll have to think about that." She sat in silence for several seconds, resting her chin on her knees. "I wish Kent were here. He'd know what to do."

Val turned away so Amy couldn't see her roll her eyes. "Don't be so sure about that. Look, why don't you think about this for a day or so? Whatever you decide, I'll do what I can to help you. Okay?"

Amy sprang forward, wrapping her thin arms around Val. "Thank you, thank you, thank you!" she said, crushing Val in yet another suffocating hug. "You're the best. I knew I could count on you!"

Val fought off the urge to push Amy away and instead patted her back. She even murmured reassuring syllables, that things would all work out all right, but she didn't believe her own words. Like Val, Amy had made a powerful enemy in Curtis, and Val had no clue how to help her fight him.

Chapter Twenty-Eight

A tearful yet much-calmer Amy departed Val's place ten minutes later, and Val soon grew restless hanging out alone in her apartment. She tried burning off some steam by cleaning the kitchen. That didn't fill the need. Not when she'd also neglected so many other parts of her life by overdoing it at work.

Time to rectify that.

Uncle Val had willed her a Honda Civic, new when he'd bought it twelve years before, before his untimely death on Val's thirteenth birthday. For lifestyle and cost reasons, she left it parked in her father's garage. Chad often warned her that letting the car sit idle for too long would invite trouble: dead battery, condensation in the gas tank, brittle belts breaking, and worse. Today seemed like a perfect day to give it some air.

She caught a bus to her dad's house and, to her relief, the car started on the first try. Dad's Ford was missing from the driveway. Meaning, she hoped, that he'd gone to an Alcoholics Anonymous meeting or some other productive endeavor and not back to rehab.

Val drove to the suburban dojo where she'd earned a black belt in jiu jitsu five years before. She signed up to resume her training, something she'd been meaning to do for over a year. She even engaged in a brief refresher lesson, enough to break a sweat and to prove to herself how rusty she'd gotten.

As often happened, the workout cleared away the clutter in her brain and restored her focus. Showering afterward at home, she went over missing clues in her mind, and kept coming back to two things: Charlene Washington and Kent Mercer.

She focused first on the Washingtons. What Gunner had told her needed follow-up, and only two people could fill in the details: Charlene's parents. Repeated calls to their number got no answer, and she dared not leave a message. If Petroni caught wind of her continued meddling on the case, Val's troubles would multiply.

But she had a hunch where and how to find Kent: at Diego's 1:00 arraignment hearing. She grabbed a quick lunch and drove to the courthouse.

Val entered the courtroom, a thirty-foot square of drab white walls, low ceilings, and dark mahogany railings and pews. The chamber seemed to embody the sense of despair that so many accused criminals feel when sitting on the wrong side of the bench. The judge's desk loomed high over a vacant rectangular section of marble flooring that separated His Honor from the attorneys. Beside the judge stood the bailiff, a stout forty-ish white man with the build of a linebacker. In front of the bailiff, a court stenographer sat at a keyboard, ready to record the proceedings.

Val sat in the back row of the cramped gallery, alone. Detectives O'Reilly and Grimes, sitting with the prosecutor's team, caught her eye and nodded to her. No hostility. No camaraderie, either.

She scanned the courtroom. Diego Collier, dressed in a crisp gray suit, sat beside a fifty-something white man with a crown of salt-and-pepper stubble surrounding a bald pate. Diego looked tired and scared, his face ashen. If he saw Val, he made no sign of it. Behind him sat Dr. Mangal and a well-dressed Black man in his late 40s—Diego's father, Val guessed. The next row back contained a few reporters, whispering to each other, pens and notepads at the ready. In the fourth row, one ahead of her on the far side of the room, sat Kent Mercer.

The hearing proceeded with greater dispatch than Val expected. The prosecutor read off the charges. At the judge's prompting, Diego stood and pleaded Not Guilty. The prosecutor summarized the evidence against Diego, much of which Val had played a part in finding. Citing the increasing frequency of the murders, the prosecutor demanded that the court hold him over without bail. The balding attorney objected that Diego was not a flight risk. The prosecutor countered that he routinely left the state, either to visit his father in Rhode Island or to attend college in Massachusetts. The judge ruled with the prosecutor, remanding Diego back to county lockup while awaiting trial.

Val couldn't watch the tearful goodbyes offered by Diego's parents. She slid to the center aisle of the gallery and met Kent's gaze, doing the same from the opposite side. He left the courthouse a step ahead of her and confronted her outside on the building's thick granite steps.

"Are you happy now?" Kent said, his face curled up in a snarl. "Is this what you wanted?"

Stunned by Kent's vitriol, it took Val a moment to respond. "Look, I just did my job and followed the clues where—"

"You 'just did your job,' eh?" Kent said in a mocking tone. "Locking up an innocent man? Yeah, that's the job of a cop, all right."

"You have some evidence that would exonerate Diego, then?" Val said, fighting to keep the heat out of her voice. "If so, I'm all ears."

"Hah! Like I'd help you." Kent turned to leave.

"Don't help me," Val said. "Help Diego. If you know anything, or can provide an alibi—"

"I've told you people everything." Kent glared at her. "If I think of something that could help him, I'll share it with his lawyers, not *you*." He strode down and off the steps.

Val caught up to him on the sidewalk. "All right, then. I'll tell you something I probably shouldn't." She walked beside him, not facing him, talking loud enough for only Kent to hear. "The department took me off the case. They thought I was biased...in favor of Diego's innocence."

"Then why show up this morning?" he asked. "Guilty conscience?"

"Something like that." Val sped up and cut him off before they reached the corner. Facing him, she spotted Shannon and Grimes in the distance, chatting with the prosecutor on the courthouse steps. She slid over so that Kent's body shielded her from their view. "I know I didn't give Diego much of a chance. That's all on me, okay? Something didn't feel right about dating him. Given what's come out since, with the drugs and his connections to so many of the murdered girls, I'd say I was vindicated."

"I knew them, too. Does that mean you think I'm a murderer?" Sarcasm dripped from every syllable.

Val inhaled a steadying breath, careful not to reveal what she really felt: Maybe, Kent. "I'm telling you, I don't think he *is* the Slayer. Unfortunately, my gut feeling carries no weight in police headquarters, nor in court. Actual evidence does." She folded her arms, waiting. With every moment that he didn't run off, her hopes rose.

"What *does* your gut tell you?" Kent asked, less suspicious now.

"That something about this doesn't add up," Val said. "At the same time, Diego brought some of this onto himself—holding back information. For example, not telling us about his relationship with Charlene."

"Diego had a relationship with Charlene?" Kent's surprise sounded disingenuous.

"Don't bullshit me," Val said. "I know how guys talk. You knew about it ten minutes after he did."

Kent started to object, then shut his mouth and bent over to scratch an itch on his lower right leg. Her uncle had always told her to watch people for furtive movements like that. *Tells,* he called them. Indicators of someone lying or holding back.

She pursued it. "See, that's what I'm getting at," Val said. "You were going to say something, but you stopped. Again."

"What do you mean, *again*?" His face betrayed guilt and doubt.

"You said you met Amy on April 1," Val said. "She says it's a week later. Which is it?"

He shrugged. "What's the difference?"

"Credibility matters," Val said, hoping he wouldn't notice her evasiveness.

"Whatever she says," Kent said. "Girls are way better at keeping those sorts of details straight."

"Like your mom?"

Kent cocked his head, confused. "My mom?"

Val shrugged. "She said you've been home studying every Monday night since the dawn of time. You told us you worked late with Curtis on Monday, March 18. Who's right?"

He blanched and seemed to shrink in size right in front of her. "Uh, my mom, I guess. Maybe I worked late on a Tuesday? What does this have to do with Diego?"

"Did Diego ever work late with you and Mr. Iverson?" Val asked.

Kent licked his lips. "Uh...not with me, no. He's a marketing intern, I do portfolio analysis. Outside AFE stuff, our paths never cross at work." He scratched his leg again.

"Can you vouch for his whereabouts this past Monday?" Val asked.

Kent thought for a moment. "No. We didn't hang out that night. He said he had to finish his taxes, and I had to study."

Val eyed him, noted the suspicion in his eyes. Time to back off. She smiled at him. "He needs help with his alibis, and they have to be independent. Meaning, you need to come up with dates, times, and places on your own of when you two spent time together. Can you do that? For Diego?"

He relaxed, relief evident in his expression. "I'll do what I can," he said. His phone buzzed, and he took it out and checked it. "I, uh...I gotta go. It's Amy. She's been blowing up my phone all morning." He tapped the phone and the buzzing stopped. He paused before turning away again. "Who do you think killed all of those girls?" His tone seemed sly, calculating. As if testing her.

Val gave it a moment's thought. "A guy who's very intelligent, who perceives women his own age as too controlling—too manipulative," she said. "So he prefers younger, less confident women. That means he's older than these girls—maybe much older." She leaned in as if confiding in him. "I think he feels women should submit to his will—and when they don't..." She let her voice trail off.

"So, a *much* older guy, huh?" he said with a nervous laugh. "Kind of old-fashioned?"

"Maybe," Val said. "It's just a theory, though."

"Diego's definitely not that," Kent said.

"Agreed."

Kent shuffled away, an extra spring in his step. Val shook her head. Diego didn't strike her as a Power-and-Control type. But Kent?

Maybe.

***

Val's phone rang on the way to her car.

"Dawes. Gibson here." The lieutenant's loud, gruff voice hurt Val's ear. "Petroni let me know what's going on. Looks like I've got you back in my shop."

"Y-yes, sir," Val said. "When should I report in at Liberty Heights? Tomorrow? Swing shift, as before?"

"Nope. Day shift. Take the weekend off and report in at 7:00 a.m. Monday, my office. Except I have an assignment for you." Gibson's tone softened. "Today, if you're up for it."

Val frowned. So much for time off. "Yes, sir." She grabbed a pen and notepad. "Fire away."

"At 2:00 sharp, I want you at Mercy Hospital. I need you to provide secure transfer of a patient being discharged to his home."

Val's mind raced. "Sir? Is this for Gil?"

"Who else?" Gibson laughed. "I figured you'd like this job. And Dawes? Make sure you book your hours. A full eight. Got it? Okay. Take good care of our boy." He hung up without a goodbye.

Val arrived at Gil's hospital room as a team of orderlies transferred him from his bed into a wheelchair. He wore a button-down shirt, untucked, and loose-fitting thigh-length shorts over the bulky cast that stretched from mid-abdomen to his knee.

"Val! How the hell—? I wanted to surprise you," Gil said with a gigantic grin. He settled into his chair and waved away the orderlies. "Did Gibson blab? That SOB never could keep a secret."

"I'm your chauffeur," Val said, bowing from the waist. "Name your destination, Your Highness."

"How about I name *your* destination, which is right here!" Gil spread his arms wide and wiggled his fingers, motioning her in. His powerful arms held her in a firm yet gentle grip, and his unshaven stubble bristled against her skin.

She drew a deep breath, taking in his scent: musk,

medicine, and masculinity. "So good to see you," she mumbled into his shoulder.

"You too, partner," he said. "Now get me out of here!"

Val filled him in on recent events during the drive, saving the big news for last: her dismissal from the WAVE Squad. "I barely lasted a week!" she said after parking her Honda behind Gil's Ford Explorer. "Though some days passed like months, and others fled by."

"Good times always go by too fast," he said. "Like the few months we had as partners. Damn, I miss those days."

"Me too. Do you think we'll ever get that chance again?"

Gil laughed. "If I can avoid doing stupid things like re-breaking my bones! Come on, help me inside." He pushed open the passenger side door.

She fetched the wheelchair from his SUV and helped him into it, then rolled him up to the garage. He entered the code, then clucked his tongue after the door opened. "What a mess," he said, shaking his head at the pile of boxes where Val had found him five days before. "Once again, the elves failed to clean up after me."

"I'll take care of that once we get you inside the house," Val said.

"The hell you will," Gil said. "You and I have more talking to do."

Val helped him to the sofa and sat next to him, her heart still in her mouth. She had so much to tell him, but didn't know where to begin.

Instead, she took in her surroundings. She'd been to Gil's a few times to pick him up or drop him off, and hadn't really noticed the decor. No surprise, though, that his choices demonstrated pretty good taste. Modern, comfortable furniture filled most of the living room. A bookshelf occupied most of one wall, jammed with books, framed photos of family members and friends, and a single sports trophy: first place in a police softball tourney. Tasteful modern prints and an old-fashioned clock with chimes decorated the remaining muted-gray walls. He even had a wine rack. Full, of course.

"I can't help but think that Petroni's making a big mistake here," Gil said, leaning forward on the sofa. "Sounds like you were instrumental in breaking the case, and it's not like their work is done. There have to be other unsolved murders and assaults of women on the books."

"Thanks, but I'm not so sure," Val said. "All I can remember right now are my mistakes. Which are legion."

"Everybody makes mistakes," he said. "Including Petroni. She'll regret making this one, I guarantee it."

"Aw." She blushed a little and looked away. "Right now, though, it feels like I've failed in my first true test as a detective."

"I get why you feel that way, but you haven't," he said in a calm, reassuring voice. "Where would they be without you? Nowhere. Plus, when you're a big shot detective someday, you'll look back on this experience and appreciate the hell out of it."

"If I ever get there," Val said. "Right now, I have my doubts."

"You will," he said. "I know it."

"How can you say that?" Val said. "As it stands, I'm a disaster."

Gil shook his head. "Because, Val, you're a true talent—a natural detective. Still green, sure. Everyone is, to start. But you've got all the tools: you're intelligent, intuitive, relentless, and gutsy as hell. Petroni probably wishes she had seven more of you."

"Ten, according to her," Val said, laughing. "Come on, don't stop now. You're just warming up."

"I will," Gil said, his expression serious. "I've seen you in action. You have great empathy and understanding for victims, and the less fortunate. Like those gang members, and that young girl, abused by the son of a bitch that shot me. You're great at getting inside the head of these perps, particularly the serial offenders. You've saved a lot of lives in a short time, Val. A *lot*."

"Can you be on the committee that reviews my detective exam?" Val said, blushing. "Better yet, can you write it for me?"

"I would if I could," he said, his expression lightening. "Val, when I say you're smart, I mean that you're good at learning from your mistakes."

"My dad used to say that there are no mistakes—only teachable moments." She shuddered. "After this week, I may have earned a Master's degree."

He waved her off. "Nobody's perfect. Cut yourself a little slack, okay?"

Val sighed. "I can't help it, Gil. I may have blown my big chance."

"You'll get more chances. And you'll do better." He edged closer to her, wincing. "Trust me."

She took a deep breath, thought about that. "Let's say that I do," she said. "How do I make sure I don't screw up the next opportunity? Be honest with me." Her gut clenched a bit. "You mentioned my strengths. What are my weaknesses as a detective candidate?"

"Your biggest weakness is inexperience," Gil said with a shrug. "Which you can only fix with time on the job."

"My biggest, you say. Meaning, there are others?" Val's ears burned. She didn't want to hear this, but she needed to.

He scoffed. "Don't worry about it."

"I'm not worried," she said. "Come on, Gil. Tell me what I need to work on."

He sighed, a long, heavy exhalation of breath. "There's one thing that makes me worry about you. Don't take this wrong, okay? Promise?" He waited for her to nod, then continued. "Sometimes, you rush in, as the saying goes, where angels fear to tread. A little blind, before you know all the facts or have assessed the situation as much as you should." He stopped short, as if he'd meant to go on.

Val drew a heavy breath. She knew what he meant to say. "Like the day you got shot, you mean?"

"I wasn't thinking of that—"

"You should," she said. "It's a great example." Now her face burned with humiliation. Gil's shooting wouldn't have happened if she'd exercised more discretion.

"Let's continue to agree to disagree on that, okay?" Gil smiled. "Which brings me to weakness number two: how stubborn you can be."

"Pot, meet kettle," Val said, poking him in the ribs.

"Guilty as charged." He grabbed her hand before she could pull it away, wrapped it up in his, and held on. So warm and comfortable. She didn't resist. "But we're talking about you. Which reminds me of number three: your casual relationship with respect for authority. Here I am, your mentor, and you're punching me in the ribs. An injured man, no less!"

"You call that a punch?" she said, laughing. "Okay, snowflake, let go of my hand and I'll show you a punch!"

Gil didn't let go, and she didn't pull away. Not at all.

"I'm serious, Val," he said. "As my old man would say, you don't suffer fools gladly. Unfortunately, insufferable fools abound in management positions, including in police departments. That type of attitude is not only bad for your career. It can, literally, get you killed."

"That's a bit melodramatic," Val said. Not with any force in her voice. His hand felt so good around hers.

"Not at all," Gil said, and he traced a finger around the back of her hand. "You lose the confidence of management, suddenly you find yourself partnered with the type of cops that…well, nobody else wants to partner with. People feel you don't have their back, so they don't have yours. It's not where you want to be, particularly at this early stage of your career."

Val swallowed a lump that somehow had appeared out of nowhere in her throat. "Okay. I hear you."

"Do you?" He peered at her, his brown eyes like dark pools in an icy cave.

She sighed. Damn, he could always read her like a book. "Sometimes it's hard," she said. "They make decisions that are clearly wrong. They let Curtis Iverson walk all over us, interfere with the investigation, and meanwhile, this Shoeless Slayer dude has killed five or six girls—and counting. What am I supposed to do, Gil? Bend over and take it, and keep letting innocent girls die?"

"That's not what I'm saying," he said, taking a firmer grip on her hand. "Give the devils their due. The folks in charge aren't complete idiots, Val. Most earned their positions through hard work and experience. They have skills you don't—like the ability to play politics, for example."

She scoffed. "I wouldn't call that a plus."

"But it is." Gil frowned for a moment. "Let me give you another example. Remember when we first encountered Richard Harkins? We knew little about him. Turns out he's a serial child abuser, with a mean streak a mile deep and ten miles wide. And, who'd-a thunk it, he's a great shot with a pistol." He pointed to his shattered hip. "We underestimated him, and it cost us. Once you learned that about him, you appreciated how dangerous a foe he was. Armed with that knowledge, you beat him. Right?"

Val blushed. "I had help."

"Enough of the false modesty. You nailed his ass, and the world thanks you for it. Here's another example. You reached out to Gunner and The Disciples, gained their trust, and got inside their heads when nobody else could get near them. Why not apply that same ability to your 'foes' on this case? If Petroni's in your way, and Curtis Iverson, work on getting inside their heads. Figure them out the way you did Gunner and Harkins. You do that, and neither of them are a match for you."

Warmth spread from Gil's touch on her hand, up her arm, and filled her chest. Gil's confidence in her was contagious and uplifting. Of course he was right. She could outsmart and outmaneuver them if need be.

His remarks also reminded her of Amy's situation with Curtis Iverson. She related a brief version of Amy's tale, then posed the question: "Should I help her?"

Gil frowned. "Your instincts are good on this, Val. Helping her is a risk, and here he's not just an obstacle to get around. He's the enemy, and a powerful one. Not only because of his wife's position, either. He's rich, entitled, and used to things going his way. There's a reason he has the reputation that he does."

"What reputation is that?" Val asked, her mind now on full alert. "What don't I know?"

"He's very aggressive in any sort of business deal or legal fight, anything to do with his reputation," Gil said. "A few years back, an employee sued him for harassment, and he dragged her through the mud, and ruined her. Despite that, rumors persist about him being a 'ladies man,' or so he'd like to call it. Predator is a better term, in my opinion."

"So Amy's claim probably has merit," Val said.

"I wouldn't doubt it," Gil said. "As you said, he made sure there were no witnesses. It's tough to prove. If you help her, you're taking on that risk, too."

"So I shouldn't help her?" Val said, her body feeling heavy.

"I didn't say that," Gil said. "There are risks. But I couldn't warn you away from this if I tried. Helping people is what you do, Val. It's who you are. It's why I like you and respect you so much."

"Ditto," Val said. "So, what you're saying is, follow my heart and not my head?"

"Listen to both," Gil said. "Just keep in mind what your head is saying. Taking on Curtis is dangerous. And it's not your responsibility."

Val took in Gil's serious gaze, the worry in his face, the caring in his eyes. It reminded her of the one man in her life that cared for her an equal amount. The one man who understood her, who taught her as much or more than Gil: Uncle Val. The man who inspired her at a young age to become a cop, to aspire to the rank and role of detective. What would Uncle Val advise today?

Val knew the answer. She reached out with her free hand and rested it on Gil's shoulder. "I'm afraid, Gil, that you're wrong about that," she said. "It's not about Amy. It's about right and wrong, and protecting the vulnerable from the powerful. That, my dear friend, is, and always will be, my responsibility."

Chapter Twenty-Nine

Val lay awake in bed, staring at the ceiling. A hundred times she closed her eyes, only to have them bounce open again. As if they followed their own will, not Val's. Another glance at the clock seemed to validate that. Since the last time she looked, fewer than five minutes had ticked by.

Do. Not. Think. About. Work.

R-i-i-i-g-h-h-t. Kind of like telling a child, Don't think about pink elephants.

No matter what anyone said—Gil, Beth, Petroni, Shannon—getting tossed from the WAVE Squad would look awful on her record, tarnish her reputation, and set back her career. Perhaps worse, she couldn't shake the feeling of utter failure, and of letting the team down. Reassuring words from Gibson notwithstanding, Val had disappointed her boss, and her partner. Their confidence in her would take a deep hit— but not as deep as the hit to her self-confidence.

So much for her becoming the youngest detective ever in Clayton.

Val rolled over, glared at the bare walls of her bedroom. She'd lived in this apartment with Beth for almost a full year and still hadn't hung a single decoration. Not a photo, not one piece of art, not even a poster celebrating her favorite band or actor. She should do that. Take advantage of the time off, go shopping, buy something pretty to hang on the wall.

Except that would require having enough good taste and cultural awareness to even choose a favorite movie, band, or artist. Which meant having a life. Which she didn't, outside work, unless working out and resuming jiu jitsu training counted as having a life.

That set her mind off on the worst possible tangent: why she'd gone whole-hog into martial arts training in the first place. Uncle Val had gotten her started, but that's not what ignited her passion for self-defense. That "honor" belonged to Milt, and all the potential Milts out there—men she seemed to find under every rock and around every corner.

Sometimes, for real, even. Sometimes, like Richard Harkins, they carried guns and shot at her partner.

Frustration boiled over. She wanted to scream, but waking up her roommate at oh-dark-thirty two days in a row would prompt Beth to move out even sooner. And Beth represented the only true close friend in her life—the only one that stayed close, anyway. So far.

By contrast, Beth had made dozens of friends in high school. Hundreds. Val had...Beth. Even her teammates on track and soccer remained just that—teammates. Not through any fault of theirs. Val never opened up to any of them. The boys in high school—the few that ever expressed any interest in her—she never regretted keeping at arm's length. Children with testosterone problems, all of them.

She scolded herself for that bit of snarkiness. She had to break out of that way of thinking. They couldn't all have been idiots. Her brother's friends seemed like decent guys, for example. Too old for her then, of course. But everyone at the reunion would be five years older, five years more mature. Maybe now they'd be okay to hang out with.

Amy flashed into her mind, and she shook her head. Maybe not.

That reminded her of something Amy had mentioned that morning—something that slipped by at the time, and stood out now. When getting away from Curtis at his apartment, Amy had tripped over shoes in the closet. Whose?

Kent's, who also used the place? Curtis's? The women with whom they'd enjoyed other, more successful secret trysts?

Or…their victims?

She checked herself. She assumed Curtis had kept his affairs secret—from his wife, at least. She recalled reading biographies of politicians and tycoons from the past—people like the Rockefellers and Kennedys. They didn't bother to keep them hidden. Low-key and out of the press, yes—even now, voters frowned upon blatant infidelity. Rich and powerful men—and sometimes women—often married for wealth and connections, and exercised their passions elsewhere. Maybe Curtis and Megan had a similar arrangement.

Her imagination wandered farther down that rabbit hole. Who would sleep with Curtis Iverson? Lots of women, no doubt. He was wealthy, well-connected, and, she supposed, attractive in that silver-fox sort of way. He probably went for younger women, and she understood the allure of older men—case in point, her own attraction to Gil.

What if those women were *really* young? As in, not yet legal age? Were those shoes the "trophies" that the killer kept from his victims? Could that be where the murders were committed? If so, was it Curtis, Kent, Bo, or someone else?

She got out of bed, grabbed a pen and paper, and sat at the rarely used makeup table against the wall. She jotted down notes of what she knew, and what she guessed, about the Shoeless Slayer. A trophy-keeper wouldn't fit the Power-and-Control profile, but he would fit the Thrill-Seeker type. That would raise the probability of a younger perpetrator, more obsessive, more prone to mistakes. What mistakes had he made? She wrote: *Tattoos—mistake?* The ink jobs seemed to dare the police to find him. Find the tat artist, find the killer.

Also: the body types. Not your typical skinny Hollywood model figure, but athletic girls with solid builds. All ambitious, smart, and working-class. And one more thing: Val had convinced herself that the girls all knew and trusted the killer. That suggested either a friend they all shared in common, or a man of authority and good standing. A teacher or adviser, perhaps. Or a mentor, like Diego or Kent. Or a wealthy aristocrat, like Curtis. However, each of them had alibis for at least one of the murders.

She recalled a phrase from a Sherlock Holmes mystery: "Once you eliminate the impossible," Holmes had said to Watson, "whatever remains, no matter how improbable, must be the truth."

She stared at the names again and realized her mistake: She hadn't eliminated the impossible.

Yet.

***

To Val's surprise, the Depression-era Liberty Heights precinct building, despite its shabby, unimpressive veneer, seemed to welcome her when she arrived a few minutes before 7:00 a.m. on Monday. Unlike downtown headquarters—an imposing, impersonal concrete behemoth—the city's smallest precinct office's earthy, simplistic Minimal Traditional style reflected the homey, if gritty, character of its working-class surroundings. New anti-cop tags appeared on the side of the concrete steps, replacing markings that the Facilities department had sandblasted off since her last time there. Most days, such vandalism frustrated her. For whatever reason, this day she marveled at the graffiti artist's boldness and persistence.

As soon as she pushed open the rear employee entrance door by the women's locker room, the faint, welcoming aroma of coffee greeted her, mixed with fresh donuts. How that could happen over the omnipresent aromas of scented lotions and shampoos, she couldn't fathom.

Minutes later, she found Lieutenant Gibson in his cramped office, a shaded-glass enclosure trimmed with dark wood and beige government-issue metal chairs, desk, and filing cabinets. He appeared tired, the lines in his face deeper than she remembered, his dark eyes bloodshot behind his black pince-nez glasses. "Welcome back to the people's precinct, Dawes," he said with a growl, waving her into a seat. "I hope your time at headquarters hasn't ruined you for real police work."

She smiled despite the trepidation she carried with her into this meeting. If Gibson wanted to lessen the humiliation of being bounced off the WAVE Squad, he'd struck the right chord. "It's good to be back, sir. I certainly learned a lot in the last week and a half."

He laughed. "Don't let it go to your head, rookie." He seemed relaxed—jovial, even. Strange. "Still. Job well done, Dawes."

"Go to my head, sir? Job well done? I don't understand."

Gibson shot her a puzzled look. "You helped close out the biggest case in the last half-century in just over a week. What, you think you deserve a medal or something? Well, a pat on the back is all I've got for you. Deal with it." He scowled, pawed through the mess of papers and files on his enormous desk, found the folder he wanted, and opened it.

"I didn't expect any sort of praise at all, Lieutenant, considering how things closed out there for me."

He looked up at her over his glasses. "You mean, because they sent you back here? Sorry, there weren't any openings in the mayor's office."

"Sir, I'm very confused. Didn't Sergeant Petroni explain why I got kicked off the task force?"

Gibson leaned back in his chair, pushed his glasses up to the bridge of his bulbous nose. "Kicked off? That's not what I understood from her report." He pulled open another folder, shuffled through the pages, lifted one and read from it. "Says here, 'Officer Dawes completed her temporary assignment as requested. As current caseload of the WAVE Squad no longer requires full staffing levels, Officer Dawes is returned to previously assigned duties.' It's not high praise, but does that sound like a boot in the ass to you?"

Confusion rose in Val's mind. It sounded like pure bureaucratese. "What about...?" She wasn't sure she should continue.

"The so-called IA investigation? Yeah, she mentioned that. Those idiots can't find their dicks with both hands. Don't worry, I won't let them scapegoat you over those supposed leaks." Gibson spit something unpleasant into a nearby trash can. "You know how those two became IA inspectors, Dawes?"

"No, sir."

"Because they couldn't make it as real detectives," Gibson said. "So now, everything looks like a crooked cop to them. The way the mayor's office and her grandstanding husband inserted themselves into that mess, I'd bet my mortgage that the whole thing was political. Getting you out of there is the best thing Petroni could've done for you."

Val nodded, and relief flowed out of her, along with a breath she hadn't realized she'd been holding. "That's good to hear, sir. So, what's my assignment going forward?"

Travis Blake's massive form filled in the doorway before Gibson could answer. "Am I late?" Travis asked, running a hand through his short, salt-and-pepper curls.

Gibson waved him in. "Perfect timing. We're talking about your new partner's temporary duties now that she's back."

Val's heart stopped for a moment. "Partner?"

"That a problem?" Travis said, thumping his massive frame into a chair next to Val.

"No, no," Val said, a smile spreading across her face. "I figured…well, in situations like this, I've been stuck on—I mean, assigned to desk duty."

"Yeah, we know how much you love that," Travis said with a chuckle. "Don't worry. As much as I prefer field work, I still have management responsibilities. So while I'm pushing paper, you will be too. Hopefully that's less than half-time. Right, Gibby?"

"Depends how efficient you are as a manager," Gibson said with a grin. "In that case, Dawes, you might never see the streets again."

"Ten bucks says we're on the street before noon," Travis said.

"You're on." Gibson slapped a ten on his desk. "I'd be thrilled to pay off that bet. Now, listen, Dawes. I don't want you answering phones. We want to deploy your talents in a more strategic fashion." He reopened the folder he'd been reading when she entered and scanned the top page. "WAVE is still treating the Sierra Stapleton case as open." To Travis's puzzled frown, he added, "That's the girl murdered this past Monday."

"I thought they pinned that on Diego Collier," Val said.

Gibson shook his head. "Internally, they still like Bo Rousseau for it. They asked for help from the precincts in mopping up some details." He handed Val and Travis each a copy of a two-page list of questions, single-spaced on each side. "Some of it's desk work, some of it's field. Mostly confirmation and documentation, but I thought you'd be perfect for it."

"Sergeant Petroni is okay with that?" Try as she might, Val couldn't keep the doubt out of her voice. She scanned the list. A bunch of make-work. Resentment grew inside her. She'd fallen from rising detective to mop-up-girl.

"Beggars can't be choosers." Gibson shook his copy of the report in the air. "Besides, she's the one that complimented your research skills. She can't renege now."

"No shit?" Travis said. "I've known her fifteen years and she's never paid me a compliment once."

"Not true," Gibson said, grinning again. "Once, she said you're not as stupid as you look."

"I feel so much better," Travis said, rolling his eyes.

While their banter continued, Val's mind wandered off. Something that Gibson had said struck her like a ton of bricks. If Bo killed Sierra—a suspicion she shared—then that meant the Shoeless Schoolgirl Slayer had *not* killed again this past Monday.

Which meant he was overdue.

***

Travis showed Val to a semi-private workspace outside his office, essentially a desk surrounded by three walls, with the fourth side exposed to a low-traffic passageway. "The noise-canceling headphones will help minimize interruptions and distractions," Travis said.

He disproved his own claim minutes later, appearing beside her desk with a grim expression on his face. "I thought you'd want to know," he said, and dropped a printout on her desk—an email forwarded from someone in county lockup.

Her heart sank. In dry, clinical terms, the email revealed that Diego had gotten beaten unconscious during his outdoor "free" time the previous afternoon. He'd arrived at the facility only a few hours before.

"He's at the secure wing of the hospital, recovering," Travis said, his voice somber. "The kid suffered a concussion, a few broken ribs, a bruised kidney, and lost a tooth or two.

Believe it or not, with all that, they consider him in 'fair' condition."

"I'd hate to see what they'd call serious." Val's throat ached. "Who did it?"

"Nobody's talking," Travis said. "I guess it all happened pretty fast. I'll let you know if we learn anything more."

She almost asked if she could visit him in the hospital, but guessed she'd be one of the last people he'd want to see. She dove into her list of research topics Petroni had given her on the Stapleton case. Sierra's mother had provided some personal items that the WAVE Squad had requested, including her yearbook from the prior academic year. Photos showed Sierra, already taller than most of the seniors, spiking the ball in a varsity match, with Olivia Lambert next to her. Seeing both girls together—one she'd met and spoken to, another whose body she pulled out of the river—put a lump in Val's throat.

Val looked closer at the photo. She made out several attendees' faces in the stands behind them—mostly students, but not all. One jumped out at her: Sierra's mother, Connie. Behind her sat two forty-something white women, one of whom bore a striking resemblance to Olivia. Beside them sat a round-faced white man with curly brown hair, a little too old for high school.

Kent Mercer.

As Diego had theorized, Kent had attended at least one Liberty High volleyball match to support his family friend, Olivia Lambert. He could have met Sierra at that match, or any other.

Val logged onto the case file system, hoping against high odds that IT hadn't yet revoked her access to WAVE Squad records. She couldn't remember the case ID, so she searched for "Lambert, Olivia." The monitor responded: *One record found.* Beneath that useless, happy statistic, the screen displayed a live link to the Lambert file. Moments later, she had Olivia's mother on the phone.

"Mrs. Lambert, Officer Dawes of Clayton PD. I'm sorry to call so early," Val said, only then noticing the time: 7:47 a.m. "I'm following up on a few details of our investigation—"

"For heaven's sake," she said, "can't you people coordinate your efforts a little? This is the fourth call I've gotten from you people in as many days." Her voice broke, and Val felt her pain with every syllable.

"So sorry for the inconvenience. I'll share your feedback with the team," Val said. She understood then why the WAVE Squad had sloughed this task onto her. She also recalled the woman's defensiveness when discussing Kent Mercer, so she tried an indirect tack. "We wanted to confirm a few details with you about your daughter's after-school activities. To your knowledge, has Olivia had any contact with the accused, Diego Collier?"

"Obviously," she said, her tone turning nasty. "He killed her."

"Did you ever see them together, or hear her talk about him?"

"No. I told your detectives this. I thought you had something new to discuss."

Val sighed. So much for the indirect route. "Diego is a friend of Kent Mercer's," Val said. "Might he have joined Kent to watch one of her volleyball matches?"

"Hell if I know. No, I'd say definitely not. Kent always came with Margaret."

"Margaret?" Val scribbled the name on a notepad.

"Mercer. His mother." Mrs. Lambert's tone softened. "She and I have been friends since high school. She was Margaret Spencer then."

"Great. Thank you." Val jotted down a note: *Kent attended V-Ball often. Not Diego.* "Did Olivia socialize with other girls on the squad?"

"Sure, sometimes," Mrs. Lambert said. "Who do you have in mind?"

"Sierra Stapleton?"

Mrs. Lambert paused, sniffled. "Once in a while," she said in a choked voice. "After matches. Not otherwise. Livvy didn't take to her so much. I didn't either. That girl had a foul mouth and a bad attitude. She was trouble, you know?"

Val's ears perked up. "In what way?"

Mrs. Lambert sighed. "She hung with the wrong crowd. The rough kids, who got into trouble with the law sometimes. Livvy tried to steer clear of those types. She tried to stay...safe." Her voice broke again. "I guess it didn't work out."

After offering a few consoling words to the poor girl's mother, Val ended the call and made a note to follow up with Olivia's other teammates after school. She spent the next few hours searching online for additional background on Bo Rousseau, finding little of consequence they didn't already know.

Travis interrupted her again around 10:00 a.m., waving an empty coffee cup at her. "Let's hit the field for a while," he said, "and get some drinkable coffee. I can't stomach another drop of the crud in the break room."

Still working off of the list of follow-up items from WAVE, they drove through a mild rain shower to Connie Stapleton's house, stopping at two different Dunkin' Donuts on the way. Even so, Travis had drained both of his coffees before Val got halfway through her first. "Your blood pressure must be through the roof," Val said when he finished the second cup.

"Staying alert when I'm out on the street is a much bigger concern," he said. "I figure some punk with a gun or a drunk driver will get me long before hypertension does."

They hurried up the walk to the Stapleton front door

through the steady rain. In their haste, they nearly tripped over a loose pile of newspapers, still in their clear plastic delivery sacks, scattered around the base of the steps. "Either she's not home, or she doesn't want to read any headlines," Travis deadpanned. Val, unused to his morbid humor, only shook her head in response. She glanced around the yard. It hadn't been mowed since her first visit.

Connie Stapleton's voice drifted through the closed door. "Go away," she said. "No press!"

"It's Clayton Police," Travis said. "We have a few questions."

"Ask," came her response.

"Can you open the door, please?" Travis asked. "It'd be much easier."

"For who?"

Travis sighed and shook his head. "Go ahead, Dawes. You've got the list."

Val raised her voice. "We'd like to know if you recognize these men," she said, readying some photo prints. Surely that would convince her to open up.

"Hold them up where I can see them."

Val looked to Travis for guidance. He nodded. She leaned over the rail and pressed a mugshot photo of Diego against the rain-drenched picture window.

"Yeah. From TV."

"Ever seen him in person?"

"Nah."

Val frowned, pressed a photo of Kent up in place of Diego's. "How about him?"

"Nope!"

"Sierra never—"

"I said no!"

One more that Val had grabbed on a whim: Gunner.

"Sierra don't hang with no Black guys," Connie said. "Not

in my house."

Travis grunted, made a face. Val sighed, fighting her own anger, and put the photos away. Then she leaned close to Travis and whispered, "I want to try one more."

His eyebrows arched. "You have another mugshot in that folder?"

She cocked her head. "Trust me?"

He smirked. "What choice do I have?"

Val opened her phone and tapped a name into the search bar. Once she had the face on screen, she pressed it against the window.

"Who's that?" Connie yelled out at them. "Your grandfather? Get the fuck out of here."

Val pulled the phone away and nearly had it in her pocket, but Travis caught her hand in time. "Let me see," he said.

Chagrined and unable to overpower his grasp, she relented and showed him the picture on screen.

Travis let out a low whistle. "Curtis Iverson? You kidding me?"

She shrugged. "I thought it was worth a shot."

He rolled his eyes and headed toward the cruiser. "Let's get out of here."

Val had almost reached the car when Connie Stapleton opened the door. She stood in the doorway, wearing a faded pink robe and slippers, her hair a tousled mess, a cigarette dangling from her lips. "Let me see that last picture again," she said.

"The last mugshot?"

"The one on your phone."

Val glanced at Travis, who still stood with the car door open. "You go ahead," he said. "I'm getting drenched." He slid into the vehicle.

Val strode up to the door and brought the picture back

to her screen. Connie squinted at it, took a deep drag on her cigarette, and exhaled. "Yeah, I recognize him now," she said. "That's the mayor's husband, isn't it?"

"Right," Val said. "Did she ever mention him? Ever see them together?"

Another drag, another cloud of blue smoke. "He called me a couple of days ago."

Val started. "He *called* you?"

Connie nodded. "Said how sorry he was about my girl. Offered to help with funeral expenses, things like that."

Val's mind whirled. Was Curtis trying to gain political points with this move—or assuage his own guilt? "And has he?"

Connie held up her hands. "No money's showed up yet. I told him, I would appreciate any help. I ain't got no savings, and no insurance, you know?"

"Would you let me know if that money comes through?" Val slipped the woman her card.

Connie nodded, took a final drag on her butt, and tossed it onto the wet grass. "You ask me, they got the wrong guy." She pointed toward Bo's house next door. "That's the son of a bitch that killed Sierra. Not that cute little Black kid."

"Mr. Rousseau is still under investigation," Val said. "I'm sure they'll hold him until—"

"Bullshit!" Connie laughed, a sound filled with more anger and sadness than mirth. "He got out yesterday on bail. Here." She trudged down the steps and poked through the newspapers, finally finding the one she needed. She ripped off its plastic delivery bag and opened to the City News section. She stabbed the page with a chipped fingernail. "See? It's on TV, too." She hurried back up the stairs.

Val glanced at the news story, then back at Connie Stapleton. "Is he home, then?" A quick glance at his driveway showed no car.

"Hell, no," Connie said. "He was packed and gone before dinnertime yesterday. I guarantee, you won't see his face in Clayton ever again. I already told his landlord, don't expect no rent check this month." She lit another cigarette and slammed the door shut behind her.

"Travis," Val said when she returned to the car, "we've got a problem."

***

The police cruiser whizzed past, driven by that giant grizzly bear of a cop, with Dawes riding shotgun. Neither appeared to notice the black sedan parked a half-block from the house they'd exited, nor the man slouched behind the wheel. Good. He'd taken a tremendous risk following them to this place. But he had to confirm for himself what he'd learned at the courthouse: that Dawes was no longer working the case.

Instead, he confirmed the lie. Valorie Dawes, like a dog with a bone, couldn't let go.

She had to be stopped.

Because, he knew deep down, *he* could not stop. Not now. Not after having tasted the ultimate thrill. Experienced the power he had over those girls, once he'd gained their trust and lured them into what they assumed was safety.

They couldn't be more wrong. And he couldn't let that stupid cop get in his way. Not when the urge for more burned inside him, smoldering, ready to explode like wildfire on dry tinder.

Dawes, it appeared, wouldn't go quietly. She'd proven herself tenacious, insightful, suspicious—a formidable foe. He hadn't counted on that. The quick sacrifice of Diego Collier, what anyone else would celebrate as an easy win, should have satisfied her—all of them. Focused them elsewhere.

Dawes was too smart for that. She wouldn't be fooled,

she wouldn't quit, and when told to back down, she'd gone rogue.

There was one thing, though, that he hadn't yet tried. One emotion he hadn't tapped in her. One that worked on all women.

Fear.

Which meant striking closer to home. The sooner, the better.

Chapter Thirty

Something's bugging me," Travis said on the drive back to the precinct. "Diego Collier supplied Sierra with the pills—that's clear. Yet she also had enough pot and coke to keep all of Liberty Heights stoned for a month. Where'd she get all that?"

"Another supplier, I suppose," Val said.

Travis shook his head. "In my experience, street dealers have one supplier. Two reasons: reduce the risk of getting caught or ratted out—on both sides—and, suppliers are super territorial. They find out you're buying from someone else, often that's a death sentence."

Val snapped her fingers. "Bo!"

Travis glanced sideways at her. "I thought she was supplying *him*," he said. "She got the pills he flushed from Diego, right?"

"So it appears," Val said. "Maybe we've been looking at this wrong. What if Sierra's not a dealer? What if she was just helping Bo, as a go-between to Diego?"

"Still a dealer, in my book," Travis said with a grunt.

"Not if she wasn't actually selling," Val said. "What if Bo got spooked by our first visit a few weeks before Sierra's death and thought we were onto him? He might have asked her to hold on to most of his contraband until it all blew over. We don't know what he flushed before we broke down the bathroom door, but what we found barely met the standard for possession with intent to sell."

"Interesting idea," Travis said. "So, how does that stack up as far as motive?"

"Sierra and her mom are struggling financially," Val said. "Suppose she dipped into the cash, and Bo found out? Worse, what if Bo needed the money to pay his own suppliers, and he didn't have it? Because Sierra did. So he arranges a meet-up, expecting her to bring it. She doesn't...and pays the price!"

Travis rubbed his chin for a few moments. "Plausible, but that's a lot of ifs," he said. "What about his Peeping Tom stuff? How do you explain that?"

"Maybe *that's* why he was peeking into her room—to find out where she hid the cash and drugs," Val said.

"That's backwards," Travis said. "Remember, Connie complained about his peeping *before* I first interviewed Bo."

"All right, so he's a creeper *and* a dealer," Val said. "I can live with that explanation."

Travis nodded. "So, we have a stronger motive for Bo in Sierra's case," he said. "How about the tattoo connection?"

"She had tats, but not the *Chingona* design," Val said. "Good point, though. Let's follow up."

Travis nodded. "First thing tomorrow, we go tattoo shopping."

***

Travis pulled the cruiser up in front of Ink Complete, the tattoo shop where Pinkie had her work done, at 9:00 the next morning.

"He's in there," Val said, peering through the shop's front windows. "With a client."

"Good. He won't run, then."

Val led the way into the tattoo parlor, wrinkling her nose at the shop's acrid smell. Bells hanging from the doorknob announced their entrance. A pudgy, curly-haired man in his twenties jerked to attention, his pen still buzzing. He mumbled something into the ear of a young blonde woman whose arm he'd been inking and set down his tattoo gun. Then, aloud, he said, "Help you, officers?"

"Topher Brooks?" Travis said.

"That's me," the man said. A panicked expression flashed over his face.

"We'd like to ask you a few questions," Travis said.

Topher, sweating, indicated the blonde in the chair. "Not a great time. C-can you come back—?"

"Relax, we're not here to shut you down," Travis said, then added in a more ominous tone, "unless you hold back from us."

"Should I leave?" the blonde woman said.

"Only if you don't want tetanus," Travis said.

"Hey, fuck off," Topher said. "I run a clean shop."

Val gazed around his shop, confirming how much cleaner and well-organized it was than the others they'd visited. Nestled in among a handful of espresso shops, clothing boutiques, and nail salons in a gentrifying area of the Alphabet Soup neighborhood, Ink Complete appeared high-end—even classy.

Travis showed him a photo of Sierra Stapleton. "Know her?"

Topher peered at the photo. "Don't think so. Now can—"

"What about this one?" Travis walked him through the photos of all six victims. "I never saw any of those girls, no way," Topher said, his eyes darting in all directions. "I don't do underage work. If they don't have IDs, I send 'em home. It ain't worth losing my license over."

"One of your customers, Alexa—you may know her as Pinkie," Val added when Topher's face expressed puzzlement. "She said that you could help us find the artist responsible for this design." She showed him the *Chingona* image.

Topher laughed. "Yeah," he said, "it's called D-I-fucking-Y-dot-com." He shook his head. "Freaking cartoons. Amateur bullshit."

The woman in the chair, who'd craned her neck to see the photo, spoke up. "He's right. I wouldn't come to a shop that put crap like that on people. Topher here does much better work than that."

"DIY?" Travis said, ignoring her. "People tattoo themselves?"

"Sure," the woman said. "You can buy kits online."

"Who the hell would do that?" Travis said.

"Kids," Topher said. "It's an underage thing. Teenagers who can't get parental permission send off for a DIY kit. Lots of times they do it on a dare." He chuckled. "That's mostly boys, though. Design like that, probably a girl thing."

"Why do you say that?" Val asked.

Topher's lips curled into a condescending smile. "What boy is into Girl Power?" He rolled his eyes. "The image, and the act of inking themselves or each other, makes girls feel empowered. New thing is, too, girls ink their boyfriends, see if he can take it."

The woman laughed. "DIYers make it hurt more. In a legit shop like Topher's, you barely feel it."

Val's mind raced. No wonder they hadn't found the artist who'd applied the tattoos to the Slayer's victims. He'd probably done them himself, or gotten the girls to do it.

Perhaps in a secret apartment set up for romantic trysts.

***

Val practically raced Travis to the cruiser from Topher's tattoo shop. "We've got to get a warrant to search Curtis Iverson's condo," she said once the car doors slammed shut. "See if he has a tattoo kit, see who owns those shoes—"

"Based on what evidence?" Travis said, pulling the car into traffic. "We have no sworn witness statements, no probable cause linking him to any crimes—"

"What about Amy Yang's story?" Val said. "He tried to rape her, and she said he had all those shoes, and—"

"Iverson didn't actually rape her," Travis said, shaking his head. "He tried to get her into bed, yes, and failed. Unless she testifies, we have no evidence he forced her. Do you want to base a warrant on the fact that he owns too many shoes? We could imprison my wife, plus every woman and half the men in the city, for that heinous crime."

"This isn't funny," Val said, anger rising. "He could be using that condo to lure his victims in. What if we find a tattoo kit there? Wouldn't that implicate him, or Kent Mercer? He used the place, too."

"Too speculative," Travis said. "Plus, almost every judge in the state owes Iverson favors for his campaign donations and fund-raising. He'd know about the warrant ten minutes before we do, and we'd most likely search an empty apartment. Besides, you don't even know the address or suite number."

"I'll get it from Amy. Failing that, put me on a computer and I'll know that factoid within thirty minutes, tops."

Travis scoffed. "Don't get cocky, kid."

She stuck out her hand, a defiant offer of a handshake. "Ten bucks says I have it by 4:00 today."

He laughed. "You're on."

Val's repeated calls to Amy on the drive back went straight to voicemail, and her texts went unanswered. Kent probably poisoned that well for her already, dammit.

Back at the precinct, she found the waterfront building Amy had described and had the manager on the phone within minutes. There she hit a stone wall.

"I'm sorry, I don't have any record of any unit being leased to the Iversons—nor to Constitution Finance," the nasal-voiced man said in a strong Boston accent.

"How about a Kent Mercer?" Val asked.

"No, definitely not."

Val named a half-dozen other people on Megan Iverson's staff. No hits.

"Look," she said, "I don't want to take up all of your time. How about you send me your list of tenants and let me go through the names myself?"

"Got a warrant?" the man said.

She hung up, frustrated. She asked the public works department for customer data, only to learn that all service ran through the building's owner, a holding company in Texas. Nothing on individual tenants. Ditto for the local cable TV provider and garbage hauler. The electric utility refused to even talk to her. By the time Travis leaned over her desk with an inquisitive expression on his face, most of the day shift had punched out and headed to the Blue Line for happy hour.

"Sorry, Val. We don't have enough to ask a judge for a warrant," he said. "Besides, it's almost 5:00. We'd have more luck finding friendly judges at the Blue Line than in their offices."

"I'll buy their drinks, if it helps," she said.

He responded with a bemused grimace. "Go home," he said. "Get some rest. We'll start fresh tomorrow. Unless you want to try the tavern."

She begged off and sank into her chair. A five-mile run sounded more inviting, even in the rain. Besides, the risk of running into unfriendly WAVE staff at the police-friendly bar outweighed the near-zero odds of sweet-talking a magistrate over beers. The dead-end search had soured her mood, and she'd never excelled at cocktail chatter on her best days.

And this, clearly, was not her best day.

***

The Observer spotted Dawes a few blocks from the precinct, jogging in rain-repellent clothes and running shoes, white stripes reflecting the irregular flashes of sputtering street lights. He detected a pair of thin cables dangling from earbuds into her jacket. Good. Listening to music or podcasts, she'd pay less attention to someone following her. Especially in his invisible little VW.

He waited for her to get a quarter-mile ahead of him before pulling into traffic, filling the gap between a noisy pickup truck and a slow-moving sedan. She turned a few blocks later, and he lost sight of her—already! He tailgated the pickup until he reached the corner, and spotted her moments later.

His relief disappeared, however, when he realized her objective: the well-lit running trail that meandered through the city's greenway, a path that made following someone by car next to impossible. Dammit. This could turn into a quick night, and as a result, a tiny paycheck.

He pulled over after watching her disappear through the gates to the running trail and checked his GPS. About a mile ahead of her, the path connected to the Torrington River Loop, a pedestrian walkway built a decade before as part of a downtown revitalization campaign. Maybe he'd get lucky and catch up to her before she crossed the bridge.

He found a parking spot a few minutes later, and sure enough, Dawes emerged from the trail's east-end spur, loping along at a brisk pace. She crossed the busy riverfront thoroughfare mid-block, a few feet ahead of him, her eyes focused on approaching headlights. She zig-zagged and turned her body to scoot behind the lone vehicle coming her way, and her gaze swept over his darkened car. For a moment, she seemed to stare at him. He ducked his head, covered his mouth and beard with one hand, hoping the visor of his baseball cap would hide his eyes.

Waited. Listened.

He lifted his gaze, expecting to see her standing in front of his car. Or perhaps running up the trail. But he found no sign of her. He peered ahead, toward the bridge, then back upriver, toward the bend. Nothing. She was gone.

He sighed, opened his message app, and tapped in his disappointing report. *Lost sight of subject jogging on TRLoop.*

The reply: *Go home. Your work tonight is done.*

Chapter Thirty-One

As always, running cleared the clutter out of Val's mind, the obfuscating details melting away like late winter snow. Still, the core question remained as she showered off afterward at home: what should her role be moving forward?

She trusted only one person's advice on that, and he lived a twenty-minute walk from her house. She knocked on his door as the last rays of sunset sank behind the clouds on the horizon.

"Friend or foe?" Gil's voice called from inside.

"Depends on your frame of mind," Val answered. "Have you skipped taking your pain meds again?"

"Door's open. Get in here," Gil said with a good-natured growl. "I need my bedpan changed."

She found him on the sofa and bent over to give him a quick, awkward hug, not half long or tight enough. She wanted an immediate do-over. Instead she sat across from him, wondering how to begin.

"What's on your mind?" Gil said. "Something big, I can tell."

"Oh, nothing," she said, her voice taking on a tone of mocking indifference. "Just my tail-spinning career, this minor detail of a serial killer attacking young girls left and right, and Sergeant Petroni going from being my biggest cheerleader to hating me. What's on TV?"

"Wrong," Gil said. "I'm your biggest cheerleader and always have been. Petroni can suck it."

She laughed, tension bleeding out of her. "Rah-rah, I stand corrected. But the rest is all true."

He shook his head. "You've already forgotten our chat from a couple days ago, I see."

Her shoulders fell. "A lot's happened since then." She filled him in on her new role, chasing down dead leads on the Sierra Stapleton case. "Gibson and Blake have been great, but it's clear Petroni doesn't want me anywhere near the serial killer. It's so frustrating."

Gil eyed her a moment, folded his hands across his lap. "Tell me something. What does catching this Shoeless Slayer mean to you?"

The remark surprised her. Gil had never struck her as the philosophical type. She met his gaze, and for the first time she noticed how haggard he looked—unshaven, his face pale, sweat beading on his forehead, his short brown hair flat against his skull.

"I mean, why this case?" he said. "WAVE has the responsibility, budget, and talented staff dedicated to finding this guy. Why has it become such a crusade for Valorie Dawes?"

"He's a killer. Isn't that enough?" she said.

"There are lots of open cases you could work on," he said, "including other murders that have happened since the first Shoeless victim. Why him?"

Val stammered a moment, then found her voice. "Well, for one, I found one of the bodies," she said. "Plus, he's preying on young, innocent girls. That sort of resonates with me."

"Okay," he said, "I buy that, as *part* of the reason to do this. Still, I think there's more. And there *needs* to be more."

"I don't understand."

"Val," Gil said, "you're one of the most talented young cops I've ever met. You'll be an outstanding detective someday—officially, I mean. In reality, you're already pretty damned good."

"But," she said, waiting.

"But," he said, smiling and nodding, "there's more to life than that. Hell, there's more to being a detective than that."

"Such as?"

He paused a moment, scratching his stubbly face. "Val, why do people become cops? Why did you, for instance?"

She tossed her hands in the air. "We've had this conversation before. To help people."

"Great. How do cops help people?"

"Protect them from criminals who intend them harm."

He frowned. "How are we doing on that front? Are we *preventing* criminals from committing crimes? How many Shoeless Schoolgirls have we saved?"

"None, yet. Not until we catch this guy." Doubt crept into her voice. She didn't like where this was going.

"Right. So, do we prevent crime, or respond to it?"

"Both, of course." Her confidence returned.

"I'll submit that we spend more time chasing perps than stopping them from their next heinous act. Wouldn't you agree?"

Val shook her head. "Isolation is getting to you, isn't it?"

He laughed. "No fair changing the subject. Let me ask this a different way. Why do you think the killer has eluded you thus far?"

Her shoulders drooped, and her heart felt like lead. "He's smarter than me, I guess."

"No. Definitely not. But he is *different* from you." He leaned toward her and rested his hand on her leg. She stared at it, but didn't push it away. This was Gil, not some drunk jock.

"You keep thinking about him in rational terms: what would he do and why would he do it, as if he were a reasonable man," Gil continued. "A man with the same human motivations and needs as you or I, except for this weird obsession with killing young girls. Right?"

She nodded. "I guess so."

"But is he?" Gil shook his head. "This guy has a hole somewhere in his heart where compassion ought to be. Ask yourself: how does that change a person's thinking? How does it affect how he relates to other people? How would you feel if you lost the capacity to love your fellow human being?"

Surprised by the blunt personal question, Val's breath caught in her throat. She rolled it around in her head and didn't like what her mind came up with. "I sometimes feel like I have lost that piece of me," Val said.

"Bullshit." Gil squeezed her leg and held it in a firm grip. "You're a loving person. Romantic? Not one bit. But that's not the same thing. Val, you're selfless, generous, and empathetic. I've seen you connect in surprising ways with the widest range of people, from the toughest gang members to frightened little girls and grizzled old shopkeepers. That's not possible without the capacity for love of one's fellow human being."

"Where's this all going?" Val cleared her throat, tried to think of a way to divert the conversation away from herself.

"In the eight months I've known you," Gil said, "your focus has always been on other people. Stepping back and observing you since my injury, though, I've noticed the one person you never help. And that's you."

"I'm fine. I don't need help."

"Bullshit again." His hand left her thigh, and her skin tingled in memory of his touch. "I'll cut to the chase. Solving this murder is important, and if that's all you accomplish, well, that's a glorious thing. But it's not enough."

"What would be enough, smart guy?" Val said with more heat than she intended.

He sat back, clearly affected by the force of her words. But he didn't cower. "What the world needs from Valorie Dawes isn't another solved murder case. What we need is the same thing you need: a *better* Valorie Dawes. One that can change the landscape of this city, one that can shift our role from chasing bad guys after the fact to making a real difference. Every case you take is an opportunity to learn—not just better investigative technique or police procedure, but to learn what's inside here." He tapped her chest with an index finger. "Find the best part of you. That's the key. Let that inform the Valorie that interacts with this community every day. When you tap into what's inside you—the talent, the smarts, and most importantly, the love—you'll make this city safe for everyone *except* men like the Shoeless Schoolgirl Slayer. I guarantee it."

"I don't understand how that even matters," she said. "He's not thinking about me when he kills. What does—"

"It matters more than anything," Gil said. "You're better than he is, Val. You don't believe it yet. There's something stopping you from exploiting your own awesomeness. I don't know what it is. Until you solve that, you're always going to be a step behind this guy, and all the other bad guys out there. And when you do..." He smiled and rested his hand on hers. "They won't stand a chance."

Val stared at him, allowing the warmth of his touch, of his words, to flow over her. On its surface, Gil's speech amounted to little more than a pep talk. But something about it—something about *him*—resonated deeper than that.

Only when she'd taken several deep breaths of the crisp night air on her walk home did she realize what that something was. It was the virtue that he'd just extolled in her, the virtue that made him available to her on a moment's notice late on a weeknight.

Love.

***

Val rose at 6:15 the next morning, taking a quick but appreciative glance out her bedroom window. The rays of a beautiful sunrise brightened a shredded blanket of low-lying clouds in pink light. She slipped into a loose-fitting "Property of Clayton PD" sweatshirt, moisture-wicking tights, a thermal headband, and gloves. After starting a pot of coffee, she sprinted out the door, letting it brew on the counter while she ran. Two miles out, two miles back in the crisp, 40-degree spring air had her body refreshed and her mind racing.

A conclusion formed in her mind while she passed the run-down mix of mom-and-pop shops, neighborhood taverns, and 1940s Art Deco buildings converted into overcrowded apartments in Liberty Heights. The key unknowns in the Slayer case revolved not around Sierra Stapleton or Olivia Lambert, but Charlene Washington. Charlene linked all the known pieces together: the killer's MO, Diego, Kent, the Association of Future Entrepreneurs, and Curtis's company, Constitution Finance. Charlene also knew Sierra, which meant she knew Bo. Her brother, Gunner, linked her to a major information resource that she hadn't yet tapped enough: The Disciples street gang. With Travis tied up in meetings all morning, she could do a little freelancing.

She showered, wolfed down a plate of scrambled eggs and a mug of coffee, and almost made it out the door when Beth's voice stopped her.

"Before you leave," Beth said, yawning, "I wanted to check in with you about Friday night." She trudged toward the kitchen and stretched, smiling at Val's obvious confusion. "The reunion, dummy. You *are* going, right?"

Val's body deflated, like her mood. "I'm...not sure," she said. "It depends on how today goes."

"Come on, Val. I need you to support me on this," Beth said. "I spent weeks planning it. If my best friend in the universe stiffs me—"

"All right, all right," Val said. "What time?"

"Be here and ready to go at six," Beth said. "I could use your help with last-minute setup. What are you wearing?"

"Pick something out for me," Val said, her hand on the door.

"You don't have anything sexy in that closet of yours," Beth said. "How about we go shopping after work tomorrow? I can get you thirty percent off at Macy's with my employee discount. Are you still a size four?"

Val barked out a laugh. "I hope I can squeeze into a six—wait, are you expecting me to wear a dress to this thing?"

Beth rolled her eyes. "The theme is 'Prom Night,' remember? Nobody wears slacks to a prom."

"I wouldn't know," Val said, rushing out the door. "I never went to one, remember?"

She clocked in at the precinct, followed up on a few more dead-ends on the Stapleton case, and slipped out to the motor pool a little after 8:00 a.m. She checked out a squad car and drove downtown, slowing as she passed the abandoned theater parking lot on MLK Boulevard. In the center of the lot, a crowd of young Black men huddled together, clapping in rhythm and chanting something in unison. Something about having each other's backs—she couldn't make out the exact words. A few stared at the car as it passed. She drove on, parked a few blocks away, and walked back. She wanted a low-key entrance, one that wouldn't scare anyone away.

As usual, only a few cars dotted the perimeter of the lot, old junkers that hadn't moved in weeks or months. Moving past them, Val felt vulnerable and slowed her pace. She recognized the ranking member in the middle of the group,

Cardinal Thomas, a giant of a man with four gold rings in each earlobe. Six-four and over three hundred pounds of muscle, he looked like he could stop a runaway semi-trailer with a flick of his wrist. Like the others, he wore a light jacket, unzipped over a plain black T-shirt and baggy jeans.

"Well, if it ain't the Copette," Thomas said without looking up at her. "You never come just to visit, so what is it you want this time?"

"Looking for Gunner," Val said. "He around?"

Thomas waved a hand around his head. "See him?"

She didn't. "So, where might I—"

"I ain't his fucking social secretary." Thomas hocked up a giant glob and spit into a nearby trash can. It hit the side and sizzled away into gray steam. Only then did Val notice the orange tongues of fire flickering above the can's rim.

Val waited for more explanation. Nothing came. After a long moment, she sidled up next to Thomas and extended her hands toward the fire. They warmed instantly in the intense heat.

"The fuck you doing, Copette?" Thomas asked.

"Warming my hands," Val said. "The fuck it looks like?"

One of the young men across from them laughed, but stopped under Thomas's withering glare. Thomas slapped her hands away, scowling at her. "You want to stand at the front of this army, you gotta earn it."

Val rubbed her hands where Thomas had smacked them, holding her flaring temper in check. She reminded herself to take the long view, not get pulled into a pissing match with the gang's Number Two man. "I'm not here to arrest Gunner, or anybody," she said. "I'm here to help find the guy who killed his sister."

"Ha!" Thomas glared at her. "Tell you what. When *we* find that cocksucker, we'll send you his remains. Now get the fuck out." He turned his massive body away from her.

Val sighed and stepped back. Sometimes, Uncle Val often said, the better part of valor was found in retreat. She glanced around the group one more time and caught the eye of a slender young man she'd encountered a few months before. A single gold earring dangled from his left lobe. Not yet seventeen, she'd caught "Dog" trying to rip off a convenience store as part of his initiation into the gang. Val had let him walk, a risky move that paid dividends later when he helped her find serial rapist Richard Harkins. She smiled at Dog, then indicated the outer edge of the lot with a wag of her head. He joined her there moments later.

"You know I'm not going to bust Gunner's balls, right?" Val said in a low voice.

Dog nodded. "He ain't been around much since his sister…" His voice trailed off.

"I get it," Val said. "So, where has he been?"

"I guess looking for the dude," Dog said, avoiding eye contact.

"Where, Dog?"

No response.

"Listen, this guy, this killer, he's already killed five, maybe six girls. He's not going to stop on his own. We've got to stop him. If we don't—"

"Pope and Thomas say we gonna stop him ourselves." Dog drew a circle in the gravel with his toe. "They say you cops don't give two shits about Charlene or any of us."

"If I didn't care, would I be here?"

Dog looked up at her, cast a quick look toward Thomas and the rest of the Disciples, then stared off to his right. He pulled out a cell phone, holding it so Thomas couldn't see it, and tapped it a few times. Moments later, it buzzed in his hand. He read the message and shoved the phone back into his pocket.

"Be in that laundry place across the street in five." Dog walked back toward the fire, his hands still shoved into his pockets.

Val waited a moment. No one in the group paid the least bit of attention to her, even Dog. She spun around and walked back the way she came, up MLK for a block, then crossed the street. She circled around another block, and found her way back into the laundromat Dog had pointed out. Two of the dozen washing machines on the right side of the room churned, making enough racket to raise the dead. None of the dryers lining the left side spun at the moment, and half of them had "Out of Order" signs taped to their front windows. A young Asian woman sat near the front of the shop, holding her baby and reading a magazine. Sure enough, Gunner sat on a long wooden bench in the back, wearing an unzipped hoodie, sweatpants, and Reeboks.

"If I'd have known I could find you here, I'd have brought my dirty underwear," Val said, sitting next to him.

"Dog said you're looking for the dude done killed Charlene," Gunner said.

Val nodded. "Thomas says you're going to find him first."

"He better hope I don't."

Val studied his face. Gunner's dark brown skin shined with a patina of sweat in the dim fluorescent lighting. Little emotion showed in his face, and his sharp eyes appeared focused and resolute. Like his voice.

"You gonna beat him up too?" she asked.

Gunner shot her a puzzled frown. "The fuck you mean?"

"Like Diego Collier. He got the shit kicked out of him in jail yesterday. Put him in the hospital."

Gunner stared at the dirty tile floor. "Don't know no Diego Collier."

"The guy arrested for killing your sister."

Gunner scoffed, making a hissing sound between his teeth. "Fucking maggot. He didn't kill Charlene. Everybody knows it except you assholes."

"So, why the beating?" Val asked.

"I didn't have that done, okay? They done that on their own."

"Who did?"

Gunner shook his head and looked away.

"Okay, then, why?"

Gunner glared at her. "Tell me what you gonna do when you find out some motherfucker done fucked *your* little sister." He spit on the floor, creating a white line on the dirty tile. "She barely sixteen, Copette. Six-fucking-teen!"

Val drew in a deep breath, let it out. She recalled the name of the boy Charlene had dated before Diego. "So, maybe Jamal had it done?"

"You find his Black ass, I'm gonna kick it, too." Gunner's eyes seemed to grow even harder, if that were possible. Val decided to believe him.

"So. What about Sierra Stapleton?"

"Who the fuck is Sierra Staples?"

"Staple-*ton*. The latest victim, we think."

Gunner shrugged. "Oh, yeah. Lady Beanpole. I heard that was a drug thing."

"You heard? How?"

He shook his head, seemed to focus on the young Asian woman across the laundromat. "Word travels."

"I see." Val put two and two together. "So, since Diego was supplying Sierra with pills, cutting in on your action—"

"Not us. That ain't our territory. And, uh, we don't deal no drugs." He grinned at her, a lazy smile of contempt over the necessary lie.

"Right. So you all wouldn't care about that." Val leaned back, thinking. "But somebody would. Who?"

Gunner half-smiled, half-frowned at her. She knew that expression well: *Are you an idiot?* "Copette," he said, "who uses that pharmaceutical shit?"

"Amphetamines? Coke? I don't know. Everybody."

Gunner laughed. "In *your* world. Not mine."

Realization dawned. "You mean, white people."

"That's money, Copette."

Val considered that for a moment. Some white person, or group, had Diego beat up, then. Great. That narrowed the list down to, oh, forty percent of the city. "Any idea who had it done?"

Gunner shook his head. "Sorry. But, you know, not sorry. That asshole had it coming."

She let that sink in a moment. "So, who do you think killed your sister, then?"

"Some other fucking white dude. She liked white dudes."

"Diego's not white. Neither was Jamal."

"She didn't fuck Jamal, I guarantee you. I'd-a cut his dick off."

"Okay. Who else?"

His expression grew dark and mean again. "You'll know when I do."

"Gunner, don't."

"Fuck you."

"Gunner, if we find him dead—"

"You ain't gonna find him, dead or alive. Not if I find him first. He and his little white dick be fish food, that I guarantee." Gunner stood and shuffled toward the exit. Halfway to the Asian woman, he spun around, his finger in the air. "I remembered one thing you asked me about. That older guy she was hanging out with? The one she had to meet with to talk about her ideas and shit for that internship? I remembered his name."

Val stood and walked toward him. "Was it Curtis, by chance?"

Gunner's expression turned to puzzlement. "No, no. Close, though. It was *Kent*. She wrote about him in her little book, a journal or whatever."

Val's eyes widened. *Kent Mercer!* "She kept a journal? Can you get that to me?"

Gunner shrugged. "If I can find it. I got pissed off, and, well, I might have burned it."

"Jesus, Gunner, that's evidence! You can't destroy stuff like that." Val fumed a moment, then calmed. "You're sure about the name?"

"Totally. I remember she mentioned him one time, too. I gave her shit about it 'cause it's such a bullshit white-boy name. She got all pissed off 'cause I called him 'Cunt Mercy.'" He laughed, turned, and strode out of the laundromat.

Val sank into a chair. Kent had claimed he barely knew Charlene and had an unconfirmed alibi for the day she died. On at least one count, Kent had lied.

Chapter Thirty-Two

Val gave up on trying to reach the Washingtons by phone and opted for a more direct approach. She parked in front of their modest home, recognizing its boxy style and trim lawn, everything well-maintained and portraying a sense of middle-class normalcy. Inside, though, sadness and tension had reigned on her last visit. That, and the press hysteria around the Shoeless Slayer case, would explain why they weren't answering their phones. But she needed to speak to them.

She approached the door and knocked. Reverend Daryl Washington opened the door, wearing a dress shirt that matched the snow-white hue of his tight, short curls.

"Who is it, honey?" called a woman from inside. Val recognized the voice of Natalie, Charlene's mother.

Reverend Washington squinted at Val, as if unsure of the answer to his wife's query. "Officer Dawes?" he half-asked of Val and half-called back to his wife. "I, uh, didn't recognize you at first."

"Sorry to intrude on your morning," Val said. "I had a chat with your son this morning, and I'd like to follow up on a few things."

"You talked with Gunther?" Natalie appeared beside her husband and rested her hands on his shoulder. "Where? When?"

"Please come in," the Reverend said, recovering. "Would you like some coffee?"

Val followed them inside, taking a seat on a well-loved armchair across from the leather sofa where Natalie sat. A framed, oversized enlargement of Charlene's high school yearbook photo rested on the coffee table in front of them. A chain necklace draped around the edges of the picture frame, centering a gold cross over the girl's chest.

"When did you see my boy?" Natalie asked Val in a choked voice.

"This morning," Val said. "Has he been around?"

Before Natalie could answer, Reverend Washington joined them with a tray containing a white porcelain coffee service. After sitting next to his wife, he poured each of them a cup and waited for Val to pour a dollop of milk into hers before stirring milk and sugar into the other two.

"We haven't seen Gunther since...*before*," Natalie said. "We spoke, briefly, long enough to tell him the news. Which, somehow, he'd already heard."

"Bad news travels fast," Reverend Washington muttered into his coffee.

Val frowned. That didn't quite add up. Somehow Gunner had obtained Charlene's diary after she died, presumably from her bedroom. Either he'd done so without their knowledge, or they had lied to Val's face. To protect him, or possibly themselves. But calling them out in that moment could derail their talk, if not her entire strategy of focusing on Charlene. She chose a more indirect approach.

"Gunner—er, *Gunther*—said that Charlene may have kept a diary or journal," Val said. "Do you know where those writings might have ended up?"

Reverend Washington took Natalie's hand in his and they exchanged a long, sad gaze. At long last, he nodded and turned away, tears welling in his eyes. Natalie squeezed his hand and faced Val. "We didn't allow our children on social media. Instead, we encouraged them to find other, more traditional ways to express their innermost thoughts and emotions," she said. "We promised Char that we'd never pry into her journals. However, on occasion, she shared some writing with us.”

“Anything that you could share with me could help the investigation,” Val said.

“We *gave her our word*,” the Reverend said in a steely tone. “Even telling you that these diaries exist feels like a violation.”

Val suppressed a sigh of frustration. The department could force them to turn the diaries over under the warrant already issued for the search of the property. Val preferred a more cooperative approach. “I understand,” she said. “Don’t you think she’d want us to have every clue at our disposal to catch the man who did this?”

“I don’t understand,” Natalie said. “Haven’t you already arrested the man who…?” Her voice trailed off.

Val’s insides tightened. She had to walk a tightrope here. “We need to build the strongest case possible,” she said. “Eliminate all doubt and counter any arguments his lawyers might make. If she mentioned any other boys besides Diego, we should investigate those leads.”

The Reverend stared at the floor, fuming. Natalie waited several long moments, then gave his hands a gentle shake. “Char’s gone,” she said in a quiet voice to him. “We can’t hurt her now.”

Reverend Washington lifted his head, focusing on some distant star in the universe, and let the tears flow down his cheeks. “I know,” he whispered. “And it’s about time someone paid attention to our girl. All the news talks about is those other girls.”

Val’s stomach churned a little. Those other white girls, he meant.

“Daryl?” Natalie said.

He exhaled and rubbed his temples. “Go ahead, Nattie.”

Natalie brushed away his tears and kissed his cheek, then hugged him and whispered something into his ear. He patted her hand and nodded, his eyes clenched shut.

"I'll get them for you," Natalie said. She disappeared down the hallway, passing the gallery of framed photos of their three children.

Val sipped her coffee, already getting cold. The Reverend continued to gaze into nothingness, every so often exhaling a frustrated, audible burst of air. After a long minute, he fixed Val with an intense stare, his lips working on forming words.

"Gunther's a troubled boy," he said.

Val nodded and set down her coffee, her fingers trembling. "He loved his sister," she said. "And she apparently trusted him enough to share her diary with him."

"Charlene did no such thing!" The fierceness of the Reverend's reply took Val aback. "Gunner stole that book from us! Which is why the rest are locked away." He punctuated his words by pointing an angry finger at Val's face.

"He came here?" Val asked. "After she died?"

Reverend Washington shrugged. "Not while I was home."

Natalie reappeared, carrying three dark green journals, about 5x8", clasped shut. She sat next to her husband, holding the books close to her chest. "We haven't read them," she said. "Nor have we read the missing volume. I hope, when you do, you'll refrain from sharing her words with anyone except those who absolutely must see them."

"I promise," Val said. "And the most recent diary...did you ever get that one back from Gunther?" Left unspoken: Did Gunner lie about burning them?

"No," Natalie said. "We've asked him to. He hasn't responded."

"He didn't even attend her funeral service," Reverend Washington said, bitterness edging his voice.

Val swallowed the painful lump that formed in her throat. That didn't sound like Gunner. She glanced at the diaries, still in Natalie's firm grasp. She searched for words of consolation, of understanding. Thought back to what people said after Uncle Val died. Did any of it help? Did any words ease her pain, allow her to trust her fellow human beings again? No. Not from her parents, her brother, her counselor, even Beth. Words didn't matter. Nothing mattered, except that he was gone.

One thing did matter. People showed up. They were *there*. And that's what Gunner hadn't done for his parents and sister.

In that moment, Val realized what she had to do—even though she did not know how.

"I will bring Gunner to you," she said.

The Washingtons stared at her, open mouthed. "He won't come," the Reverend said at last.

"If he wouldn't come before, why would he now?" Natalie said.

"Because he needs you," Val said. "And you need him."

"Pfft," Reverend Washington said, spittle flying. "Like that matters."

"How would you do this?" Natalie said with what sounded like a tinge of hope. Lots of doubt, but also hope.

Val stood. "I'll ask him," she said.

"We've asked him," the Reverend said. "Why would he listen to you, and not us?"

Val heaved a deep breath, let it out slowly. Memories flooded in of her father, demanding that she tell them what was wrong. Demanding explanations. Pleading, scolding, belittling. Then she recalled the image of her mother, walking out the door, cigarette in one hand, suitcase in the other. Giving up on her, on their family.

"Sometimes when parents ask, it sounds like telling," Val said. "So asking him to come here wouldn't work. However, that's not our only option." She faced Reverend Washington, who also stood. "You said you have a difficult relationship with Gunther. Because of that, I'm going to ask you a favor."

Puzzlement clouded his face. "What kind of favor?"

Val reached out to Natalie, who stood up next to Reverend Washington. She took Natalie's hand. "I'd like you, Reverend, to stay here. And for you, Mrs. Washington, to come with me. I'll show you where to find Gunther. Then you can tell him, face to face, how much he means to you."

The Reverend squirmed away from them. "Gunner should come to *us* and tell—"

"Daryl." Natalie let go of Val's hand and pressed a finger to his lips. "We're the parents." She paused, glanced at Val, then back to her husband. "Let's act like it."

Reverend Washington stared at her for an infinity of heartbeats. Val held her breath, waiting. Then, without another word, he nodded and left the room.

Natalie turned to Val, her hand resting on Charlene's black-bound journals. "I will give you these diaries," she said, "when you bring me my son."

***

Val's return trip to The Disciples' street headquarters ran into a stone wall, with the few loitering gang members professing ignorance of Gunner's whereabouts. Or of Cardinal Thomas's, or Dog's, or anyone else who might be able to locate him. "Come back tomorrow," one of them said with a dismissive sniff.

With Travis again tied up with administrative duties, Val returned the next day, this time a passenger in Natalie Washington's Toyota Camry. A half-block shy of the abandoned theater's parking lot, Val pointed to an empty metered spot on the street.

"Gunner lives here?" Natalie said, doubtful.

"I don't know where he lives," Val said. "I only know that I can usually find him here."

She led Natalie to the edge of the parking lot and stopped there, searching each face. Again, no Dog, Gunner, or Thomas. Frustrated, she turned toward Natalie—

And came face to face with the man known as Pope, a hulk of a man in his late twenties with a broad, expressionless face. Easily six-four, two-fifty, probably bigger. He sported seven large, gold rings in each earlobe, the mark of ultimate authority among The Disciples. Despite the chilly spring temperature, he wore a sleeveless black T-shirt with the word "Resist!" stenciled in white letters and baggy, black canvas pants. As always, two shorter, bulkier giants, similarly dressed, stood on each side of him, the positions of rank in the gang, each with a smaller set of gold earrings.

"The fuck you doing down here, Copette?" Pope said, arms folded across his massive chest. "This ain't no place for a unarmed cop out of uniform."

Val pointed to Natalie with an open palm. "This is Gunner's mom. We're trying to find him."

Pope scowled and shook his head. "All due respect, Gunner's Mom, if he wanted to find you, he would. And if you're toting a dumb little white girl around with you, he ain't gonna want to." His lieutenants chuckled and exchanged knowing glances.

"All the same," Val said, "if you know where we can find him, I'd appreciate a heads-up. It has to do with finding Charlene's killer."

"Why don't you look in your city jail?" Pope said. "Ya'll cops said you done found the dude and arrested him already."

Val cursed herself for the slip. "There are some loose ends we need to wrap up," she said. "To make sure we have the right guy."

Pope laughed. "You arrested a Black dude for killing a bunch of school girls, most of 'em white. My guess is you *don't* got the right dude. But that never stopped ya'll before."

"Mr. Pope," Natalie said, stepping around Val to face him. "Please. Gunther told me you have a younger sister. Wouldn't you do everything you could if someone brought harm to her? Wouldn't you expect us to help you, in that situation?"

Pope squinted at her, biting his lip. He twisted his body back and forth, making eye contact with his beefy bodyguards. Both glanced away in silence.

"Aight," he said. "Wait here." He snapped his fingers at one of the men beside him. The man slipped away into a dark, narrow alley between the theater and a taller, mixed-use building. What seemed like hours later, but was probably only a minute or two, he re-emerged. A short, stocky man trudged along behind him, screened by the large man's bulk until they drew close. Then he stepped aside, and Gunner stepped forward, his face full of sadness and doubt.

Natalie stepped forward, her arms extended. Gunner stared at her, thumbs hooked in his pockets, then glanced back at Pope and his lieutenants. "What the fuck?" he said in a low voice.

"Gunther?" Natalie swayed a bit on her feet, her arms drooping. "Can we talk a minute, son?"

Gunner blew out a noisy breath, arched his back. "Bout what?"

Tears formed in the corners of Natalie's dark eyes. "About you...about Char...maybe you coming home to see Alysha," she said, her voice breaking.

Gunner rolled back on his feet, his eyes downcast. He leaned to one side, then the other, scraped the pavement with his toe. "The Rev don't want me there," Gunner said.

"I spoke to him," Natalie said. "If you need, I'll—I'll make sure he's not there."

"In his own house?" Gunner's voice betrayed his disbelief.

"It's my house, too," Natalie said.

Gunner looked away from her, said nothing.

"Your sister needs you," Natalie said. "*I* need you."

Gunner's gaze fell back to his feet, his eyes moist.

"Please," Natalie said in a whisper.

Finally, he glanced up at her. "Aight," he said.

Natalie stepped toward him and drew him into a long, fierce hug. Tears splashed down her face. Gunner's body shook, and he patted his mother's back several times, rocking her from side to side.

"Officer Dawes," Natalie said without breaking the embrace, "the books are in my car. It's unlocked. Take good care of them." With that, she buried her face in Gunner's shoulder.

Val backed away and caught Pope's eye. "Thank you," she mouthed.

"You owe me," Pope mouthed back, and with that, he joined his comrades in their circle around the ever-burning fire in the trash can in the center of the lot.

***

Val pored through Charlene's diaries, holed up in her cubicle at the Liberty Heights Precinct office. The first two volumes, spanning from the previous summer until almost Christmas, contained the girl's musings about how her parents would kill her if she earned only a B in Algebra II. Others detailed how much she loved volleyball practice and how much her little sister bugged her. Typical girl stuff, and nothing of obvious relevance to the case.

She changed tactics and scanned the latest diary in reverse order. The last entry, dated in mid-February, made vague references to a boy she had a crush on. She didn't reveal his name. Another entry mentioned meeting up with Gunner, but provided no details. She cursed Gunner's impulsive destruction of the most recent volume. If any of the diaries had something of relevance, that would have been it.

Val glanced at the clock, shocked at how long this had taken her. Protocol demanded that she log the diaries into evidence ASAP. The paperwork would take at least an hour, which would make her late to meet Beth at Macy's. She shrugged it off. She could secure them in her locker overnight, book them in later when she had more time.

Which meant she could read a little more right then. She skimmed back through the next few entries, mostly details about Charlene's school workload, yearbook responsibilities, and volleyball. One seemed promising, but turned into a long rant about how strict her parents were, not letting her get her ears pierced—again. But another entry, from mid-January, yielded paydirt.

> Met with my AFE mentor today, Diego. He's so nice! Such a gentleman, and OMG is he cute. But get this: he brought a friend along, who said he could get me an internship at Constitution Finance. I guess I got pretty excited because the next thing you know, all three of us are heading over to Constitution Tower! My parents would kill me if they knew I went to Hartford without permission but I couldn't pass up this opportunity. And I'm so glad I went.

Val turned the page, and a printed photo slipped out from between the pages. The picture showed Charlene posing in front of Constitution Tower with two young men: Diego Collier and Kent Mercer, all three arm-in-arm and smiling.

We get there, and it's like a palace, and Kent walks in like he owns the place! I met his supervisor, Ms. Schofield, and before you know it, I'm interviewing with Curtis Iverson himself. The husband of the mayor! He asked for my resumé and sounded so excited to hire me, I almost peed my pants. And get this: they said that Olivia, from volleyball, had recommended me. That girl never said two words to me outside of practice and meets! I start next week and I am SO EXCITED!

Val set the diaries down, a dizzying pair of realizations coming straight to mind. One: Kent had lied again, this time denying that he knew Charlene. And two: every one of the Shoeless Schoolgirl Slayer victims had interned for Curtis Iverson and LeeAnn Schofield.

Chapter Thirty-Three

Stuck behind a desk all day Friday answering phones, Val left work early for the first time in her brief career, mindful of her promise to help Beth set up for the reunion.

First, she had to get herself ready. Val had succumbed to Beth's good-natured haranguing and shelled out a hundred bucks for a violet, knee-length sheath dress the night before. Aside from its scooping neckline, which she remedied by wearing a lacy camisole underneath, the dress was modest and even flattering to her wiry figure. More important, it was comfortable. As a bonus, Beth suggested she could wear it to her wedding in four months.

She changed into it after an early dinner and joined Beth and Josh in the living room. Beth, as promised, had squeezed into her prom gown, a glittery, floor-length sleeveless affair with a plunging V-neck that showed off her ample curves. Beth pinned back her brown curls with a slender, tortoise-shell clip, giving her a distinctive throwback look.

"Man, you both look *hot!*" Josh said, close enough for Val to smell the booze on his breath. He put a scrawny arm around each of the women and pulled them into an uncomfortable hug. "I've got the two hottest dates to the whole reunion!"

"Easy, boyfy," Beth said, slapping his butt. "You're spoken for. And I'm the one speaking." She slathered a wet kiss on his face, and Val escaped the embrace before getting crushed between them.

"Didn't you say we needed to get there early?" Val said, grabbing Beth's car keys off the coffee table. "Come on, I'll chauffeur so you two can get this out of your system on the way."

Liberty Heights High, the oldest and second-largest high school in the city, carved its decaying footprint out of a cramped, 35-acre campus in the heart of the city's working-class industrial core, two miles from the Torrington River. The main building, a two-story yellow brick eyesore, somehow had survived nine decades of neglect. Patches of English Ivy hid about half of the black smoke stains from now-retired factories. Still the heart of campus, it contained over 80 classrooms, a handful of administrative offices, a drafty auditorium, an undersized cafeteria, and a boys' and girls' gym.

The cafeteria and gym served as Reunion Central. On the drive over, Beth fretted about whether they'd fill their designated space. Of the 560-odd seniors in the 2014 graduating class, Beth predicted that fewer than 70 would attend—close to 100 total attendees with spouses and dates.

"You never know," Josh said. "People suck at RSVP-ing."

That size crowd meant they'd split the cafeteria with the class of 2009, with an accordion-style folding divider bisecting the room. "We almost got relegated to a classroom," Beth complained. "Like we could dance in a science lab?"

"How many reunions are there tonight?" Val hadn't considered the idea that other graduating classes would share their, ahem, special night.

"Every five years, back to 1959," Beth said. "Can you imagine going to your sixty-year class reunion?"

"What the hell would you do?" Josh said. "Have six-legged races with your walkers tied together?" He and Beth dissolved into laughter, which soon led to more audible kissing. Val sighed and stared straight ahead.

Once inside, bad news struck: the committee member who'd volunteered to check people in called in sick. Val, looking for any alternative to mingling and small talk, stepped in without hesitation. The job soon expanded to include directing traffic for more senior graduates wandering the school, cursing their planning committees who had sent out less informative invitations than Beth.

"Are you sure we're not in the cafeteria?" a white-haired graduate of the class of 1969 asked, clutching to her husband's frail arm. "We've always held our reunion in here."

"No respect for their elders, these kids," clucked another member of the wrinkled regality. "Taking over our space like this!"

Val calmed the old folks down and directed them to the proper location before fragile fists went flying. Over the course of the next hour, one well-dressed happy couple after another sharpened Val's self-consciousness over having come stag to the event.

One classmate proved a welcome exception. A dark-haired young man, dressed in casual slacks, a blue blazer, and a crisp button-down shirt, cast her a shy smile when he approached. "Guess I missed the part about 'prom theme' on the invite," he said with a wry grin, pointing at the poster on the wall. "Will you still let me in, Valorie?"

Val searched her memory but didn't recognize his face. He had deep-set brown eyes, almost-black hair shaved close on the sides, a trimmed dark beard lining his powerful jaw, and dimples when he smiled. "Um...did you RSVP?"

"Of course. I should be on the list." His eyes sparkled, and those dimples returned. So. Damned. Cute. Val scanned the list, turned the page...nothing.

"You don't remember me, do you?" he said, getting way too much enjoyment out of her predicament. "Even though I sat behind you in AP English class three years straight."

She tried to recall a boy meeting that description. Nothing.

"Imagine longer hair, no beard, glasses, braces..."

That did it. "Oh, my God! Nicky! You've...changed!"

He laughed again and opened his arms. Shit. Another damned hugger. Val stood, leaned over the table, accepted the awkward pat on the shoulders, escaped. "You, um, look great," she said.

"Amazing what gaining half a foot in height and losing twenty pounds will do," he said. "I finally took the advice you gave me in junior year and started running. Even did some intramural sports at Yale."

She confirmed his improved physique in appreciative silence. Nicky's jacket hugged his broad shoulders and tapered waist in all the right ways. Either he'd whipped himself into terrific shape, or he'd spent good money on a tailor.

"You look the same as always. I mean that as a compliment," he added, blushing.

"Uh, thanks," she said, blushing right back. She found his name on the list. "Evans, Nicholas." Checked his name off the list. "Party of one tonight, Nicky?"

He sighed. "Some things haven't changed since high school. By the way, I go by Nick now. See you inside?"

"I hope so," she said before she could stop herself. He disappeared inside the noisy room.

Around 7:30, she studied the roster. Beth's prediction had proven conservative. Already, over 90 of their classmates had checked in, most with significant others in tow. Standing room only, and she suspected that the cash bar's inventory of beer and wine wouldn't last past 10:00. The food, no doubt, was long gone.

"Vaaaalll!" Amy Yang's nasal voice echoed in the concrete-block hallway, and her slender form skittered on stiletto heels along the gray tile floor. "I'm so glad to see you!" She reached over the table and wrapped Val in what she meant as a hug. Instead it turned into an uncomfortable headlock that lasted about five seconds too long. "I didn't think you did reunion-type things!"

"I didn't either," Val said. "You look beautiful." Which she did. Resplendent in a chiffon sleeveless ankle-length gown, no doubt the exact dress she'd worn to the prom five years before, Amy hadn't gained a single pound since high school. She'd wrapped her long dark hair into a towering bun, accentuating her high cheekbones and coal-black eyes. "Are you here alone, or...?"

"No, Kent just ducked into the men's," Amy said. "He'll be along. Can you get us checked in?"

Kent. Val's gut tied itself into knots. She hadn't counted on seeing him there. Nor Amy. But she had to act on the opportunity before he returned. "Amy, real quick, I was wondering...that condo that you told me about, of Curtis Iverson's...do you remember the unit number of that place?"

Amy's painted-on eyebrows arched even higher on her forehead, her mouth forming a tiny "O". She fidgeted on her feet and clutched her purse, color-matched to her perfect dress. "The number? Um...no, I don't. Why?"

"Just curious," Val said. "If you think of it, could you maybe ask Kent tonight? He brought you there too, right?"

Amy's voice dropped to a whisper. "Valorie, please tell me you're not pursuing charges against Curtis over that...thing that happened. I told you that in confidence, and—"

"No, no," Val said, her ears burning. Shit. She'd handled this all wrong. "I, ah, know someone else looking for a place, and thought, maybe it'd be comparable."

"Comparable to what?" Amy stared at her, suspicion growing in her expression.

Val searched for words to escape the uncomfortable rut she'd talked herself into. The airy hallway felt hot and crowded.

She blinked, and Kent emerged at Amy's side, stuffed into a powder-blue tuxedo he'd outgrown since his own prom three or four years before. Fitness-wise, he and Nick had gone in opposite directions. Sweat dotted his brow, matting curly hair against his scalp in front.

"Officer Dawes," he said in a curt voice. "Fancy meeting you here."

"Mr. Mercer. Welcome to Liberty Heights, Class of 2014." Val turned the pages of the check-in sheet, finding Amy's name near the bottom of the last page. "Two tonight, then, Amy?"

"Isn't that what I RSVP'd?" Amy asked, a hint of concern creeping into her voice.

"Indeed it is. Have fun tonight." Val checked the box next to Amy's name and avoided their gaze as they walked past her into the party.

Beth brought her a glass of merlot twenty minutes later. "I looove Amy's boyfriend!" she said. "He's hilarious!"

"*Kent?*" Val said. "Are we talking about the same person?"

"He talked my ear off in there," Beth said. "I can't believe you didn't go out with him instead of that Diego guy. They're friends, right?"

"They are. Uh...trust me. It's very believable." She showed Beth the list. "We're way over projections, but nobody's shown up for a while now."

"Go ahead and shut down registration," Beth said. "If anyone else wanders in this late, they'll have missed out on the free food anyway. Come on, we're going to sing some karaoke. Josh and I want you to join us for 'Love Shack.' You can sing backup."

"I think I'd better stay here a little longer," Val said. "A lot of the old-timers keep finding their way over here by mistake."

"Speaking of which," Beth said. "Look! It's Mayor Iverson."

Megan and Curtis Iverson appeared at the building's entrance, a twin set of massive, glass-and-metal double doors, now swinging shut behind them. Megan, as always, looked dignified in a flowing blue gown. Curtis strode arm-in-arm with her, wearing a black tux, his dark hair coiffed, and that creepy smirk of a smile plastered onto his tanned face. Both looked out of place in the dingy confines of Liberty Heights High.

"What the hell are they doing here?" Val asked in a low voice.

"Probably looking for the '94 reunion, in the gym. She graduated valedictorian," Beth said, in a voice loud enough for the mayor to hear. Val cringed. Sure enough, Megan flashed a broad, campaign-worthy smile at them and tugged Curtis over to the registration table.

"What year is meeting in the cafeteria this year?" Megan asked, as if very pleased with herself.

"Class of 2014 here, and 2009 on the far side," Beth said, accepting the mayor's offered handshake. "Welcome, Madam Mayor. I'm Beth Holland, and this is—"

"Pleasure to meet you," Megan Iverson said, and narrowed her eyes at Val. "Ms. Dawes and I have met. Curt, you remember Officer Dawes?"

"Indeed I do." He accepted Val's reticent handshake, then took Beth's hand in his. "But this is the first time I've had the pleasure of meeting Ms. Holland."

"I hope it's not rude to pop in and say hello to your classmates for a moment," Megan said. "I love to meet all of my constituents, and I prefer informal settings like these."

Voters, she means, Val groused in silence. She caught Curtis staring at her with those steely gray eyes. He looked away and fussed with one of his gold cuff links.

"Of course you can!" Beth said. "We'd love to have you!" She opened the cafeteria doors, and the blast of the DJ's dance tunes flowed out into the hallway. "I hope you like dancing, Madam Mayor!"

"Please, call me Megan," the mayor said with a laugh. She tugged at Curtis, whose steely gaze had returned to Val. He let it rest there a moment longer, then smiled and joined his wife inside the party.

"Coming, Val?" Beth said, holding the door open.

Val sipped her merlot. Cheap crap from CostCo. She left it on the table and followed Beth inside. After all, both Kent and Curtis were in there—and both needed watching.

And so was Nick Evans, who'd be a lot more pleasant to watch.

***

Some days, things just go right.

Across the crowded cafeteria, he recognized the girl Dawes had run with a few Sundays before. The first minute of small talk revealed how perfect she was. Dawes would fall on her sword for this girl. No doubt about it. As much as Dawes disliked him—she'd proved that many times, and it was mutual—she'd set that aside in a heartbeat, if necessary, to protect her friend from harm.

Which she could not. Not even the tenacious, fearless Dawes could stop a young woman from falling for his charms.

Beth wasn't perfect, but almost. A few years older than he preferred, yet still young. Vivacious. With spirit. Passion. Powerful, yet vulnerable. And, he could tell, willing to take risks.

Physically perfect, too. A body with curves. One already dotted with ink—enough of her skin showed to confirm that—so she wouldn't fear the needle.

He chided himself for having flirted with a candidate as weak as Amy Yang—a sweet girl, but lacking substance. Physically, intellectually, and emotionally. How could he ever have considered *her*?

He recalled his logic. Amy would throw the cops off the scent. But that was unnecessary. They were lost. Fixated on Diego Collier. They had no idea.

Even better: once he lured the roommate in, Dawes herself would fall prey.

That prospect sent a shiver down his back. Strong, smart, fierce, and determined, Dawes wouldn't succumb easily. And normally, targeting a cop would mean taking on the whole department.

But Dawes was a loner, and a bit of an outcast—as the department proved when they tossed her off the squad assigned to finding him. The Brotherhood of Police might not rally as fast to support an ambitious woman among their ranks.

Besides, with great risk came great rewards. Exerting his power over her would raise his game—and the thrills he would thus enjoy—to new levels.

He gazed at her across the dark room, chatting with her voluptuous friend. Dawes's body had never enticed him before, but perhaps he'd judged her too harshly on that score. At least in that dress, her legs and hips looked powerful, making up for her smallish breasts. An athletic shape, substantive enough to satisfy his cravings. Her hazel eyes, unique and intense, revealed an indomitable spirit.

Indomitable until now, that is. She'd make quite the conquest.

First, though, the friend.

The DJ announced he was "slowing it down for the ladies," and a fragile hand rested on his elbow. "Come dance with me, honey," she said. He cringed. The voice belonged to a woman most men would consider beautiful.

Most men, though, were idiots.

He nodded and let her lead him onto the dance floor, closing his eyes so he wouldn't have to gaze upon her absurdly skinny body. He reopened them once their bodies pressed close, and fixed his stare on the swaying figure of Beth Holland.

Soon. Soon.

Chapter Thirty-Four

Slow songs had always terrified Val at high school parties. Invariably, some boy she had never met would ask her to dance. The few times she succumbed left her wanting to escape his sweaty, groping hands even before she gagged on his unnecessary after-shave. So, when the DJ announced his intention to "slow it down for the ladies," she slipped into the shadows near the cash bar, pretending to get into line.

But her lifelong friend knew her habits, and soon Beth and Josh danced close by.

"I think that guy over there wants to dance with you," Beth said, leaning away from Josh. She nodded toward the tall, bearded guy Val had checked in an hour before. Nick stood by the DJ's table, sipping a dark beer.

Val shook her head. "If he wanted to ask me, he'd have asked me." She pointed to the long line ahead of her at the bar. "Besides, I doubt I'll get served before this song is over."

"Valorie?"

Shit. In the time it took to dish out her lame excuse, Nick had noticed them looking at him and wandered over.

Nick cleared his throat and smiled, showing those cute dimples again. "One dance? Or, at this point, half of one?" He extended his hand.

Val sighed. Anybody else, she'd have said no, but he intrigued her. She surrendered a shy smile. "Okay. Half a dance." She followed him a few feet to the edge of the dancing area, where he stopped and held his hands in a slow-dance pose. She took his right hand in her left and rested the other on his shoulder, then braced for the inevitable too-cozy placement of his arm around her waist. But he proved shyer than expected, his hand resting like a feather halfway up her back. They swayed side to side, bodies a foot apart, to a John Legend song, popular the year they'd graduated.

"I didn't think you'd say yes," he said after an eternity of awkward left-right wobbling.

"I didn't think you'd ask," she heard herself saying. As flirty of a thing as she'd uttered to any man in years…other than Gil. She looked away from Nick.

"Are you sorry?" Mock horror flashed across his face, replaced by a quick smile.

"Not yet." Val blushed. "I mean, no. Thank you for asking." Wobble, wobble. Hours ticked by.

"Are you having a good time?" he asked.

"Sure," she said. "Everybody's been friendly." Meaning, they'd left her alone. Until now.

They danced, if one could call it that, for another half-minute of eternity. Val closed her eyes, then noticed his scent. It reminded her of Gil. A pang of guilt made her pause for a moment.

"Are you okay?" Nick asked.

"I'm fine," she said, reopening her eyes. "A little tired."

"Yeah, I didn't expect to stay this long," Nick said. "None of my friends showed up." She must have given him a disapproving look, because he added, "That I hung out with in high school, I mean."

"Me either. Other than Beth."

"Yeah, Beth's cool. I always liked her." He glanced over at her, dancing with Josh. Val followed suit. Beth grinned at her, mouthed something like "Yay for you!" and went back to snuggling Josh.

The song ended and she withdrew from their embrace, or pose, or whatever people called it. People who actually danced. "Thank you," she said.

Someone tapped her arm. Turning, a halfway-familiar, clean-shaven male face cast a drunken gaze her way. She seemed to recall him playing football and running for class president junior year. "Hey, cutie. Can I have the next dance?" he said, slurring his words.

"Gonna take a quick break," the DJ announced, right on time.

"Sorry," Val said.

"I'll find you," the jock said. "Buy you a drink?" He wandered off toward the bar, looking back at her with expectation in his smile, turning to disappointment when she stayed put.

"I'm going to get some air," Nick said. "You're welcome to join me."

"Sounds good." Anything to get away from drunken jocks.

The exit in back opened to a parking lot, and beyond it, practice fields for the various varsity squads. A rubber running track circled the closest field. For whatever reasons—security, Val guessed—the maintenance crews had left the field lights on. "Shall we take a lap or two around the track?" she said, slipping off her 1-inch heels.

Nick froze, glancing at his jacket and slacks. "I'm not really dressed for a run."

She laughed. "I meant walking. If you'd rather race, name your poison."

"Walking's fine." His eyes glistened, and those cute dimples returned.

Val smiled and stepped out at a brisk pace. "I haven't seen you around Clayton since graduation," she said. "Where have you been?"

Nick fell into step beside her. "Yale, until December. Switching majors cost me—and my parents—an extra semester."

"From what to what?"

"Pre-law to telecommunications, minor in journalism." His voice gained strength and confidence. "I hope to land an internship at WCLA-TV this summer."

"Do you remember Amy Yang?" Val said. "She interned there. Maybe she'd help you." As soon as the words left her mouth, she regretted it. She hoped to keep her distance from Amy for the time being.

"You think so?" Nick turned toward her, excited. "I didn't talk to her much in school, but at this point, I'll talk to anyone."

"Obviously." Another blurt she wanted back.

To her relief, Nick laughed. "Do I seem that desperate?" he said.

"No, no, sorry about that," Val said. "I meant, in your position, you kind of have to be open to anything."

"That's what my dad keeps telling me. In fact, he's the one who convinced me to come to this thing tonight. Said it might be good for networking. I expected nothing to come of it, but, well, here we are."

"Yes...here we are." Val swallowed, wondering where they were. That left them with an awkward silence until they rounded the third corner of the track.

"I think the music is starting back up," he said. "Want to dance again?"

"S-sure," Val said, though she couldn't hear anything from their half of the cafeteria. "A faster song, perhaps. Get the heart racing, you know?"

Nick nodded, but he let the distance increase between them.

"How do you like being a police officer?" he asked after they turned the final corner on the track.

Val cast him a sideways glance. "How did you know I became a cop?" she asked.

"Everybody knows you're a cop. Anyone who reads the news around here."

"I like it...most of the time," she said. "Less so when my name gets in the papers." Or when people like Gil take bullets for her.

"I can imagine," he said. "I have to admit, though, it was pretty cool to see you on the news when you got that award a few months ago."

"Thanks." Her face warmed. No need to remind him that the award recognized her for shooting a guy in the balls. Maybe he remembered that, too, though, as he grew silent while they walked back toward the cafeteria.

"Where have you guys been?" Beth called from outside the door. As always, Josh's arms remained locked around her waist. Nearby stood Amy, Kent, and a few other alums.

"Walking around. Amy, do you remember Nick?" she said. "He's interested in interning at WCLA. Perhaps you could provide him with some contacts?"

"Why would you want to work there?" Amy said, resting her hand on Kent's arm. "Long hours, and they don't pay squat!"

Nick shrugged. "It's the only game in town, unless I'm willing to move to Hartford or New York." He glanced at Val. "Which I'm not ready to do, yet."

Kent murmured something in Amy's ear and tugged at her arm. "C'mon, let's bounce," he said, louder.

"We should talk more about this another time," Amy said. "Val, will you set something up?"

"Going somewhere?" Beth asked, a little peeved. "Somewhere more fun, I take it?"

"Kent's having an after-party at his place," Amy said. "You all should come. We can go party without all the..." She cleared her throat. "*Restrictions* of being on school grounds."

Val sighed. Getting high, she meant. Not her thing, long before she became a cop and had to suffer random drug testing. She glanced at Nick, saw the hope in his eyes.

"Josh and I will go after we clean up here," Beth said. "You guys should totally join in."

"You can," she said to Nick. "I think I'll make it an early night."

"Next time," he said. Then, to Beth: "I'm willing to help clean up, if you need extra hands."

"Always!" Beth hid her face behind Josh and mouthed to Val: "He's awesome!"

Val smiled. Nick did seem pretty awesome. So why didn't she feel anything?

"Whatever," Kent said in a grumpy tone. "Whoever wants to come, Amy will send the address." He shuffled off to the side, bent over, reached down, and scratched an itch on the lower part of his right leg. The hem of his slacks rode up his calf, revealing what appeared to be a fresh, crude tattoo. Only a small portion of the image showed, and only for a moment.

Val recognized the design, though.

Rosie the Riveter, with an inscription beneath: *Chingona.*

***

The *Chingona* tattoo on Kent's calf stunned Val into immobile silence. Up to this point, she'd only seen the image in photos on Shoeless Schoolgirl Slayer victims. Despite what Topher at Ink Complete had said about the popularity of do-it-yourself tattoos, she'd never expected to see it in person, much less on a man.

Plus, even in the dim light of the parking lot outside the cafeteria, it looked pretty grotesque. All around the crude drawing, his skin had turned puffy and red. Where he'd scratched, a trickle of blood ran down to his black socks.

Amy's movement toward him startled Val out of her trance and into action. If Kent had applied the tattoo to himself, Amy would be next. "Amy!" she said, her voice high with tension. "Before you go...would you help me with something?" She gestured toward the cafeteria.

Amy halted her approach to Kent, still a few feet away, and cast him a wistful smile. "Give me a minute, honey?"

Kent scowled at Val. "I gotta take a leak anyway," he said. "Meet you back here?"

Val led Amy inside the cafeteria, but the DJ's booming voice over the intro to an Ariana Grande song drowned out any further conversation they might have attempted. She pulled close to Amy's ear and shouted, "Meet me at check-in?"

Amy stared at her, puzzled. "Can't hear," she mouthed.

"Follow me," Val shouted back, and dragged her by the arm through the gyrating bodies crowding the dance floor. Val shut the heavy double doors behind them once they reached the hallway where her registration table still stood.

"You want me to help you pack this up?" Amy said. "I'm not dressed for physical labor."

"That's okay," Val said. "I wanted to ask you something. About Kent."

"You need the address to the after-party?" Amy pulled her phone from her purse. "I'll text it to you."

"Not that. It's..." She took a deep breath. "I noticed he had a fresh tattoo on his leg."

"Don't you love it?" Amy's eyes lit up. "It didn't come out as good as I'd hoped. It was my first one, and—"

"Wait. *You* put that on him?"

Amy grinned. "He's going to do me too. When I saw how red and puffy his got, I asked him to wait until after the reunion. I didn't want my leg all gross like that, you know?" She propped her leg up on a chair. Her dress's side-slit, which reached above her knees, put her entire calf on display. The tattoo would have wrapped halfway around Amy's slender limb.

"Amy," Val said, her voice hoarse with tension, "promise me you won't let him tattoo you."

"Valorie, don't be such a prude," Amy said, laughing. "Everybody's doing it. It's no big deal."

"It *is* a big deal," Val said. "Please, this is important. Do. Not. Let. Him."

Amy's smile morphed into an irritated frown. "I don't see how it's any of your business."

Val's frustration mounted. The WAVE Squad had withheld the tattoo detail to help identify any would-be copycats. She couldn't reveal it to Amy now—she'd tell Kent in a microsecond. But Val had to protect her. "You'll have to trust me," she said. "I can't explain."

Amy slapped her foot down off the chair. "I can. You're jealous. Things didn't work out between you and Diego, so you don't want anyone else to be happy. How childish of you!" She took a few wobbly steps toward the big double doors of the cafeteria.

"For God's sake, Amy!" Val caught up and blocked her path. "It's not about Diego, and it's not jealousy. I want you to be safe, okay?"

"It's safe," she said. "We sanitize everything and it doesn't even hurt. I've gotten tats before." She turned and pulled her hair aside, displaying a colorful flower inked onto her neck.

"That's not what I mean," Val said. "Amy, how well do you know Kent?"

"Enough to trust that he wouldn't poison me with an unsanitary tattoo pen," Amy said, huffing. "Besides, he said that if I wanted, he'd anesthetize the area. Kent doesn't want to hurt me."

Val bit back an angry reply. Amy had no idea. And Val couldn't be sure. She had to warn her, though, somehow.

"How did this all come about, anyway? Why tattoos? Why now?"

"It's a commitment thing, and sort of an April Fool's joke," Amy said. "People do it all the time. You get the same tattoo as a bonding thing. A symbol of our love."

Gag. "Okay, I get that," Val said. Kind of. She understood the odd logic of it, but couldn't imagine doing it herself. "Why that image? Why not pick something more romantic? A heart, or a knot, or a red rose, perhaps?"

Amy laughed. "Hey, Valorie, the 1950s are calling and they want their 9:00 p.m. curfew back." She rolled her eyes. "Our love is not a Hallmark card. Stop trying to force us into that box. Anyway, it has to be the same image, and he already has his."

"Okay, okay," Val said. The whole thing was probably moot. If Kent was the Slayer, the tattoo wouldn't matter either way now. Besides, she had time: he wouldn't do anything that night. Not with other people around. And not until Sunday or Monday, if he held to the same pattern.

Something else Amy had said triggered a new question. "What was that about it being an April Fool's joke?" she asked.

"Oh," Amy said, her frown softening into a coy smile. "We came up with this idea on our first date...well, sort of date." She blushed. "If you get what I mean."

"Yeah, sure. Go on."

"Kent volunteered a week after I started on the campaign," Amy said. "We hit it off later that night, and we both wanted to be together right away. So we, um, *got together* the next night, and...anyway. It was a week after April Fool's day, and we kind of dared each other to do something to...show our commitment. I think getting the same tattoo was my idea, or maybe both of us. He said he knew how and it would save us a bunch of money, and it'd be wicked sexy, and I fell in love with the idea...and with him." Amy's voice trailed off, and a satisfied smile crossed her face.

Val weighed Amy's words. They made sense at one level...and raised a million red flags at another level. Something about the story didn't ring true, but she couldn't put her finger on it.

Before she could figure it out, the big double doors to the cafeteria opened, and an Ed Sheeran song echoed through the hallway. Kent's head popped out, a scowl on his face. As always, it seemed.

"Are you ready to go?" Kent said, his tone as impatient as his facial expression. "I have to stop for more drinks and stuff before everyone gets there."

"You should come, Valorie," Amy said, walking toward Kent. "Bring Nick. The two of you look good together."

"Thanks." Val watched them go, arms around each other's waists, down the hallway toward the building's exit.

Someone else exited the cafeteria, and Val spotted Beth and Josh dancing close, their smiling faces inches apart. They looked so happy together. A twinge of jealousy crept up inside her. She'd never experienced that feeling. Not really.

Except, sort of, with Gil.

Val tried shaking that off, without success. She wondered if he would still be up this late—almost 10:00— and considered calling him.

"Valorie?" Nick's voice interrupted her reverie, and he appeared next to her. "They're playing kind of a fast song. I thought I should take you up on that second dance?"

She listened. The music had shifted to a Nicki Minaj tune. Fast enough. "Sure," she said, and followed him inside.

Chapter Thirty-Five

The DJ maintained the fast pace, spinning tune after tune that kept the twenty-something bodies moving around the floor. Val kept up with Nick, who proved an able and agile dancer, and he seemed to get the message to keep his paws off her unless invited.

That invitation didn't come. Not yet, anyway. Still, she grew curious about him, wanting to learn more about the guy she'd ignored five years before.

When the tempo slowed on a song Val didn't recognize, she headed out the doors to the parking lot, letting the cool spring air cool her glistening skin. She heaved in a deep breath and marveled at how good she felt. "Whew!" she said when Nick joined her again. "I've never been much of a dancer, but that's a pretty intense workout."

"Fun, too, right?" Nick said with a hopeful smile.

"Yeah, sure," she said, nonchalant. A moment later, she grinned. It really *was* fun.

They sat on a bench, a foot or two apart, and gazed out in silence over the line of cars making an early exit. Mostly older folk from the prior-year reunions. So, not early for them. The white-haired crowd probably quit by 10:00.

As if on cue, a parade of older couples pushed through another exit at the far end of the school building, a sign that their party had ended altogether. A minute later, another group, somewhat younger, what Val guessed to be the fifteen-year reunion crowd—thirty-something parents with babysitters to send home. She wondered if she'd ever fit into that married-with-children demographic, much less at such a young age.

One couple—or rather, the female half of a couple—looked familiar as they moved closer up the sidewalk. A statuesque platinum blonde with pale white skin leaned on the arm of her husband, a dark-haired man with chiseled features and a premature stripe of gray running through his sideburns. Val didn't recognize him, other than that he could have replaced any of a thousand actors on Viagra commercials. On the other hand, the woman's face reminded her of someone she'd met in recent weeks. In this setting, though, she couldn't place her.

When the couple reached the parking lot, a male voice called out something unintelligible to them, and the woman paused, facing the source of the voice. A young man, a little too pudgy for his ill-fitting powder blue tux, jogged toward them.

"Is that Kent Mercer?" she asked Nick. "What's he doing back here? He left over a half hour ago."

"Remind me, who's Kent Mercer?" Nick said. "Was he in our class?"

Val shook her head, looked closer. Definitely Kent. In that instant, she recognized the woman: LeeAnn Schofield, Curtis Iverson's executive assistant.

"I didn't realize LeeAnn Schofield went to Liberty Heights," she muttered aloud.

"Schofield? As in the wife of Brandon Schofield?" Nick said.

"Who's Brandon Schofield?"

Nick laughed. "Only the best point guard who ever played ball in Clayton!" Nick shook his head. "All-state three years in a row, then led UConn to the national championship. Come on, I thought you were into sports?"

"Playing them, not watching them," Val said. "Google him for me, would ya?" She maintained her laser focus on Kent and LeeAnn. They chatted for a moment, and her husband crossed his arms, a cross expression on his face. LeeAnn patted him on the arm and nodded at Kent. Their car lights flickered on. LeeAnn opened the passenger door, reached in, straightened, and handed something to Kent. He shuffled off a moment later, getting into a black sedan, already running. A dark-haired woman who resembled Amy Yang occupied the passenger seat. Kent drove off in a hurry. Meanwhile, the Schofields remained outside their car, talking. No, arguing. Mr. Schofield seemed upset with her, and LeeAnn appeared to be trying to calm him down.

"This is him," Nick said, showing her his phone. The screen showed a much younger version of the man with LeeAnn, wearing a UConn basketball jersey. According to the accompanying text, Brandon Schofield flamed out of pro basketball after a single season, victim of a career-ending ACL tear. He married LeeAnn a year later and joined a Hartford insurance firm.

"What did she give Kent just now?" Val wondered aloud.

"I don't know, but it sure pissed off her husband," Nick said. "I wouldn't want to be her right now."

"What, you don't think married couples fight?" Val frowned. Okay, if she wanted to learn about him, she might need to go first. "I think my parents fought more than they drank. Which was a lot."

Nick sighed. "Sorry to hear. That can be tough to live with."

Val shrugged. "I only had to live with half of it. After I turned fourteen, anyway. Mom couldn't take it anymore, and she left. Dad...he's still fighting. The bottle, I mean. Winning lately, so I hear, but I can't baby-sit him, you know?" She stopped, and her heart skipped a beat. "Damn, I haven't told anybody about that, besides Beth and my grief counselor when I was sixteen. What the hell, Nick? Did you cast some sort of magic talk spell on me tonight?"

Nick grinned and waved an invisible wand. "You are under my spell," he intoned in cartoon-wizard-like fashion. "Speak!"

"Nope, your turn," she said. "What was it like in the Evans household growing up?"

His smile faded and his eyes clouded over. "My parents didn't fight, for the simple reason that my dad never dared contradict Mom. Nobody did. To call her overbearing would be the understatement of the century."

"Are you close?" Val asked.

"To my dad, yes," Nick said. "To my mom's everlasting horror, I resented her, chafed at her bossiness, at her always telling me I wasn't good enough. Mom had high standards. I never met them, and she let me know it."

"Hence, you went away to college," Val said in a soft voice.

"Bingo. And changed my major in sophomore year so it took me an extra semester to graduate."

"So, why not go to grad school, or move somewhere else?" Val said. "I mean, it's not like there are a ton of jobs around here."

"I thought about law school. But..." Nick grew serious, his eyes downcast. "Mom's stage four, liver cancer," he said. "Inoperable. She has less than six months left."

A football-sized lump formed in Val's throat. "I'm so sorry," she said.

"It was a mistake," he said. "When I visited her in the hospital, at first she refused to see me. Told me I was an idiot for getting such a useless degree, and why wasn't I married? And, was I gay? She actually asked me that, out loud, and not in a loving, understanding way," he said, his voice bitter. "By the way, in case you're wondering, I'm not."

"I kind of guessed. Anyway, I'm sorry. That sucks."

"You're telling me!" Nick jumped up from the bench and crossed his arms, facing Val. "I wanted to tell her the truth—that she's the reason I'm not married, why I can't seem to relate to women, particularly strong women, in a healthy way. Of course I can't, because...I don't know. I just can't. Even though I find strong women attractive. I can't relate to the wilting flowers out there, who want their husband to do all their thinking for them—and yes, they do still exist. Especially in Ivy League schools, I think."

Val stood and, smirking, pressed her hand against Nick's folded arms and gave him a gentle push.

He stumbled but regained his footing, arms flailing. "What the hell?"

"You seem to be cured," she said, her grin widening. "Here you are, with a strong woman, and you're relating just fine."

Nick stared at her, then burst into laughter. "Touché," he said. "Damn. Thousands of dollars spent on shrinks for the past eight years, and you cure me with a simple shove. What do I owe you, Doc?"

"About an hour of your time, helping with cleanup," Val said. "Come on, let's get inside. This party's almost over, and Beth's probably about ready to send out a search-and-rescue team for me."

He smiled and bowed low. "After you, m'lady."

Val led him back inside, and a thought struck her. Nick's difficult relationship with his mother led him to idealize strong women, yet unable to relate to them. In a sense, so did the Shoeless Schoolgirl Slayer.

Could that be the missing link needed to round out the killer's profile? Might that provide the clue she needed about his background to narrow down her search?

⁂

The reunion ended with more of a whimper than a bang. Guests followed the lead of Amy and Kent, ducking out early for after-parties around the city. That left only a few dozen hangers-on in the space when the DJ announced the last song—a slow one, of course. The final few desperate singles eyed each other, weighing the pros, cons, and odds of a hookup with the remaining eligibles. A few took the plunge, along with the couples who'd arrived together. The drunk jock from earlier in the evening found another victim before he could reach Val. Nick cocked his head at Val, a questioning look aimed her way. She pretended not to see him and got a jump on clearing off and breaking down the unoccupied tables in the room's dark corners.

Beth joined her after the event ended, sending Nick off to help a group of guys remove decorations that required ladders to reach. "I hope that's okay," Beth said. "I don't want to mess up your plans with him, if you had any."

"No, that's cool," Val said. "No plans to mess up."

"That's too bad." Beth swept a stack of empty plastic drink cups into a garbage bag and paused a moment. "I was kind of hoping you and he…"

"Don't you have, like, a dozen volunteer teams to supervise?" Val said, rolling a wad of used napkins into a ball and tossing it into a garbage can. "I've got this."

"The more I get my own hands dirty, the sooner we get out of here," Beth said. "So, why *not* Nick Evans? He's smart, good-looking, athletic, and socially awkward. You're two peas in a pod."

"Thanks. You should create a Tinder profile for me. I'm sure I'll get all swipe-lefts. Or is it right? I can never remember which one I want."

"I'm not sure which one you'd want, either," Beth said. "Most gals would def swipe right for Nick. Come on, what's wrong with him?"

"Who said anything's wrong?" Val said. "Not everyone knocks boots with a guy five minutes after meeting him."

"So you do like him." Beth followed Val to the next table.

"Sure. He's a nice guy. All the things you said. Help me get this tablecloth off." Val picked at the tape attaching the plastic to the underside of the table.

"Why not bring him to Kent and Amy's after-party, then?" Beth said. "Get to know him a little better."

"Because I'm not going."

"Why not? You have better things to do at midnight?"

"Yes. Sleep." Val tugged at another piece of tape, once again without success, and wondered if Gil had gone to bed yet.

"Come on, Val. Live a little. You have tomorrow off, right? You can sleep in."

"I'm helping Gil in the morning." Val gave up on peeling the tape and ripped the plastic, leaving a tiny stub behind.

"Helping him what? Hey, don't tear the tablecloths like that. We're hoping to reuse them."

"Whatever he needs. Look, I can't go to the party, okay? For a lot of reasons." She checked to make sure no one was looking, then mimed smoking a joint. "I can't even risk second-hand exposure. One positive drug test as a rookie and I'm fired forever."

Beth frowned and stacked up some plastic chairs. "Sorry, I forgot about that. Well, the two of you could go get a drink or something."

"Beth, please. I know you mean well, but I can take care of my own dating needs."

Beth exhaled a gust of air and sat down in the only remaining unstacked chair. "Val, I worry about you. You're an amazing person in so many ways, but in this one important way, you're so...hard. On yourself, I mean."

"Not this again." Val pulled the table away from Beth and flipped it onto its side so she could fold its legs in.

"I'm sorry." Beth thought for a moment. "I know I'm a broken record, but ever since Josh and I got together, I've realized how fabulous it can be when somebody gets you. When you *let* somebody get you. It's something I wish everyone could have—especially you."

"Why me?" Val said. "Why does my being single bother you so much? Because I'm such a weirdo?"

"No," Beth said. "Because you're my dearest and closest friend. It wouldn't bother me if you were *happily* single. But you're not. You're miserable being a loner. There's a big difference. Look, I saw how you were when you partnered with Gil. When you saw him every day, you were a different person. Happy. Energetic. It thrilled you to go to work each day, and it wasn't because you loved arresting people. You two were a great team, and it meant a lot to you."

"Where did that get me? I nearly got him killed." Val dragged the folded-up table over to the wall next to some others, where a crew could come by to gather them later.

"It didn't diminish how he feels for you, or you for him."

"You don't know that." Val moved to another table.

Beth followed and grabbed a paper towel to wipe up a spill. "Here's what I know. Whether it's Gil, or Nick, or some other guy or gal, you owe it to yourself to open up your heart to another person. Let yourself love someone else and let them love you. It'll change your life. I promise you."

Val stopped cleaning and rested both hands on the table, palms down. "You know why I don't feel open to that. You, of all people."

Beth circled the table and stood next to Val, hands folded in front of her. "I also know that you haven't let that stop you from caring about other people. I know what motivates you to find that schoolgirl killer and protect the girls who haven't yet been victimized. You have a big heart, my friend. Someday, somebody besides me deserves a chance to see how much love lies within it." She wrapped her arms around Val, squeezed her tight for several seconds, then stepped away, wiping a tear from her cheek. "I need to go supervise the idiot boys over there. Someone needs to teach them how to mop." She walked away, head held high, as if they'd been discussing the weather or travel plans to Europe.

Val reached under the table and peeled away the tape, careful not to tear the plastic cover.

Chapter Thirty-Six

Cleanup of the cafeteria took only about a half hour. Beth and Josh offered to drop Val off at home, but she declined. "It's the complete opposite direction," she said. "I can take an Uber."

Nick Evans stepped in. "I can give you a ride," he said. "Please."

Beth's eyebrows danced on her forehead. *Do it!* she mouthed. Then she mimed a kiss and raised her eyebrows again.

That settled it. "Thanks. I'd rather not this time."

His face fell, and Val felt horrible. She did like the guy and he shouldn't suffer rejection because of Beth's pushiness. She smiled at Nick and extended her hand. "Give me your phone."

He eyed her with mock suspicion, unlocked his phone, and placed it in her palm. Val punched in her digits and handed it back. "Call me next week?"

"I'll wait with you for the Uber," he said, smiling.

Fair enough. She assented.

When the car came, she braced for the inevitable kiss or inappropriately long hug. Instead, he took her hand in both of his and squeezed it. "I'll talk to you soon." Then he walked away with a slight spring in his step.

The driver, a young Asian man, chatted aimlessly as he drove. Val ignored him. Beth's words ran through her mind, and the truth underlying them blasted through her friend's intrusiveness. Val did put up a protective shield around her heart, never letting the slightest vulnerability show. She'd done it her whole life—since the rape, anyway.

Except once. Or, rather, with one man. The only man that made her feel better about herself, who understood that she needed to be about something more than just herself. That it was all about what she could do for others, especially for young women at risk from male predators. One man, and only one, celebrated who she was, and made her feel that was enough.

She sent a text. He was probably asleep, but no big deal if he saw it in the morning instead: *Talk?*

The reply came moments later. *Anytime.*

Now?

Several seconds passed. A minute. The driver chatted on about God-knows-what.

I said ANY time. Now, tomorrow, next week. ANY.

"Driver," she said, interrupting him mid-sentence, "change of plans."

***

The lights in Gil's house shined like a welcoming beacon when the driver let her off, and she found the front door unlocked. "Burglar!" she shouted into the living room before letting herself in.

"S&W .45," came the response from the kitchen. Gil limped in, paused, and extended his arms, resting his elbows on the pads of his crutches. "Get in here, you."

She didn't remember crossing the room, or opening up her arms and wrapping them around his thick, muscular torso, or him pressing her close. Didn't remember dragging him to the couch, still enclosed in his embrace, or how long it all took. Didn't remember seeing the pot of coffee already on the table, or letting go of him long enough to pour them both hot, steaming mugs of the delicious brew. But she believed him later when he insisted that's how it happened. It explained the lightness in her heart, how her body shed the exhaustion and tension she'd borne all evening, and how she couldn't. Stop. Smiling.

"I've missed you so damned much," he said some minutes after Val's sense of time and reality returned.

"It's only been three days," she said. "Hasn't it?"

"If by days, you mean eons," he said. "Fill me in on everything. Don't leave out a single detail. Start with why you're wearing such an amazing dress. Hell, why you're wearing *any* dress. I didn't know you owned one."

"It's brand-new," she said. "I bought it for the high school reunion tonight."

"Seriously?" Gil laughed. "First off, you went to a reunion? I didn't think you did stuff like that. Much less in formal dress. And those fancy shoes!"

"Long story. The short version is, Beth," she said. "Here's the curious thing, though. Guess who showed up?"

"The mayor?"

She smacked his chest with the back of her palm. "Spoil sport, guessing right off. How did you know?"

Gil pointed to the TV. "It was on the news. They missed the real story, though. They should have led with 'Val Dawes wears a hot dress.' Seriously, you look, dare I say it, *sexy*."

"Stop it. The news? I didn't see any crews there."

"They didn't show your graduating class." He winced and shifted his weight on the sofa, her sign to break the embrace with him. "Everything Megan Iverson does is news these days. Her poll numbers are looking good—thanks to you and the WAVE Squad, I might add."

"That's kind of what I want to talk to you about," Val said. "Not about Megan, though. It's her husband. Curtis still creeps me out, and something tells me he has something to do with these Shoeless murders."

"Lay it on me," Gil said, wincing again. "This sounds good."

"Are you feeling okay?" Val said. "You look like you're in pain."

"I am. Hot tip from a pro: don't re-break your hip." He grimaced again and leaned back on the sofa.

"Do you need your meds or anything?" Val asked.

"No!" His arm shot out, bumping her chest and preventing her from getting up. "I mean...I'm taking myself off the meds. Too freaking addictive."

"Gil, is that wise? Shouldn't you consult with your doctor first?"

"I will if it gets worse. I'm fine. Talk to me." He stretched out his good leg and let out a slow breath.

"Okay." She kept an eye on him as she talked, glad that she'd come over after all. If he needed a trip to the hospital, she could ensure he got one. "I analyzed the case from the point of view of the victims. What did they have in common? And whom? What did each of them need that would let them get trapped by a serial killer?"

"Good approach," he said. "What did you come up with?"

"First, the obvious stuff," Val said. "They're all high school juniors or seniors. All active in school sports and clubs—things that build a resume. All had ambitions to go to a top-of-the-line college—Ivy League or close to it. Yet they all came from families that could never afford it. Not in a million years."

"Right. So they needed help to get in, and to pay for it. Like that last girl, Sierra—she did some drug dealing, right?"

"Right," Val said. "Now, I don't see Sierra as a Shoeless Slayer victim. I think she's the victim of a copycat. Drug deal gone bad, and they dressed it up to look like a Shoeless case. But they missed an important detail we withheld from the public."

"What's that?" Gil said. "You can tell me. I'm still on the force."

"Technically I shouldn't," Val said, "but they threw me off the WAVE Squad, so screw them. The Slayer tagged each of his victims with a tattoo on their lower leg. We call it the *Chingona* tattoo—Rosie the Riveter's face and arm with *Chingona* written underneath."

"Why that?" Gil asked. No more wincing in pain. Maybe police work made it all feel better.

"It translates, roughly, to 'Girl Power.' I think it's an ironic reference to the Slayer's attitude toward women. He's selecting victims who appear strong—empowered—and who are also vulnerable. Girls who need a little help to bust through the glass ceilings holding them back. Financial limitations, gender expectations, and racial bias."

"Exploiting their vulnerabilities somehow to gain their trust," Gil said, nodding. "How does he get them tattooed, though? That'd take some time, and word would get out."

"Here's the weird thing," Val said. "The tattoos are amateur jobs, or even DIYs. All of them appear to be fresh at the time of death—within the last 24 hours."

"That is weird," Gil said. "Imagine half a dozen girls, each trusting the same guy enough to let him tattoo them...then all dying the same way. Drowning, right?"

"In the river. Some were suspected to be suicides at first. And the tattoo morphed over time. The first few victims just had Rosie's image. No label."

"Which one first had the word added?"

"Yolanda." Val snapped her fingers. "Spanish word, Latina girl. Of course! Why didn't I realize that before?"

"It also suggests that he's deliberately morphing his MO with each victim to throw off the investigation," Gil said. "Tell me, was Yolanda's death a suspected suicide?"

"Not sure," Val said. "My first brush with the case was the next victim, Olivia Lambert. The one whose body I found." A realization popped into her mind. "She was the first one wearing a parka! Then Charlene was, too. Damn, you're right. There's got to be something added with each victim that gets carried over to the next one. I need to go, Gil. I need to figure out what these things are!"

"Not so fast," he said. "Keep working this through with me. Get the complete picture in mind, and your next steps will be a lot more coherent. What else links the girls together?"

"Curtis Iverson," she said. "They all interned, or applied to be interns, at Constitution Finance through the Association of Future Entrepreneurs scholarship program. He had to have met them all."

"That's a good clue," he said. "But hundreds of people work at that company. Who else might have met them all there?"

Val thought a moment. "Kent Mercer," she said. "He's a college-level intern, and a buddy of the guy they arrested. And LeeAnn Schofield, Curtis's executive assistant. Probably others, but that's all I know of, for now."

"Good. Scratch LeeAnn, at least as the main perp. We know it's a guy, because of the sexual abuse, right? Wasn't that part of it?"

"It was with Olivia and Charlene," Val said, snapping her fingers. "And Yolanda, and Jaden. Not Hannah, the first victim. Another morphing of the MO!"

"So tell me what differentiates Curtis and Kent. Be specific."

Val got up and counted off differences on her fingers. "One: age. Curtis is in his forties. Kent is half that. Two: access to power and money. Kent's family is wealthy, but it's his parents' money, not his. Curtis earned his own fortune, from what I understand."

"He was never poor, but sure, he went from well-off to rich. Agreed."

"Three: Curtis is married. Kent's single. Most serial killers are single. Loners, even."

"Most. Not all," Gil said. "Being single makes it easier to hide the trophies...wait, are there trophies?"

"The shoes, I'm guessing. And the tattoo, sort of. Markers work much the same way."

"Have you found a stash of shoes in his possession, or Kent's?" Gil asked.

She shook her head. "Neither. That said, we haven't searched—wait. Amy tripped over a bunch of shoes in the condo!"

"Who's Amy?" Gil asked. "What condo? I can't keep up with the players without a program!"

"Amy's a fr—er, former classmate of mine, who's dating Kent," Val said. "Curtis lured her into his secret condo and she had to cut through a walk-in closet to get away from an almost certain rape. He called it a 'misunderstanding,' and he's full of it." Val's voice grew heated, and she took a few deep breaths to calm down.

"That settles it, then. It's Curtis," Gil said. "Or am I missing something?"

Val sighed and sat again. "Yeah. Two things. One: Kent has the same brand-new tattoo."

"Him? That's weird," Gil said, pensive. "The killer wouldn't do something that bold. Or stupid."

"Huh. I didn't think of that."

"And the second thing?"

"It wasn't Amy's first time in the condo," Val said. "She'd been up there with Kent, too."

"To the same apartment? Jesus!"

Val nodded. "Kent uses it for the same purpose Curtis does. Unfortunately, the bozos in charge don't think I have enough for a search warrant to see if any of the shoes belong to the victims. They're afraid of ruffling powerful feathers, is my guess."

"That's outrageous!" Gil started to get up, then yelped in pain. "Shit. I keep forgetting! Anyway, I can't believe they haven't raided that place ten times over. With or without a warrant."

"There is one problem," Val said. "We haven't pinpointed which unit it is. Curtis covered his tracks well, probably to avoid his wife and the press finding out about his little peccadilloes."

"Piece of cake," Gil said. "Put somebody on him and Kent, 24/7. They'll lead you right to it within a week."

"We don't have a week," Val said. "He's overdue to kill again. And—holy shit! He was at the reunion tonight! I mean, both of them were."

"So?" Gil shrugged. "They were with dates, right? And don't they target much younger girls?"

Val's alarm subsided a bit. "I...guess you're right," she said. "Sorry. I panicked a moment."

Gil smiled. "Better safe than sorry. Who knows? Maybe that's his next morph. An 'older woman,' if that term applies to women in their early twenties. Which raises the question: Were they at *your* reunion tonight? In the room?"

Val's blood ran cold again. "Yes. Both of them."

"Any other reunions?"

Val cocked her head left, then right. "Curtis was, for sure. Kent...I don't know. I didn't track his whereabouts."

Gil blew air out between his lips. "Okay, priority one has to be to get inside that condo. How?"

An image snapped into Val's memory: LeeAnn handing something to Kent, long after Kent had left the reunion. He'd come back for something—something that LeeAnn had. Something that had upset her husband, too. Could it be...?

"I think I understand why we haven't found the condo's address," she said, excitement building. "It's not registered under Curtis's name, nor Kent's, nor Constitution Finance. Five gets you ten, LeeAnn Schofield leased that condo. And I know how to get inside without a warrant."

"How?"

Val stood and rested her hands on Gil's shoulders. "Gil," she said, "I was invited."

Chapter Thirty-Seven

Despite the late hour, traffic moved at a snail's pace through downtown Clayton. "I wish they'd synchronize these traffic signals," the Uber driver groused. Then he went off on a rant about the "Deep State" and how the "liberal media" controlled everything. Val put earbuds in and cranked some old Linkin Park tunes while scanning local news reports on her phone.

She found nothing focused on the Slayer case, but an unrelated headline grabbed her attention: "Mayor Claims Crime Down in Busy Campaign Swing." The article noted that Megan Iverson had given several speeches at fund-raisers that day, including at least two after her reunion stop. A photo of Megan at the last event showed her surrounded by campaign aides—and not Curtis. That struck Val as odd.

A text message from Nick interrupted her reading: *Still up?*

Val's initial response was irritation. She'd told him to call *next week*. Then again, she'd also told him she didn't want to attend the after-party. Showing up alone could prove awkward if everyone else attended with significant others. Decisions, decisions.

She swallowed her pride and replied: *Changed my mind about Kent's party. Join me?*

Her phone remained quiet for thirty, forty seconds. Then: *Meet you there.*

Committed now, she sent a quick note to Beth. Her phone rang a moment later.

"Oh thank God," Beth said in a hushed voice before Val could say hello. "When are you getting here? I'm stuck here alone with Amy!"

"Can she hear you?" Val asked, horrified.

"No, I'm hiding out in the bathroom. Where I might stay until you arrive or the boys get back, whichever happens last. Jeez, this girl makes me crazy. She does not shut up!"

"Where did Kent and Josh go?" Val asked. "And isn't anyone else coming?"

"To get ice and more liquor," Beth said. "Kent invited a couple dozen people, but no one else RSVP'd. So either we'll have enough to play tackle football, or barely enough for a hand of bridge. Neither of which I know how to do, so...can you get here any faster?"

"We would, but my driver is convinced that the government, the Illuminati, and the Tripartite Commission are conspiring against him," Val said. She got an angry glare from the driver in response. "Remind me: which unit is it in?"

"1507," Beth said. "Top floor. It's beautiful, Val. Magnificent view of the river...shit, Amy's banging on the door. Hold on." Her muffled voice came next, something like "a few more minutes," and then she returned. "Amy's worried. The boys have been gone for over a half hour and won't answer our texts. And it does seem like kind of a long time."

"Traffic's a mess tonight," Val said. This time, the driver nodded in approval. "I'm sure they'll be back shortly. There aren't many liquor stores open after midnight."

"We should raid the wine rack," Beth said. "There must be 100 bottles of French and Italian reds here alone. But Kent said we can't. Which makes no sense. It's his condo, right?"

"Um, maybe not," Val said. "Okay, I see the Tower in sight. I should be there in less than ten. Hang on."

The driver let her out in front of the elegant, all-glass entryway to Trillium Towers a few minutes before 1:00 a.m. Val gazed up at the gleaming citadel of pink glass, a monument to the town's newly rich and vain, trying to pick out unit 1507. Moments later, a silver VW Jetta pulled up next to her and powered down the driver-side window.

"I'll park and meet you back here in a minute," Nick said, and drove off without waiting for a response.

Curious timing. She'd thought Nick wouldn't get there for another ten minutes, since he lived in the far North End.

Then something about his car caught her eye: a pair of stickers on the rear windshield for car-sharing services. In an instant, a lot of coincidences fell into place.

Nick found a visitor parking spot in front and rejoined her, cradling a bottle of wine in his arms like a baby. He still wore the same clothes as he had at the reunion.

"You didn't tell me you were an Uber driver," she said.

"You never asked," he said with a sheepish smile.

"Have you ever given me a ride?"

The smile widened to a grin. "And here I thought you hadn't noticed."

Something about that nagged at her. Felt...weird. Probably her own guilt, bringing him along to a party so soon after falling into Gil's arms.

However, that conversation had to wait. She needed to get inside. But the second set of glass doors leading from the foyer to the lobby were locked.

***

He parked his black sedan at the scenic viewpoint overlooking the river, on the east side, with its fine view of downtown. On a clear day, this view provided a beautiful vista of the river's blue waters and occasional whitecaps, framed behind by rolling hills tumbling up to the Berkshires in the distance.

At this hour, only the gleaming glass towers overtaking the city's decaying brick slums and factories remained visible. With the aid of high-powered binoculars, he could see not only the exterior frames, but also the interiors of certain buildings.

One in particular. A domicile used not as a full-time residence, but as a discreet getaway, where hungry, illicit passions could be slaked. With the right company, of course.

Trillium Towers, despite its forgettable glass-and-steel contemporary architecture, provided views of incomparable value—both from within, for its tenants who sought the pretense of escape from Clayton's urban blight, and from without, for those who knew where to park to view the goings-on inside its plush accommodations.

He focused the specs on the fifteenth floor, fourth unit from the left, one of the few lit at this hour. He knew the interior layout well—the master bedroom and bath to one side, the living room with its sliding doors opening to the iron-railed balcony on the other. One of the women, Beth, fussed with something on the bar that separated the kitchen from the living room—drinks, perhaps. The other, Amy, sat on the sofa, legs crossed, the slit in her dress revealing toothpick-thin legs. Legs that had fallen into disfavor with him of late. Particularly when he could have the other girl, whose dress did not reveal as much, but advertised the curves of a body that promised so much more.

They were alone now. In a space he knew well. One he'd set up to be as private as possible.

Which reminded him. He retrieved his cell phone and typed in the code that revealed the hidden folder. That folder contained a single, high-end home security app that enabled him to control every aspect of that Smart Home environment from anywhere on the planet. With a few taps, he enabled the silent, signal-blocking device inside the unit. A beep confirmed that it had disabled all connectivity—internet, phone, even the building's security cameras—from within the unit to any part of the outside world, without alerting the women inside. Another tap locked the unit's front door, preventing passage even to someone holding a key—any key except his own electronic one.

Two women, alone and unprotected, though they no doubt believed themselves safe, expecting their men to return and entertain them. Two men they thought they knew well. Instead of one, who would surprise them with a persona they could never imagine.

Two women. He'd not tried this variant before.

A shiver ran up his spine. This was going to be fun.

***

Val lifted the beige security phone on the wall of the glass-enclosed entryway of Trillium Towers. The display underneath lit up with instructions to dial the tenant's code or search. She tried "1507." The screen read: "Invalid code. Try again or press # to search."

She pressed the "#" key. A short list of names and unit numbers appeared, with up and down arrows off to one side. The names, sorted alphabetically, ranged from "Lancaster, A." to "Myers, T." No "Mercer." She scrolled up for "Iverson." No luck. She scrolled back down and confirmed what she'd suspected. The name for Unit 1507. "Schofield, L."

She tapped the screen for 1507. Ringing sounded over a background of static. Again. Five, six rings. Eight.

"What's the deal?" Nick asked. "Why aren't they buzzing us in?"

"Maybe I pressed the wrong button." Val hung up, waited ten seconds, and repeated the process. This time she let it ring ten times before giving up. She texted Beth: *We're here. Can you buzz us in?* "Should have done that in the first place," she said.

No answer from Beth.

"This is ridiculous." Val lifted the receiver again and dialed "0." A sleepy male voice answered. "Hi," she said in as sweet a voice as she could muster in her irritated state. "We were invited to a party in unit 1507, but the host isn't answering. Could you let us in?"

"Bullshit," the man said. "Go 'way."

"I can show you—"

"No noisy parties allowed after 11:00," the man said. This time she detected a strong Boston accent. "Get outta here 'fore I call the cops."

"I *am* the cops," Val said. "Officer Valorie Dawes, badge number—"

"I can see you, you know," the man said. "You don't look like no cop to me. Now get lost." The line went dead.

Val glanced up and spotted the security camera mounted near the ceiling. "Yeah, nobody's mistaking this dress for a Clayton PD uniform," she said.

"Try Beth again?" Nick suggested.

She did. Again, no answer. Her irritation mounted, compounded by worry. Either Beth was ignoring her, had phone problems, or was in danger. All three options, bad.

"What now?" Nick said. "Should we see if there's another party somewhere?"

"Wait." She tried Amy's number. Again, no response. She doubted that both women would ignore her calls or have simultaneous phone failure. That left only one possibility: danger.

Which meant she needed help. Yet she couldn't call in for backup on a case she'd been kicked off of, to get inside a place where she'd been denied a warrant, on a hunch rather than actual evidence of a crime. Or could she?

What had Gil told her? Take risks. Make herself vulnerable. No doubt that meant in her work relationships as well as her private ones.

She dialed, hoping she remembered the number correctly.

***

He pulled his black sedan into the entrance of Waterfront Towers, driving around the outer fringe of the front lot toward the driveway to the rear of the building. He glanced to his right before his car's hood eclipsed the edge of the building. Two figures occupied the well-lit entryway, an all-glass enclosure that jutted out from the building. They looked familiar. At least the woman did. Especially her violet dress. He'd noticed it earlier that night.

Dawes.

That complicated things. She'd come to join the party— or worse, to pull her close friend, Beth, out of the mix. He couldn't let that happen. Either thing.

He parked in a visitor's spot behind the building on the surface lot, eschewing the underground resident parking garage. Its gated entry was one thing his smart app couldn't disable.

He had an idea. Not the usual plan, but he'd already diverged from that plan in so many ways. He could make it work, but he needed to improvise.

He retrieved the phone he'd found in the parking lot at the high school when leaving the reunion. It had buzzed a half-dozen times in the last hour, before he'd cut off the signal in the condo, and he read a few of the texts. Each one from Beth to her missing boyfriend, the owner of the phone. He smiled. Perfect.

He replied to the last text: *Locked out. Come open back door of building.*

Waited. No response. Dammit. Then he remembered he'd need to turn off the signal blocking from his own phone. He did, and resent.

Moments later came the reply: *I'll send Amy. She knows the way.*

He grunted and pecked out a new message: *No, you come. I want to talk to you—privately.*

A few seconds later: *OK.*

He re-blocked the signal, double-checked that he'd turned off the building's security cameras, and circled around to the trunk of his car. Popped it open, retrieved what he needed: a one-liter bottle of chloroform, a muslin cloth, and a couple of long zip ties. He poured chloroform onto the cloth and returned the bottle to the small storage box in the trunk. He left his trunk ajar, then took up his position by the back door.

A minute later, the door opened toward him, shielding him from her view. He predicted her next steps: lean out further, look around, realize that she needed to come out further...

When it happened, as predicted, he moved fast. Grabbed her from behind, covered her mouth with the cloth, and wrapped an arm around her beautiful, thick body to trap her arms against her sides. He held her until her kicking and wriggling ceased, and she lost consciousness.

Chapter Thirty-Eight

Travis answered Val's call on the third ring, his voice as alert as she'd ever heard it. "You'd better be standing over a body or looking at the wrong end of a gun," he said, his voice loud enough to wake up the entire building.

"I'm hoping to prevent another body from dying," Val said in a low voice, turning away from Nick and holding the phone closer to her ear. "I wouldn't call at this hour on a whim."

"Okay. Talk." Travis harrumphed, and she imagined him slumping into an uncomfortable chair, away from his sleeping wife and kids.

"I'm at Trillium Towers. I was invited to a party in Iverson's unit, and nobody's answering to buzz me in."

"Sounds like the party got canceled, then. Got any other social problems for me to solve?"

"It's not canceled. Something else is going on. Travis, I need to get inside."

"So, what do I look like, a locksmith? Call the manager."

"Already tried that. Listen, the apartment belongs to LeeAnn Schofield. She works for Curtis Iverson. If I can get her on the line—"

"At 1:00 in the morning?" Travis laughed. "Dawes, I almost hung up on you, and I *like* you. What's Plan B?"

Val took a deep breath. Think, think. "Um...we try again on that warrant?"

"You want me to wake up a judge, based on what fresh evidence?"

Val lowered her voice. "It's Kent Mercer's party, and he has the *Chingona* tattoo."

"He what? Wait, are you saying he's the next victim? The Slayer's going for boys now?"

"No, of course not," Val said, frustration growing. "Isn't that suspicious, though?"

Travis grunted. "Or stupid. And you heard Topher. Everybody and their brother has that DIY kit. What else?"

Val calmed herself and concentrated. "The Washingtons gave me Charlene's diaries."

"What? *When?*" Travis's voice grew animated. "Have you read them? Please tell me you've logged them into evidence."

"Of course—I did that today." She didn't feel obliged to mention that she'd gotten them on Thursday.

"What did Petroni say about them?"

Val cleared her throat. "Well, I'm sure someone over at WAVE will see my entry, and—"

"Jesus, Dawes!" Travis covered the phone, but she could make out some choice swear word combinations. Scatological, biological, and sexual, with enough blasphemy to curl even Gil's short hair. "You've got to let people know about finds like this. Petroni will be pissed you didn't tell them, and she'll have a right to be."

"I'll phone them tomorrow, I promise. First I have to get in here."

Travis fumed another moment. "What did these diaries reveal that convinced you there's evidence in that condo?"

"Charlene knew Curtis—and Kent. And both are connected to this place."

"That connects the people, not the place. Come on, do better. Think like a judge."

"Okay, um…" Val gritted her teeth. Her head ached from exhaustion. She could barely think like a cop, much less a judge.

Then a realization struck her. Not from the diaries, though. Something about the date of Charlene's death. Kent's alibi didn't line up. Why?

The tattoo pledge. According to Amy, they made it on their second date. Their first date was the evening of the day they met at the campaign—April 8. Kent claimed he started on April 1, the night Charlene died, and that he'd studied at home on April 8. One of them had lied, and Amy had no reason to.

Curtis, meanwhile, had claimed Kent and he worked late on April 8—an unusual occurrence that Kent should have remembered, and didn't.

Which meant Kent wasn't working that night. Which meant LeeAnn and Curtis both lied to cover for him.

That blew up Curtis's alibi as well, because Kent could no longer vouch for *him*, either. And LeeAnn lied for Curtis, too.

Travis huffed and spoke up. "I'm listening, and not hearing anything."

"This is where the killer takes his victims," Val said. "I'm almost certain. I need to get in there to verify it. The problem is the manager doesn't believe I'm a cop. I'm not in uniform and don't have my badge."

"If you expect me to get dressed and go down there—"

"No. I don't want sirens and uniforms. I just want to get in and do a little informal search. By invitation. But I need help getting in the front door of the building."

"That's why we get warrants. Which we can't do until tomorrow. Good night, Dawes." The line went dead.

Val cursed and gripped her phone tight until she feared it might break. Damned Travis. What was the point of partners if they didn't come through in emergencies?

"So, are you working, or are we going to a party?" Nick asked, looking up from his phone.

Nick had a point. She had to come clean. "I *also* have a work-related reason to get inside," she said. "I was hoping I could look around a little during the party. Discreetly, of course."

He smiled. "I don't mind. It's kind of exciting, actually." He paused, scratching at his beard. "Maybe I could help."

Val's ears perked up. "Cool. How?"

Nick made a face, like he hadn't yet decided to make the offer. "I heard you say the Schofields rented this place?"

She nodded. "Do you know them well enough to get us inside?"

He grinned. "In a way. Let me try." He led her outside, away from the door, and tapped on his phone several times, then held it to his ear. "I Googled the main number for this place," he said. "So I—hello?" His voice changed to an even deeper pitch and he slowed his cadence, meanwhile boosting his volume. "Hi, sorry to bother ya," he said into the phone. "Who do I got here?"

Val cocked her head. He was imitating someone else's voice. Whose?

"Yeah, hiya, Frank. This is Brandon Schofield. Hey, I'm wicked sorry, bud. I had a few drinks tonight, and for the life of me, I can't remember the front door code. Wassat? Unit 1507. No, my wife's upstairs, she's got people over. I stepped out for a minute and locked myself out. I'm an idiot!" Nick laughed, and to Val he sounded like a jock in a locker room. "Aw, geez, Frankie, do me a solid, would ya one time? Yeah, I tried calling. She's not answering. We kinda had a fight, ya know? Which is why—oh, you're the best, man. Man, I knew that, too. Stupid me, I got the last two backwards. I typed 98 instead of 89." He hung up. "120489, then pound."

"That was amazing," Val said. "How is it you can do a perfect Brandon Schofield impression?"

He grinned. "I told you, I'm a big fan. And remember me saying I was in communications? Before that, theater. I can impersonate anyone. But I sucked as an actor. Turns out I had paralyzing stage fright."

That made sense. Good-looking, yet introverted. That wouldn't wash in the dramatic arts. Still, she had the sense he wasn't telling her something. Something important.

Val shook it off. She had things to do, and she couldn't think straight due to exhaustion. She pushed through the outer doors and punched the numbers into the keypad. The door buzzed, and she pulled it open.

***

Val and Nick rode up the elevator in silence, each deep into their own thoughts. His reaction to learning of her subterfuge seemed too mild. As if he'd almost expected it.

Or, she was letting her imagination run wild. Maybe he believed, like many people, that cops never really went off the clock. Which beat all to hell the folks who believed the opposite.

Nick stepped aside when the doors opened and she led him to Unit 1507, the fourth unit from the end, facing the water. She pounded on the door. Moments later, Amy flung it open, her face full of excitement. Upon spotting Val and Nick, her expression turned to disappointment.

"So glad to see you, too, Amy," Val said. "May we come in?"

"Of course," Amy said, her face flushed. "I'm sorry, Val. I was hoping it was Kent and Josh."

"Where's Beth?" Val scanned the spacious living room. Furnished with spare, Danish-style modern furniture and decorated with tasteful oil paintings on walls of muted gray, it looked like a page right out of House Beautiful Magazine. The living room opened to a gleaming modern kitchen, with an island bar separating the two rooms.

"Josh texted her a short while ago to ask her to help carry stuff. They must have bought out the entire liquor store," Amy said.

"Great," Val said. Beth ignored *her* messages, but not Josh's. She couldn't help but grow a little annoyed at that. "Where's the bathroom?"

"Down the hall to the right," Amy said. She sat on the sofa, her hands intertwined, her gaze unfocused.

Val pulled Nick aside. "I might be a few minutes," she said. "Take care of her, okay? She's been through a lot lately." In this very condo, she could have added.

"Sure," Nick said. "Amy, how about I fix you a drink?"

Val disappeared down the hall, passing the main bathroom, opting to start in the master bathroom. While letting the water run in the sink, she searched the medicine cabinet. Nothing of interest there. She left the door to the hallway closed and snuck into the walk-in closet that connected to the master bedroom. Unlike when Amy had fled through it to avoid Curtis, Val turned on the light, took her time. Sure enough, several pairs of women's shoes lined the shelves and floor along one wall. She whipped out her phone and snapped photos of all of them, then sent them to Travis, just in case. *I got in,* she added in a text. *We need to check these against shoes missing from the victims.*

What the hell, I'm not sleeping anyway, Travis texted back.

Val smiled. It felt good to have someone backing her up, even from a distance.

She entered the bedroom. Another paragon of the good taste money could buy. A dark walnut frame for the king-sized bed, matching double dresser drawers holding a giant mirror, and a half-dozen books on a shelf, all by well-known authors. An end table by the bed held a half-filled bottle of lube and a nearly empty box of condoms. Of course! She noted the brands and shut the drawer.

Val liberated a pair of men's socks from the top dresser drawer, which she pulled over her hands, and then wiped the knobs clean of her fingerprints. The end table, too. She rifled through the remaining drawers and found nothing of interest, except to notice that all the clothes bore high-end brand trademarks and logos. Not a single thread had ever graced the shelves of Target or Walmart.

Then, another realization: three-quarters of the clothes were men's. She returned to the closet and found the same ratio. None of the women's clothes would fit a woman with a physique like Amy's, LeeAnn's, or Megan Iverson's.

On the other hand, they would have fit most, if not all, of the first five victims of the Shoeless Schoolgirl Slayer. The smallest dress was probably a size 10, and they went at least as large as 14. Too large for Sierra Stapleton. Large enough to fit someone like Olivia, or Charlene, or—

Beth!

She shook off that thought. Beth didn't fit the profile. Too old, not filled with enough anxiety or self-doubt, not vulnerable to the advances of a man flashing wealth and prestige. Val laughed at her paranoia and returned to the master bathroom and reached for the door, then remembered the socks. What to do with them? She wanted to search the other rooms, but she couldn't parade down the hall wearing them as mittens.

Val removed the socks and stuffed them into her purse. She pulled the door open enough to verify that the coast was clear. Laughter emanated from the living room, followed by the clinking of glasses. Good. Nick and Amy were focused on the wine, not on her. He'd done a good job of settling her down and distracting her.

Val slipped across the hall to the second bedroom, closing the door behind her. This one held more functional, less elegant furnishings: a queen bed, a smaller set of dresser drawers, one end table with a lamp, and a closet with vented sliding doors. None of the drawers contained anything at all. She turned to the closet and slid open the door, and the items in plain sight surprised her: four 50-quart coolers, stacked two-high on the floor. She lifted the lid of the closest one. Filled with ice. The second one as well. Probably all four. An odd time and place for that.

Kent had gone out for ice. Which meant he didn't know about this stash, or didn't want to admit to knowing. So why was it here?

She stood on tip-toes to examine the shelf over the empty curtain rod. In the back, against the wall, she found a roll of brown paper and a ball of rough twine, the cheap brown stuff that disintegrated with age. Weird. What would somebody want to tie up with twine in a luxury condominium?

The shelf contained one more oddity: a paper bag with about a dozen virgin wine corks. Each bore a stamp on the side, an insignia or logo of some sort in light red ink. On the floor, a hand-held corker. She made a mental note to check for homemade wine in the wine rack.

On to the second bathroom, which necessitated another quick dash down the hall. Clean as a whistle, like the rest of the apartment, except for a few fibers stuck in the tub drain. She fished one out. It sort of resembled the twine she'd found in the closet. An odd place to find that.

The medicine cabinet yielded more tangible dividends. On the top shelf she found a small, clear bottle containing liquid that looked like water at first glance. She turned the label toward her and read: *Flunitrazepam.* Val searched her memory—had it really been two years since her forensic chemistry class? She Googled it on her phone, and confirmed her suspicion of what it was: the liquid form of Rohypnol, more commonly known as "roofies," the illegal date-rape drug. A plain white cardboard box on the lower shelf held a half-dozen unused syringes. The length of the needles—about an inch and a half—made her shudder, imagining getting stuck by one of them.

Heart racing, she texted Travis again: *Check coroner's reports. Did vics blood have elevated GHB? Any needle marks on skin?* She sent him a photo of the bottle and replaced it in the medicine cabinet.

She checked the cabinet under the sink. Its contents sent shivers down her spine: a small black case containing a home tattoo kit. Inks, tat pens and needles, latex gloves, alcohol wipes, gauze pads, medical tape, and a pamphlet on tattoo design, with templates. She leafed through it. No Rosie the Riveter, much less *Chingona*.

The buzzing of her phone interrupted her search. Travis, responding about the shoes: *The black flats might match Olivia. Size 8?* A moment later: *Blue ones might be Charlene's. Still checking the others.*

Val's heart raced. She needed to rejoin Amy and Nick, but she couldn't pass up the chance to verify the clues. She speed-walked back to the main bath and into the walk-through closet. Sure enough, she found a few pairs of black flats. *Which black flats? Mary Janes, ballet-style, or Jelly style?*

His predictable response: *Hell if I know. Shoes!*

She opened her notepad app, estimated the size of each pair of black flats. Two eights, and one seven. Thank God there was only one blue pair, kitten heels in a size six. They could figure the rest out later, when they searched with a warrant.

Another text from Travis: *Confirmed slightly elevated GHB levels in Charlene, Olivia. Need all 5?*

She responded with a *No, thanks so much! Let's get that warrant tomorrow?* She exited through the main bathroom again and rejoined Amy and Nick in the living room. "Sorry that took so long," she said. "I feel better now."

"Try Nick's wine, it's delicious!" Amy said, jumping up to fetch her a glass.

Val smiled at Nick, gave him a thumb's-up for raising her spirits. "Any word from Beth or the boys? They should be back by now."

Amy shrugged and gazed out the window. "I keep looking for his car, but black BMWs are a dime a dozen in this place," she said, pouting.

"Where are all the other guests?" Nick asked. "I thought he invited a big crowd."

Amy rolled her eyes. "He kind of threw the invite out there to a group that we didn't know very well," she said. "I'm not surprised no one else showed." Her face took on a worried expression. "Valorie's right. They've been gone a long time."

"Should I go look for them?" Nick asked.

"Let's not add to the problem by spreading out, ourselves," Amy said, bringing Val a generous pour of Nick's red wine. "I'll call Kent and see where they are."

Nick toasted Val with his glass and caught her eye. "Did you find anything?" he whispered, indicating the back rooms with a toss of his head.

Val nodded. "We need to get Amy and Beth out of here," she whispered back.

He furrowed his brow. "Now? Before Kent and Josh get back?"

Val's phone buzzed before she could answer. Travis. *Interesting: several vics had signs of frostbite. Even vic #1 from September. Also rope burn?*

Suddenly, the contents of the closet and bathroom cabinets all made sense. The ice. Twine. Paper. Roofies. She pieced together a plausible scenario. The killer drugged his victims, raped them, marked them with the tattoo, then tied them up with the twine and dumped them in the bathtub. With the ice, to slow down their metabolism. Or drowned them in the tub rather than the river and used the ice to slow down post-mortem effects like rigor mortis and tissue decay. That would throw off time of death estimates and give the killer the opportunity to establish an alibi.

Cold sweat dotted Val's brow. Kent had planned to get Amy here, alone. He'd gotten cross when Amy invited them all to join the party—because he'd never intended to host an actual party. He somehow got Beth and Josh out of the way, never expecting Val and Nick to come along...

A loud knock sounded on the front door. Val jumped, caught herself before she fell over. Amy rushed to open the door. Josh stepped in, his black tie loose around his neck, his white ruffled shirt unbuttoned halfway down his chest. He held a paper bag filled with bottles in his arms. Val exhaled a long sigh of relief.

"Man, what an ordeal!" he said. "Scoring liquor this time of night is impossible. I hope you all like beer." He set down the bag on the kitchen counter and produced a 40-ounce bottle of malt liquor. "Hey, Val! Glad you made it."

"Where's Kent?" Amy said.

"Getting ice from the machine on the ground floor," Josh said.

Ice! Val started again.

"Where's Beth?" Josh continued, looking around.

"Isn't she with you?" Val said. Fear built inside her chest.

Josh cast them a puzzled stare. "Of course not. Why would she be? We left her here. Come on, what's going on? Is she hiding in the bedroom for me?" He laughed and stared down the hall.

"You texted her fifteen minutes ago or so, telling her to–"

"No, I didn't," Josh said, opening the malt liquor and taking a long sip. "In fact, my phone's been missing since we left the reunion. It may have dropped between the seats in my car."

"She got a text from you a short time ago," Val said, her tone insistent. "Telling her to meet you out back to help carry stuff."

More puzzlement from Josh. "You're crazy. I couldn't have. I didn't have my phone."

"Then who did?" Amy asked.

Val met Nick's gaze, and his eyes widened with hers. "Josh. You don't suppose Kent has it, do you?"

Josh laughed. "Why would he? Anyway, I was with him almost the whole time. I'd have noticed if he had my phone."

Val ran to the sliding doors leading to the balcony facing the riverfront, overlooking the rear parking lot. As Amy suggested, she saw several black sedans, all appearing to be high-end models like BMWs or Mercedes. Damned rich people. None had an iota of independent taste. No Beth, either. Where was she?

In danger, that's where. Val knew it deep down, and it made her nauseous. She bent over the rail, taking deep breaths, calming herself. She had to do something. She considered tossing the coolers, twine, drugs, and brown paper off the balcony to at least slow the killer down, then thought better of it. They'd need it as evidence.

The killer. Before that evening, she'd narrowed it down to Kent or Curtis. Kent was with Josh, so he wouldn't have sent those texts. And he wouldn't be getting ice if he knew about the loaded coolers in the bedroom.

Curtis had been at the reunion. Maybe he'd found Josh's phone.

Which meant Curtis had Beth, and Val needed to find her.

Chapter Thirty-Nine

Val hurried out of the condo unit, shouting "Everybody stay here until I get back!" over her shoulder and slamming the door behind her. Someone—Nick or Josh—opened it and shouted her name, but she never looked back. The elevator arrived moments after she pushed the button and whisked her to the first floor. On the way down, she tried Travis again. No answer. Dammit!

She ran to the rear of the building, as best she could in her dress and flats, and located the exit door, ignoring the warning not to open it after 10:00 p.m. She guessed opening it wouldn't set off any alarms—after all, it hadn't if, or when, Beth had tried it.

Holding the door open, she scanned the lot. No signs of any people. Just lots of expensive cars. A gated entry to the underground parking level prevented unauthorized vehicles from entering, but left plenty of room for her to slip through. She propped the door open with a small stone she found nearby, no doubt stashed there by tenants desiring a quick in-and-out to their cars or a private smoke in the parking lot.

The garage had three levels with a circular layout around a central elevator and stairway shaft. It took her only a minute at half-sprinting speed to survey the entire level. Nothing. Just more expensive sedans and SUVs.

She recalled elevator buttons labeled "P1" through "P3." Two more levels to check. Each one, including the stairs, took another minute and a half. No signs of Beth, or of a struggle anywhere.

Val punched the elevator button. Nothing. A beige phone and keypad, a replica of the one in the building's entryway, beckoned. She keyed in the code Nick had sleuthed from the manager, and the panel lit up. Good. While waiting for it to arrive, she texted Beth again. Maybe she'd returned to the room already.

Several seconds passed. The elevator opened and she stepped inside, holding the doors open for an extra moment, just in case. No answer.

Val let out a long breath. The doors remained open. She pressed the "Close Door" button several times. Come on, come on—

Dammit! Security again. She re-entered the damned code. This time, the doors obeyed.

Moments later, she raced through the doors on the fifteenth floor and down the hall, banging on the door for 1507. Amy flung the door open, anxiety written all over her face.

"No Kent?" she said.

"No Beth," Val said, rushing past her. "Listen, everyone," she said when Nick, Josh, and Amy gathered around her in the living room. "We've got to get out of here. Everyone. Now!"

"What?" Nick and Josh said at the same time.

"Why?" Amy said. "What about the party? Shouldn't we wait for Kent and Beth—"

"No. Now. We are all in danger. Do you understand me?" She growled in frustration at the look of confusion on their faces. "There isn't going to be any party."

"If you don't want to party, you don't have to," Amy said. "The rest of us can do what we want. Right, guys?"

"I dunno, I'm kind of worried about Beth," Josh said. "She should have gotten back by now."

"We can't ditch out on Kent's party," Amy said, plopping onto the sofa with a pouty expression on her face. "That would be so rude."

"Amy, listen to me. You're not safe here," Val said. "Not alone, and the rest of us are leaving. Right?" She glanced at the two men. Nick nodded. After a moment, so did Josh.

"I won't be alone," Amy said. "Kent will be here. He'll protect me if Curtis comes back and tries anything."

Val clutched both hands behind her neck, rubbing the stiff cables of muscle that held up her aching head. This woman had a freaking death wish. "You're not safe with Kent here, either. Please. Come with us."

"You're just trying to ruin Kent's party," Amy said. "No way. God, why do you hate him so much?"

Val gritted her teeth, contemplating a snarky answer, but swallowed it.

"I'll stay behind with Amy," Nick said.

Amy's eyes widened, alarm filling her face. "No!" She jumped up, holding out her hands like a shield. "Sorry, I don't know you well enough to be alone with you, in some strange condo—No. Uh-uh." She glanced away from Nick. "No offense."

Val hung her head in frustration. "Which is why you should come with us," she said through gritted teeth.

"I'm not leaving until Kent gets back," Amy said, resolute. A long silence ensued.

"Tell you what," Josh said. "Val and Nick, you go looking for Beth and Kent. I'll wait here with Amy. Whoever finds them, call or text. I'm sure it'll only be a minute or two. Okay?" He wandered over to the island dividing the living room and kitchen and picked up a bottle of red wine off the counter. "I need a drink, anyway. Amy, is this one okay to open?"

"Yes, Kent said we should start with that bottle. I'll find you a corkscrew."

Val considered interrupting and insisting that they all leave, but realized she'd never convince Amy now. "Come on,

Nick," she said. "With two of us, we can cover twice as much ground."

"Sure," Nick said. "Let me hit the bathroom first." He disappeared down the hallway.

The cork popped out of the wine bottle and Josh poured two glasses three-quarters full. "Val? One for the road?"

"No, thanks." She sat on a tall bar stool to wait for Nick. Josh set the corkscrew on the counter, without removing the cork, and brought Amy her drink.

Something about the cork caught Val's attention. She picked it up and examined the insignia stamped in red on the side. She'd seen it before. Where?

She flipped it around in her fingers. Something else was wrong. The end once exposed to the wine should have turned red after several years of storage. It remained as white as the side exposed to the air, still entombing the shaft of the corkscrew.

A bit off-center, she found a tiny puncture in the cork. Flipping it around, she found a matching hole in the top, next to the entry point of the corkscrew.

The size hole that, say, a syringe would make.

"Don't drink that!" She jumped off the stool and grabbed Josh's and Amy's wine glasses by the stem. Wine splashed onto both of them, the floor, and the sofa.

"Val! What the hell are you doing?" Amy shouted, rising off the couch. But she let Val take the glass from her, as did Josh. "Look what you've done to my dress!"

"I'm sorry," Val said. "This wine is tainted. Don't drink any!"

"Too late. I already took a few sips," Josh said.

"Me, too," Amy said. "What do you mean, tainted?"

"Wait here." Val ran down the hall to the second bedroom and grabbed the bag of corks off the closet floor. Sure enough, the logos stamped on each cork matched the one they'd opened. That convinced her: Josh and Amy had ingested some drugged wine.

She dashed out into the hall—and nearly collided with Nick, standing outside the bathroom, texting someone.

"Sorry!" Val said, clutching him so neither one would fall over. "I was…wait, who are you texting this time of night?"

"M-my folks," Nick said. "Letting them know I'll be out late, and not to worry."

"That ship sailed hours ago," she said. "Wait. Your parents, plural? I thought your mom was in the hospital."

"Yeah. Uh, I guess I mean my dad," he said. "Slip of the tongue."

"And your dad cares, why? What, are you on a curfew?"

Nick laughed. "They—I mean, *he* worries. Sorry. I'm a dork."

Val stared at him a moment, shook her head. What-*ever*. She didn't have time for his issues. However, it reminded her of something. She and Beth had traded "Find My Phone" data years ago. It had come in handy a few times before. She opened the app and activated the trace on Beth's phone. In seconds, the app zoomed in on its location.

She grabbed Nick by the arm. "Found her!" she said. "Come on!"

"Where?" he asked, putting his phone away.

"Based on this map," Val said, "she—or at least her phone—is only a few yards from the rear exit of this building. Let's go find her!"

***

He'd panicked, and that bothered him.

Fleeing showed weakness. And a failure to plan. How embarrassing. How…unprofessional.

He stared across the river from his favorite viewpoint, toward Trillium Towers. The condo unit remained lit. Even without binoculars, he could make out shadows moving about in the space. Space he needed, and soon.

The chloroform wouldn't keep Beth out for long, despite the heavy dose. He'd given her too much—could have killed her, in his haste. He guessed that she'd had a few drinks, which would help keep her out for a while.

Sooner or later she'd regain consciousness, although she'd appear drunk on her feet for several minutes after. If he timed it right, he could get her back inside the condo without drawing attention to them. If not, his security hacks would wipe away the evidence.

With that, a pang of horror jolted through his body. He'd turned off the signal blocking in the condo, but had he turned it back on? He checked the app. Dammit! A slip-up.

Two slip-ups: he'd also left the door lock unjammed. Meaning they could come and go if they wished.

Well, he needed them to go. Even Amy, if necessary. Clueless Amy might even unwittingly help him. If not her, then the dupe of a boy who'd become so helpful lately.

Would she, or he, remember which wine to open? If so, their party might become a sleepover. For a short while, anyway. After which, the sleep would become permanent.

Regardless, he needed to regain control. He reset the signal block and door lock, reviewed the other settings, and realized how he could get them to leave at the moment of his choosing.

He headed back to Trillium Towers and, again, parked in the rear lot. He verified with a glance that people still occupied the condo, still moved around, unaware of his surveillance.

That movement meant they hadn't opened the right wine yet. His dupe had failed him. The cost of doing business with people to whom he couldn't give overt orders. Only suggestions.

No matter. He had his girl. Now he needed his space, his *laboratory,* to work in. Time for them to leave.

He activated his security app, disabled signal blocking and unlocked the door. Then he texted his guy: *Trouble. Get out!*

That gave him a narrow window in which to operate. If they exited the rear of the building, they could encounter him. He needed to get her inside, fast.

He checked his surroundings. Nobody in visual or audible range. Good. He opened the trunk. The dim lighting of the parking lot illuminated the blonde highlights in her long brown hair, the light freckles peeking through her makeup. But opening the trunk disturbed her slumber. She winced and stirred, mumbled something.

"Come on, beautiful," he said. "Time to party." He lifted her by the shoulders—not an easy task, given the awkward angle—and got her on her feet, her arm slung over his shoulder. A practiced pose. She'd look like a typical bar babe who'd drank too much and said yes to the first guy who offered to take her home.

He fumbled for his keys at the building's back door—hard to do with the girl on his shoulder, and she squirmed a bit. Another timing problem to manage. He couldn't afford for her to regain full consciousness. Resist. Fight him. Create a scene. Force even more delay.

He got the door open and pulled her into the dim hallway. On each side of the corridor, closed doors led to a series of utilitarian spaces: a small gym, a laundromat, a janitor's closet, some others whose purpose he didn't know. The doors to the gym and laundromat had glass panels on top, enabling him to check inside. Both empty. Good. He needed a moment to rest. The gym required use of the keycard, another security system outside his control. By contrast, the laundry room unlocked with a traditional metal key, issued to each tenant. Even so, he found the door ajar. Typical sloth. Sometimes his precautions seemed unnecessary.

He dragged the girl inside and shut the door. She murmured and pawed at him, grabbing his arm. Alarmed, he dragged her farther into the room. She slipped out of his grasp and slid backward, falling to the floor. He sat her up against the wall behind a vending machine, hiding her from any prying eyes that passed by. Then he turned off the lights and locked the door.

Just in time. Voices echoed down the hallway—a man and a woman—along with footsteps, drawing closer.

Chapter Forty

Val and Nick again exited the back door of the building, propping it open with the rock she'd used earlier. The "Find My Phone" app's beacon led them to a parking space some twenty feet away. Val found the phone on the ground between two cars. The hood of the black Mercedes to her right felt warm. Someone had parked there in the last few minutes.

"Why would she have come out here?" Nick asked. "She was just supposed to open the door and help them carry stuff."

Val rolled her eyes, exhaustion chipping away at her patience with him. "That was a bogus message, I'm pretty sure," she said. "Hush a moment." She woke up the phone from its hibernation state and keyed in six quick digits. Since high school, against Val's advice, Beth used the same PIN for everything: bank ATMs, her laptop, and every phone she'd ever owned.

The phone unlocked, and the screen displayed the last several text messages Val had sent her. With a few taps, she accessed the ones sent from Josh's phone as well.

"Beth's phone has probably been here since she left the condo." Val shivered. "Where is she?"

They searched the rest of the lot, between and under every parked car, as well as the few empty spots. No sign of Beth anywhere. Val had feared that they'd find something horrible—her shoes, for example—and finding nothing brought her as much relief as frustration.

"Let's check the garage," Nick suggested.

"I already did," Val said.

"Yeah, you checked the parking lot before, too," he said, his own impatience showing. "What's the harm in another look?"

"Wasting precious time, that's what," Val snapped. "Whoever took her wouldn't leave her in plain sight. My guess is, given where we found her phone, she got into a car with someone—possibly against her will." A chill ran down her spine. Until speaking those words out loud, she hadn't internalized how much danger Beth could be in.

"Still," Nick said, "we should make sure—check other common areas, or spaces accessible only to tenants."

Val nodded. Smart thinking. "Let's go wake up the manager," she said. "What the hell, he hates me already."

***

The young couple passed by the darkened laundry room without so much as a glance. The back door groaned open. He waited for the sound of it slamming shut...which didn't come. Which meant they'd propped it open and planned to return soon. He had to hurry. He grabbed the girl by the armpits to lift her. She pushed away, mumbling something about being "tired, leave me alone."

"Come on, baby," he said, his voice soft. "I'm bringing you up to bed."

"Kay, Josh," she said, smiling, her eyes still closed. She remained dead weight. He almost dropped her, but by propping her against the wall with his body, managed to steady her.

The press of her flesh against his distracted him a moment. He loved how soft she felt, her scent, how she gave up the fight and relented—

No. Not yet. Not here, not now. He had a place, and a process. He must follow it.

He carried her to the door, checked the hallway. All clear. He swift-walked her to the elevator—a moment of vulnerability he'd never had to encounter before. All the other girls had come to the condo willingly. Excited, even. This one felt...different. He hadn't had time to make the sale, so to speak. To gain her trust. Her commitment to secrecy. Her discretion.

No matter. What's done is done. The doors opened, and he pulled her inside. Once the pull of gravity and soft whir of the motor indicated their ascent, he texted the dupe again. *Are you gone? Trouble imminent!*

He waited. Worst case, he stops at the fourteenth floor and pauses in the stairwell. A pain, but low risk, this time of night.

The elevator passed the fifth floor. Eighth. Tenth. Eleventh. His finger hovered over the "14" button—

The text came as the indicator lit on "13." *All R out. TY for the warning.*

He sighed in relief, then realized with a pang of regret: no threesome tonight.

No matter. This one would be more than enough.

He glanced at her shoes, and shivered.

***

Nick redialed the building's main number he had called earlier and handed his phone to Val. The sleepy and grumpy voice of the manager said, "What now?"

"Clayton PD. This is a police emergency. I need to search every vacant unit in this building right now."

"You got a warrant yet?" he said, even more irritated than before.

"Did you hear me say emergency?" she said. "Meet me in the lobby. Or do I have to call in a dozen squad cars with blaring sirens?"

"Okay, okay. Jesus."

They reentered through the back door and met the haggard, unshaven man, dressed in a robe over faded flannel pajamas, in the building's main lobby.

"Where's your badge?" he said.

Dammit again! Val dialed the main dispatch number and put the call on speaker. "This is Officer Valorie Dawes," she said. "Off-duty and out of uniform, responding to an emergency at Trillium Towers. Could you please verify for the building manager my active duty status and badge number?"

"Enter your date of birth and social," Dispatch said in a bored tone.

Val typed the digits into her phone. "Confirmed," Dispatch said, and rattled off her badge number. "Active since September 2018."

Val sneered at the manager. "Believe me now?"

"You're a damned rookie, eh?" the manager said with a nasty grin. "No wonder you forgot your damned badge."

"What's the emergency, Dawes?" Dispatch asked.

Val turned off the speaker and spoke in a low voice. "Missing person and probable connection to the Schoolgirl Slayer case," she said.

"We'll send backup," Dispatch said. "Stand by until units arrive."

Val hung up. No way she'd wait around while some creep had her friend, doing God-knows-what to her.

"This is all about those high school girls?" Nick said in a hoarse whisper, eyes wide.

Val waved him off and spoke to the manager. "Show me those empty units," she said.

"There's only two," he said. "306 and 705." They rode up to the third floor and he opened the vacant unit for them, a one-bed, one-bath apartment with a view of the street, and clean as an operating room. Same for the seventh-floor unit, a two-bedroom with the same layout as LeeAnn's top-floor condo.

"What common areas are there?" Val asked. "Storage, laundry, anything."

The manager grunted and took them back to the first floor. He pointed down the hallway that led to the back exit. "Laundry and gym back there if you want to look. Restaurant's in front—closed since eleven," he said. "Storage bins in each parking level. I can't get you in those. You break in, you pay for the damage."

"Cameras on all that?" Nick asked. Val let her irritation slide over his butting in. She should have asked that.

"Of course," the manager said. "And yes, you can see footage…as soon as I see that warrant."

Val cursed under her breath. "Show me the gym and laundry room," she said.

He opened the dark gym first, a small space with about a dozen electric-powered machines, a few stationary bikes and ellipticals, and some dead weights. Otherwise, empty and clean. The laundry room, across the hall, held about a half-dozen washers and dryers with credit card payment slots—no cheap coin-op jobs. It reeked of bleach and laundry soap. A few random socks, dryer sheets, and lint balls hugged the corners and baseboards. It was the only space in the building that wasn't pristine.

"Seen enough?" the manager said in a raspy voice.

"Not yet," Val said. The room's minor clutter and funky odor drew her in deeper. She opened each washer and dryer, as if their cavernous bellies would somehow surrender a clue. Nothing.

As she turned to leave, though, something reflected in the corner nearest the door, under a giant lint ball. The glint of metal. Gold, in fact. She squatted down and retrieved it. Turned it over in her hand.

"It's a cuff link," Nick said over her shoulder. "My dad used to wear those with his tuxedo."

"Who would come do laundry dressed in a tux?" Val said. "Nobody, that's who."

"Give it to me," the manager said. "One of our tenants must have lost it. I'll get it back to him."

"What was Kent wearing tonight?" she asked Nick, turning her back on the manager.

"A tuxedo," he said. "Powder blue."

"Who else wore a tux, that you remember? Anyone?"

Nick searched his memory for a moment. "That rich guy, Iverson," he said. "Maybe others, but he's the only one I remember."

Val nodded. That confirmed her memory, too. She scanned the floor for the other cuff link and spotted a slender, tortoise-shell hair clip in the nearest corner. She picked it up. Her knees grew weak, and for a moment, she couldn't speak.

"This is Beth's," she choked out. "She wore it to the reunion. Beth and the Slayer were both in this room tonight!"

"Where are they now?" Nick asked, blanching.

Val shook her head. "That," she said, "is the ten-million-dollar question."

***

The elevator opened, and he half-carried, half-dragged the girl toward number 1507. Just a few units down the hall. His electronic key unlocked the door, and he pushed it open with his elbow. The girl slipped from his grasp into a heap at his feet.

Somewhere down the hall, another door opened. Someone leaving their condo—at this hour!

Sweat gathered under his armpits. He tugged at the girl's arms, but she slid off him like a jellyfish, dead weight on the floor. Voices echoed from the open door up the hall. A man and a woman. He stole a glance in that direction. Still an empty corridor, but the voices grew louder.

Desperate, he pushed her through the open doorway, intending to follow her in. But she fell to the floor, blocking his path and preventing the door from closing. She moaned and rolled to her side, tried to get up. He slid inside next to her, grabbed her under the arms, and dragged her onto the sofa. The door clicked shut behind him.

His heart pounded, as much from exhilaration as from exertion. A man paid a price, consorting with girls with a little meat on their bones. No tossing a curvy girl over his shoulder and dropping her on the bed. He liked it when they put up a bit of a fight, too. Not too much—not enough to scratch or bite or otherwise snag some of his DNA. Enough to pay off the work he put in.

Beth lay back on the sofa, her eyes open a slit, her head lolling to one side. "Wha...where's...how'm I..." Then gibberish. Still, she'd regain full faculties soon. Time to put her in the proper frame of consciousness.

He grabbed the wine off the counter, a cheap Chianti that someone had opened. The kind he'd prepared for nights like these. Someone had consumed a few glasses. He shook his head. They'd better not drive with this in their system. Still. Not his problem right now. He poured a glass and returned to the girl, who'd grown more animated. Held it to her lips. She turned her head away. He grabbed her by the hair, forced her mouth open, and poured. Covered her mouth, pinched her nose, and stroked her neck with his pinky finger. Her eyes opened wide with fear and the obvious intention to resist. They always did when it came to this.

But she had no choice. She needed air. To get that, she had to clear her airway. Which left her only one option: to swallow.

Finally she gulped the liquid down. She choked and coughed, spraying the drugged wine all over both of them.

He cursed and held her down again, pouring more wine into her mouth. As much onto her as into her, but enough. Made her swallow again. Straddled her, holding her down with his weight, pinning her arms to her sides. Come on, come *on!*

She struggled, breathing hard, wriggling, and losing her fight with every deep breath. Minutes later, she lapsed into unconsciousness.

Time to mark her.

Chapter Forty-One

Val and Nick followed the manager to the main lobby, a small space that functioned as a wide crossroads to the rest of the building. Besides the elevators, stairways, and the hallway they'd just traversed, the lobby bled off into a few more short corridors. One led to the manager's office and apartment, and a wall full of mailboxes. Another led to utility closets and storage areas, along with a stainless steel ice machine. An Italian restaurant occupied a quarter of the building's footprint, its glass walls revealing a dark, empty dining room.

"Would a resident have access to any of those spaces?" Val asked.

The manager responded with an emphatic shake of his head. "Nope. The only keys are on my person or locked up in my office. Always. I lock all the spares in the safe every night before I close up shop, including tonight."

"Can you verify that for us, please?" Val asked.

"I just told you they're there!" the manager shouted, his face turning red. "How many times—"

"Val!" Josh's slurred voice interrupted them. A moment later, he and Amy stumbled out of the elevator, each leaning on one of Kent Mercer's sloping shoulders. "Where's Beth?" Josh continued. "I thought you were finding her."

Val grabbed Nick by the shoulder, nearly knocking the phone out of his hand. "Help Kent with those two," she said. "The drugs in the wine are kicking in. All of you, get to the car and get out of here!"

"What about Beth?" Josh said. "I can't leave her..." He slumped like a bag of rice to the floor. Nick stepped forward and, straining, got Josh back to his feet.

"Drugs? What the hell are you all doing up there?" the manager said, pointing a finger at Kent.

"Easy," Nick said. "It wasn't their fault."

"I'm calling the cops!" the manager shouted, and hustled back to his apartment.

Val shook her head. Finally, he'd found a way to be useful.

"What the hell is going on?" Kent said, holding Amy tight against his body. "What are you doing here, Dawes? And where's Beth?"

Val crossed over to him in two long strides and poked him in the chest. "I'm searching for her, that's what. Where have you been all night? What kind of host leaves his own party for an hour and doesn't even answer his damned phone?"

"Like I told Amy, I was looking for booze and ice," he said, defensiveness creeping into his voice. "Which isn't easy, this time of night."

"Where is all this booze and ice?" she said, heat still rising.

"Josh brought the booze up with him," Kent said, his voice now as hot as hers. "I struck out on the ice. Even the machine on this floor was empty, God knows why."

"God knows, and so do you," Val shot back. "It's in the ice chests in the spare bedroom closet!"

Kent's face curled up in confusion, and surprise replaced anger in his voice and demeanor. "What ice chests? What closet? In the condo, you mean?" He threw his free arm up in frustration. "Why didn't anyone tell me?"

Val glared at him, her breathing returning to normal. As much as she hated to admit it, Kent seemed to be telling the truth. "Tell me something," she said in an even tone. "Why didn't anyone else show up to this so-called party? And why did you tell Amy to drink the bottle of wine on the counter?"

He paled a bit, grasping for words. "I didn't tell her she *had* to," he said, stammering a bit. "I told her it was okay to drink it. Cur—er, the owner gave me permission. Why?"

"It's laced with Rohypnol, that's why," Val said. After a moment of registering his blank expression, she explained. "Roofies. The date-rape drug from the '90s. Don't tell me you aren't aware of it."

"I'd never do that," Kent said, defensiveness returning.

That seemed less genuine, but his surprise and confusion registered as true. And he'd confirmed what she suspected all along: Curtis Iverson was behind the whole thing. He'd somehow manipulated Kent, LeeAnn, and probably a dozen others to do their part, none of them knowing the overall scheme or the impact of their actions.

"Whatever," she said. "The point is, the police are on their way. That condo unit is now a crime scene. You need to get these two to a hospital and make sure they haven't overdosed. I'll send officers there to take their statements. Now go!"

Kent's mouth opened in a little "O," and his gaze landed on Amy's slumping figure on his arm. "Amy's in trouble, isn't she?" Tears leaked from his eyes.

Nick hefted Josh up a bit in his arms and edged closer to Val. "Don't you think I ought to stay here with you? I mean, I'll help get Josh to the car, but—"

"No," Val said. "Like I said. Crime scene. You all need to go. I'll catch up with you later."

"But—"

"*Go!*" She grabbed Nick's arms, spun him around, and pushed him toward the front exit. He stumbled forward, nearly falling into a heap with Josh. Kent didn't wait for her to tell him again, instead picking Amy up and carrying her like a baby to the front door. After one more backward glance, Nick followed, half-carrying, half-pushing Josh along with him.

Once the doors closed, Val returned to the elevator. In order to find Beth, she needed some clues as to where the killer—Curtis Iverson—might have taken her. Which meant she needed to get back into that apartment before he did.

***

He emptied the contents of the four ice chests into the tub and opened the cold water spigot, at the last second remembering to close the drain. He cursed himself for the near miss. He'd made that idiotic mistake once, costing valuable time—and risk—fetching more ice and refilling the tub. He could afford no sloppy mistakes this time.

His secure messaging app notified him with an update: Dawes hadn't left the Towers yet. No matter. He'd locked down the condo, good and tight. He didn't dare leave until it came time to get rid of the body. He had much work to do before that moment arrived.

While the tub filled, he returned to the girl, laid out on the bed, on the edge of consciousness, too drugged up to refuse his manifold requests. The perfect state. Awake and pliable.

He lifted the hem of her dress up above her knees. Removed the thigh-high nylons that darkened her pale skin. Rolled her over to expose her calves. Her left calf already sported some playful ink, a flowering, climbing vine that reached around the back of her knee. The right remained untouched, for now. A bare canvas for him to claim with his own work.

He laid out his tools on the bed and lay the pair of henna decals on her skin. Positioned them, soaked them with water, fixed them into place with Band-aids. In a few minutes, they would yield the perfect pattern for him to trace with his tattoo pen. On top, an image of Rosie the Riveter, the iconic, apocryphal industrial hero of World War II, a symbol of women's power and independence. Under that, the Spanish word *Chingona*, for "Tough Woman," or something like that. The Hispanic girl, Yolanda, had explained it to him before losing consciousness a few months before. Her last words, ironically. She'd been anything but tough that night.

While the decal set, he checked the tub—still less than half-full—and prepared a second dose of Flunitrazepam, this time in a syringe. Its long needle, necessary to penetrate all the way through the corks in unopened wine bottles served to most of his unsuspecting girls, required careful handling. The tattoo would hide the needle marks, and her unconscious state would keep her from squirming around during the precision work about to come.

He returned to the bedroom, peeled off the decals, and picked up his pen. Clicked it on and savored the gentle humming sound it made. The sound of a man taking ownership of his woman.

***

At the door to the condo unit, Val realized her mistake, another one borne out of exhaustion: she had no way to get in. She needed a key, which remained in Kent's possession, now on his way with Amy to the hospital. Forget the manager. He'd made it clear: without a warrant, he wouldn't let her in. Which left her with only one more option: wait for backup to arrive.

Her frustration mounted, as did her fear for Beth's safety. Every minute counted. Waiting around did no good— she had to try. She rushed down the hall toward the elevator. Before she reached it, the doors opened, and a familiar figure stepped out.

Nick Evans.

"What are you doing back here?" she hissed at him.

He held up a credit-card-sized piece of hard, white plastic. "Amy forgot her purse," he said. "She'll need ID when she gets to the hospital. I told Kent to go ahead and I'd catch up with them there."

Val's relief at the unexpected help mixed with irritation at him for ignoring her instructions. And a certain dose of skepticism: he had a knack for always being nearby with a flimsy excuse when she'd explicitly told him to get lost.

At the moment, though, he had what she needed. She held out her hand. "I'll get the purse," she said. "You wait here."

"But—"

"Don't argue with me, okay? Stay out here and warn me if anybody comes."

He glared at her, but surrendered the key. He crossed his arms, huffing. "Fine. Whatever."

She rolled her eyes and returned to Unit 1507, Nick a few steps behind her. She inserted the key into the slot.

Nothing.

"I think it goes the other way," Nick said.

She flipped the card around, inserted it again. Still nothing.

"Hmm," Nick said. "Let me look."

Val stepped aside, willing to try anything.

Nick leaned closer, examined the lock, and nodded. He pulled out his key ring and flipped open the blade of a tiny penknife. He inserted it into a crease on the metal casing of the door handle, twisted, and popped a small portion of the casing into his hands.

"Whoa," Val said. "Is there something about your past you're not telling me?"

Nick surrendered a shy grin. "Remember me saying I never went home during semester breaks? Instead, I got a job working security in a hotel. They used the same system." He set the metal casing onto the floor and pointed inside. "Electronic systems are required to have workarounds in case of emergency, like loss of power."

"What? That's all it took to unlock it—popping off the cover?"

He chuckled. "No. Look." He pointed to a tiny ten-key numeric pad inside the handle. "Now, we need to guess the passcode."

"How long will that take?" Val asked.

Nick shrugged. "Assuming any random four-digit code, it could take up to ten thousand guesses. At two seconds per guess, that's five or six hours. Six digits, a little over three weeks."

"We don't have that kind of time," Val said. "Thanks, anyway."

"Ah, but never assume a random code," Nick said. "People generally choose codes that are easy to remember. Few are dumb enough to pick 1-2-3-4 or 1-1-1-2-2-2, for example, and even fewer pick a sequence that has no meaning to them."

"Such as?" Val failed to keep the irritation out of her voice. Beth could be anywhere, suffering almost unimaginable humiliation and pain—or worse—and he picks this moment to get all pedantic on hotel security systems.

Ignoring her frustration, Nick smiled and pecked at the pad four times. He paused and tried again. "Ah," he said. "Did you see the lights blink? Right after the sixth number I entered. That means I entered the wrong six-digit code."

"You seem happy about that," Val said.

"We're learning the system," Nick said. "So, we need a six-digit code that's meaningful to the owner."

"Curtis Iverson," Val said.

Nick glanced at her, a quizzical expression on his face. "Why him?"

Val fretted a moment. "He's the one who uses it," she said, her voice fading. "But he wouldn't have set the code, would he? LeeAnn Schofield rented the place."

"And rarely uses it, right? So she'd pick a code that she'd remember no matter what. Six digits, so probably a date—a birthday, anniversary, something like that." Nick touched a finger to his temple. "Got it." He pecked at the keypad again. Waited. Again, and again. Val grew more restless. He was wasting valuable time.

But a minute later, something clicked, and a tiny green light lit at the top of the keycard reader.

"Of course," he said. "The day that the Nets drafted Brandon Schofield into the NBA."

"You're either a genius or an incredible nerd," Val said.

"Not both?" He smiled and turned the handle. "Let's go."

"No," Val said. "Sorry. Police business. You stay out here. I'll find the purse and hand it out to you. Please?"

He made a face, then held up his hands in surrender. "I'll be right here." He stepped to the side and leaned against the wall. "I should get to the hospital soon, anyway."

Val nodded and pushed open the door. The first thing she saw blew her plans to search for clues right out of the water.

Draped over the sofa lay a black tuxedo jacket. On the floor rested a pair of women's shoes.

Beth's shoes.

Chapter Forty-Two

He ran his hand over the spot on the girl's leg where he'd created the template for his work. So smooth and strong, it was almost a shame to spoil it. Then again, it wouldn't last long, spoiled or otherwise. He would leave his mark on her in other, less visible ways, as well.

Besides, it had become a tradition of sorts. Ever since the first girl, Hannah, who'd come by her ink before they'd met. She'd shown it off to him as he massaged her bare feet, tempting him in that innocent-but-mature way of hers, daring him to take their flirtation further. Her devil-may-care dares led them from the office to this secret den, one where he'd indulged in marginally kinky dalliances in the past. Never anything more dangerous than the occasional tie-up and blindfold, but things that conservative, uptight Megan would never have tried in a million years.

Hannah convinced him to drop his inhibitions, displaying appetites and skills he never would have expected a seventeen-year-old to know, much less have mastered.

Then things had gone awry. Sex in the bathtub, which this young woman—this *girl*—insisted on filling with ice-cold water to "heighten the sensation." That move made it nearly impossible for his body to perform, and led to trying positions with which even he, an informal student of the Kama Sutra, was unfamiliar. Positions that, it turned out, were too risky to try in a full bathtub, where the excitement of impending orgasm could lead a man to neglect the danger it presented to his partner. And to discover, to his horror, she'd drowned while yielding to his pleasure.

Not one to panic, he'd taken great care in disposing of the body, and only later discovered her shoes still in the condo. A slip-up—or an unconscious choice? He never resolved that question in his mind. Not for Hannah.

Until girl number two. Jaden shocked him with her youth—barely sixteen—but so smart, so dynamic, and harder to convince that her path to financial freedom necessitated a detour through his bedroom. The first one he'd needed to subdue, and the one that reminded him of the value of pharmaceuticals, an approach he'd not resorted to since exploring the nightclub scene during college. Not knowing how the tattoo would appear on her dark skin, he'd almost skipped that step. But no. No shortcuts. No skipping the homage to how she yielded, her power no match for his.

Oh, how tattooing her had heightened the experience!

Alas, he'd been too slow in applying it. As a result, she'd recovered from her alcoholic haze, and her resistance led to unintentional disaster—for her. He'd intended to wash her body clean after their sweaty excitement in the bedroom. She tried to escape, and he panicked, envisioning the disaster that would ensue. So he had to end it for her.

He hoped Beth would show as much spirit. Beth and Jaden shared many traits—an athletic, curvy body, high energy, a fun-loving flair—despite their differences in age and race. His hand shook, still caressing Beth's leg. Yes, please be like Jaden! While Hannah had started it all, Jaden had brought the excitement he so craved.

Then came the little Latina. Yolanda had put up the most fight of all and had talked all night about *Chingona*—Girl Power—which inspired the addition of that word to the drawing. Which became yet another new tradition. Her claims of sexual experience bore out later. A magnificent girl. Such a shame to lose her.

Beth's experience—he assumed, since she was engaged—enticed him. Made him think tonight could surpass what he'd felt in February, with Yolanda.

By contrast, Olivia had put up no fight at all. So disappointing. He'd tried to elicit more of a reaction from her by getting a little extra rough. However, whether from an overdose of the drugs or because of her unexpected passivity, she lay so still that he almost wasn't sure if he needed to push her head under the water after all. The entire experience left him so unsatisfied that he'd later succumbed to seducing his wife. That memory made him shudder.

Then, Charlene. Such a darling girl. She'd fallen for his appeals to her vanity, to how "grown-up" she was. So naïve that he almost felt guilty about lying to her. So inexperienced, she told him that the drugged wine he'd given her was her first alcoholic beverage. She even remained awake for the tattoo, so excited to do something so "grown-up," and only resisted a little, at the very end.

Beth would resist a bit more, show her spirit, if he managed the dosing right. He reached for the syringe—

A noise in the living room stopped him. He listened to see if he could identify it. After a few seconds, he doubted himself, blamed his over-active imagination.

Then he heard it again. Or, rather, something similar. The door, clicking shut.

Someone had gotten inside.

He crept out to the hallway to investigate.

***

Val slipped off her shoes and tiptoed across the living room toward the sound of running water, fatigue draining away as adrenaline surged through her body. Unarmed, alone, and dressed for dancing rather than confronting a serial killer, she'd put herself in a dangerous position. Every instinct told her to flee, or to wait until backup could arrive.

But fleeing would leave Beth in danger. Even a few minutes could spell the difference between her living and dying, or suffering less fatal yet horrible consequences. Consequences Val herself had suffered at a much younger age.

Val's small size put her at a disadvantage. She needed a weapon. She wrapped her fist around the business end of a corkscrew someone had left out. It would do.

Besides, she also possessed a few key advantages: her youth. Her rusty martial arts skills. And if she played it right, the element of surprise.

Something moved in the master bedroom. She recognized the sound—the slight creak of a body rising off of a bed. She had one chance.

A few steps away, the main bathroom door lay ajar. Val dashed inside and pulled it almost shut behind her. She stumbled over an empty ice chest lying on the floor beside the tub, itself loaded with ice and filling with water. Getting ready for its next victim. Beth!

Footsteps sounded in the hallway. She needed to hide—fast. In here, she had only one option. She stepped barefoot onto the edge of the tub, pulling the shower curtain closed, hoping the faint metallic scraping noise wouldn't alert her attacker. She slipped and nearly fell, righted herself, and readied her weapon.

***

Curtis crept down the hallway, glancing at the doorways to the second bedroom and both bathrooms as he passed. All seemed quiet and as he'd left them. His intruder, then, hadn't begun to explore this end of the condo.

The intruder had to be Dawes. His informant had warned him she'd remained in the building and hadn't updated him since. Somehow, she'd found a way past his considerable defenses. Who else but Dawes could accomplish that?

He smiled. His little threesome might happen, after all.

At the end of the hallway, he sidled up against the wall to avoid detection, and peeked around the corner.

Empty! How?

Ah. The kitchen. She'd hidden behind the island bar. He crouched low and made his way to the passageway separating the two rooms. Again he peeked around the corner of the low bar—

Again, empty.

Somehow, she'd made her way past him. Which meant she'd gained an advantage. She'd positioned herself between him and Beth.

He hurried back down the hallway and peeked into the master bedroom. Beth still lay on the bed, face-down, drooling onto the pillow, her dress hiked up high above her knees. No one else. Dawes, had she gotten that far, would not have left her friend undisturbed.

Which left the other bedroom or one of the two bathrooms.

He closed the master bedroom door and slipped through to the walk-in closet. Locked it behind him and continued through to the master bath. All clear. He exited into the hallway, checked the second bedroom. Empty.

That left only one room: the main bathroom.

Inside the bedroom, a faint bell rang. His alarm, telling him to turn off the water in the tub. As if fate itself had decided to intervene.

He pushed open the bathroom door with his elbow. In moments he spotted proof of his deductive power: the shower curtain, drawn closed. Not how he'd left it. Near the center of the tub, a shadow became visible through the semi-opaque plastic. The shape of a body—a woman's body. Hiding. Lying in wait. Not expecting him to notice her.

He placed himself in position of maximum advantage, then lunged toward the shape, arms outstretched as if making a football tackle. As expected, his shoulder made impact, right where a person's waist might be. A moment later, the human-shaped form splashed into the tub's icy water, covered by the shower curtain, ripped off its rod by the falling bodies.

***

The sudden impact knocked Val off balance. Her body bounced once off the opposite wall and her feet slid off the short walls of the tub. She grabbed at the air and snagged only the top edge of the flimsy plastic shower curtain. Before she could catch a breath, her body tumbled into the icy water, dragging the curtain down with her.

The shock of the impact, the fall, the icy cold water, and the plastic sheet enveloping her body paralyzed her for a moment. To make matters worse, in her panic, she dropped the corkscrew. Strong hands gripped her through the shower curtain, finding her head and pushing her under the surface of the water. She gulped in a breath, but got as much liquid as air. She choked, tried to lift herself up. The weight of the man and the confining straitjacket of the plastic kept her underwater.

Unable to breathe. Cold water, already in her mouth, filled her throat and lungs. So painful! She needed to expel the water, find air. Now!

Panic rose inside her. With her heart pounding, her lack of air, she'd lose consciousness within seconds. Val fought against the man's grip, but he overpowered and outweighed her. He didn't need to hold her tight, just keep her head under for a short time. Soon her body's instincts would take over, try to suck in another breath even though her head knew she could not. He'd win. She'd die in the frigid bath, unable to save her friend from the same fate. Because of her failure to prepare for his attack.

The icy water still splashing from the spigot into the tub drowned out all other noise, giving voice to the threat against her, as if the universe itself screamed at her: Drown! Give up! Die!

Anger replaced panic inside her. No. She would not give up, would not let him win. Could not let that happen to Beth…assuming he hadn't killed her already.

Her Sensei's teachings came to mind. While he'd never addressed a drowning scenario, the same principles of jiu jitsu applied: use your enemy's force against him.

Val stopped flailing and resisting, and instead allowed his weight and pressure to shift her body to one side. That enabled her to wiggle her arm free and out of the stifling cocoon of the shower curtain. Her hand brushed against something floating in the water. Her fingers curled around a long, slender object. A plastic tube of some sort, with a long, sharp needle. A syringe! Curtis must have intended to jab her with it and dropped it in the struggle. She gripped it, thumb on the plunger, and swung at him, swatted only air. Swung again, and her forearm hit something firm—his back or shoulder. She adjusted her aim and arced her arm in a third attempt.

This time, the needle found purchase, and she drove it deep into his back. He screamed, and his weight on her lessened. She pushed her body upward, enough to break the water's surface and suck in a deep gasp of air.

With another roar, his grip tightened again, and he pushed her head back underwater. She closed her mouth in time, and the single, deep breath of air she'd gulped renewed her strength. She bucked against him, felt him weakening. Broke the surface again for a second breath. Found the syringe still stuck in his back, and pressed its plunger to the hilt, forcing the remainder of the full, massive dose into his bloodstream.

He yelped in pain and arched his back, reaching one arm behind him to yank the needle away. Val pressed harder, holding firm. Using his momentum, she lunged her body against his, knocking him backward, and they landed hard on the tile floor. She tried to wriggle free of the shower curtain, still wrapped around her, but he somehow rolled on top of her, his weight crushing her. He tried to punch her. She dodged his clumsy attempt with ease. He wriggled and kicked, but with her one free arm, she held onto the syringe, still penetrating his back. After several seconds, his struggling weakened, then ceased.

Taking deep, delicious breaths, she freed her other arm, pushed him off her, and stripped the plastic curtain away from her body, its metal rings jangling like tiny bells. She got to her knees, breathing hard. Curtis lay slumped over the side of the tub, his head submerged in the water, his arms waving in a slow, clumsy attempt to lift himself up. Air bubbled up from his nose and mouth.

Soaking wet, shivering, and gasping for air, she stared at him, her teeth chattering. If she left him there, he would suffer the same death he'd intended for her and Beth. The same death he'd inflicted on at least five other young women in the last year.

More bubbles escaped. Curtis lifted his head up for a moment, then splashed back into the frigid water.

So tempting to let him die.

The bubbles stopped.

Val screamed in frustration, then grabbed him by the shoulders, tugging at him. His body, at least a half-foot taller and seventy pounds heavier than hers, refused to budge. She swore, grabbed his hair, lifted his face out of the water, then wrapped her other arm around his neck in a choke-hold. She pressed her knees against the side of the tub and yanked her body backward. Reluctantly, it seemed, his body followed hers into an upright position. She pushed him away, and he sprawled in a heap on the cold, wet tile floor.

Val cursed aloud. Why couldn't she let him die?

Dammit. She knew why. Unlike Curtis, she took no joy from watching someone die. But she would take great joy from bringing him to justice.

Val turned off the faucet in the tub. The condo filled with an eerie silence, broken only by her own deep breaths and the sputtering gasps of the nearly unconscious man next to her.

A shadow darkened the room, blocking the light from the hallway. A bear of a man wearing the uniform of the Clayton Police Department crouched in a shooter's stance, weapon drawn.

"Hey, Travis," Val said. "Welcome to the party."

Chapter Forty-Three

Travis holstered his weapon and helped Val to her feet. "What happened to you?" he said. "You get the hots for Iverson and decided to shake it off with a cold shower? Most people undress first."

"Shut *up*," Val said, shivering. She couldn't suppress a grin. "And hand me a towel."

"Got a live one!" someone shouted from another room. She recognized the voice: Shannon O'Reilly.

"Beth!" Val pushed past Travis and rushed into the master bedroom. There she found Shannon leaning over Beth's body on the bed, one hand checking her wrist for a pulse while the other hovered over her mouth.

Val sat on the bed and held her lifelong friend's hand. "Beth," she said, her teeth chattering from the cold. "Can you hear me?"

Beth mumbled something and moaned.

"She's breathing," Shannon said. "She appears heavily sedated, and her pulse is weak." Shannon pointed to the red, puffy skin on Beth's calf, where the image of Rosie the Riveter appeared in faded blue, except for the crude, black-ink outline of Rosie's head. Shannon picked up the tattoo pen from the bed. "Looks like our boy fancies himself an artist."

"We'd better get her to the hospital," Val said, fighting tears.

"You should go home and change into some dry clothes," Travis said. "You look like a drowned rat."

"Thanks, *pal*," Val said. "What about the evidence here?"

"We'll take care of it," Travis said. "Go get some sleep."

Shannon slipped her jacket over Val's shoulders. "Get it back to me tomorrow," she said. "And Dawes? It's good to see you."

"You, too, Shannon," she said. "That goes for you, too, Travis."

"Get out of my crime scene," Travis said with a growl, but he was smiling, too.

The commotion that greeted her in the front parking lot of Trillium Towers stood in marked contrast to the spooky, nearly empty patch of dimly lit pavement she'd encountered less than an hour before. Squad cars blocked every entrance and exit, lights flashing, with uniformed police on alert nearby, scanning the grounds. One of them took a statement from her as to what had happened in the condo while the paramedics drove Beth away in an ambulance. Every fiber of Val's being wanted to join Beth on that ride to the hospital, but she couldn't leave until giving the investigators what they needed.

As they concluded, a tall, bearded figure strode toward her. "Valorie!" Nick Evans said. "Thank God you're okay!"

"What are you still doing here?" she said, evading an offered hug. "Aren't they expecting you at the hospital?"

"I was still waiting for you to hand me Amy's purse when the cavalry arrived," he said, indicating the crowd of uniformed officers nearby. "They made me wait outside. What happened in there?"

"Curtis Iverson happened," Val said. "He had Beth, and he got the jump on me. It...was a close call."

Nick's mouth gaped open, and he covered it with his hand. "Holy shit!" he said. "I'm so sorry."

"Why are you sorry?" Val said. "It wasn't your fault."

Nick stared at her. His mouth moved, but no words formed.

"What's the matter, Nick?" Val said. Concern turned to alarm when his face blanched and he collapsed onto a bench with a heavy thud. "Is there something you aren't telling me?"

"Val, I...I think I may have fucked up, big time," he said. "Oh, God." He buried his head in his hands and rocked his body from side to side.

Val sat and shook him by the shoulder. "Nick, tell me," she said. "What did you do?"

Nick uncovered his face, his cheeks wet with tears. "First, you gotta believe me. I didn't realize," he said. "I mean, I should have suspected—"

"Stop explaining and start confessing," Val said in a sharp tone. "Come on, I'm too cold and exhausted for bullshit. Get to the point."

Taken aback by the force of her words, Nick blinked and wiped away his tears. "Okay," he said, collecting himself. "First, I didn't run into you by accident tonight at the reunion. It was planned."

"It doesn't take a detective to know that you've been checking me out," Val said. "Go on."

"I wasn't checking you out. I was...following you. For...someone." Nick gave his head a few sharp shakes, as if throwing off a mental burden. Or an emotional one. "I was on a job."

"A job?" Val stood and moved a few steps away, arms crossed. "What kind of job? I thought you were in PR or journalism or something."

"That's what I thought, too," he said. "A blogger contacted me. Clayton Copwatch. Heard of them?"

"Unfortunately, yes," Val said. "An online tabloid of the worst kind. They hired you to follow me? Why?"

"I don't—I mean, I *didn't* know," he said. "I answered an online ad for a writing gig. It paid well, and all I had to do was 'report in' every so often on what you were doing. Where you were, who you were with, that sort of thing. They made it sound like some sort of exposé on police corruption." He heaved a deep breath before continuing. "I-I didn't expect to like you."

"Sorry to disappoint," Val said. "Jesus, Nick! How skeezy is that? For God's sake, you could have gotten me—all of us—killed!"

"I'm so, so sorry." He stood and moved toward Val.

She backed away, and he stopped. "Holy shit," she said, realization dawning. "You're an Uber driver. What did you do, camp out on my account?"

Nick sighed, and after a pause, nodded. "I'll cooperate fully with the police. I'll tell them everything, no matter what. I won't accept the pay." He swallowed hard. "Not a dime."

"Of course," Val said. "I'd expect nothing less. Officer!" She waved a uniform over.

"Valorie," Nick said, "before you go. I just want to say thank you for spending time with me tonight. I realize now that nothing will come of it, but it was nice to hang out with one of the cool kids for a little while."

Val laughed. "Dude, I'm a cop. The opposite of cool."

"You're cooler than you realize," he said. "Anyway, you've got a guy, right? So it was never in the cards."

Val held up her hand to pause the approach of the officer she'd waved over and faced Nick again. "What are you talking about?"

"That guy whose house you went to after the reunion. Before you texted me."

"*You* texted *me*," Val said. "You even followed me to Gil's house?" She shivered, and this time, not from the cold.

"That was the job," he said. "Anyway, when I saw how you two embraced, and the way you acted with him—"

"Okay, that's enough," Val said. "This whole stalking thing is creeping me out."

"I wasn't stalking. Okay, I guess I was," he said. "The point is, I could see that you love that guy. I realized right then that I didn't have a shot with you. Which kind of hurt, and made the rest of the evening even more awkward, but...at that point, I was committed."

Val glared at him, disgust rising in her throat. She waved the officer over again. When he drew near, she pointed to Nick. "Please take this man in for questioning," she said. "Tell Sergeant Petroni that he has information useful to her investigation." She spun back to face Nick. "Tell them everything," she said, pointing a finger at him. "Every fucking detail."

She shook her head, watching him go. *Fucking* men.

***

Val drove Beth's car home and tried to sleep, but her over-active brain wouldn't let her. After a couple of fitful hours, she showered and changed into dry blue jeans, a sweatshirt, and running shoes. She made it to Mercy Hospital as the first orange rays of sunrise peeked over the rolling hills to the east, reflecting on the placid current of the Torrington River. Her dad, at one time an avid amateur photographer, would have gushed over such a picturesque springtime scene.

Whoa. That bit of introspection surprised her. When had she last thought of her father in connection with something positive and beautiful? She should call him, let him know she was all right.

Val found Beth's room with no trouble, and a nurse assured her that Beth would recover just fine. "She's awake, if you want to visit for a minute," the nurse added.

Val didn't hesitate. She took a seat by her friend's bedside and cleared her throat.

Beth's eyes opened. "Hey, girl," Beth said, a smile filling her beautiful face. "You found me."

"I've been looking for you all night long," Val said, chuckling. "You scared me a little."

"Now you know how it feels to live with a cop." Beth held out her hand, and Val took it. Squeezed. God, how she loved this woman.

"Has Josh been by?" Val asked.

Beth's expression soured. "Yes," she said, with an edge to her voice. "The jerk."

"Whoa," Val said, alarmed. "Did you guys fight or something?"

"Fight? Jeez, I wish he had some fight in him." Beth's face darkened. "I can't believe I almost married that man."

"Wait, what?" Val's heart stopped for a moment. "Almost? Aren't you—tell me you didn't—Beth, what's going on?"

"What's going on is that my best friend risked her life to rescue me from a weirdo rapist killer, and my fiancé couldn't be bothered to try," she said. "The man who 'loves me more than the air he needs to breathe,' as he once claimed. Where was he when I needed him most? Partying with that stupid girl *Amy*." Beth spit more than spoke the final words, and her face twisted with anger.

"To be fair," Val said, "I asked him to watch her while Nick and I—"

"Yeah, Nick and you," Beth said. "Not my fiancé. Do you see the problem? He should have insisted. Instead, the little chicken shit stayed behind and drank. What did I ever see in him?"

Val sat back in her chair, too stunned to speak. She'd often asked herself the same question about Josh. The guy never seemed a good fit for Beth. Still... "Maybe this isn't the best frame of mind to be making these types of decisions," Val said. "After you rest and recuperate—"

"I don't need more time. I told him to get his crap out of our place. We're done." Beth closed her eyes and tears dripped down her cheeks. "Done."

"I see." Val gave Beth's hand another squeeze and a shake. "Okay, then. I guess I'm glad I never got around to finding a new roommate."

Beth sighed and opened her eyes again. "I've been thinking about that, too."

Uh-oh. Val's dread returned. "What are you thinking?" she asked in a measured tone.

Beth grimaced. "This whole thing crystallized some feelings I've been having about our living situation," she said. "This was...a horrible night, Val. I almost died." Tears flowed again, this time in rapid succession. "I can't go through another episode like this. I just can't."

"What does that have to do with—"

"You're a cop," Beth said. "In less than a year on this job, you've been in mortal danger at least three times that I'm aware of. I feel like an anxious spouse, always wondering if you're going to come home alive each day. That's one reason I've spent so much time at Josh's place. Some days, I don't want to know. Whether you've..." She turned away and let go of Val's hand. "I can't do it anymore. I can't worry about you being safe, and...I can't spend each day worrying about me staying safe, either."

Val folded her arms across her chest, hugging herself to drive away the choking sadness welling inside her. "I see. So, you want me to move out?"

Beth shook her head. "I can stick it out until the lease expires in June. After that...we should go our separate ways. Living-wise, I mean." She faced Val again. "I'm not dumping you as a friend! I would never, ever do that. Please don't take it that way."

"Of course. Never." Val smiled and nodded.

But that's not how it felt. Not at all.

***

Val left Beth's room shaken to the core. Her closest friend since middle school had dropped two big bombshells—her broken engagement and a major shift in the terms of their relationship. In the past, announcements of that sort would have led to hours of deep, meaningful exchanges over copious amounts of coffee, drinks, or boxes of chocolate. This time, the decisions themselves—particularly the one about her moving out, and, in effect, moving on from how they'd engaged for the past several years—precluded any such conversation.

Which, Val realized, was the point—one that Beth had understood better than, and before, Val did.

That lent an extra heaviness to her step, adding to the weight of sadness, fatigue, and stress of the day...and it wasn't over yet.

Val passed by a private room guarded by a uniformed police officer sporting a seven-day beard. In her exhausted state, his familiar face didn't register at first. Only when his eyes narrowed in disapproval did she recognize her former partner.

"Hey, Rico," she said.

Rico nodded at her. "I heard you had a rough night."

She stole a glance at the name written on the whiteboard outside the room. *D. Collier.* "You could say that. How's Diego doing?"

Rico frowned. "Word is, he's getting released today. From the hospital, I mean. He's still facing a drug charge, from what I gather. You busted that Iverson guy last night for the Schoolgirl Slayer thing, didn't you?"

Val nodded again. "Would it be okay if I said hello?"

Rico laughed and shook his head. "If there's one person he doesn't want to see, it's the cop who put him in here. In jail, anyway, which is what got him beaten up." His expression softened. "Word of advice, Dawes? Don't get emotional about your perps. Once you've arrested them, move on. You'll live longer and happier that way."

Val sighed. "Thanks." She stole one more glance at the closed door, grateful for the privacy it provided in both directions.

A text message from Brenda Petroni interrupted her plans: a request to meet at WAVE Squad headquarters. Immediately.

***

Despite her serious reservations, Val reported to the WAVE Squad office as requested, finding Shannon O'Reilly and Brenda Petroni in the Bullpen, waiting.

"Thanks for coming over so quickly," Petroni said. "We wanted to get more details on what happened last night, and fill you in on a few things. First, though, we wanted to apologize for what happened last week. We mishandled that situation, and we should have been more forthright with you about it."

"Thanks," Val said. "What do you mean? Forthright about what?"

The two women exchanged glances. Shannon ducked her head, and Petroni took a deep breath. "We knew you weren't the leak," Petroni said. "We needed to get you out of there, both to prove it, and to protect you. That was a toxic situation. Some powerful people were out to get you, and they had allies. We wanted to isolate you from that."

"It worked, too," Shannon said. "We found the source of the leak. Any guesses?"

"Grimes?" Val said, then shook her head. "Nah, forget that. He's too much of a straight shooter. So, Dion Woodson?"

"Bingo!" Petroni slow-clapped and surrendered a grim smile. "He tried to pin it on you, but he tripped himself up within days of your leaving."

"Turns out, he owed Curtis Iverson big time for getting his captain to recommend him for the WAVE Squad assignment," Shannon said.

"They twisted my arm pretty hard to get him assigned," Petroni said, venom dripping from her voice. "I couldn't say no."

"Didn't they also do that for me?" Val said. "Didn't that raise your suspicions, too?"

"The mayor requested you," Petroni said. "But I already wanted you."

"Both of us did," Shannon said.

"Thanks," Val said after a long moment. "That means a lot. And I'm sorry I got so angry with you. That was unprofessional."

"And understandable," Shannon said.

Petroni's phone chirped, and she held up an index finger while she answered it. "Petroni...Oh, he did? Excellent! What's the skinny? No kidding...Wow. That's great. No, wait for us. I have something in mind for that." She hung up, beaming. "Fantastic news! Kent Mercer spilled to Grimes. He's going to be charged as an accomplice."

"Kent?" Val's mood, already lifting, skyrocketed to the moon. "How did that come about?"

"When the doctors found elevated GHB in Amy's system, Grimes smelled blood. He asked Mercer a few innocent-sounding questions and didn't like what he heard," Shannon said. "Grimes hauled his butt downtown and started grilling him."

"Grimes broke him in under an hour," Petroni said. "Mercer admitted to scouting girls for Curtis Iverson through the Future Entrepreneurs group, not realizing what Curtis was really after. He thought it was just for late-night trysts in the condo. In exchange, he got to use the place for his own rendezvous."

"Didn't he get suspicious when they all turned up dead?" Val asked, incredulous.

"They didn't *all* end up dead," Petroni said. "Kent apparently found him a dozen or two over the past year. Only a few died, and Curtis found some of the victims on his own. But what Kent Mercer revealed is enough to put Iverson away for a long, long time."

"I thought what I found tonight would do that," Val said in a dull voice.

"You're right," Shannon said. "Which is why we want you to do a little paperwork for us."

Val rolled her eyes. "My reward for nearly getting killed is to type up a report? Gee, thanks."

"Not *type* it." Petroni slid a sheaf of papers over to Val. "Sign it."

"Sign what?" Val took the papers and scanned them. "Wait, this is the arrest report for Curt Iverson."

"That's right," Petroni said. "We think you deserve the collar. After all, you did all the work—including physically taking him down."

Val, her chest swelling with pride, accepted the pen Petroni offered. "Okay, I'm game."

"There is one other thing," Shannon said, expectation in her voice. She seemed to be prodding Petroni with her tone and her facial expression.

"Yes, there is," Petroni said with a heavy expulsion of air. "Another plateful of crow for me to eat, but what the hell. Dawes, with Woodson getting kicked off the team, that opens up another slot. We'd like you to fill it, if you'll have us back."

"Seriously?" Val stared at each of them in turn, dumbstruck.

"Back on the fast track to detective," Shannon said. "We promise, this time, everything's above board. No tricks to trip up your double-dealing colleagues."

"Scout's honor," Petroni said.

Val leaned back, considering their offer. She'd loved the short time she'd spent on the WAVE Squad. However, her rough departure had scarred her, and the long hours meant no social life.

Hell. She had no social life in the best of times, and she'd done nothing except work since returning to Liberty Heights precinct, anyway.

"Can I think on it for a day?" Val said. "I really need some sleep."

"Take two days," Petroni said. "Hell, take a week. We only have one active case—Sierra Stapleton—and we think Bo Rousseau's good for it."

"Only one case, thanks to you," Shannon said. "You did amazing work last night."

"Thanks," Val said. "There's someone I want to talk to before I decide."

Petroni and Shannon smiled at her. They knew exactly who she meant.

***

Val's second attempt at sleep succeeded only slightly better than the first. She managed a few hours of fitful slumber, marked by nightmarish dreams of tattoos, syringes, and deep pools of icy water.

She roused herself with a quick breakfast and two cups of strong coffee. With cream, of course. One thing her uncle had always told her: only psychopaths drink coffee black. Probably to excuse the excessive amounts of cream and sugar he stirred into every cup. Whatever. She'd worshipped Uncle Val and his advice for two decades now and had no plans to stop.

Val walked to Gil's, not minding the warm, steady rain. She needed the fresh air to clear her mind of the clutter and to help her frame this conversation.

All of which flew out the window the moment Gil opened the door.

"So, you are alive," he said with a good-natured growl, holding the door open with one of his crutches. "You could have sent at least *one* text message."

"Why spoil the surprise?" Val squeezed past him and waited for the door to slam shut.

Then she kissed him.

She hadn't planned on that. She'd planned to sit on the sofa, four feet from the recliner he favored, with her hands folded on her lap. Then she would explain how important it was that their friendship remained platonic. To prioritize their professional partnership above all, and how much she valued his mentorship.

All of that melted away in an instant, once her lips met his. His powerful arms wrapped around her, and the warmth of his body gave her the emotional strength she needed. Gil's words from the hospital echoed back to her: Man plans, God laughs. Something Uncle Val always used to say. She held him tighter, their bodies rocking in smooth rhythm.

"Well, hello," he said after their embrace cooled. Might have been minutes, might have been hours. She had no idea. "How was your day?"

Val laughed and guided him to the sofa, where they sat together. Touching. Not four feet apart. Close enough to smell his masculine scent, see the reflection of the lamp in his dark eyes. "Oh, typical," she said. "Inhaled some freezing bathwater, stabbed a rich and powerful bad guy with a drug-laden syringe, and made an enemy for life out of our next governor. How about you, honey?"

After a moment of open-mouthed surprise, he laughed, too. "A syringe? My dear, I've always loved how unconventional you are, but this takes the cake. Whatever happened to a good, old-fashioned service revolver?"

"Meh. I thought it'd clash with my dress."

His eyes darted down to her casual outfit. "I already miss that dress."

"Hush. We have work to discuss." She related the events that transpired since she'd left him the night before. Only when she finished did she realize they'd held hands the entire time.

"One question," Gil said. "How did you know to go back to the condo?"

Val thought for a moment. "It's hard to say," she said. "I guess I did what you suggested: I learned to trust myself and my instincts."

He cocked his head. "I'm impressed," he said. "Not only by what you did and how you figured it all out. You also showed incredible courage, and you did it not just because you wanted to catch the perp." He paused. "You did it out of love for your friend."

"I would never let anything happen to Beth," she said.

Gil let go of her hand and tapped her forehead with one finger. "My dear," he said, "you are going to make one hell of a detective someday."

Val drew in a deep breath. "Yeah, about that," she said. "Petroni offered to put me back on the WAVE Squad. After how things went down last week, I'm not so sure I should do it."

"Do it," Gil said without hesitation. "You want to make detective? They're greasing the skids for you. You'll be the youngest detective in Clayton history, and you'll make your uncle proud." He gestured skyward with reverence.

"Not everyone's so happy with my career choices." Val related Beth's decisions and reasoning. "Gil, we've been friends as long as I can remember. How can I repair this?"

He pulled her in for another long hug. Damn, it felt so good. "You don't," he said. "You can't fix what's past. Just keep moving forward." He loosened his embrace, but kept his face close to hers. "Your relationship with her isn't ending. It's evolving." He paused, and his expression shifted, revealing an enigmatic smile. "Like ours."

Val cocked her head, allowing her puzzlement to show. No inhibitions, no secrets, no hiding her emotions with Gil. "What does that mean? Evolving, how?"

"How do you want it to go?" Gil's thumbs kneaded the tensc muscles in her back. Felt so. Damned. Good.

"Uh...I thought I gave that away a few minutes ago. Or have you already forgotten?"

"Remind me," Gil said with a sly smile.

Val smiled back at him, easing her lips closer to his. His subtle woodsy scent flooded her senses. Her heart pounded harder with every inch that they drew nearer. For some reason, a planned kiss seemed so much more difficult to pull off than a spontaneous one. Finally, their lips met again, just a touch. Then another, and again, this time lingering, her shyness dissolving, overtaken by emotion.

"Why are you crying?" he asked her, pulling back again.

"Am I?" She wiped tears from her cheeks. She hadn't cried in what seemed like forever. Not after her near-death experience of the night before. Not even after her difficult exchange with Beth.

"Please tell me those are tears of joy," he said, his voice as soft as his cashmere sweater.

"Must be my allergies," she said with a weak laugh.

"Better not be," he said. "So far as I've seen, the only thing you're allergic to is stupidity."

"You know me too well."

Gil shook his head. "Not well enough. I hope we can fix that. Assuming you don't mind being the strong, able-bodied one in the relationship."

"I always have been." Val grinned and poked him in the ribs.

He jerked his body away from her fingers, playful alarm on his face. Puzzled, she touched him again, on his abs. He jerked away again, emitting a nervous giggle.

"Holy smokes," she said. "Big, tough Gil Kryzinski...are you *ticklish*?"

His sheepish expression answered for him.

Despite the temptation to continue, she slid her hands around his back, holding him close. "All right," she said with what she hoped was a devilish smile. "I can keep your little secret. Out of respect for our friendship."

Gil gazed down at her. "Good," he said. "Val, I don't want...whatever we do next...to get in the way of that. Because, my dear, you are an amazing friend. Whether or not Beth realizes it."

She paused, letting his meaning sink in. "You know," she said, "a few months ago—hell, a few weeks ago—I'd have said no way to this."

"And now?" He fixed his gaze on her, anticipation welling up in his eyes.

"Now," she said, "I'm in a much better place. In so many ways."

"Yes, I think you are," he said, nodding.

Val returned his gaze, focusing on the dark pools of his eyes. She searched for guile there and found none. Instead she found affection, trust, and strength—the best parts of a man. The things she'd hoped to find in another person all her life, since the loss of her uncle. She closed her eyes and looked deep inside herself. For the first time she could remember, what she found pleased her: the better part of herself, coming to the fore.

She pulled him close again and held him for a long, long time.

From The Author

Thank you for reading *A Better Part of Valor*. If you enjoyed reading it, won't you please take a moment to leave me a review at your favorite retailer? And please, tell your friends!

Questions to consider when posting a review:

What made me first decide to read this book was...

As I started reading, the first thing that drew me into this book was...

What I liked most about the main character was...

What I liked most about the plot was...

What I liked most about the author's writing style was...

My favorite part of the story was...

Compared to other books in this genre, this book was...

__ Among the best __ Better than most

__ About average __ Not as good __ Among the worst

I would / would not recommend this book to a friend because...

ACKNOWLEDGMENTS

Writers often get approached by readers with "great ideas for a book!" Most often, we listen politely, nod, and don't bother to explain that ideas for books are not hard to come by. Ideas we've got. Time to write them all, not so much.

But that's exactly the way the *Valorie Dawes Thrillers* came into being.

My father, Donald Corbin, first dreamed up the basic story of *A Woman of Valor*, the book that inaugurated this series. He pitched it to me, and I loved it from the start. But rather than just go off and write a book based on his idea, I proposed that we write it together.

We completed the first rough draft together, but we weren't able to get it into publishable shape before he lost his battle with lung cancer in 2006. It took years for me to get past the emotional wall that kept this project tucked away in a drawer for over a decade. I hope, Dad, that the result does you justice.

Dad and Mom helped in an infinite number of ways, but not least was driving me around Hartford on one of my infrequent visits home so I could revisit their old haunts. That exploration led to the creation of Clayton, Connecticut, and the neighborhoods in which the action of this novel occurs.

Several members of the Hartford Police Department assisted me in my background research for this book, and helped ground this fictional story in reality. In particular, Detective Buyak and Officers Mulroy, Kent, and King gave generously of their time, expertise, and personal perspectives, and I thank you all. The *Valorie Dawes Thrillers* would not have happened without you.

Many other friends, colleagues, and family members—too many to count or even remember—have contributed ideas, feedback, critique, encouragement, and love. I thank you all.

Special thanks goes out to my critique group partners—Erick Mertz, Jenny Furniss, Laura Mahaffey, Debb Stanton, Randal Houle, Rankin Johnson, Kate Kort, and Joe Walters—whose scene-by-scene critiques improved this story on a weekly basis.

Thanks also to my Beta Readers—Judith Bottorf, Danielle Faucheux, Erick Mertz, and Randal Houle—who gave me invaluable late-in-the-game feedback.

No writer can survive without a great editor, and I have two. The keen eyes of Laura Lee Bennett and Patsy Silk caught many errors long after my own eyes glazed over. If errors remain, they are my fault, not theirs.

I can never give kudos enough to Steven Novak, whose creativity and patience with me once again yielded an amazing cover design.

Nobody contributed more to my writing career than my dear mother Patricia Corbin, who awakened in me the love of books and reading, and always encouraged my love of writing.

But most of all, thanks to Renée, the kindest, most patient, most beautiful person I've ever known, whose smile lights up the darkest night and brightens the sunniest day. Your support makes all of this possible. I love you.

Book Group Discussion Questions

Characters

1. What do you think of Valorie? What terms would you use to describe her?

2. Do you think you would like Val if you met her in person?

3. Which of the other police officers did you like? Which did you dislike? In each case, why?

4. What do you think happens between Val and Beth after the end of the story?

5. Do you think that the author – a middle-aged white male – portrayed Val, a young woman who struggles with her memories of abuse by older men — authentically and sympathetically?

Scenes and plot

6. Which scene or scenes stood out to you? Why?

7. Were you satisfied with the conclusion of the story? How would you describe the state of Val's healing at the end of the book?

Personal connection

8. For the most part, what emotion(s) did the story evoke in you as a reader?

9. Did you identify with Valorie? Any other character? How did that affect your enjoyment of the book?

Writing

10. *A Better Part of Valor* crosses genres, blending some character-driven aspects of literary fiction with the plot-driven aspects of police procedurals and crime novels. Did this work for you, as a reader?

11. If you could change something about the book, what would it be and why?

12. Describe what you liked or disliked about the writing style.

General

13. Name your favorite thing overall about the book, and your least favorite.

14. At what point in the book did you decide if you liked it or not? What helped make this decision?

15. If someone asks you what this book is about, how would you answer them?

About The Author

Gary Corbin is a writer, editor, and playwright in Camas, WA, a suburb of Portland, OR. In addition to eight published novels, his creative and journalistic work has been published in *BrainstormNW*, the *Portland Tribune*, The *Oregonian*, and *Global Envision*, among others. His plays have enjoyed critical acclaim and have been produced on many Portland-area stages.

Gary is a member of the Willamette Writers Group, Nine Bridges Writers, the Northwest Editors Guild, PDX Playwrights, and the Bar Noir Writers Workshop. He serves as treasurer of *The Pulp Stage*, and participates in workshops and conferences in the Portland, Oregon area.

A homebrewer and home coffee roaster, Gary is a member of the Oregon Brew Crew and a BJCP National Beer Judge. He loves to ski, cook, and root for his beloved Patriots and Red Sox. And when that's not enough, he escapes to the Oregon coast with his sweetheart.

Connect with Gary Corbin

Keep up to date with the latest at
http://www.garycorbinwriting.com

Follow me on Twitter:
http://twitter.com/garycorbin

Follow me on Facebook:
https://www.facebook.com/garycorbinwriting

Follow my Amazon Author Page (and review this book!)
http://smarturl.it/GaryCorbinAuthor

Favorite me at Smashwords:
https://www.smashwords.com/profile/view/GaryCorbin

Also by Gary Corbin

Valorie Dawes Thrillers

In Search of Valor

*The action-packed prequel to **A Woman of Valor***

Valorie Dawes fights an international kidnapping syndicate on behalf of a new college friend—and harbors serious doubts about her future as a police officer.

Anxious to prove herself worthy as a cop and a friend, Val puts her own life on the line, and discovers the kidnappers will stop at nothing to get rid of obstacles like her.

ISBN: 978-1-7346152-0-3

A Woman of Valor

A rookie policewoman, who had been molested as a young girl, pursues a serial child molester—and struggles to control the anger his misdeeds awake in her.

Can Valorie overcome the trauma she suffered as a child and stop this dangerous criminal from hurting others like her—or will her bottled-up anger lead her to take reckless risks that put the people she loves in greater danger?

ISBN: 978-0-9974967-9-6

*All **Valorie Dawes Thrillers** are available in hardcover, paperback, audiobook, and all eBook formats at garycorbinwriting.com, and at your favorite local retailers.*

*Read a sample chapter from the fourth novel in this series, **Mother of Valor**, forthcoming (2022), at the end of this book!*

The Mountain Man Mysteries

The Mountain Man's Dog

In the small town of Clarkesville, in the heart of the Oregon Cascade Mountains, Lehigh Carter, a humble forester, stumbles into the complex world of crooked cops and power-hungry politicians...all because he rescues a stray, injured dog on the highway.

ISBN: 978-0-9974967-1-0

The Mountain Man's Bride

In this thrilling sequel to *The Mountain Man's Dog*, Lehigh's wedding plans get put on hold when the authorities arrest Stacy for the murder of popular acting Sheriff Jared Barkley. Mounting evidence of a secret affair causes Lehigh to wonder how innocent Stacy really is.

ISBN: 978-0-9974967-3-4

The Mountain Man's Badge

Appointed to fill out the unexpired term of disgraced sheriff Buck Summers, Lehigh battles the mistrust of the community's powerful elected elites, the sheriff's department he leads, and his own wife—until he finds shocking evidence of who really killed Everett Downey.

ISBN: 978-0-9974967-7-2

*All three **Mountain Man Mysteries** are available in hardcover, paperback, and all eBook formats at garycorbinwriting.com, and at your favorite local retailers.*

Lying Injustice Thrillers

Lying in Judgment

A man serves on the jury trying a man for the murder that he committed!

Peter Robertson, 33, discovers his wife is cheating on him. Following her suspected boyfriend one night, he erupts into a rage, beats him and leaves him to die...or so he thought. Soon he discovers that he has killed the wrong man—a perfect stranger.

Six months later, impaneled on a jury, he realizes that the murder being tried is the one he committed.

ISBN: 978-06926426-8-9

Lying in Vengeance

Peter's worst nightmare comes to fruition: Christine, his beautiful and charming fellow juror, knows his dark secret and uses it to blackmail him.

The price of her secrecy: Peter must kill again, this time to stop Kyle, the man who torments Christine and threatens her very existence.

ISBN: 978-0-9974967-5-8

*Both **Lying Injustice Thrillers** are available in hardcover, paperback, audiobook, and all eBook formats at garycorbinwriting.com, and at your favorite local retailers.*

Chapter One

A tall, slender woman in a tank top, tight shorts, heels, and a silver wig sashayed past the parked SUV in Clayton, Connecticut on East Chestnut Street, making eye contact with the man behind the wheel. The model of the car—a Lexus LX—indicated wealth—doctor or lawyer. Dentist, maybe. The sun had just set, but sufficient ambient light remained to allow her to make out the driver's key features: white, middle-aged, well-dressed, and probably lonely. With any luck, a hard-up suburban husband who didn't know how much this business transaction ought to cost.

In other words, perfect.

She stopped, jutted out her skinny little hip, and smiled at the man. He smiled back and nodded at her. Bingo. Time to negotiate the specifics and close the deal. She sauntered back to the driver's side and leaned into the open window, in a pose that would maximize the exposure of cleavage. Cool air washed over her, giving her goosebumps but providing welcome relief from the relentless late June humidity. "Wanna party?" she said, smiling.

"I heard this is the party district," he said, returning her smile. Up close, he looked a little older—don't they all?—and maybe not quite as wealthy. A businessman, rather than a lawyer or dentist. Balding, a little out of shape. Nice suit, tie, wedding ring. "I was hoping maybe we could party together a little. Privately?"

"Sounds good. I know a good place." She wiggled an eyebrow at him and sashayed around the front of the car to the passenger side. He clicked it open and she slid in, immediately reaching across to grab his leg. "Whatcha in the mood for tonight, honey?"

"I...I'm new at this," he said. "I'm not sure how this all works. Do I pay you now, or—"

"We'll get to that," she said. "First we gotta work out what you want. While you drive. Take us to 16th and Fir Street."

He started the car, then placed his hand on hers—still on his leg—and pressed it into his crotch. Already hard. This one might not take more than ten minutes. He leaned toward her, tried to kiss her.

"Whoa! Baby, wait a minute," she said. "No kissing, okay? Come on, don't be so nervous. Drive."

He nodded, said "sorry sorry sorry," and put the car in gear. Pulled away from the curb. "So, is there like a standard package, a price list? I mean, that's how we do it in my business. Home security stuff, you know? You want alarms, it's X, automatic alerts is Y—"

"Sure, sure," she said. "You just tell me what you want, I tell you what it costs. And don't worry, you'll love what I can do for you."

He nodded. "I'm sure. My ex-wife, she would never do anything other than the, how do you call it, 'standard' stuff. Religious and all, you know? So, half the stuff, I don't even know what to call it. What do you call when you, uh, when I, um...when it's not regular front-to-front, but kind of front-to-back...?" Sweat rolled off his scalp, dripping onto his expensive suit. "You know...up the bum?"

"Anal?" She laughed. "Sure, sure. But that's extra." Dollar signs floated in front of her eyes. He probably wouldn't last past applying the lube.

"You do? Oh, great. How much would...and I assume it's all cash...?"

She laughed. "You're not trying to pay with Bitcoin, are

you, honey?"

He laughed too, a nervous titter. "No, no, of course not," he said. "Don't worry, I have cash. I hope *enough*. If not I can stop at my ATM. So, how much would I..."

She sighed. Her pimp had told her always, *always* make them ask for the service first, explicitly, but this guy might take all night. And he was so ready to pop, he might take longer to pay her than screw her.

And he was so desperate, he might pay anything.

"Six bills," she said. "Touching my titties or anything else is extra. No kissing, and you wear a condom or it's double."

"Six?" He gulped. "Okay, I might be a little short. But that's okay, my ATM is right up here." He pulled the car over to the curb, unbuckled his belt. "I'll just be a second."

"Dude, hurry," she said. "You're on the clock."

"I sure am," he said, smiling.

She gazed at him, puzzled, for just a moment. Then realization struck. She scrambled to find the door handle. Pulled it. Nothing. Tried to unlock the door. Nothing. Turned back and saw his face...in duplicate. The second one being on the Clayton Police Department ID he'd shoved into her face.

"You're under arrest," said Police Detective Robert Grimes, "for prostitution. You have the right to remain silent..."

***

Val Dawes opened the passenger door to the Lexus and tugged the young woman by the arm onto the sidewalk. She flashed her badge and ID, then slipped them into the back pocket of her jeans. "Hands on the roof," she said. "And spread 'em. Come on, you know the drill."

The girl complied, cursing but not resisting.

"You've Mirandized her?" Val said to her partner, Bob

Grimes, still sitting behind the wheel.

"Of course," he said. "I ain't the rookie here, you are." He jumped out of the car and circled around, taking his sweet time. "You got her cuffed?"

Val secured the handcuffs and spun the woman around, for the first time getting a look at her face. It looked familiar.

"Destiny?" Val said when recognition dawned.

The woman's eyes grew wide, and she cowered a bit. "Do I know you?"

"Another of your high school classmates?" Grimes wise-cracked, opening the back door of the SUV. "At the rate we're going, you might have to have your next reunion at county lockup."

"No. Hold on a sec." She pushed the door shut with her foot and lifted the woman's chin with two fingers. Tears wet the woman's face. "Destiny Mathers? It is you, isn't it?"

"What is this, the fucking Masked Singer?" The woman spit onto the pavement. "Check my ID, you want to know my name."

Val cursed and stared off into the darkening sky for a moment. A few months before on patrol, she'd stopped a man from beating Destiny to a pulp in her apartment building. "How the hell did you end up here?" Val asked her.

"The fuck you care," Destiny said. "Come on, let's go get this over with. I gotta make my one phone call."

Val re-opened the back door, pushed her inside, then slid in next to her. The SUV, repossessed from a drug raid, lacked the usual security features of a departmental cruiser, so procedure required one of them ride in back with the suspect. "You heard her, Bobby," Val barked at Grimes. "Let's go."

***

They booked Destiny at the downtown precinct,

otherwise known as Clayton Police Headquarters, and met on their fourth floor office, also known as the Women's Anti-Violence Emergency Squad Office. The mayor had established the WAVE Squad three months before in an effort to stamp out violent crime against women. In recent weeks, with violent crime rates suddenly dipping in the city, the police chief had requested WAVE's help in addressing a sudden upswing in prostitution in the so-called "Alphabet Soup" district, so-called because the street names progressed in alphabetical order, each for a tree species that no longer graced the district's decaying urban core.

"Another newbie," Grimes told their boss, Sergeant Brenda Petroni, a solidly built forty-something woman with short brown curls. "No priors. Dawes here says she was an assault victim a few months back, unrelated to her profession."

"So far as I know," Val said. "No indications arose then that she turned tricks for a living. Not even in court, so far as I know. In fact, her attacker's been living in Clayton Cottage for two months."

Brenda smiled at Val's use of the term Clayton cops used for city lockup. "All that means is, he wasn't, or isn't, her pimp. But I get your point, you guys. It seems everyone we haul in from the Alphabet Soup District is new to the game. It makes me wonder if something bigger's going on."

"One thing that's different about this Destiny Mathers chick," Grimes said, "is her age. She's twenty. Most of the others from Soupland have been teenagers. Some as young as fourteen."

"Destiny looks younger than her age," Val said, and when Grimes scoffed, she added, "at least, she did a few months ago."

"Okay, let's look into it," Petroni said. She turned to Val. "You have a history with her. Think she'll talk to you, or did busting her poison that well?"

Val shot a glance at Grimes, who made a face of disgust, but said nothing.

"It's worth a shot," Val said.

***

Val joined Destiny in a tiny cement-block interrogation room, guarded by a tall, silent uniformed cop named Price, standing at attention. With a nod from Val, Price exited, standing guard just outside the door. Grimes, meanwhile, observed from behind a one-way mirror that lined the far wall of the hot, stuffy room. The chamber reeked in equal measures of sweat and disinfectant, and slightly cooler air flowed from a noisy vent near the ceiling. The room's flickering overhead lights seemed to make the room even hotter.

"So, Destiny," Val said, taking a seat across a small table from her. "I didn't expect to meet up with you again like this."

"Yeah, well, I must've missed all those party invites," Destiny said with a sneer.

Val sighed. "Okay. I guess I deserve that. How've you been doing since we last saw each other?"

"Fucking peachy, as you can tell," Destiny said, indicating her skimpy attire.

"What was that, a month ago, or two, in court?" Val asked.

Destiny shrugged. "You say so."

Val waited, and when no more words came, she leaned back in her seat. "Come on, girl. Help me out. How did you get from there to here in such a short time?"

Destiny shot her a sharp, questioning look. "It's not like 'there' was such a hot place to be, Officer."

In spite of herself, Val smirked. The woman had a sense of humor. "Were you turning tricks back then?"

"Who's turning tricks?" Destiny said, snarling. "Fucking hell. I ain't talking without no lawyer."

Val nodded. "Yeah, I get it. That's your right, of course. But listen. I'm not here to 'get you to talk,' so to speak, about what you did tonight. I'm interested in your story. How this all started. You had a job when I last saw you. What happened?"

"I lost it, obv."

"Okay. And then?"

Destiny glanced around her as if hoping someone would rescue her from the Idiot Brigade. "And then I fucking got hungry, okay? I have bills to pay. Rent. The state said I can't get unemployment because I was fired, and that's bullshit anyway. So, what options does that leave a girl like me? I ain't a user, so dealing's pretty much out. What's left?"

Val heaved a deep breath. "So, it's just a money thing?"

Destiny scoffed and shook her head. "You think it's about changing the world or some shit?"

"No, I guess not." Val tapped a pencil on the table, thinking. Somehow, she had to break through to this kid.

She stopped herself at that thought. *Kid.* The woman was three years younger than Val, and clearly hadn't enjoyed the benefits of a college education or police academy training. And, still a rookie uniformed cop, Val lacked the masterful interrogatory skills of her partner, Grimes, or their boss, Sergeant Petroni. But they'd trusted her to tap into something to connect with this woman. Shared age and gender, perhaps? Intuition? Empathy?

She searched her memory for something she knew about Destiny, something that would connect them. Such as, the first time they'd met, during her assault.

"You still living at Merrybrook Apartments?" Val asked.

Destiny shook her head. "That was Rafe's place." Her ex-boyfriend.

"So, where will you stay tonight?"

Destiny shook her head in disgust. "I hadn't planned on sleeping, dude. I was planning on working."

"Right. But that's out. So, where will you go?"

Destiny gazed at her in amusement. "Back to the Bar and Grill, is my guess."

Val chuckled. Cops had their pet name for lockup, inmates had theirs. "What if I told you that you had other options?"

Laughter. "I'd tell you you're a liar."

"I'm serious."

"Yeah, so'm I. We done?" Destiny rattled the cuffs still binding her wrists.

"Who's coming to get you? Anyone?"

Destiny said nothing, just shook her head.

"Your Man isn't upset that you're off the clock, not earning him his eighty percent?"

Destiny locked eyes with her, new respect showing there. "If I'm in here, he can't kick my ass. Know what I'm saying?"

Val nodded, reappraising Destiny's appearance. Her pale skin, almost translucent where the makeup had been smudged off, stretched thin over her bony jaw and cheeks. Her eyes appeared hollow and tired. For a non-drug user, to take Destiny's word for it, she looked unusually emaciated.

"You hungry?" Val asked her.

Destiny's eyes lit up, her posture straightening. "Always."

"Let me get you some food," Val said. She stood and rapped twice on the door. Price opened it. "Get her a sandwich and a drink from the machines," she said, handing him some cash. Price nodded and closed the door.

"I'll believe it when I see it," Destiny said.

"That you will," Val said.

Sure enough, Price returned with a tuna sandwich, Coke, and a bag of chips a few minutes later. He stood guard inside the room and Val unshackled one of Destiny's wrists, locking the other to the arm of the chair. "Eat," she said. "That's yours."

Destiny blinked, then tore the wrapper off the sandwich and ate half of it in four bites. She sucked down half the soda in one gulp and shoved fistfuls of chips into her mouth.

"Better get more," Val said to Price. He returned just as Destiny finished off the last of her first course. This time, ham and cheese replaced the tuna, with popcorn instead of chips.

"Figured I'd mix it up some," Price said with a smile.

Again, the food disappeared in under two minutes.

"Feel better?" Val asked her.

"I ain't doing nothing for that," Destiny said. When Val shot her a questioning look, Destiny mimed a humping motion. Price laughed.

Reddening, Val waved her off. "On the house," she said.

Destiny offered her unshackled wrist to Val. "You gonna tie me back up?"

Val shook her head. "I trust you."

The woman's shoulders rose, fell, as if taken aback.

"Does your pimp ever feed you when you're out of funds?" Val asked.

"He likes me to call him my manager."

"Okay. Does he?"

A wry smile, and a shake of her head. "Not anymore."

"He used to? When?"

"At first. Like, three, four weeks ago. Says dudes like girls with a little meat on their ass."

"No doubt. I get that a lot, too." Val indicated her wiry frame, recalled the unkind names boys taunted her with back in high school: Titless Wonder. Broomstick. The Androgynous One. "So, what does he do for you, then? Your Manager, I mean."

"Customers."

"Seems like he takes more than he gives on that front. Did I get his cut right? Eighty percent?"

Destiny nodded, thought a moment. "Protection."

"From whom?"

"From..." Destiny fought for words. "Bad dudes."

"The customers he's so proud of sending you? And if he's supplying clients, why do you have to walk the streets?"

"It's just...he's got other girls, too, you know."

"Right." Val huffed. "You don't have to repeat what he tells you. It's bullshit, anyway, and you know it."

"You don't know." She looked away, a sour expression on her face.

"Yeah, I do know, Destiny." Val kept her voice soft. "And you know I know. Don't you?"

She squirmed in her seat, biting her lip. Finally, she gazed back up at Val. "Any chance I could squeeze another Coke out of you?"

Val waited a moment before answering. "Maybe. If it means we get to talk some more."

Destiny lowered her eyes, folded her hands in her lap. "We could talk some," she said after a while. She glanced back at Val for a moment, then at Price. "Alone...if that's all right."

Val nodded at Price, who exited with a look of respect on his face for Val.

"Okay," Val said, "it's just us girls, now. What do you want to tell me?"